W9-AGI-247

RAVE REVIEWS FOR LISA CACH!

THE CHANGELING BRIDE

"This charming and whimsical tale will leave you laughing with glee!"

—*Romantic Times*

"An excellent debut novel—cleverly plotted, genuinely funny, and featuring two endearing leads."

—*The Romance Reader*

"I laughed throughout and even shed a tear at the end. Brava!"

—*All About Romance*

BEWITCHING THE BARON

"An engaging tale of love's power of redemption. . . . A story rich in humanity and emotional intensity. 4½ Stars!"

—*Romantic Times*

"WHO ARE YOU?"

"Serena," he said, raising his eyes and looking straight at her. "I have had enough of your childish games. I have felt you following me, lying beside me in my bed, and watching me bathe." He leaned back in his chair. "I have even dreamt about you, and what you may look like."

Her lips parted, a chill running up her body.

"I even thought, once or twice, about how fascinating it would be to speak with you."

What?

"Now, though, I am not at all certain that I want to know anything about you. I have doubts that you retain any more of your humanity than its worst qualities. I fear you may be nothing but the echo of a disturbed mind."

She was not disturbed! That was unfair. And she was more human than not—why else would she feel this pain? He did not understand her or the purpose of her haunting. He understood nothing!

He sighed. "Which are you, Serena? Are you a beautiful woman caught halfway between life and death, or are you nothing but an echo of the ugliest parts of humanity?"

Silence stretched to the corners of the room, trapping her mute in its bonds. She was neither, but she wished she could be one of those two, wished it as she always had, with all her heart. She wanted to be a beautiful woman about whom men dreamt.

"If you are indeed a woman, I should like to know you."

OF MIDNIGHT BORN

LISA CACH

LOVE SPELL BOOKS   ✦   NEW YORK CITY

To Kelly and Jürgen

A LOVE SPELL BOOK®

September 2000

Published by

Dorchester Publishing Co., Inc.
276 Fifth Avenue
New York, NY 10001

ISBN 0-505-52399-X

The name "Love Spell" and its logo are trademarks of Dorchester Publishing Co., Inc.

Printed in the United States of America.

OF MIDNIGHT BORN

Chapter One

Clerenbold Keep, England
1350

"God's heart, Thomas, enough with your daydreaming! I cannot be expected to do this all myself," Serena complained, catching her brother wielding his sickle as if it were a sword, slashing at imaginary Frenchmen. She hacked at the wheat in front of her, the heavy-headed stalks falling with a whisper to the stubbled ground at her feet.

"I should be fighting under the Black Prince," Thomas said, standing with feet spread wide, "not cutting corn like a peasant."

"Then find me a peasant to take your place, and I will happily see you go," Serena answered. "What? There are none?" she continued in mock surprise. "Wherever could they have gone?"

"We can't keep living like this, Serena. We weren't born to work in the fields. We are not made for it, and we know nothing of farming."

Serena took one more slash at the wheat, then dropped her sickle, standing straight to her full six feet, glaring down at her shorter brother, anger rising in her. "Do you think I like it?" she asked harshly. "Day after day in the sun, bent double, sweating and stinking like a pig, going home to that filthy, crumbling shell of a keep, weary to the bone, and supping on nothing but water and whatever we have scrounged from the fields? Do you think I like it? I don't, Thomas. I hate it. But I do it, and you're going to do it, too. I'll be damned if I'll die of starvation after all we've been through."

Thomas let out a cry of angry frustration and threw his sickle across the field, the blade glinting in the sun as it twisted in the air, then fell, disappearing into the wheat. "Look at this field, Serena. Look at it!" he shouted, gesturing toward the acres of waving grain. "Why can't you admit that we're beaten? We can't harvest this all ourselves. We'll never find enough food to survive the winter, and even if we did, spring would find us worse off than we are now, with no one to plow or sow the fields for us."

"We have no choice!" Serena shouted back. "You're not going to get to France without armor or a horse. No one is going to come to marry me, an ugly giantess with a scarred face and no money. No one wealthy will marry a pauper like you, either, for all your pretty looks. We are stuck here. Accept it!"

Thomas threw up his hands, turned, and began to walk away.

"Thomas! Where are you going?"

"I don't know. For a walk," he said over his shoulder.

"Thomas!" she yelled. "By Saint Nicholas, come back here!"

He kept walking.

Serena turned back to the standing grain, picking up her sickle and hacking at the wheat—hacking at fate, at death, and at the few peasants who, having survived, had run off to find better pay. Sweat dripped into her eyes, ran between her breasts, and soaked through the back and underarms of her old gown. The muscles in her back and arms ached, her legs growing sore from the stooped posture.

Weariness pulling at her, she turned to survey how much she had accomplished. Less than an eighth of this one field lay cut. Rooks had already settled en masse on the ground, feeding on her corn.

"Yaa! Hee!" she screeched at them, waving the sickle and running at the birds. They scattered into the air, but did not go far, landing in shrubs at the edge of field, waiting for her to leave.

Cutting the wheat was not enough. She would need to rake and gather the grain, then dry and thresh it. She would need to do all of that and more before she could eat it, and half of it must be done before the night fell, if she wanted to protect her crop from the birds and mice.

She dropped down to the ground, sitting amid the stubble and cut stalks, the sickle falling to the side as the immensity of the task overwhelmed her.

Maybe Thomas was right. It was too much work for the two of them, and they knew only a smattering of what they should of farming and of preserving food. Add to that the fact that all that remained of their livestock was an ancient pony and three chickens, and there seemed no way for them to survive here at the keep

11

through the winter and next year, much less to recover their fortunes.

She picked up a head of wheat, feeling the grains and breaking them away from the stalk with her fingers. There had to be some alternative, some way out. There had to be. She had lived through too much to give up now. If they could not do all the work themselves, there had to be some way to get the money to pay the high wages the peasantry now felt entitled to charge for their labor.

She and Thomas had no money of their own. Their family had not been wealthy even before the Pestilence had taken so much, so selling anything from the keep was out of the question. Even if there had been something of value to sell, there were precious few who would wish to buy it. Food was all anyone cared about now, food and livestock.

There were those who sold off fragments of their land out of desperation, but that she could not do. Their father had long ago sold more than he should have to fund his warring, and there had been barely enough left to support them and the peasants they had once had. She knew she would be nothing without the remaining land and keep, would be reduced to the condition of a peasant herself. Thomas was likely willing enough to sell, though—all he could see was the glory and adventure of battle.

It was true that Thomas might possibly win wealth and new lands through war, either through plunder or the Black Prince's favor—assuming he was not killed in the process—but he could not even go to war without horse and armor. And the only horses suited to the task were dead, the only armor either outsized or broken and rusted through.

Marriage had always been a reliable source of income, but neither she nor Thomas stood much chance of finding a willing, wealthy partner. Thomas was fair enough of face, but poor and without a title. And she—she had not even the face to recommend her. She touched the thin scar that crossed her forehead, cut through her right eyebrow, then leaped over her eye to trace a path across her cheekbone. She had not forgiven her brother William for giving her that, however accidentally, even now that he was dead.

She stared out across the valley, looking for some answer in the green countryside. Its lushness was an illusion of life, for she knew that in ditches and empty hovels, in houses and along roads, even in the very fields, there lay the moldering remains of the victims of the disease that had spread like a foul wind across the land. People, sheep, horses, goats, even cats and dogs had fallen, their bodies black and putrid. Even now, one could sometimes catch the scent of death and decay on the air and wonder if the Pestilence would come back to take those it had left living.

The sun was behind her, slanting its rays across the valley as it descended behind the hills. The valley fell into shadow, but several miles away, on top of the highest hill in the range, the golden light caught on Hugh le Gayne's fortress, its squat towers rising above the trees.

Le Gayne's lands and home had been decimated by the Pestilence just as her own had, only he had money to continue paying peasants to work his fields. She had been told so by a small group of workers crossing her own land to go to his. They said they had heard he had bought new livestock, undoubtedly at outrageous prices. He had been hit hard, yet had retained his wealth. Would that his were her home, and she had no fears of starving over the winter.

She watched as the sun painted the fortress in pink and gold, the sky behind it deepening into a rich blue. Suddenly the turquoise streak of a falling star, pale and strange in the last light of day, coursed across the lower heavens and disappeared in the sky behind the fortress.

She drew in her breath. God himself had given her the answer she needed.

Serena was in the small kitchen of the keep, eating roasted apples and boiled turnips and greens, and drinking some of their precious remaining wine when Thomas at last returned, a hare hanging from his hand. There was a larger kitchen in a separate building outside the keep, but they had no need of its huge fireplaces, large enough to fit an entire ox, and the large stone room only made them feel their lack of companions. She and Thomas spent most of their time indoors in this small kitchen off the upper great hall of the keep, the rest of the chambers too hauntingly empty of life to be comfortable.

"It was in one of my snares," Thomas said of the beast, dropping it on the table and taking out his knife to start dressing it.

"Oh, Thomas," she said, setting down her cup and staring large-eyed at the animal. It had been several days since she'd tasted meat. They had been too hard at work in the fields to take the time to hunt. "I still have turnips and greens in the kettle. We can have a real stew."

He nodded, made several cuts on the hare, then with a tearing sound pulled the skin off in one piece.

She knew better than to think the rabbit a peace offering. They fought constantly, she and Thomas, and neither was wont to back down or apologize. Their desperate situation had increased the tensions that had always been between them, but it had also made them realize their dependence on one another. The empty keep was a constant reminder that they were all the family either one had left, and that no one else would care if they lived or died. Their battles usually ended in bloodless standoffs, the disagreements ultimately less important than working together to survive.

With the hare in the pot and the unusable bits cleaned away, Serena poured Thomas a cup of the wine. He raised his eyebrows at her.

"What's this for?" he asked suspiciously.

" 'Tis in celebration."

"Marry! Celebration of what?"

"Sit down, Thomas, and I shall tell you." She waited until he had sat and taken a drink of the wine before she continued. "I have thought of a way to keep us from starving: I shall marry Hugh le Gayne."

Thomas rolled his eyes and looked away, already losing interest. "He won't have you. He is wealthy enough to have his choice of women, and will likely choose one who can increase his holdings." He swirled the wine in his cup.

"He will have me. He will have no choice." Serena felt a smile playing around her lips. "You and I are going to kidnap him."

Thomas looked back at her, speechless, then gave a shout of laughter. "Ha! You think he's a virgin heiress? You can't destroy his reputation by forcing him to spend a night in our keep without chaperones. My God, Serena, you've lost your senses."

"It wasn't my thought to pluck his nonexistent virginity," she said dryly. "What I had in mind was giving

15

him a choice between death and marriage."

Thomas swallowed his wine wrong, coughing. "Are you crazy?" he said in a gasp. "You can't threaten Hugh le Gayne—he'd kill you before the words were half out of your lips." He set his cup on the table. "God's blood, I needn't worry. You'll never succeed in kidnapping him, anyway."

"He is much better off than we, but still he cannot have so many surviving men-at-arms to defend him. Everyone works in the fields—or if they can they go to war. How many could he have left to guard him? He must leave the fortress to oversee the work, and I am betting that he is accompanied by few, if any, when he does. He is likely too confident of his position, and of his authority. He cannot think that any would dare to attack him."

"You don't know that. He didn't hold on to so much by being careless. A man with so much to lose learns caution."

"We will seize him on his own lands," Serena said, hands gripped around her cup, the plan laid out in her mind's eye. "Then we shall bring him back here and lock him in a storeroom with neither food nor water until he agrees to the marriage. The next monk who comes begging can perform the service." She leaned forward, pinning Thomas with her eyes and the force of her will. "It *can* work, if we are bold enough to attempt it."

Thomas shook his head, leaning back, away from her. "It will lead only to death, even more surely than winter."

"It's life, Thomas. I'll have a husband, and we'll finally be able to outfit you for war. You can go fight under the Black Prince!"

He snorted derisively. "A man would hardly be generous with a wife who forced him to wed, much less her brother. Le Gayne! Even if your idea could work—and it can't—le Gayne would be the worst choice. I hear he is a beast of a man, Serena, hardly human."

She shrugged. "He is the only choice. A rich and awful husband is better than no husband at all."

"He is said to be godless, and ruthless with those who disobey him. I have heard that his first wife poisoned herself rather than continue to share his bed."

"Nonsense," she said dismissively. "The woman died of a fever, and there is nothing unusual in that. I am not afraid of le Gayne. Do you think I cannot hold my own with the likes of him, after living so many years amongst our brothers? He is said to be old and fat. I will be able to defend myself."

"Perhaps he is old, but old like a boar, with the same strength and temper. Serena, forget this plan," Thomas begged. "It can lead only to disaster."

"There's a chance it might work. You cannot deny that. There is a chance."

"Very small, and not worth the price of failure."

"If I were wed and your responsibilities to me finished, you would be free to go where you wished, and to sell the land and keep if that was what you wanted. You could get enough to arm yourself for war that way, even if le Gayne would not pay."

"I would be dead before I had the chance, and you as well," he said.

"And you are the one who wishes to be a soldier!" she scoffed. "There is no daring in you, no fight."

"There is none of your foolishness in me!" he answered back.

Serena took several breaths, and when she spoke again she did so in a lowered voice. "I have always wanted a husband, Thomas. You and our brothers may not have thought so—certainly you all made clear to me how unlikely it ever was to happen—but it is the truth. I am twenty years of age, and I do not want to grow old barren and untouched. I survived the scourge upon this land, and now I want a full life. I want children, and a family of my own. Le Gayne can give me that, even if he hates me. I don't care how unappealing he is, as long as he can give me children and a secure home, and keep me from starving over the winter."

"*You* want to be a wife?" Thomas asked, his face expressing his incredulity. "A mother? I cannot believe it! You begged to be trained to fight like the rest of us. You know nothing of children, and you but scarcely tried to learn the duties of a chatelaine."

"With Mother dead, who was there to teach me, except the bailiff who had no time for a girl? Who was there to encourage me? The only praise that ever came from Father's lips came for skill with a weapon. He had no time for womanish things, not after Mother died. Of course I wanted to learn to fight."

"Fat lot of good it did you," he said, and she saw his glance go to her scar. "Father didn't think much of you after *that* happened."

She pitched her cup at him, hitting him on the temple, wine spilling all down his face and shirt. Her brother jumped backward, falling off the bench, and she was up and over the table and on top of him before he could recover. She knelt with all her weight on his chest, her dagger out, pricking at the skin under his chin.

"I have told you before, Thomas," she said softly, fury burning through her, "that you are never to speak of it."

"But you always refer to your scar! You did so this very afternoon!" he protested.

"It is different when I do, and well you know it. I had enough of mocking from Father and the others: I will not endure it from you."

"It's not half so bad as you think. I don't even see it most of the time."

She moved the dagger up to the edge of his eye socket. "Would you like one to match?"

"You wouldn't do that."

"Wouldn't I, though?" she said, and for a moment did not know if she would or would not. She had so little left, it almost seemed simplest to destroy what remained and be done with it. Kill Thomas, kill herself, and be done with fighting to survive. The thought was with her for as long as it takes a spark to die, and then the full fire of her determination to live rose up within her, devouring any thoughts of giving herself over to despair.

"Serena?" Thomas asked, a wobble of worry in his voice, his eyes wide.

Her eyes focused on him anew, this, her last remaining kin. She lowered the dagger and climbed off his chest. "Get up, Thomas."

She went to go check the stew while he found his feet and picked up the fallen bench. She used serving bowls to serve them, there being no bread for trenchers. When she came back to the table, she saw that Thomas had refilled her cup.

They ate in silence, and despite the luxury of the meat, Serena did not taste it. She would survive, and she would get Le Gayne. She would not starve here over the winter, scrounging for scraps of inedible food. She would have children whom she would love, and who would love her the way she had loved her mother, without regard to beauty or size, intelligence or grace. Her mind began again to run through and discard possible scenarios for how to capture her soon-to-be husband.

"We will need to lure him away from whatever men ride with him," she said, staring into the growing dark of the kitchen, then turning her gaze on her brother.

Thomas, his face half-lit by the orange flames of the fire, said nothing.

"What will draw a man away from others?" she asked. "And what will take down his guard?"

Thomas took another bite of stew, chewed, and swallowed. A long moment went by, in which all that could be heard was the crackling of the fire. "A woman will draw him away," he said at last, quietly. "The weak and helpless take down his guard."

Serena smiled.

Chapter Two

"He's coming!" Thomas said, crashing through the bushes to where she waited by the stream. "And he'll be alone this time. He's left his two men to oversee one of the fields. He must think it's safe, this close to his home."

"At last!" Serena said, relief and apprehension mixing together, her heart beating a rapid tattoo. "Do I look all right?" she asked, nervously combing her fingers through her loose hair.

"Pull the dress down a little lower on your shoulder."

"Like this?"

"That's perfect. Now, quick, get in position," he said, and ran to the hiding place they had constructed earlier.

Serena went and sat at the edge of the creek, pulling her skirts up to midthigh and putting her bare feet in the water. She put her bandage-wrapped wrist in the sling around her neck, and rearranged the too-small gown again, so that plenty of shoulder and half a breast were showing.

It was the first time in her life she had made an attempt to attract a man's sexual attention, and she had her doubts that it would work. Thomas had assured her that her hair alone would be enough to catch le Gayne's eye, fair and silky as it was, growing down past her hips. He had also managed to embarrass her by pointing out that her breasts were quite respectable, and had a good swell to them.

They had overcome her height by putting Serena on the ground, a position that only increased the false impression of vulnerability given by the sling.

She started to sing, her voice not particularly lovely, but of sufficient strength to guarantee that their quarry would hear it from the narrow road passing nearby.

> "There were three ravens sat on a tree,
> Down a down, hay down, hay down,
> There were three ravens sat on a tree,
> With a down."

She and Thomas had been spying for nearly a week, moving about through the pockets of forest to avoid detection, and masquerading as wandering peasants to avoid questions while out in the open. They were both growing frustrated with being unable to find le Gayne alone, having decided that that was the safest chance of abducting him. This was their first real opportunity.

> "There were three ravens sat on a tree,
> They were as black as they might be,
> With a down, derry, derry, derry, down, down."

"The Three Ravens" was the only ballad she knew by heart, so there hadn't been much choice in what to sing. Thomas had insisted that the words wouldn't matter— all le Gayne would care about was seeing a young woman alone.

> "Then one of them said to his mate,
> 'Where shall we our breakfast take?
> Down in yonder green field
> There lies a knight slain under his shield.' "

She saw movement through the trees. It was their quarry. She sang louder, bending over and splashing water up her calves with her unbandaged hand, as if she were a resting traveler washing her weary feet.

A few moments later le Gayne came through the woods and drew his horse to a halt on the other side of the narrow, shallow stream. She looked up from the water and stopped her singing, her hand going to her throat as if she were startled. "Good sir!" she exclaimed, as breathily as she could manage. She made a fumbling, ineffectual attempt to push down her skirts.

"What are you doing here in these woods?" Le Gayne was a large man, plainly overfed, his jowls and fat neck bulging beneath his cleanly shaven jawline as he spoke, a massive, rounded gut hanging over his belt. His hair was the dark gray of unpolished steel, and she guessed his age to be in the late fifties. Despite the age and the fat, it looked as if there were muscle under his padding, and she thought he was likely as strong as Thomas had warned.

Serena bowed her head forward, letting her hair cover half her face and the scar, and looked up at him from under her brows. Thomas had said it was a most pleasing, beseeching look. "I have been wandering in this wood half the day," she said. "I have lost the road."

He laughed, swinging down from his horse. "You are alone then?"

"Aye, sir, and growing terribly hungry. I am looking for work. Do you know of where I might find some?" She blinked innocently at him.

"How can you work with an injured arm?" he asked, his eyes on her breasts.

"Sir, I will do whatever I must. Is there not some use you could find for me?" she asked, per Thomas's direction. She arched her back a bit, thrusting her breasts into plainer view. She felt the creeping heat of embarrassment coming up her neck at both the whorish role she was playing and her poor performance in it. Surely he must think her ridiculous.

His eyes went up and down her body. "I might be able to think of something," he said, and dropped his horse's reins.

She made herself stay still as he leaped the narrow stream and walked up beside her, not quite believing that the man was falling for their trap. She felt his fingertips touch the hair on the top of her head, stroking her lightly as if she were a dog.

"Sir?" she said, trembly voiced, and looked up at him helplessly, being sure to turn slightly toward him so he could get an unobstructed view down her neckline.

Looking up into le Gayne's eyes, she saw for the first time in her life a man lusting for her. She shivered, as much from a true sense of fear as a feigned one. Thomas had said that a man like le Gayne would enjoy a bit of cowering and protesting, but she found she need hardly pretend. It was as startling to see that lust as it was terrifying, for she knew right then that this man did not see her as Serena Clerenbold, a sister and a daughter, a person with her own thoughts and feelings. He saw only a female with breasts, a body to be used. She might as well have been a sheep, for all the care he would give her sensibilities.

"I am a maid, sir," she said, covering her cleavage with her hand and looking down bashfully. "I have never known a man." Thomas had promised that those words would do away with any of le Gayne's remaining hesitation. Deflowering peasants was great sport among those who could get away with it. She knew her own brothers had occasionally done so, when they got the chance.

"Today must be your lucky day," le Gayne said roughly, and grabbed a fistful of her hair, jerking back her head as he dropped on top of her, pinning her to the ground.

The attack took her by surprise, both her arms caught under his weight on her chest, and she kicked and struggled, trying in a panic to push him off her, forgetting that this move by le Gayne was exactly what she and Thomas had hoped for. All she knew was that the man's huge weight was on her, and his hand was up her skirt, poking blunt fingers at the most intimate area of her body. She grunted with the effort to dislodge him, silently screaming for Thomas, her fear skittering out of control.

"You like a fight, do you?" le Gayne said into her ear, one hand still wrapped in her hair. "I like that. You'll be giving me a wild ride," he went on, and ran his tongue across her face.

The scent of his stale saliva on her skin made her gag, her stomach heaving. She thought she'd choke on her own bile.

There was a sudden loud *thunk,* and le Gayne collapsed on top of her.

"Get him off me!" she shrieked, seeing Thomas over her assailant's shoulder. She squirmed beneath the weight. "Get him off me!"

"Shh! Serena, for God's love, be still!" her brother said in a hiss, dropping the iron pot with which he had clubbed le Gayne, and moving to help push away the fallen man.

The moment his weight was off her she scrambled to her knees and to the edge of the stream, her stomach heaving, trying to keep from retching. She bent her head down, not caring that her hair trailed in the dirt, and tried to gain control of herself. She heard Thomas working behind her, shackling their prey.

"Are you all right?" Her brother's voice sounded a few moments later, as he came to kneel beside her, his hand lightly touching her back.

She moved out from under his touch, reaching down into the stream for water with which to splash her cheeks. "I'm fine," she said coldly. "Go get the cart."

Her brother hesitated until she turned to meet his eye; then he nodded and got to his feet, dashing into the woods. He must have seen the hardness she felt in her own face.

She rose and went to get le Gayne's horse, well trained enough to have stood its ground throughout the melee. If nothing else, they could ride it to another county and sell it if their plan fell apart. Or eat it.

She recrossed the stream, leading the mount, and forced herself to look at their prisoner, lying like a dead pig in the brown leaves, his mouth open and dribbling saliva, his hands trussed behind him.

This was the man she had chosen to be her husband,

the man who would plant his seed in her, and own her body. He would share her bed and put those blunt fingers on her whenever and wherever he wished, and lick her face with his foul-smelling tongue.

It wasn't too late to back out. They could remove the shackles and leave him here to wake on his own. He had not seen Thomas, and perhaps would not think to look to Clerenbold Keep to find her.

But then she and Thomas would be back where they started, minus a week's worth of harvest time.

She heard the rumble of the cart, and Thomas appeared a moment later, leading their one ancient pony.

"It's not too late to leave him," Thomas said, echoing her own thoughts. "You don't have to go through with this."

She looked at le Gayne again, this time taking note of the thickness of his flesh that denoted a well-stocked table, and the finery of his clothes that said he wanted for nothing. The horse whose reins she held was a finer creature than any that had been at Clerenbold for many a year. No one would be starving in le Gayne's fortress this winter.

She knew what sons the man had sired had died in the Pestilence or the war, just as had her own brothers and father. He would want heirs. He would provide for their children, and keep both them and her safe and fed in his fortress, however much he hated her, and she him. Marriages had never been matters of love, after all.

She would have children. She would not starve.

"We will continue," she said.

"Damn you, show your faces, you cowardly whoresons!" le Gayne shouted through the small barred window in the door of his cell. "God rot your filthy souls."

"It doesn't sound like a good time to talk to him," Serena said.

"I doubt he'll get any better tempered as time goes on," Thomas replied.

"No, but at least he'll be a little more desperate, a little more willing to listen." They were in the cellars under Clerenbold's main kitchen, around a corner from where le Gayne bellowed in the dark. His "cell" was a storage room that had once held wine and spirits, its door heavy and fitted with a lock.

"We may as well talk to him now," Thomas said. "It will give him something to think about as he gets thirsty."

Thomas spoke as if indifferent, but Serena could feel his tension, an echo of her own. Le Gayne's incessant ranting had an unnerving effect, and she was half-afraid he would find some way to break through the door and come after them.

There was a rising voice inside her saying that this had been a huge mistake, that however rich the man was or however well equipped to father and provide for children, marriage to him would not be worth the price she would have to pay.

She doubted he would try to kill her. Even a rich man like le Gayne could not automatically get away with killing his wife, and she had no intention of making herself an easy target. She knew how to be on guard. But there were other ways le Gayne could take his revenge out of her hide—like beatings, or in the marriage bed—and no one would lift a hand to stop him.

Having gone this far, though, there seemed no way to stop, and she quashed the rising voice of her fear, focusing instead on what the marriage could bring them. Life with le Gayne, in however miserable a marriage, was surely better than death in the winter. Besides, he would likely get used to her in time and learn to ignore her, and she would have children to love and raise. She could not let le Gayne's shouted threats frighten her from her course.

"Good morrow, sir," Thomas said, coming around the corner, the light from his torch reaching le Gayne's face in the hatchwork of iron bars. The man squinted from the light, stepping back from the opening.

" 'Good morrow,' he says," their prisoner returned in a mocking voice. " 'Good morrow' my ass. Who the hell are you? Do you know who I am? There will be soldiers searching for me, and when they find you they will disembowel you before your own eyes. I'll have them rip out your tongue first, so that you may not pray to God to take your black soul and save you from your torment. Hot irons will—"

"Your pardon, sir," Thomas interrupted, "but we will gladly answer your questions."

Serena felt her heart pounding painfully in her chest, le Gayne's ire infecting her with an echo of the panic she had felt at the stream.

"—burn out your eyes. With my own dagger I shall flay—"

"He's not going to listen," Serena said, quietly enough that le Gayne could not hear. "It's been only two days. Give him two or three more without food or water, and at least he will be too hoarse to shout."

"I do not like the waiting," Thomas whispered back. " 'Tis making me nervous as a cat. I have eaten no more than le Gayne since we took him."

"Nor I," Serena admitted under her breath. It had been so much easier to be brave when this was all a plan and not reality. She had not counted on being frightened of her prey. Where was her courage now?

They began to move away from the door, but were halted by a sudden shout. "Wait, you dung-eating sheep buggerers!" he commanded, and then was blessedly quiet for a long moment. "Who the bleeding hell are you?"

Serena waited for the verbal abuse to continue, and when it did so only in low, muttered tones she and her brother moved once again toward the cell door. They had agreed beforehand that Thomas should do the talking, as it was unlikely le Gayne would listen to a single word from a woman's mouth in this situation. He would probably see it as adding insult to injury. They'd also decided to pretend the kidnapping was Thomas's idea, in hopes of lessening any revenge the man might take on her.

"I am Thomas Clerenbold, and this is my sister, Serena."

Le Gayne squinted at them through the window, a further stream of curses dribbling from his lips before he gave an intelligible answer. "Clerenbold. You are Robert's whelps?"

"Aye."

"Or what's left of them," le Gayne said. His small, raisin eyes moved to Serena. "The strumpet by the stream. I should have known. All of the countryside knows of Robert's scarred monster of a daughter. You're even bigger than the stories say. Good God, girl, what do they feed you? Horses' oats?"

Her nervousness disappeared under a growing wave of furious humiliation, pinpricks of light appearing in the corners of her vision as blood rushed to her head. Her mind filled with a vision of her dagger at his bloated, frog-belly throat, cutting a bright and bloody swath through the stretched skin of it, digging deep and severing his vocal cords. She could see the yellow fat bubbling out the open wound, mixing with the crimson of his blood.

She felt Thomas take hold of her hand, out of le Gayne's sight, whether in warning to keep quiet or in comfort she was not sure. His palm felt hot against her skin. Her own must have felt cold as snow.

"What are you hoping to get from this stunt?" le Gayne demanded, and peppered them with another string of insults, most involving the sexual organs of animals. "Are you hoping for ransom? You're stupider than you look, if that's the case."

"Not ransom in the way you think," Thomas said. "We do not want your gold."

That caught him up short. "Christ's curse, what else could you want?"

"My sister needs a husband. I have decided upon you."

"*What?*" le Gayne exclaimed, his eyes going to Serena. Then he started to laugh. He fell back from the door, his voice moving farther away as he stumbled about the room in the dark, howling with laughter.

His mirth cut through to her bones, settling deep. She could remain standing there only by clinging tight to her will and to her anger. It didn't matter what this donkey's ass thought of her, she told herself harshly. She was not in search of his affections. She would have her revenge on him for this humiliation when he was forced to accede to their wishes.

When the laughter had died down to intermittent giggles—creepy and repulsive, coming from such a large man—Thomas spoke again.

"You will have neither food nor water until you have agreed."

"What?" le Gayne said angrily, his giggles stopping. "I will be of no use to you if I die!"

"You are of no use to us alive and unwilling, either," Thomas said. " 'Twould be safer to have you dead than to set you free at this point."

" 'Tis a fool's plan! You will gain nothing from it!"

"Perhaps not," Thomas said, and began to lead Serena away, carrying the torch and leaving le Gayne in darkness. "But be assured that all you shall gain from refusal is a slow and painful death."

Serena sat on the floor of the bedchamber, going through her chest of treasures. There were not many.

There was an ivory comb, several of its teeth broken, with a mermaid carved upon it. There was a small silver mirror, tarnished now, reflecting nothing. She lifted out the gold links of a girdle, finding the place on the medallion at the end of the chain belt where she had put her teeth marks in the soft gold as a baby. Any of the three items could have been sold, but for her doing that would have been worse than selling the land.

These three things, and a white and gold sleeveless surcoat, were all she had left of her mother. Her memories were almost as sparse: a bee sting that her mother had soothed; being held on Lady Clerenbold's lap while she talked to one of the serving women; her face illuminated by a candle after she had tucked Serena in for the night; and, near the end, seeing her pale and weak against her pillow, after Thomas was born. She had died within the year, never having recovered her strength from the complicated birth.

Serena remembered as well the love she had felt for

her mother, the warm sense that all was well when the woman was present. She wanted to re-create that with her own children. She missed the softness that had gone so early from her life.

She doubted she could ever become a graceful lady, pious and soft-spoken, her fingers skilled with a needle and her hands at healing: she was too well used to the ways of men for that. She knew she had it in her, though, to be a loving mother. She loved Thomas, for all that they were constantly at each other's throats, and she would love her children. There was nothing more she would ask from life than the chance to do that, and to remain free from hunger.

"Serena?" Thomas interrupted her thoughts from the doorway.

"Yes?" she said, turning from her seat on the floor, the white silk surcoat spread over her lap. Her brother had been down to see le Gayne on this, the man's fifth day of captivity.

"He has agreed."

She closed her eyes and gave thanks to God.

Chapter Three

Le Gayne's Fortress
1809

"This is the haunted castle?" ten-year-old Alex asked in
disgust, still panting from the long climb up the hill.

His cousin Rhys looked affronted, the locks around
his own face damp with sweat. "What were you expecting? I told you it was a ruin."

Alex dropped down onto the springy turf, shaking his
head at the sight before him. Random stones were scattered over the hilltop, innocent and bland in the cheery
June sunlight. Rabbits grazed among the low grasses and
wildflowers, and blue butterflies danced in the warm
golden air. A few eroded, low walls gave hints of the
fortress that had once stood here, protector and oppres-
sor of the farmlands below, but there was nothing left

to impress a boy who had been expecting towers and torture chambers.

"It's nothing but a pile of rocks."

"Don't let the ghost hear you say that."

Alex made a rude sound. "There's no such thing as ghosts."

"We'll see how brave you are when it gets dark, city boy," Rhys taunted.

"London at night is more dangerous than your stupid ruins will ever be."

Rhys threw a rock at him, hitting him on the shoulder. Alex scrambled up and tackled him, setting off a scuffle that left Alex with a fat lip and Rhys's shirt torn. Honor satisfied, they set about exploring the ruins, looking for remnants of armor, swords, and battle-axes. As they scrounged about, Alex slowly wandered away from Rhys, his mind lost in thoughts of knights and battles.

A black-and-white bird standing on a rock made a harsh *weet-chak-chak,* and small bees buzzed among yellow and pink flowers. A grasshopper leaped away as Alex poked at the ground with his stick, seeking the clank of metal. The sun, hot on his neck and shoulders, felt as if it were seeping through the fabric of his shirt, baking his skin. He paused in his search a moment, standing straight to see where Rhys was.

His cousin was nowhere in sight, and as Alex looked around he saw that he had wandered into what might once have been the kitchen garden. It was a walled area, and made up one end of the U-shaped castle foundations. Like most boys his age, he could never get enough of reading about castles, and his schoolmaster had taught him a good deal about the history of the structures.

The garden was a mass of wildflowers and small

shrubs, its grasses buzzing with insects. A small snake sunned itself atop the wall, waking and slithering quickly into a crack when his approach disturbed it. The garden was bare of trees except for one, an old monster with a massive trunk several feet around.

Alex squinted through the sunlight at the tree, its branches sparse, thick, and stunted, as if they had been broken off in storms. It looked ancient, as old as the ruins themselves. It had gray-white bark, with rough horizontal ridges where it was not split and breaking away in black wounds or covered in pale lichens. The bark looked like that of the cherry tree he had sat in yesterday with Rhys, gorging on ripe fruit until he was ill. Only this tree was still in blossom and without leaves, whereas those in the orchard were already bearing fruit.

The blossoms didn't look quite like anything he'd ever seen. They were vivid pink, with dozens of petals on each flower. He continued to stare at the tree, which was massive and rough, blooming out of season with its profusion of feathery pink blossoms, and an eerie sense of the tree's wrongness began to creep up his spine.

The hum of the insects grew louder in his ears, and in their chattering he imagined he could hear another voice, softer, female, calling to him.

Alex, she called. *Alex . . .*

His body trembled, his legs going weak. He wanted to run, but could not move. It was as if some silvery energy ran through his nerves, turning his muscles to jelly.

"Alex!" Rhys shouted from somewhere behind him. "Where are you?"

The sound of his cousin's voice, impatient and real, broke the spell. "Here!" he called, and backed away from the tree. "Coming!" He was unwilling to turn his back on the cherry tree, possessed by the certainty that it was somehow aware of his presence: that there was some alien sentience living within it.

When he was a safe distance away, he turned and ran.

They built their campfire in the shelter of one of the low walls, and as the sun set they sat around it, devouring the supper that Rhys's mother had packed, both of them as hungry and well mannered as a pair of wolves.

Alex knew his mother and elder sisters would throw a fit if they saw him gnawing on a slice of roast beef bare-handed, as he did now. He growled in low pleasure, ripping at the meat—imagining it was a leg of boar, imagining Philippa, Amelia, and Constance having a fit of the vapors, moaning and fanning themselves, waving a burned feather under each other's noses at his display of barbaric manners, all the while bewailing their fate at having been given a brother to endure. Mother would look on, helpless and disapproving.

The food was well finished by the time full dark fell upon them, late in coming at this time of year. As weariness crept up on them they grew chilled, and they crawled into their blankets, lying at right angles to each other, nearly head-to-head around the fire. They said little, staring into the flames and occasionally throwing a stick into the pit or poking at the embers. Eventually even that grew to be too much effort, and Alex drew his hands into the warmth of the blanket.

It was the first time he had camped out-of-doors, and he felt his senses expanding into the night around him, hearing the crackle of the fire, the breeze around the low walls, and the night insects buzzing faintly. A sense of his own vulnerability slowly began to tingle over his skin as he lay exposed on the ground, without the shelter of walls or roof.

"Her name is Serena," Rhys said into the quiet.

"Who?" Alex asked, his half-mast eyes opening full again.

"The ghost."

Alex gave a loud, disparaging sigh, but felt a shiver along the back of his neck. "And when the moon is full you can hear her weeping for her lost love," he mocked. "It's the same story everywhere."

"Serena is not that type of ghost. She is a murderess," Rhys said, his voice low and ominous.

Alex tucked the blanket more tightly under his neck, his hands fisted in the wool. "Oh? And whom, pray tell, did she murder?"

"Her husband, upon their wedding night, in their bed while he slept. He was in love with her, wildly so, even though she had professed a great hatred for men and vowed to become a nun."

"Then why did she marry him?" Alex asked.

"It was her brother who forced her to marry. Except for her brother, the entire family had been wiped out by the Black Death, and they were desperate for money. When Hugh offered for her, the brother agreed. The brother beat Serena into submission, and, helpless to do otherwise, she married Hugh, swearing revenge on them both all the while."

"She could have run away," Alex said.

"To where? And that would not have been good enough for Serena. Like I said, she wanted revenge. The final straw was what Hugh did to her under the bedcovers on their wedding night. When he was finished, and slept in blissful satisfaction, she took her dagger and stabbed him through the heart."

Alex craned his neck to see his cousin's face. "What *did* he do to her . . . under the covers?"

"Some say he did something unnatural. Others that it was only what a maid should have expected."

Alex frowned. But what *was* that, exactly?

"The next morning," Rhys continued, "when a serving wench came in with their morning meal, she found Serena covered in blood, laughing. The girl screamed, and Serena ran past her, darting from the room, her naked body red with her husband's blood. She tripped at the top of the stone stairs to the great hall, and tumbled down them, breaking her neck and half the bones in her body, her crumpled body finally coming to rest on the floor of the hall."

Alex flicked his eyes to the remnants of a stone staircase, not four feet from where he lay. He inched closer to the dying fire.

"The castle has been haunted by her crazed spirit ever since. She will not harm a woman, but any boy or man who ventures onto the grounds at night had best fear for his life. 'Tis why the place came to be called Maiden Castle."

Alex stared wide-eyed at his cousin for several long moments, until it occurred to him that if Serena was so dangerous, Rhys would not be lying so calmly in his blanket across the fire. He forced a laugh. "That's a clever story. Did you make it up as you went along?"

"It's God's own truth, and it's why I'm wearing this for protection," Rhys said, pulling on the chain around his neck until a silver crucifix emerged from his blanket. "My sister's nurse is Catholic, and she gave it to me after hearing where we would be spending the night."

Alex's eyebrows went up in concern, and he chewed his lip. He had no such talisman, coming from a family that only went through the motions of religion. "There's no such thing as ghosts," he said.

Rhys smiled, and tucked the crucifix back into his shirt. "Sleep well, city boy." He made a show of flopping about, getting comfortable, then gave a loud sigh of contentment and closed his eyes.

"There's no such thing as ghosts," Alex repeated in a whisper. He closed his eyes, shutting out the shadows of the castle walls, and the staircase so near. In his mind the lumps of ground beneath him slowly became the crumpled body of Serena, her broken limbs jutting against his own small frame, the cold earth her own cold, dead flesh. He could hear her calling him, a breathy whisper on the night air, calling like the voice from the cherry tree, *Alllll-exxxx . . .*

His eyes flew open. The fire was but burning coals now, and he could hear his cousin's relaxed breathing. Rhys was truly asleep. His cousin's blithe ease at sleeping in the ruins of a haunted castle, protective crucifix or no, reawakened Alex's suspicions. He narrowed his eyes at this country relative who had already tricked him into trying to milk a bull—he'd been lucky not to get his skull kicked in—and who had persuaded him to wade in stagnant water infested with leeches. And an encounter with a patch of stinging nettles had led to a serious fistfight.

This time when he closed his eyes, he kept away the images of broken bones. Instead he drifted off to sleep imagining the grand revenge to be had if Rhys ever came to visit London. It would be a wonderful thing if he could be knocked into the filthy Thames.

When Alex awoke again it was to chilled darkness, and he did not know for a moment where he was or what had stirred him. A streak of light, present but for an instant, flashed by the corner of his eye. He turned his head, then rolled onto his back as another streak, then another flashed across the deep blue-black sky above.

His lips parted, and his eyes widened in amazement. Streak after streak—five, ten, twenty at a time—burned their way across the heavens, their white light illuminating the castle ruins like silent fireworks.

"Rhys!" he whispered, not turning to look at his cousin, unwilling to take his eyes off the miracle above. "Rhys! Wake up!"

Not waiting for a response, he stood and stumbled his way to the remnant of stairs, climbing them up onto the tallest fragment of wall, where he stood atop the uneven stones. It was the highest point of the ruins, above even the tops of the trees that crept up the flanks of the mountain. He tilted back his head and took in the blue-black sky.

Stars fells down by the hundreds in a cloudburst shower of light, illuminating the mountaintop and the valley below.

Another glow of light, larger than the stars, closer, brought his gaze back down. He caught a quick impression of long pale hair floating in the breeze, a white hand reaching toward him, and a glowing face with eyes like empty wells, black with pain. Startled, he lost his balance, the stars above briefly filling his gaze once more as he fell through empty air.

He hit stone, and then there was nothing.

Chapter Four

Maiden Castle
August, 1832

"Serena must be rubbing her ghostly hands in anticipation," Rhys said.

Alex's index finger lightly touched his temple, and the streak of white in his midnight black hair. The scar from where his head had struck one of the stone stairs twenty-odd years ago was hidden there, at the edge of his hair-line. "Sometimes I almost think you believe that story."

"I didn't, you know. Not until I woke up that morning and found you with your skull cracked and a broken arm. It's a miracle you ever got off this hill alive. It's beyond me why you would choose to live here now."

Alex sat atop one of the crenelated parapets of the tower of the rebuilt castle, oblivious to the sheer, hundred-foot drop at his back. He could see for miles,

over downs and small pockets of woodland, sheep-
dotted fields and hedgerows, the river and the gray village of Bradford-on-Avon, which nestled along its bank.
And he could see the sky, all of it, a glorious blue dome
stretching from horizon to horizon and into the endless
realms of space beyond.

A breeze through his hair drew him back to earth, and
he smiled at his cousin. "You still think it was Serena
who pushed me from that wall."

"It makes no sense to me how even an ignorant child
of the city like you could have come to such grief without help."

"Ah, but the wonder of the stars . . ." Alex said,
sweeping his hand above him at the sunlit heavens.

Rhys snorted rudely. "There's not a romantic, fanciful
bone in your body."

"Why, darling, what an unfair statement to make,"
Beth Cox said, her bonneted head appearing above the
trapdoor of the tower. Rhys went to assist his wife up
the final steep steps, grasping her hand and pulling her
up. "Whoop!" Beth gasped as she found herself suddenly standing, her fluffy skirts billowing in the breeze.
"Oh, good gracious," she said, taking in the view.

Alex watched as Rhys put his arm around his wife,
steadying her. It reminded him that he'd had that once,
that closeness with a woman, ripe with the hopes of
family and a long life. Death had taken it from him with
the hot touch of a fever, sweeping pretty, petite Frances
away as if she were so much dust. Sometimes it felt as
though every step he had made since that day was a step
away from the possibility of ever having such a life
again, and having to risk the pain of loss.

"I don't see what was unfair about it," Rhys was saying to his wife. "The man would rather spend his nights with a telescope than a woman."

Beth rolled her eyes, shaking her head at his obtuseness. "You have only to take a look around you, my darling, to see the truth."

Alex and Rhys both raised their eyebrows, their twin expressions forcing Beth to elaborate. "It's a *castle*," she said, as if speaking to simpletons. "A medieval castle atop a mountain, pennants waving, portcullis raised as if awaiting the return of its lord from the Crusades." She sighed, moving a little closer to the edge and looking out over the body of the fortress. "If Serena does still haunt this hill, I am certain she is glad to see her home occupied again, especially after the Briggs family abandoned her so abruptly. There were rumors that Mr. Briggs did not like sharing his home with a ghost. You wouldn't mind though, would you, Alex? Not a man with your kind sensibilities."

Alex raised a single eyebrow at his cousin, who responded to his wife's words with a shrug and a helpless expression. Beth could find romance in a pigsty; a castle held a host of wonderful imaginings, even one with a murderous ghost for a caretaker.

"I took the place only for the view," Alex said. "It's the perfect spot from which to study the night sky. And you already know it was Mr. Briggs who rebuilt Maiden Castle, so I can't take credit for that bit of your fancy. I would have been content with the tower and a one-room cottage."

Beth wrinkled her nose at him. "Pish."

He smothered a smile. *Ah, well.* Let her think him a dashing, romantic figure in his castle on the hill if it pleased her. No doubt she would slowly drive Rhys up a wall with her thoughts.

"Uncle Alex?" a small voice asked, and he turned to see his niece Louisa, age nine, poking her blond head above the hatchway. "Uncle Alex, Mummy is looking for you. She said to come right this minute," the little girl said imperiously.

"Did she?" He raised his eyebrows at her.

"She did. She said to tell you she is waiting in the library." Louisa frowned at him. "I shouldn't keep her waiting, if I were you," she said, and then ducked back down the hatchway, her message delivered.

Alex turned a wry smile on Rhys and Beth. "Duty calls."

Serena stood amid the spring flowers in the garden, staring up at the new stone walls of the castle as if their solidity were a personal challenge. She would rip them down with her bare hands if she could. God knew she had done her best to keep them from going up.

She'd worked hard to chase out the new occupants, too. For all the good it did her. The Briggses and their staff had moved out, but now someone else was moving in, and she'd have to start all over.

Didn't anyone understand that this place belonged to her now, and that she wanted to be left alone? She had been at the fortress for nearly five hundred years. She had earned it with her own blood and determination. It was hers, and she was not inclined to share.

Living people. How she loathed them.

She jerked her chin up and flicked back a long tress of pale blond hair with the back of her hand. As her father had once said, the first step to defeating an enemy was to know him. It was time to reconnoiter.

She walked through the flowers to the stone path, and followed it the length of the garden to the new iron gate at the end. The only thing she could thank Briggs for was having the garden replanted and cleaned up. She had grown used to it being wild, and had not known how lovely cultivated flowers could be. There were many growing here now that she had never seen before, their hues brilliant, their blossoms huge and exotic to her eyes.

She walked through the iron gate, wincing as it shivered through her. The folktales about iron holding in a spirit were not true, but the metal was unpleasant to encounter nonetheless.

The courtyard she stepped into was filled with wagons and people moving about, unloading furniture and supplies and shouting orders at one another. The noise they made had her cringing back, the voices a vibrating, ringing assault on her head.

She had forgotten how loud they were, living people. The six-month respite since Briggs had left had allowed her to forget, and she had luxuriated in the quiet of a vacant building.

She clenched her teeth and wove her way through the milling servants, careful to avoid being stepped through. No one turned to look, no one commented that she was dressed oddly, and no one made way for her, for no one could see her. She paused to drag her fingers across the nape of a man's neck, and was rewarded by his startled jump. He turned around, but, seeing no one, could only rub at his neck and wonder.

She could have floated above the servants had she wished, like thistledown on the wind. She could have gone from the garden straight through the castle walls, and avoided them altogether. Thomas would have said it was stubbornness that had her walking among them, stubbornness and her own peculiar form of defiance against the obvious truth that she was no longer completely human.

In part he would have been right.

The rectangular courtyard formed the center for the long, U-shaped castle that surrounded it, the open end leading to a drive that, through a modern, ingenious bit of engineering, wound down like a tunneling spiral staircase before opening out below at the gatehouse on the side of the steep hill. That dark passage had made an excellent place in which to spook horses and terrorize Briggs and his coach and footmen.

Serena climbed the stairs to a pair of the castle's doors, held open by wooden wedges. She paused to the side, waiting for workers to pass through with their crated burden. She felt something brush against her leg.

"Beezely!"

The orange cat meowed, staring up at her unconcerned as a workman put a boot through him.

"Beezely, silly kitty, you're in the way." Serena squatted down and picked up the phantom cat. She pressed her nose to the space between Beezely's ragged ears, hugging the animal close, protective even though she knew the cat was past all harm. The feline, her first and only pet, had been her one true companion through the centuries. Twenty years into her ghosthood, the cat had dragged himself into her garden, wounded from battle with some unknown animal. He had died a few hours later, but his spirit had stayed with her. "I don't know how you can be so unconcerned, with all this disturbance all around us," she said to him.

Beezely purred and kneaded her sleeve, his sharp claws pricking her skin. Being a ghost like her, the cat always seemed solid to her touch—more so than "real" things, which she could pass through at will. It usually

47

took an intentional effort on her part to touch or move solid objects, or to make herself visible or heard.

The doorway now empty, Serena went through and into the ancestral hall. It was an empty room with a big fireplace, but on the walls were painted the twining, twisted branches of a family tree, with spaces for portraits and names among the leaves. Men were on the north wall, women on the south. Briggs hadn't had time to finish, so it was just his own red face peering out from the leaves on the men's wall. Mrs. Briggs, opposite, looked wan and frightened. *Spineless wench.*

The next room was the king's hall, with a marble diamond-patterned floor and a gilded, royal blue groined ceiling that made the display of ancient, blackened weapons on one wall look as out of place as a dead rat on a banquet table. Briggs and his wife had taste that even she could recognize as showy.

Serena could hear voices coming from the library at the other end of the king's hall: the enemy. She went toward the sound.

Beezely tensed in her arms. An enormous hound had appeared in the doorway to the library, head raised, eyes staring straight at them. Beezely hissed and clawed his way loose from Serena's arms, dropping to the floor with his back arched, hair on end.

The hound's ears lowered uncertainly as he looked at Serena, the beginning of a whine starting in his throat, but then Beezely trotted away from her. The hound gave a tremendous bark, and the animals were off, Beezely an orange streak heading for the door. The hound's claws scrabbled for purchase as he gave chase on the polished floor, nails clicking and clattering as he galloped after the cat.

Serena had seen it before: dogs had a natural fear of

48

ghosts, but their instinct to chase and kill animals smaller than themselves often overrode it. Especially where Beezely was concerned. Either that, or the cat somehow taunted the beasts into going after him. Serena had thought that was the case more than once over the years.

"Otto! What in God's name—" The speaker came into the hall in time to see the rear end of his dog disappear through the door to the ancestral hall. The man halted, staring straight through Serena for a long moment, then gave a facial shrug, as if to say the mind of a hound could not be fathomed.

He was a tall man, perhaps even an inch taller than Serena herself, with broad shoulders and a sturdy frame. He was neither thin nor fat, having instead that solidness of form that bespoke a man past the first gangly flush of youth. He had dark hair with a white streak, dark blue eyes, and a shadowed jaw that spoke of a heavy beard if left unshaven. He was dressed in a jacket of dark forest green, the collar of his white shirt coming only halfway up his neck, his cravat tied without flamboyance.

She had often spied on Briggs as he dressed with the help of his valet, and had grown familiar with this modern mode of dress. Briggs's clothes had been much brighter, however, and his collar points had reached halfway up his cheeks. She'd marveled that he didn't put an eye out on one of them.

This man looked much more competent than had the castle's last intruder. There was intelligence in his eyes, and a relaxed confidence. He was a great deal better-looking, too.

A faint sense of familiarity floated through her, coupled with a distant, long-suppressed yearning. The con-

49

fusing, unexpected combination brought a sudden panic welling up inside her.

He had to be gotten rid of, as quickly as possible.

A female voice with all the melody of a crow's suddenly rang out at him from behind, and Serena watched him close his eyes briefly, lips tightening as he summoned patience.

"It's foolish, Alex. Foolish and irresponsible," the woman said, coming into the hall. She looked older than him by a handful of years, and there were deep lines from the sides of her sharp nose to the corners of her sour mouth. "How can you trust others to run the mills for you? We shall be robbed blind, while you sit up here and play at being an astronomer. Do you think you will discover a planet, like your hero, Mr. Herschel?" She had her hands on her hips, looking at the man as though he were a recalcitrant child. "This is just another of your childish fantasies, like the time you tried to run away and join the navy."

"I am no longer twelve years old, Philippa," he said, turning to her. He spoke softly, calmly, yet there was a sure strength in his words. "And you know, as well as do Amelia, Constance, and Sophie, that I would never make a decision that would result in a reduction in your or their incomes. Your well-being has always been my primary concern."

Philippa looked as if she wanted to say more, her lips pursed tight with discontent, but apparently his words rang true. "Well. You have shown more business sense than Father ever did, I will grant you that. But it's a good thing you only leased this monstrosity, instead of buying it outright. We should surely have all been in the poorhouse then, with the upkeep."

Alex gave a half smile. "Mr. Briggs wasn't quite

ready to give up the idea of being lord of the manor. I think he likes to tell his friends that he owns a castle. He claims to be descended from a line of German princes."

The comment coaxed a twitch of a smile from Philippa's lips.

Serena studied the man, her eyes narrowed. There must be something wrong with him. He was placating this woman who cast doubt upon his good sense, when he should instead be telling her to hold her tongue. From what they'd said the woman must be his sister, but that should mean nothing. Thomas had never lacked the backbone to argue with her when he disagreed, even though she usually had been right.

She had been mistaken to think it was strength she heard in this man's voice. He was obviously some form of coward, weak and trembly as jelly.

Square shoulders and a strong jaw did not make a warrior. She would have him out of here within a week. The fluttering panic in her chest quieted, and she buried that faint, painful sense of yearning.

He surely would be no more difficult to evict than Briggs had been. Easier, as he had nothing but a lease to hold him, unlike Briggs, who had invested huge sums of money in building this "monstrosity," as the Philippa woman so aptly called it. Briggs's weak-willed wife had at first pleaded to stay, but when her husband had started reporting to her each of his ghostly encounters, she'd become a sniveling, nervous mess, more eager than he to leave the place.

What a pair of cowards they had been.

Philippa gave a sudden shiver. " 'Tis a drafty home you've chosen, Alex," Philippa said, rubbing her arms. "I shouldn't like to be here in winter, if August is so

51

chilly. Why anyone would build on top of a mountain, exposed to the wind, is beyond me."

Alex began to move toward the open door to the ancestral hall, where two workmen were fumbling with a crate. "I find it quite warm, myself," he said, and then to the workmen, "Careful there! Get that to the tower in one piece, and there's a shilling in it for each of you."

Philippa hissed out a note of disgust, barely waiting until the men were out of earshot before addressing her brother. "You spoil them. Why pay them extra for doing their job? You are too soft, Alex. Too soft by half."

"As you've said before," he replied calmly. "Have you any notion where Sophie may have gone off to?"

Serena came close to Alex, until she was right beside him and could stare into his eyes. Was there any anger there at all for this overbearing sister? A flicker, perhaps. Or was it cunning she saw? Or perhaps he was deaf to her insults, and there was no flicker of emotion in him at all.

He turned his head suddenly, his eyes meeting hers, boring into her. She started, letting out a small yelp of surprise.

"She's probably taken Louisa into some dreary cellar, to fill her head with superstitious nonsense," the one called Philippa was saying. "I'd best find them, else that child will be screaming of monsters and goblins into the wee hours yet again. Why either of them take such delight in scaring themselves silly I shall never understand."

Alex turned back to his sister, the faint crease of a frown visible between his dark brows. "They behave more like sisters than aunt and niece," he said, but sounded distracted.

Serena, feeling slightly shaken herself by meeting his

eyes, let herself fade away into the unconscious oblivion that was her only form of rest. He couldn't have seen her, but some people seemed able to sense her—as he had. She would have to think on this peculiar man, and on how she could most easily be rid of him.

Chapter Five

"No moon, clear skies, and nary a female voice to be heard. A man could ask for no more," Alex said to his Great Dane Otto as he set down the small, red-shielded lantern on the portable desk. He went to the crenelated wall of the tower and looked out over the dark countryside. There were few lights visible, much of the populace having gone to bed with the setting of the sun. They had work to do at dawn.

He, on the other hand, had but recently awoken, and only the rising of the sun would signal the end of his work for the night.

"Would they think me mad, Otto, if they knew what I was about?"

Otto looked at him, jowls hanging, then turned his shoulder to his master and went to go lie down on his favorite horse blanket.

"As if you are one to talk," Alex said to the animal,

who tucked his nose into his paws and gave a great sigh. "At least I have not been chasing shadows all week, barking at nothing."

He pushed away from the parapet and went to the table, arranging the star charts and clock within easy reach from the reclining chair he'd had brought up when it became apparent there would be no rain or clouds tonight. A sense of delight, mingled with a trace of guilt, tickled at his chest. It was the same feeling he had known as a child, abandoning schoolwork for games.

"Perhaps Philippa was right about me," he said aloud. "Not that it matters." The wool mills were in capable hands; Sophie was at last engaged and presently living under the watchful eye of Philippa; Amelia and Constance had their own households to concern them; and he was finally free to do as he wished. There was no reason he shouldn't sit and count stars until he was ninety.

He made himself comfortable in the chair, lying almost supine upon its lowered back, and turned his eyes to the sky. He felt as if he had been waiting twenty-three years to do this, here in this place where he had first been struck by the wonder and mystery of falling stars.

His hand went to the scar above his temple, his fingertips running along it in unconscious habit. Little memory of which he could be certain remained from that night. The falling stars, yes. Rhys and his damnable ghost story, yes. But what had caused him to fall—of that he could not be certain.

There had been something he'd seen, some other light, but whether it was only a brighter star or Rhys's ghost Serena, he could not say. Logic demanded that it all had been his own imagination upon waking from the fall, that there had been no light, but there was a part of him that wanted this place to hold a mystery, a bit of the unknown that had touched his life on that extraordinary night.

It had touched his life, cracked his skull, and broken his arm. It might be better for him, he reflected, if it were a certain thing that ghosts did not exist—and Serena most particularly.

Serena roamed the quiet corridors and rooms of the castle, many of which had not been touched since the Briggs family left. What type of life was this Alex Woding trying to lead here?

Woding. The name made her smile. Did he know it meant "the mad one"? He would understand by the time she was through with him.

His was a most peculiar household. It was composed completely of men and boys. Where were the women? Her own home had been predominately male, but even so there had been a fair complement of females, for everyone knew they were needed.

Who was going to do Woding's laundry, mend his clothes, and do a proper job of cleaning? Who would tend to the kitchen herbs and the stillroom? Keep track of the stores and maintain order among the servants? And what would all these men do without the distraction of women? They would descend upon a village inn and throw themselves upon the first poor serving wench they met, like hounds upon a fallen deer.

The girl could likely buy herself a farm on the coins they'd give her, if she survived the ordeal. *Poor wench.*

Still, the all-male situation was convenient for her, so she would not complain despite the curiosity it roused. With just men here, there was no reason to feel guilty about her methods of being rid of the filthy beasts. When

Briggs was here, she had taken care not to frighten his wife, or any of the female staff. He would have been gone sooner if she had, but women had a hard enough time of life without her directly adding to their grief.

But a household of men? Scaring them would trouble her conscience as much as killing fleas.

Men. Men like Hugh le Gayne. She let the old anger bubble up into her chest, heating it quickly to a rolling boil. *Murdering, perverted bastards.* She stoked the flames beneath her caldron of hatred, imagining le Gayne's head floating in the broth, his eyes melting in agony. *Spawn of Satan. Lying, thieving, soulless smear of pig droppings.*

To be surrounded by the living was torture enough. To be surrounded by men was not to be endured. The time had come to act.

She ran down the corridor, her footsteps gaining volume as her fury rose, breaking through the barrier between death and life, becoming audible to the living, the sound a growing pounding upon the wood. Woding, where was Woding, the head of this house and the bringer of these men?

She found his room, empty of all but furniture. Enraged, she grabbed the curtains on the bed and yanked, but they only waved under her efforts, too securely attached to rings and rails to come down unless she consciously made herself more solid. She was too angry to think of that. She jumped onto the bed, kicking at the pillows, tearing at the cloth on the underside of the tester above her head, succeeding only in leaving faint streaks in the cloth.

She leaped off the bed, landing past the bed carpet on the bare wooden floor, her feet making a deeply satisfying boom, as if a log had been dropped on the floor.

She ran to the paneled walls and banged her fists along them again and again, harder and harder, the sound growing, echoing, louder than what would have come from human hands on wood.

A narrow door in the wall suddenly opened, revealing a sleep-befuddled man in his nightshirt. It was Underhill, Woding's manservant-cum-butler.

"Mr. Woding?" he queried, staring blindly into the dark room.

Serena screamed at him, and when he did not hear her she threw herself at him, passing through him, the sensation of going through him bringing her instant nausea. The act brought her to her senses even as the man stumbled back, nearly stepping into her again.

"Who's there?" he cried.

She left him, staggering through the room out into the corridor again, feeling sick, and angry at herself now as well for being so stupid as to pass through him. The experience always cost her more than it cost the living, leaving her drained and queasy.

She moved silently down the corridor, her mind a welter of hatred and weariness. She stopped at the head of the stairs and sat, breathing deeply with her head between her knees, gathering herself together.

Where was Woding? she found herself asking after several moments had passed. She sat up straight, and the feeling of sickness subsided.

Beezely brushed against her side, purring, then stepped up onto her lap, twisting onto his back and batting at her hand as she scratched his stomach. And that hulking hound, Otto, where was he?

A door down the corridor opened, and Underhill came out, dressed now and carrying a candle. Serena pushed Beezely off her lap and followed him.

He went into one of the rooms left empty after the Briggses departure, only a few crates of unknown goods occupying it now, pushed up against one wall. Underhill went through the door in the corner, the one that opened onto the stairs that led to the tower room. He seemed to sense her presence, if only just, peering twice over his shoulder and hastening his step as he went through the door and began to climb the spiral staircase.

Serena followed, then stopped at the top of the stairs, taken aback by what she saw as Underhill set the candle upon the desk in the tower room.

What madness was this?

Taking up half the room was a contraption of polished brass made up of slender arms and balls. As Underhill bumped against it, the balls began to drift about each other, reflecting glimmers of candlelight.

She took a few steps into the room, her eyes going from the spiderish contraption to a thick cylinder of brass atop a wooden tripod placed near the window. Then she saw the maps hanging upon the walls.

Only they were not maps of the land, she saw as she came closer. They were charts of the heavens. She could see the bright points of the Bear, and the Hunter, and the other constellations she had learned to find her own names for over the centuries of watching their turnings through the night sky.

A shiver ran up her spine and she crossed herself, something she had not done since she had lived. God help her, Woding was an astrologer. He knew the secret workings of the universe in ways she could only guess at, and was likely capable of wielding great powers, for good or evil. It had been the astrologers of Paris who had unlocked the cause of the Pestilence, finding its origins in the conjunctions of the planets, and she was certain that any man who could divine such a truth could also own some control of it.

She remembered the way Woding had sidestepped his sister's bleatings, deflecting her to other topics or humoring her. She remembered the way he bribed servants to work hard. She had thought him weak. Was he crafty instead, allowing others to underestimate him? Did having a household of men in some way increase his power?

Underhill had gone up the steep wooden stairs at the side of the room, pushing open the hatchway at the top. Serena followed with trepidation, her long skirts gathered in one hand as she half floated, half-climbed behind him.

"Mr. Woding?" the servant, ahead of her, said as he came out onto the roof of the tower.

"Yes, Underhill, what is it?" came Woding's voice. It was deep, soft, and mildly surprised. She heard no annoyance at being intruded upon.

"Sorry to disturb you, sir. Is everything all right?"

Serena gained the top of the tower, standing still a moment as she tried to make sense of what she saw: the man supine in his chair/bed, the dim red lamp, the table and papers. Recalling the charts upon the walls below, she tilted her head back and took in the vast night sky, shimmering with stars.

"I might ask the same of you. I thought you had gone to bed," Woding said.

"There was . . . ah . . . a disturbance, sir."

There was movement on the other side of Woding's couch, and then the shadowed head of his hound appeared. A low growl emanated from his throat.

Serena made a face at the beast, knowing that at least with the animal she had the advantage. "Growl all you want, you heaping pile of dog meat," she said, knowing that only the hound would hear her. " 'Twill only serve to aid me."

"Otto, hush," Woding commanded gently. The dog's ears flattened, and he gave a discontented whine, shifting on his haunches. "What type of disturbance?"

"I awoke to knocking, thumping sounds coming from your chamber, as if someone were pounding against the wall. When I went to investigate, fearing you were in some distress, there was no one there and the noise suddenly ceased."

Serena went to stand beside Otto, consciously making herself solid, albeit still invisible. She reached down and scratched round the base of his ears, knowing how her presence and contact unsettled the creature. The dog cringed away from her, whining more loudly.

"You must have been the runt of your litter," Serena said, using both hands now to pet and scratch as the dog tried to scoot away from her ministrations.

"Awooo-woo-woo!" Otto howled in distress, and tried to squeeze himself under Woding's couch, bumping the man half out of his seat. Serena drifted into insubstantiality and went to lean against the parapet and enjoy the show.

"Otto! Good Lord, boy, what is it?"

"Woo woo wooooo!"

Woding got out of his chair and crouched down beside it, peering at Otto. "Here, now, what's frightened you?"

"I have heard, sir," Underhill said with a touch of diffidence, "that dogs are especially sensitive to . . ."

Woding stuck his head farther under the couch, making soothing sounds. "Yes, Underhill?" came his voice. "Sensitive to what?"

"To the presence of ghosts, sir."

Woding was silent for a long moment, and then he slowly came out from under the chair, the sounds of Otto's whimpering unabated. "Is that what you think made the noise in my bedroom, rather than, say, a particularly vivid dream?"

"I do not know," Underhill said, now sounding almost embarrassed. "When I opened your door, I felt a terrible sensation of cold, such as I have heard described by those who have been in the presence of spirits. When I checked the room after finding a light, the covers and pillows on your bed had been slightly disturbed. They were neatly made when I checked before retiring, sir."

Woding stood, still looking at the chair where his dog cowered. "If there is a ghost, then judging by Otto's behavior I would say it has followed you."

"Sir?" Underhill said, his voice cracking. Serena clapped her hands in delight.

"I find it much more reasonable, however," Woding said, turning to look at Underhill, "to assume that the noise you heard was no more than the settling sounds of an unfamiliar house, distorted perhaps by sleep. Otto, for his part, has obviously been having a hard time adjusting to his new home, but I expect he should calm down in a few weeks' time."

"But the covers . . ."

"Otto likely made himself comfortable for a few minutes, when I went to fetch a heavier coat."

"And the cold, sir?" Underhill asked, his voice filled with mingled doubt and hope.

"You had just arisen from your warm bed. Naturally my room felt cold in contrast."

Serena made a moue, not at all pleased. She did not like having her efforts reasoned away.

"Of course." Underhill all but sighed the words. "I apologize for being so foolish, sir. I should not have listened to the stories going around, or at least should not have allowed them to affect my imagination."

"Stories? What stories?"

"Various, sir. Some of the men we hired from the village have said that the Briggs family moved out because of a ghost, and they relate the legend of a woman by the name of Serena, who went mad and killed her husband on their wedding night."

"Liars!" Serena screeched, coming away from the wall. How she hated that story! She kicked the table leg with her insubstantial foot, producing no effect in the motionless table. She kicked it again.

Woding pressed his fingertips to the table, as if to keep it still, and turned toward her.

Serena stopped, looking carefully at his face, feeling anxiety rise up in her. He seemed to sense she was there, in a way that went beyond the fleshly chill she caused in many people. She kicked the table leg again. He blinked; then his eyes narrowed.

This was not good. She didn't want him knowing she was nearby except when *she* decided he should know. Her invisibility was one of her greatest weapons, and he was showing signs he might be able to take it away.

"That story has been around for years, no doubt getting more gruesome with each telling," Woding said. "My cousin tried to scare me with it when we were children, on a night we camped in the ruins of the original fortress. He did a fair job of it, too. I was barely able to close my eyes."

"I've heard there was more than that to the night, sir," Underhill said, a hint of curiosity in his tone.

Woding laughed softly. "So that tale makes the rounds

as well? I suppose I should have expected as much. Feel free to tell any who ask that I was watching falling stars, not my feet, and I lost my footing on a ruined wall. I was careless, and I fell. That is all there is to it, although I almost wish I had been pushed by the ghost of a murderess. It would have made for a better story."

What was this? She looked at the streak of white in Woding's hair, suddenly remembering a black-haired boy lying on the stone stairs, the gash on his head bleeding a river on a night when stars fell like rain. The sense of familiarity and longing, was that where it had come from?

"Yes, sir."

"Go back to bed, Underhill. Even if there were a ghost, she could do nothing to harm you."

"Yes, sir. I am sorry to have disturbed you."

Woding waved away the apology. "You might bring a fresh pot of coffee to my study, before you retire."

"Yes, sir!" Underhill turned toward the hatch, apparently happy to have this chance to redeem himself.

There was a great scraping of claws on stone, and then Woding's reclining chair was overturned as Otto scampered out from beneath it, pushing past Underhill and all but tumbling down the wooden steps to the study below.

As Underhill started down the stairs Woding handed him the dog's blanket. "Put it by the fire in the kitchen. Perhaps he'll be more comfortable down there." And then, almost under his breath, "The miserable coward."

Woding closed the hatch, righted his chair, and resumed his supine position, his figure dimly illuminated by the red-shaded lamp. He looked completely at ease, as if nothing his manservant had said had bothered him.

Serena drifted up to sit on the parapet and study him, as he in turn studied the sky.

He was sly, devious. She had already learned that much. He did not approach obstacles directly, like a normal man, using strength to conquer. He employed instead the tactics of a wily woman, manipulating and obfuscating to get his way. She had always thought such modes a sign of weakness, proof that one was not strong enough to take what one wanted. Even she, female since the day she was born, had learned to fight with strength, not wiles.

He looked strong, though. If he'd been properly trained, he might have been able to wield a sword with some skill. He had the shoulders and the height for a decent swordsman. She tried to imagine him riding a warhorse, decked out in armor, battle-ax at the ready. Physically it was not too great a stretch, but the soft tones of his voice made such an image ridiculous.

What strange forces had directed this man's life, and why had he been placed here with her again after so many years? Was he seeking revenge for the fall he had taken? It seemed unlikely, if he did not even believe she existed. Or did he only pretend to disbelieve, and to not remember that night he had seen her? He appeared as foolish as he had been as a boy, his eyes on the stars when there were dangers near at hand, but perhaps that appearance was an illusion.

Whatever the case might be, he would not be able to explain away her actions for long. His servants, by the sounds of it, had already half-spooked themselves. It would be short work to finish that job, and have them fleeing the castle as if their drawers were on fire.

As for him, if he was already aware of her presence in some manner, half her work was done there, too. It would simply be a matter of persuading him that it would be in his own best interest to leave. First, though, she'd have to be certain of what his abilities were. It was always foolish to attack without knowing the armaments of the enemy.

She would triumph in the end; of that she was certain. This Alex Woding had once nearly lost his life because of her. It would be wise of him to remember that.

Alex drew an arrow on his chart through Cassiopeia, noting the time along its length. It was the fifteenth arrow on his chart so far tonight, marking the path of a shooting star. If he were one to believe in omens, he thought it would have been a good one that his first night observing in his new home should be one so rich in data.

He sketched in another arrow, this time through the heart of Pegasus. *Time: 3:20 A.M.*

It was strange that it should yet be so early. Most nights with such a frequency of falling stars, the dawn would come before he was ready, the time having flown by with the swiftness of the wind. Tonight he was not concentrating as he usually did, and despite the falling stars could not lose himself in his observations. Ever since Underhill's abrupt arrival just before midnight, he had been distracted by the sense that he was not alone: that, in fact, someone even now watched him as he made his notes.

He had to restrain himself from checking over his shoulder. This was all probably his own imagination, fired by Underhill's tales. Ghosts *did not* exist. *Serena* did not exist. He was aware that those were the same thoughts that had gone through his head as a boy, the night he'd fallen.

At any rate, even if Serena did exist, he would not

give her the satisfaction of being noticed. Like a mischievous child, if he ignored her long enough she would likely go away. His musings on his possible childhood encounter with her were pleasant only because the incident was distant and unreal, and therefore suited to idle musing.

He returned his gaze to the heavens, and twenty minutes later marked the path of another falling star.

It would be just his luck to have deliberately surrounded himself with the undemanding, relaxed company of men, and then to find himself haunted by a woman.

Chapter Six

Serena sat on the path in the sun, amid the flowers of the garden, Beezely stretched out nearby, asleep. The leaves of her cherry tree rustled in a breeze, and she could almost feel the warmth of the sun on its fresh green leaves. The blossoms came and fell later and later each year, the tree warping and cracking with age. She didn't know what the normal life span of a cherry tree was, but it seemed reasonable to assume that five hundred years was past its limit. She tried to chase the thought from her mind.

The clank of the garden gate latch drew her attention, and she heaved a great sigh of annoyance as an old man and a boy of about thirteen came through, the boy pushing a wheelbarrow from which a hoe and shovel stuck out.

Serena stood, stepping out of their way, but Beezely slept on.

The old man suddenly stopped, looking down at the cat. "Why, hello there," he said. "I almost didn't see you." The man squatted down, reaching out to scratch Beezely, who opened a green eye to stare at the man as his hand approached.

"Grandpa, who are you talking to?" the boy asked.

"This old—" the man began, then stopped as Beezely slowly faded away before his eyes. "Cat."

The boy leaned to one side, trying to see around his grandfather. "What old cat?"

The man stood, chewing at his upper lip for a moment. "A marmalade, rough old tom by the look of him. He's gone now. Must have spooked him."

"I didn't see any cat."

"No," the old man said. "You wouldn't have."

Serena left the garden, not wanting to be around in any form while the males worked, and willing enough to leave them unmolested. She appreciated the flowers too much to disturb those who tended them.

She didn't know why the old man had been able to see Beezely. Was it something to do with him, with the weather, with the alignment of the stars? The cat had been seen often over the years, apparently without any intention on Beezely's part, although she could not be sure of that. Who knew what went on in the mind of a cat?

She herself had been seen only a scant handful of times: once intentionally, and a very few times accidentally, when her emotions were strong and the observer possessed of a nature that allowed such a sighting. That had been what had happened the night young Woding had fallen.

Serena walked along the path that went around the castle, between it and the parapet of the curtain wall.

Grass grew alongside the path, and in several of the bastions there were benches and flower beds, attesting to the castle's present use as a residence as opposed to a defensive fortification. Hugh le Gayne would be calling curses down on Briggs's head if he knew there were roses growing on his walls.

Serena sat down on the bench in the corner bastion, her favorite of the arrow-shaped outthrusts of the wall. She could see for miles over the valley from here, see the gray smudges of the villages, and the green lines of the hedgerows that fenced in the sheep, sheep that looked like so many dots of white from this distance.

The view was as lovely as it was achingly lonely, dredging up memories of what used to be. Clerenbold Keep had long since fallen to ruin and been overgrown, not so much as a crumbled wall visible from where she sat. She had watched it happen slowly, over decades, and it was as if her last link with Thomas and her family had died away with it.

It was more than the sight of her old home decaying that gave her a sweet, almost pleasurable pain in her heart when she looked over the valley, though. She had watched villages come back to life after the Pestilence, and watched them grow. She had seen, from her great distance, people at work in the fields and riding or walking along the roads. It was like listening to a story that she could not be a part of, the characters living in a world to which she could not gain entrance however much she longed for it.

That sweet ache was completely different from the pain of having living people actually share her home. That pain was a knife plunging deep into her heart, each solid step that a living person took a slap in her face, reminding her that she was all but dead. There was no

70

buffering distance with which to shield her heart, no comforting barrier of space to keep her from knowing that they were real, and lived, and ate and drank and slept, while she would never again do any of those things.

Was it that pain that had made her visible, and made her frighten Woding as a child, whether intentionally or not? She remembered observing the boys from a distance, listening to that tale of falsehoods Woding's cousin had spewed out as truth, debating whether it was worth giving them the fright they deserved for invading her mountaintop. She thought she had decided against it.

And then, in the middle of the night, with dawn but a few hours away, something had drawn her to young Woding as he stood in wonder upon the wall, his very soul glowing in his face, completely entranced by the stars. She had reached out, wanting . . . wanting to touch something she could not name, even now. And he had seen her.

Strange to think that boy was now a man, older than she herself had been when she died.

White clouds drifted in the blue sky, taking nameless shapes, as if trying to speak to her in an unknown language. Would that they could teach her all she still did not know. Would that they could tell her if there was some purpose to Woding's being the one who took the place of Briggs.

Did he sleep now, after his night of stargazing?

Alex dozed uncomfortably in his darkened bedchamber, longing for the oblivion of deep sleep. Man, unfortunately, did not seem made to dream while the sun was yet in the sky.

He rolled onto his side, the top sheet sliding smoothly over his naked skin. Little light reached him where he lay; the heavy curtains on the windows were drawn, as were those on the Jacobean tester bed in which he tried to sleep. Despite the darkness, and despite his own weariness, his body somehow knew it was day.

Disturbing images peopled his half sleep: Otto pursued by a shapeless shadow; his sisters standing with quirts in hand, supervising his kitchen staff, who toiled in front of a roaring fire dressed only in loincloths; himself locked in a dungeon room while Underhill stood outside the door, complaining that his feet were cold.

Then he was in his own bed again, lying on his side, and felt the covers being lifted behind him, and then the gentle depression of the mattress as a woman slipped into bed with him. She pressed herself up against his back: he could feel her breasts, her thighs, her arm coming over his side so her hand could stroke his chest. She was tall, able to kiss the back of his neck as her feet entwined with his.

Sighing, he rolled over toward her, his arm wrapping around her to hold her closer, and he opened his eyes. Black hollows stared back at him where her eyes should have been, black, empty wells in a face white as death.

His own shout woke him. He sat up quickly, feeling the sweat that drenched his skin, realizing with relief that he had awoken from lying on his back, not his side. There had been no phantom woman in his bed. It had been only a dream.

The sound of his own breathing was loud in the confines of the curtained bed, his eyes accustomed enough to the darkness to see the dim shapes of the bedposts and disarranged bedcovers. His breath caught. He felt it

72

again, the sense he had known last night of not being alone.

He stared into the deep shadows in the right-hand corner at the foot of the bed. He could see nothing in front of the bedpost, could see nothing but the dark, bulbous shape of the post itself, yet some sense told him there was something—some*one*—there.

Serena sat frozen. He was looking at her. Right at her: she didn't dare move. Did he truly see her, or only sense her, as he had seemed to in the king's hall that first day, and again atop the tower?

She had come to see if he slept, and had sat in the corner of the bed watching him toss and turn, curious, needing to know his secrets. She had wondered what nightmares tortured his sleep.

At last he looked away, flinging wide the curtains on the left of the bed and swinging his legs out so that he sat on the edge of the mattress. He bent over, elbows on knees, head in hands, fingers scratching through his hair, then suddenly looked over his shoulder at her once more, staring hard for a brief moment. He stood and walked naked to his dressing room.

Serena released her breath in a whoosh, still too shaken to move. She wished he would stop doing that—staring at her as if he knew she was there. It was positively unnerving. As had been the sight of his bare buttocks.

Firm, well-sculpted buttocks.

She'd seen plenty of them in her time—her brothers and the men-at-arms had never been shy about bathing, and took some incomprehensible delight in flashing their derrieres at each other and at any female servants—but buttocks had never widened her eyes the way that glimpse of Woding's smooth flanks had.

73

Smooth, hollowed at the sides, just the size to be held and squeezed.

Her mouth turned down, and she was appalled with herself. Where had that thought come from?

She could hear water flowing in the dressing room. He had to be bathing.

She had watched Briggs at the task. Her curiosity over the fittings of the bathing room, with its long, deep tub and built-in basin, had overwhelmed her reluctance to see Briggs's huge, hairy belly and the jiggling, peeping pink mouse that was his manhood, poking its puny bald head from a nest of wiry hair.

She somehow knew Woding's manhood would not look the same.

The warrior in her said this was the perfect time to investigate that issue, when he would likely sense her presence and be made uncomfortable. He would not want to remain in a home where he had no privacy, where every time he took his drawers down he felt someone was staring. As much as her brothers had enjoyed flaunting themselves, she knew that they had enjoyed it only while they had control over the baring of their nether parts. Certainly Briggs had not reacted well when she—cringing in disgust the whole while—had reached out and given that little mouse a quick yank.

Something in her balked at the idea of spying on Woding at his bath, though. She didn't know if it was fear of him that stopped her, or unease with her own desire to look upon his naked body.

She would leave Woding, his buttocks, and his stars to themselves for the present, until she decided what course to follow with him. There was always more than one flank on which to attack an enemy. It was time she herself went to battle.

* * *

"Dickie, bring up a cask of beer from the cellar, will you? There's a good lad," Horace Leboff, the cook, told his young assistant.

"Yes, sir, Mr. Leboff," Dickie said, glad enough to set down his paring knife and give his cramping knuckles a break from potato peeling.

He took a candle and went round the corner of the kitchen to the doorway that led down to the cellars. This household was small enough in numbers, and Mr. Leboff was large and strong enough that no one dared to filch spirits, and so the beer cellar door was left unlocked. Dickie liked that. Although he and a few of the other younger servants had talked about how easy it would be to steal a cask, there was some element of pride in knowing they were trusted not to be thieves.

The stone stairway to the cellar was dark and cold. He lit the candles in their brackets as he went down, the flickering flames turning his own shadow into that of a grotesque, misshapen man upon the opposite wall. He wished there were gas lighting down here, as there was in the king's hall chandeliers.

He thought of Marcy, who lived two houses down from his parents, and how her big hazel eyes would go wide with awe when he told her how he and a few of the others all but ran the castle. She had thoughts herself of going into service, but he doubted she could find a posting as plum as this one.

He did not much miss home, except for Marcy. Mayhap it was seeing no one but men all day that put her so much in his mind. Mr. Woding was a strange one, having no women in his house, but Dickie wouldn't complain. A man could let down his guard this way, and be himself. He didn't have to apologize for a belch, and no one shrieked and said he was disgusting when he passed a bit of gas.

He raised the candle high when he reached the bottom of the steps, looking over the humped shapes of the casks. Marcy would ask him if he'd seen the ghost of Serena. They had both grown up hearing the legend of the murderous lady of Maiden Castle. He almost wished he would see her, to have something other than second-hand, half-imagined rumors to tell.

He felt a hand lay itself against his cheek, the flesh as damp and cold as a corpse in the night.

He jumped, a strangled shriek gurgling out of his throat. The sensation vanished, leaving his heart pounding painfully in his chest. He stood motionless, breathing like a winded horse, bulging eyes darting about, seeking movement in the flickering shadows.

Nothing happened. He shivered, his skin chilled, the cold going to the bone. All was quiet beyond the noise of his own thundering body. Had he imagined it?

He set the candle in the last bracket, nearly dropping it before managing, with a shaking hand, to wedge it in tight. He went to heft the nearest cask onto his shoulder.

There was a slow creaking sound from the top of the stairs, and he stopped to listen, prickles running up the back of his neck. The sound quickened, the creak going higher-pitched, louder, recognizable now as hinges, and then the door slammed shut, all the candles along the stairs blowing out in a rush of frozen air.

He trembled, unable to move, the cask wobbling on his shoulder. Don't let it touch me, he thought. If it didn't touch him again, he would be all right. He could hold together. As long as it didn't touch him.

"Our Father, who art in heaven—" he began to pray,

his skin pebbled with goose pimples as if it, too, dreaded what might come.

Cold hands wrapped around his throat.

The cask fell, splitting open on the stone floor with a crashing splash. Dickie howled, scrambling for the stairs in the dark, running headlong into a wall, stumbling into barrels, knocking several off their stands before at last he found the foot of the stairs again, and scampered up them on all fours.

The ring handle of the door would not turn. He put all his strength into it, sweat coursing down his face. There were footsteps, slow and deliberate, coming up the stairs behind him.

He pounded on the door, screaming, "Mr. Leboff! Help me, God help me! Mr. Leboff!" He heard the rustle of cloth, a breath not his own stirring the air behind him, a chill like winter on his skin.

The door suddenly opened, and he fell forward onto Leboff's massive, solid frame.

"Dickie, what is it? What's happened to you, lad?"

"Sss—" he tried. "Ssss—"

"Yes? Sss—?"

"Ssserena," he yelped, regaining his feet and stumbling away from the open doorway.

Leboff peered down the dark stairwell, then turned to look him up and down, a frown on his face. "You've wet yourself. Best you clean yourself up before anyone sees you. And don't be speaking a word of this!" Leboff warned, his expression dark. "There's no need to be stirring up false rumors. I think someone has been playing a prank on you."

Dickie looked down, away from Leboff's eyes, aware now of the warm wetness of his trousers and the sharp smell that mixed with the beer on his shoes. "I dropped a cask," he admitted. He knew it hadn't been one of the other servants teasing him. It had been Serena who had come after him; he was sure of it.

"You can clean it up after you change," the big cook said. "When we find who spooked you, I'll have Mr. Underhill take the cost out of his wages."

"Yes, sir," Dickie said, and went to fetch clean trousers, wondering how he'd ever be able to make himself return to that cellar.

Daniel Padgett rubbed beeswax onto the mahogany rail of the great staircase. He was tall, strong, and blond-haired, and he knew he looked as if he should be out plowing fields or hauling blocks of granite on his shoulder. Doing men's work.

He took another dab of wax onto his cloth, rubbing the satiny rail, quietly pleased with the faint honey scent and the way the wood shone under his care. His title was footman, but he knew he was doing the work of a housemaid. Pride had urged him to protest when his duties were outlined for him, but prudence had kept his mouth shut. The wages here were better than anything to be had in a mill or on a farm, and he lacked the skills of a craftsman. If Mr. Woding wanted to pay him to sweep, dust, polish, and scrub, then sweep, dust, polish, and scrub Daniel would.

And besides, he rather liked being a maid and making things neat and orderly. Not that his mother would ever believe that, given the trails of mess he left behind at home. Somehow, though, here at the castle, it was different. Mr. Underhill showed him what to do, then left him to do it. There was no nagging, no correcting every minor flaw, no hurrying him along. As long as it was done by the end of the day, and done well, he was his own master.

Tomorrow Mr. Underhill was going to show him how to wash clothes, and give him as his helpers for the day John Flury, the gardener's grandson who did odd jobs, and Dickie Chiles, the cook's assistant. He had not decided yet how he felt about spending the day in the laundry, but it was worth trying. He hadn't thought he'd find scrubbing the bathtub bearable, and look how that had turned out. He had never really liked "men's work," anyway. Perhaps this was his calling.

He dropped his rag over the edge of his supply bucket, and with both hands checked the texture of the wood, admiring the way it reflected multicolored light from the rose window at the head of the stairs. It needed just a spot more wax.

He reached for his rag, fumbling along the edge of the pail for it. He turned to look. The rag was gone.

He peered in the pail. Nothing but clean, folded cloths. He lifted the pail. No, nothing. He turned in circles, thinking it must be beneath him, stuck to his shoe, tucked into the back of his pants—it had to be *somewhere.* He bent over the rail, looking down at the gray stone floor below. No.

He scratched at his shirtfront, frowning, turned back to the pail, and there it was, draped over the edge of the pail, exactly as he had left it.

Daniel picked the cloth up carefully, smelled it, looked around. Was he as daft as his mum had always said? He dabbed the rag into the wax and went to work again on the rail.

The next time he turned around, the pail had disappeared.

*　　*　　*

Jim Sommer, coachman, stableboy, and groom all rolled into one fifty-year-old, small, lumpish package of a man, did not like the winding tunnel that led from the castle down to the stables and the lower gate. It was dark, lit in day only by a few deep, narrow windows, and it spooked the horses. He didn't blame them. Every step echoed in the confounded passage, as he should know—every time he wanted something to eat, he had to walk its length up to the castle kitchens.

He was not given to foolish fancies, but he trusted his horses. If their instincts rebelled against a person or a place, he was inclined to think there was something wrong with that person or place.

He walked the passage now, grumbling to himself as his stomach grumbled to him. He'd like to give a piece of his mind to the idiot who'd designed the place. The sound of his own breathing bounced off the walls, sounding louder than it should.

He felt the hair slowly rising on the back of his neck as he approached the spot where the horses shied five times out of ten. There was an alcove in the wall, visible only as a darker shadow now that there were no torches lit. He did not take his eyes from that spot as he made a wide berth of it.

A sigh of pent-up breath escaped him as he rounded another turn and the alcove was out of sight, but before the last of the air left his lungs he tripped over something, sending it clanging on the stones as he stumbled, heart jumping into his throat. His knees hit the paving, his palms scraping stone as he broke his fall.

Sommer panted a moment, his mind checking through his body for injury. He was all right. His glance fell on the object he had tripped over, barely visible in the dim light: a pail, cleaning rags spilling from its mouth.

Sommer got angrily to his feet, grabbed the pail handle, and marched up the last winding curve of the tunnel, across the courtyard, and straight to the kitchens. When he got there, he stomped to the worktable that dominated the vaulted room, slammed the pail down on the wood, and turned a glaring eye to the others who were gathered there: Leboff, Daniel the housemaid, and Dickie the scullery wench.

"What fool," he began, feeling his face flaming with anger, "what utter imbecile—no, what brainless spawn of a dung-eating maggot was stupid enough to leave his cleaning pail in the middle of the tunnel, where one of my horses could have stumbled into it and broken a leg?"

Daniel made a squeaking sound and fainted.

"Hey, ho!" Sommer said in surprise, as Dickie scrambled to catch his falling comrade, managing just barely to ease the tall man to the floor. "What's wrong with him?" the coachman asked, his anger forgotten. "His bucket, was it? I wouldn't have been that hard on him," he said, pulling in his chin, frowning down disapprovingly at the man's limp form. "Thought he had more backbone to him than that, for all that he makes beds for his wages."

"Shut up," Leboff ordered curtly. He dipped a cloth in water and lowered himself heavily to one knee, where he could dab at Daniel's face.

Sommer shrugged and took an apple from the worktable, crunching into it as he watched the little drama on the floor.

"Sommer, make yourself useful," Leboff ordered as Daniel came around. "Go find Mr. Underhill."

"Eh? And tell him what?" he asked around a mouthful of apple.

"Tell him we have a prankster among us. And when we catch him, I'm going to break his miserable neck."

Chapter Seven

Golden rays of late-afternoon sunlight slanted through the diamond panes of the dining room windows, sparkling on the wineglasses and the silver epergne that held an arrangement of fruit and flowers. The rays were doing a fair job of brightening the otherwise ridiculously gloomy chamber, Alex thought.

"I do so love this room," Beth said, lifting her wineglass as young Dickie began to clear away the remaining dishes, preparatory to removing the top tablecloth and bringing in dessert.

"Good lord, you cannot be serious," Rhys said to his wife. "With that . . . that . . ." he stammered, looking up at the wall behind Alex. "What is that thing, anyway?"

Alex knew without turning of what his cousin spoke. "I believe it is a caribou."

"Caribou? Where did Briggs get a caribou?"

"Canada, I should imagine."

"I think it's clever," Beth said, admiring the head and enormous rack protruding from high on the wall. Its missing body had been painted onto the plaster work, one hoof raised as if it were about to take a step.

"The damn thing is cross-eyed," Rhys said.

"And I like the carving over the fireplace, as well," she said, nodding toward the four-foot-tall, carved and painted woodwork coat of arms.

"Briggs probably stole it," Rhys said.

"You have no imagination."

"You have too much," Rhys countered his wife.

"Alex, I insist you champion me in this," Beth said, turning her soft blue-gray eyes to him. "Don't you find that living here makes you want to don hose and doublet, and carry a sword at your side?"

He smiled crookedly. He rather liked Beth and her fancies. She was so sweetly sincere in her romanticism, it was hard to hold it against her. "I'm afraid that Briggs's taste in furnishings is not mine, but I will not deny that the castle has something of an atmosphere to it. It seems to encourage one's fancies to take flight."

Dickie, replacing the epergne and placing dessert spoons on the clean cloth, made a small sound in his throat.

Rhys caught the sound, raising his eyebrows first to Dickie, then to Alex. "Have there been sightings of the dread Serena?"

"Oh, do tell!" Beth exclaimed, clapping her hands in delight.

Dickie carelessly plunked down dishes of ice cream in front of each of the diners, barely nodded to Alex, and dashed from the room.

"Ice cream! Ghost stories and ice cream," Beth sighed on a breath of pleasure.

"I think it is a mischievous staff member we have, not a ghost," Alex said. "With the exception of Underhill and Sommer, the staff are all locals who have no doubt grown up with the legends of Maiden Castle. One of them seems to have taken it into his head to play the restless spirit: things go missing, only to turn up in the unlikeliest of places; footsteps are heard in the hallways and on stairs, strange thumpings heard in the middle of the night; doors appear to open and close on their own; and many complain of sudden cold chills. All of it, however, can be explained away by a mischievous human hand, drafts, and imagination."

"Do you have suspicions of who the culprit might be?" Rhys asked.

"Underhill is looking into it, but has not yet come to a conclusion. Ben Flury, the gardener, can be ruled out. He's seventy if he's a day, and goes home at night. That leaves Leboff and the three young men, two of whom claim to have had ghostly encounters, and one of whom, John, the gardener's grandson, seems genuinely frightened by the stories. He will no longer spend the night at the castle, and refuses to work alone. I find it impossible to believe that Leboff could be the prankster: the man is as solid as granite."

"Perhaps one of the others lied about his own ghostly encounter," Rhys suggested. "Or maybe the two young men you haven't eliminated are in it together."

Beth spoke up. "Or maybe there really is a ghost. Everyone suspects that's why Briggs left so quickly, despite the story he gave about his wife wanting to live closer to their eldest son and grandchildren. I hear he could not get a single night's rest while he lived here."

"Where did you hear that?" Rhys demanded. "I never heard that."

"From Mrs. Rogers, who heard it from Mrs. Fields, who got it from her daughter, who sold eggs to one of the kitchen staff."

"The usual reliable sources, I see."

"I'd have thought you'd be siding with Beth on this," Alex said to his cousin. "You were always all for blaming Serena for my accident."

"Frankly, I can't decide which is the more appealing of the two possibilities," Rhys said. "Having a prankster to outwit, or knowing you're being haunted by a medieval murderess."

"Many thanks for your concern."

"You're welcome."

A tingling awareness began to creep up Alex's neck, one that he had not felt since that day he'd had the nightmare. He continued conversing with Rhys and Beth, his mind only half on what he said as some internal sense tried to locate the source of his unease.

Serena came around the table, curiosity about Woding's visitors having drawn her to the dining room, and now drawing her to Beth. She sat in the empty chair to the woman's left, listening to her speak, the woman's words so fast that Serena had trouble catching them. She leaned her elbow on the cloth, resting her chin in her hand, her tangled pale hair trailing over the table and the seat of the chair as she gazed at the young woman.

She was so pretty. Such smooth skin, unmarred, and dotted with a few faint freckles across her nose and cheeks. She was a creature from a different world from any Serena knew, and led a life she could only barely begin to imagine. She had an innocent, mischievous light in her eyes, and a playful affection when she looked at her husband. Her husband, in turn, looked to adore her.

Serena felt a sadness opening up inside her, a sense of loss for all that she had never had and never been. Why couldn't she herself have led such a life? She reached out her hand to where she could almost touch the blush of Beth's cheek, then touched instead one of the woman's dark brown coils of hair, giving herself just enough substance to be able to feel the silkiness of a braid, and to touch the head of a pin holding it in place.

Beth turned slightly, her hand going to her hair, and Serena backed away, not wanting the woman to feel the chill of her presence and be frightened.

"Beth, what is it?" Woding asked sharply.

Serena saw that, once again, he was looking directly at her, his eyes trying to focus on what must look to him to be empty space.

Beth smiled, shivering slightly. " 'Twas nothing. A loose pin. It felt almost—" Beth finally noticed that Woding was staring intently to the left of her, not at her, and her eyes widened. "Almost like someone had touched my hair," she finished on a whisper. "What do you see, Alex?"

Serena drifted away, not wanting to be detected by Woding, and feeling in no mood to cause a disturbance. Now was not the time to cause trouble, with an innocent such as Beth here. She shouldn't have come to the dining room, shouldn't have given in to her curiosity.

Alex felt the sense of someone *other* move away, and as it left the room he became aware of Rhys's imploring voice and Beth's concerned murmurs.

"Alex? Are you all right? Alex? Beth, pour him some wine. Alex?"

Alex blinked and looked at his cousin, who was half out of his seat and white faced. "I am perfectly fine,

87

thank you, Rhys." He smiled. "Lost in thought for a moment, that's all. My apologies."

Rhys sat back, letting out a shaky breath. "Good lord, you had me believing for a moment that Serena sat here at the table with us."

"She did, I know it!" Beth said. "She touched me."

"You said it was a loose pin," Rhys said.

"It was her, and she wasn't frightening at all. I got a very gentle sense of her, more of curiosity, or almost of sadness . . . yes, sadness. I do think she's lonely. Perhaps, Alex, your servants should try talking to her when something goes missing. Perhaps she is only try to gain their attention. It must be very isolating, being a ghost."

"Beth, darling," Rhys said. "The man was lost in thought. Serena did not touch your hair, and is not looking for a nice chat and cup of tea." He had the sound of a man trying to convince himself more than others.

"You were ready enough to believe in her a moment ago," Beth said. "You should have seen your face."

"I am still not certain, Rhys," Alex said, "of whether you actually believe those stories you are only too glad to tell on dark nights."

Rhys gave a crooked smile and took a sip of wine. "Neither am I, cousin."

It was a few hours later, as the sun began to lower toward the horizon, that Alex stood in the courtyard with Rhys and Beth as they made their good-nights, then climbed into the small, one-horse carriage that they would drive back to their large sheep farm in the valley.

"Come to dinner some evening soon," Beth invited. "Studying stars is well and good, but I wouldn't want to see you become a hermit."

"Your list of eccentricities is long enough as it is,"

Rhys said with a grin, flicking the reins. "We can't have people saying my relatives are mad."

"Good God, you don't mean you've been telling people we're related? I shall never live it down," Alex said.

"Hush, the both of you," Beth scolded. And to Alex, "Come to dinner."

Alex watched as they drove off into the tunnel, where torches had been lit to light their way. He waited, listening, until he was sure they had safely passed the alcove Sommer insisted was haunted.

The evening air was soft, too pleasant to abandon for the Gothic gloom of the castle. He would take a stroll through the garden, then perhaps around the lower wall.

The gate swung easily under his hand, the hinges well oiled. The high walls of the garden cast much of it in shadow, but the espaliered fruit trees on the east wall still caught the light, and the top half of the old cherry tree as well.

Whoever had planned the garden had been careful to include flowers that bloomed at different times of the year, so there were many splashes of color among the dark green foliage of summer. He followed the stone flags of the path in their circuit of the enclosed area, then stopped beside the cherry.

It looked harmless, not at all the frightful tree he recalled as a boy. It had leaves just like any other cherry, and he wondered now if the tree's obvious age had had anything to do with its late blooming, or if it were simply an unusual variety. He would clip a branch of blossoms next summer and see if he could find their match in a book on botany. Perhaps he would ask Ben Flury about growing a new tree by seed—this one looked as though it had outlived its life expectancy.

He continued through the garden, then out onto the

lower wall. When he got to the corner bastion he leaned upon the parapet, looking out over the countryside. For a moment his fancy took him, and he wondered, if he were a ghost, what would it have been like to have been trapped upon this hill for centuries, so far from living beings? Heaven, or hell?

Ghosts. *Serena.* Every strange occurrence at Maiden Castle since he had moved in could be explained away. Even his own occasional feeling of being watched could be dismissed as his imagination, and lingering fears from when he had nearly lost his life here as a boy.

He would not be swayed by thumps in the night or shivers on the back of the neck. There was that in him that wanted to believe Serena existed, that wanted to believe there was something beyond the life he knew, but he would not cheat himself by letting that desire sway his mind from the facts.

Intuition was for others. He needed proof.

In their open carriage, passing between the hedgerows of beech and hawthorn, Beth and Rhys rode in companionable silence, the soft clopping of their horse's hooves punctuating the birdsong and distant *baa*ing of sheep.

"I'm worried about Alex," Beth said into the country quiet. "Did he not look weary to you, as if he had not been sleeping well?"

"He stays up all night looking at his stars. Of course he does not sleep well."

"And the way he stopped and stared over dessert, as if transfixed. I have never known him to behave so."

Rhys did not answer.

"It worried you, too."

Rhys continued staring straight ahead, and Beth could see him working on what to say. "Tell me truthfully," he said, turning to meet her eyes, "without putting into it wishful thinking or imagination. What was it you felt at the table? Was it a loose pin, or did something touch you?"

Beth touched her hair and the head of the pin, recreating the sensation. "It felt just like this," she said, "like I am touching my hair now. You will have to make of it what you will, darling. I can tell you no more."

Rhys sighed. "It would be just like Alex to get himself haunted. He never could live life the usual way."

"I wonder what Sophie would make of this?" Beth mused aloud.

"For God's sake, don't tell her! The last thing Alex would want would be to have his little sister coming to stay, sprinkling holy water about the place and holding conversations with the dead."

"I don't understand what you have against her," Beth said with a touch of affront. "If it hadn't been for my friendship with Sophie, you and I would never have met."

"She's batty, and a bad influence on you."

"As if I haven't a mind of my own! And besides, she's engaged to a vicar."

"That does nothing to reassure me of her state of mind."

"Such a typical man," Beth said, looking skyward and shaking her head. "You have no romance."

Chapter Eight

"Daniel Padgett quit today," Underhill said as he set down the supper tray.

"He could not be induced to stay?" Alex asked, looking up from where he was translating his star-chart notes into coordinates. It was a cloudy night with a hint of rain on the breeze coming through the tower room window, and he had resigned himself to an evening indoors.

"This time his bucket was hanging from the chandelier above his head. No one could have put it there without his noticing. They would have had to put a ladder right over him."

"He could have done it himself."

"I do not see what the point could have been, to keep these pranks up for so long," Underhill said.

"It may be that he is trying to drive up his wages," Alex suggested. "Although I would not have credited him with the cleverness for such a scheme, and indeed it makes no sense for him to quit now if that is so. It continues to be a puzzle."

Underhill mumbled something.

"What was that?"

"I was saying, sir, that there *is* one simple explanation for it all."

"I don't want to hear any talk of ghosts!" Alex said. It had become a sore point, his entire staff convinced that Serena stalked them. They were unwilling to listen to reason, and failed to notice that not a one of them had a mark upon their body to show for her supposed efforts. Even if there were a ghost, she was more a nuisance than a danger.

"Nevertheless, Padgett has quit. Sommer refuses to bring the horses through the tunnel. John Flury will work only at his grandfather's side, in the garden. Dickie, likewise, has glued himself to Leboff, and will not so much as cross a hall without his company. There is no one to do the laundry, to serve, to clean. We are going to have to hire at least two new staff."

Alex sighed. "Then do so. And be sure they are made of sterner stuff than this lot."

"Should I let Dickie go?"

"No, not yet. If Leboff can find enough for him to do, let him stay. Maybe he'll rediscover his backbone, given a little time."

After Underhill left, Alex leaned back in his chair and rubbed his eyes. This sojourn in the castle was not turning out the way he had expected. Yes, he was spending his nights as he wished, but his fantasy of a peaceful household was not being realized. They were almost worse than women, these skittish men.

A low, rumbling growl came from the corner where Otto lay on his blanket. Otto's head came up; then he gave a loud bark, scrambled to his feet, and leaped across the room. Whatever he was after evaded him, and Otto turned and galloped back, barking madly at something on Alex's desk.

"Otto! Hush, boy!"

The dog watched something go from the desk to his blanket, where he pounced, snapping his jaws closed on empty air.

"Otto! Stop it!"

The dog spun and ran at the desk again, crouching down this time and trying to fit his nose under the drawers to one side, his rump in the air, barking all the while. Then all of a sudden the barking stopped, and Otto's head came up, his ears flattening, his eyes going round and white as he stared at the doorway. A soft whine crept from his throat.

The skin at Alex's nape began to rise. He, too, stared at the doorway, and his eyes widened as a vague, transparent white form moved through the space between door and frame. It stopped just across the threshold, as if watching him. Otto inched his way into the well of the desk, bumping aside Alex's legs.

The white shape started to fade from his vision, as if he had lost his focus on it, and in moments was no longer visible, but he still felt a presence in the room with him.

"Will you tell me what it is you want?" he asked aloud. The room remained silent but for Otto's whimpering, yet he knew there was something listening. "You've done a good job of frightening my staff, innocent people who mean you no harm. It does seem that you are seeking something from us."

He was glad Underhill was nowhere near, to hear him talking to an empty room like this. As the seconds stretched into minutes with no reply, he began to wonder at his own foolishness. He was as bad as the rest of them, certain he was being watched.

"Perhaps you're a coward, and afraid to speak," he said, picking up his pen to go back to work. It was jerked from his fingertips and thrown across the room. His desk started to shake, papers and weights vibrating, then was just as suddenly motionless. A touch brushed through his hair, directly over the scar.

He was surprised into silence for a moment after it ended, but then his annoyance at the petty display and all the mischief this ghost had caused came alive. "You *are* a coward, terrorizing the simple and the innocent— even animals, for God's sake. You're a coward and you're cruel, and you ought to be ashamed of yourself," he said, as if scolding a naughty child. "You might succeed in frightening my staff, but you will not frighten me. I'll be damned before I'll see you chase me out of my own home with your silly tricks."

He pulled his supper tray over in front of him, gave a last, disapproving stare to where he felt the presence to be, then began to eat.

Serena gaped at Woding, so calmly forking into his cold kidney pie. She had come to his tower room to spy on him and learn what she could of his astrology work, yet once again he had immediately known she was there.

And what had he done? He had called her a coward, and then lectured her! How dared he talk to her like that? How dared he? He had no idea what she had been through, what reserves of bravery she had had to call upon during her life. She had had to fight to survive, and she had fought for what she wanted. And what she

95

wanted now was for Woding to move out, he and his staff of men.

How dared he lecture her! She wanted them gone, every last one of them.

And she wasn't going to be nice about it any longer.

Woding's staff were at the breaking point—after tonight they'd all be leaving, and then, when he was alone and vulnerable, it would be his turn. The only cowardice she was guilty of was hacking at the arms and legs of the beast that was this household, rather than the head. She'd finish her hacking tonight; then woe to Woding!

Serena moved quickly through the house. Entering the room that was her destination, she grabbed Dickie by the feet and pulled him off his bed. He woke up at the same time he hit the floor, the sound making Leboff stir. Still holding his feet, she began to drag him across the floor.

"Leboff! Leboff!" Dickie screamed. "Aaaa! Leboff!"

The big man came awake, sitting up in bed, staring blindly round the dark room. "Dickie! What is it? What's happening?"

Dickie was struggling against her, so she dropped his feet and pounced onto his chest, her form solid but invisible as she crouched on his rib cage. She lightly poked her fingertips all over his face, in his mouth, his ears, plugging his nose. He started to make bleating sounds.

A hand walloped her from behind, knocking her off Dickie. She went for Leboff's bare leg, biting down on the rounded calf. He bellowed, and she scampered out of the way of his fists and kicking legs.

She went formless and let herself drift halfway up the wall. Then, going against habit, she let herself be seen as a transparent, glowing form. When Leboff's eyes went round as fried quail's eggs, she began to float toward him. He backed away, his head shaking from side to side. He grabbed the candlestick from beside his bed and stabbed it at her.

"Lord Jesus Christ, protect me!" he cried, and she rushed him. He passed out just before she reached him, falling to the floor with a board-shaking thud.

Dickie, weeping, managed to get to his hands and knees and crawl to the door. Serena left him clawing at the handle, too weak and uncoordinated with fear to open it.

She went next to the kitchen, taking every knife she could lay hand to and stabbing them into the plaster of the high, vaulted ceiling. She found flour and dusted it over every horizontal surface, then put a single floury handprint on the black back of the fireplace. It was a pity she didn't know how to write, that she might scrawl something suitably threatening.

Sommer was sleeping down in the stables: too far for her to go. The end of the tunnel was her limit. The Flurys slept in the village. Daniel Padgett was already gone. That left Underhill.

She flew through the halls and up the stairs, getting into the rhythm of destruction, for the moment loving that she was a ghost and not human, and able to do the unnatural. She was a fighter, a warrior, and she would fight until the last of them was gone.

With each act of destruction, the rage in her grew, and as it grew she became more distant from thought and caution. She knew she was expending energies that would cost her dearly, but she was too wrought up to care. It mattered only that there was another to attack, a fresh target for her wrath.

She stopped outside Underhill's door and pounded the

heels of her hands on the wood, softly at first, then steadily louder. She used her fury to funnel energy into her noisemaking—the sound pounding, pounding, pounding, the whole hallway shaking with the force of it as it grew still louder, like the thudding footsteps of a gigantic beast.

The door down the hall opened, and Underhill dashed out in his nightshirt. Tricky devil, he'd escaped through Woding's room.

Serena pounded after him, following, and saw that he was headed for the tower. She flashed ahead of him, using the noise of her hands to herd him back toward the main stairs. He ran down them, and she followed, chasing him through the rooms of the castle, then out into the courtyard.

She continued the pounding out in the open, blocking Underhill when he tried to make for the garden or the lower wall. She wanted him in the tunnel.

He seemed to sense where she was sending him, and tried to escape to the left or right like a frightened sheep, but she kept him in line, coming up right behind him with a noise that he must have felt reverberating in every tissue of his thin body.

The black mouth of the tunnel gaped ahead, and Underhill finally flung himself inside with a howl of surrender. Serena quit the pounding, standing listening as Underhill screamed his way through the turns of the tunnel, alone now with his terror. She doubted either he or Sommer would be coming back through that passage anytime soon.

A deep tiredness began to overcome her as Underhill's echoing cries died away. The thrill of the attack was still with her, still pumping the blood through her bodiless veins, but underneath it she could feel exhaustion seeping out from her marrow. She turned toward the garden and stumbled. She was more tired than she had realized.

A fluttering panic rose in her breast. How much of her precious energy had she used? As the blood lust faded under the pressure of exhaustion, the voice of reason began to chide her for her wastefulness. Never had she expended so much at one time. Never had she allowed herself to get so carried away. She would need to spend several days in the unconscious oblivion that was her only form of rest, to recoup.

She dragged herself into the garden, then allowed herself to float, too tired to go through the motions of footsteps. Her cherry tree was silhouetted against the dark sky, clear to her night-seeing eyes.

Were those leaves there curling, drying out? She came closer, reaching out to touch them. The leaves crumbled under her insubstantial touch. She brushed her hands along the whole branch, feeling the drained wood. It was only where the limb joined the trunk of the tree that she felt life again.

Oh, God. She had killed an entire branch with her stunts tonight. She wrapped her arms around the trunk, tears slipping down her cheeks to soak into the cracks of the bark. For nearly five centuries this tree had been her key to maintaining an echo of life. Without it, death would take all of her.

Once again, if she were not careful, her efforts to live as she pleased would bring about her own destruction.

Chapter Nine

"Leboff quit, and Underhill will sleep only in the stable quarters with Sommer," Alex said, stepping around a sheep. "Dickie, who's had the worst of it, remains in the castle. Underhill hired Dickie's sweetheart, Marcy, as a maid, and I think Dickie is afraid she'll lose all respect for him if he leaves."

"We heard you'd started hiring women," Rhys said, climbing over a stile into the next of his pastures. "The word is, no man in his right mind would spend the night at Maiden Castle." He cast a smart grin over his shoulder. "So much for your plan to live in a bachelor's haven, free from the repressive presence of women."

Alex followed Rhys over the stile, and they followed the sheep path down to the bank of the river, where it ran alongside the water into the cool shade of the trees. "I begin to think an all-male house was a foolish idea. Look at Dickie: he puts on a much stronger front with

Marcy there. And Leboff could have learned a thing or two from Daisy Hutchins, the young widow woman we found for the kitchens. Do you know of her?"

"I've met her at church. A more stolid, unimaginative person you will not find."

"Leboff might have stayed if she were there to begin with, shaming him with her good sense," Alex said, pausing to look into the darkened river for trout.

"I hear there were actual teeth marks on his leg."

Alex grimaced. "So that part got out as well? Then it's no wonder only women were willing to hire on. I'm assuming they all believe the part of the legend that says it is only men Serena dislikes."

"There's an element of competition to it now," Rhys said, tossing twigs into the water. "Every woman for ten miles is using Marcy and Daisy as her proof that when push comes to shove, women have more backbone than men. They are even laying bets on it."

"I can only hope, for the sake of my clean shirts, that they win those bets."

Rhys stopped his twig tossing and looked at Alex, his brows drawn together. "Did Leboff truly have bite marks on his leg?"

Alex shrugged and resumed walking along the wooded path. "Yes, but in the chaos of the dark, I think it just as likely that Dickie bit him as that a ghost did."

"You're still trying to explain things away. God, Alex! I should think it plain even to you by now that something is wrong at that castle."

"There have been no disturbances since that night."

"Most likely because Serena got what she wanted. The only males who will sleep there now are a frightened boy and you. Have you seen nothing unusual yourself?"

"Nothing I would swear to." He could not be certain he had seen that white mist, after all, and in the light of day he could make himself doubt that his desk had shaken, or his pen been pulled from his hand. An experience was not necessarily proof.

Rhys narrowed his eyes at him. "Don't play word games with me. I didn't ask if you would be willing to tell the tale to a judge."

Alex shrugged. "I've done my share of imagining, along with the rest. I'm not willing to completely believe any of it, though."

"You should leave that place. There are other houses with good views. There's no reason to stay."

"I won't be chased out of my home by something that might not exist. Maybe there is something going on up there—but I don't know what, and I cannot be absolutely certain there is a ghost. There is no evidence."

"What more do you need?" Rhys demanded.

They came out of the woods, walking back up the sloping pasture. Alex stopped, looking over the green fields and up at the soft, hazy blue sky. "I don't know what would convince me. Perhaps being led to a previously unknown tomb, or an ancient goblet appearing out of thin air. Something concrete and unknown. I can't let myself believe in the supernatural, while there yet remain other explanations, however far-fetched."

Rhys slapped Alex on the shoulder. "You are one stubborn bastard. Serena could sit on your lap and give you a kiss, and you still wouldn't believe."

Alex grimaced. "Let us hope it never comes to that."

The clock was striking two A.M. when Alex finally lifted his eyes from the pages of *Ivanhoe,* turning the book over on his leg to hold the place while he rubbed his eyes and pushed himself up straight in his chair, feeling the ache in his neck from holding the same position for too long. He yawned, and then as he looked around the library he felt the hairs slowly rise on the back of his neck.

She—or *it*—was in the room.

It was not so strong a sensation as he had had before, else he most likely would have been stirred from his reading, but the sensation was definitely there.

The last time he had spoken to her, or whatever it was, his staff had had a night of hell. Beth's theory that Serena was lonely and simply wanted attention was obviously flawed.

Tonight he would try a far saner course than speaking to the invisible: he would not acknowledge the sensed presence in any way. He would not look toward it; he would not speak to it. This way he might even teach his own imaginative psyche that there was nothing there.

He was privately worried that the more he let himself even think about the possibility of there being a ghost, the more likely he would come to believe it to be true, whether or not there were facts to support the conclusion. He had seen the same thing happen too often with acquaintances who, like him, were interested in the sciences. Their own thoughts became more real to them than the physical world they were trying to study, and they became incapable of seeing evidence that contradicted their theories.

Clearly, the best course was to ignore any strange sensations he had of being watched. There was no purpose in doing otherwise. If Serena existed, she would have to write him a letter saying so, as well as draw a map pointing to the location of her moldering bones.

With that thought in mind, he rolled his head to work

the kinks out of his neck and then rose, taking the lamp and book with him up to his bedroom and thence to his bathroom, making a conscious effort to ignore the sense of something following him. It was much like trying not to think of a blue zebra, once someone has suggested that you not let the image enter your mind.

He stopped in front of the door to the water closet, his resolve to act and think as if he were alone faltering at the idea of tending to private needs with the presence in attendance. A dim remembrance of a childhood fear of monsters in the privy flitted to mind.

Serena stood a few feet from Woding, watching as he stepped into the water closet. She couldn't bring herself to follow. She hadn't even followed Briggs into that small chamber, remembering too well how her own brothers had made a joke of trying to disrupt and embarrass her at similar times. She'd dosed William's food with enough tansy to send him to the garderobe for a day and a half, in revenge for one particularly humiliating episode.

Her haunting of Woding's staff, although draining, was proving reasonably successful. Unfortunately, there were always more workers willing to be hired, a fact that had become abundantly clear when Marcy and Mrs. Hutchins showed up. Serena had eavesdropped on a few of their conversations, hearing their boasts that they would prove the men cowards. Knowing that, she was even less likely to want to disturb the women in any way.

It was best, therefore, that she direct her efforts to where they should have been all along: to Woding. His awareness of her presence had given her a devastatingly simple idea for how to wear him down. She would be by his side day and night. Minute by minute, hour by hour, this man who appeared to value solitude almost as much as she did would have to endure her constant company. He would feel her standing behind his shoulder, sitting across from him at dinner, leaning against the parapet of his tower, and even lying beside him in his bed. Day in, day out. It would drive him mad.

And the beauty of the plan was that she would not drain energy from her tree. She could haunt him this way for half a century, and it would be nearly effortless. She'd had centuries of learning patience, and could endure the pain of being in such close contact with the living. Woding would break long before she would.

She went and sat on the edge of the tub. It was white and perfectly smooth, and she wished she could know what it felt like to step into such a bath. She knew there would be no danger of finding a splinter in one's backside while one wallowed about in the steaming water.

She swung her feet over the edge and slid down into it. She was a tall woman, but the tub was long and deep, and with the back of her neck on the edge of the tub she didn't even need to bend her knees, her feet just reaching the end. She lay there, pretending to be covered in water, then slid down deeper, pretending to hear the water fill her ears, and to feel it close over her face.

She heard Woding come out of the water closet; then after a few moments he appeared beside the tub. She looked up at him as he looked down, faint flickers of emotion dancing in the muscles across his face. It was his habit to bathe in the evening, and she wondered if he was reluctant to do so now. It was likely he had some sense that she was in his tub.

Whatever internal debate Woding had been waging while he looked down into the tub, he settled it. His jaw tight, he reached over and twisted the cock to let in hot water.

Serena shrieked, pulling back her feet, then snorted at her own foolishness, sticking her feet back under the pouring water. It ran right through her ankles.

Woding splashed his hand under the gurgling stream, testing the temperature, then took the rubber plug and bent down to stopper the drain. Serena spread her feet apart to avoid his touch. He moved away, and she heard cloth on cloth, and uneven steps: the sounds of a man undressing.

She scooted up and peered over the edge of the tub, her one previous view of his buttocks still vivid in her mind. She had persuaded herself that spying on him at his bath was necessary to her purpose, and had little to do with her own curiosity about his body.

He had his back to her now, bent over as he stood on one foot, peeling off a stocking. All he wore was a pair of white drawers, his shirt and other garments lying over a chair. She watched the flexing of muscles in his legs and back as he balanced on one foot, then tossed the stocking atop his shirt, standing straight again.

His hands went to the waistband of his drawers. Her own hands gripped the edge of the tub. He seemed to hesitate; then, from the flexing and angle of his arms, she knew he was at work on the buttons. He slid them off, stepped out of them, and placed them on top of his other linens.

For a long moment he stood motionless, long enough for Serena to feel a blush in her own cheeks. He knew she was watching him. The thought of being known as a voyeur embarrassed her, but not enough to stop looking. As long as he didn't acknowledge her presence, she thought she could stand the shame.

He turned around. Her lips parted as her eyes roved over his firm body. She could see every flex and ripple of his muscles as he walked toward the tub. Dark hair spread across the top of his chest, then tapered to a single faint line down his abdomen. His forearms and lower legs were dusted with dark hair, but the rest of his skin was bare, somewhat pale from lack of sun, but free of a single mark or blemish.

He looked like the statue in the castle chapel of a naked, alabaster Saint George, standing with spear in hand atop the writhing serpent. Her eyes went to his manhood, staying there as he came closer, and she found herself unable to look away from the dusky form. It was longer and thicker than Briggs's, surrounded by dark hair, and the sight of it stirred some unnameable hunger deep within her. He stopped at the edge of the tub, that strangely entrancing organ mere inches from her face.

She looked up at him. His cheeks had gone pink, and he was staring determinedly at the wall, but a moment later he stepped into the tub. She scooted back toward the water cock, giving him room. The water sloshed as he sat, his face wincing at the temperature. He stretched out his legs, forcing her to climb up to the edge of the tub, out of his way. She took off her leather shoes and let her feet dangle in the water she could not feel, her toes inches from his ankles.

She sat, and she watched.

Alex had to fight the urge to don a nightshirt after his bath. The sense not only of a presence, but of an intensely observant one, had persisted all through his bath, setting his nerves on edge. It had been a battle just to ignore it, and then once he had accepted his inability to do so, a battle to accept the sensation and to try to carry on regardless.

His home growing up had been one where the male anatomy was neither seen nor spoken of. Even the lapdogs had all been female, so his sisters would not have to cast their eyes on the embarrassing evidence of male gender.

Holidays with Rhys and his few years in boarding school had loosened him up, but he still did not have the easy comfort with nudity that many of his male friends did, who when among each other seemed not to have ever heard of the concept of modesty.

His one place of freedom from his own bashfulness was his private quarters, and he was determined not to give that up to an imagined ghost. Or a real ghost, for that matter. His habit was to sleep nude, and sleep nude he would.

He had to fight not to cover his privates as he walked to his bed, feeling every bounce and swing. He slid beneath the covers with a sigh of relief, and blew out the oil lamp, sinking deeper into concealing darkness and body-hiding sheets, lying on his side facing out, the bed curtains open.

He closed his eyes and immediately felt the presence come to the side of the bed, standing for a moment near his head. It was as if he could see it in his mind's eye, a darker shadow in the dark, pausing there, then going around the foot of the bed and thence to the other side. A tingle of awareness crept up his spine as the presence climbed onto the bed and lay down beside him, just behind him.

He opened his eyes and rolled onto his back, trying to check from the corner of his eye whether there was indeed something darker on the pillow next to his. He could see nothing, but still, awareness tingled all down his right side.

What did it—or she, assuming it was Serena—want from him? From any of them?

Stop it, he told himself. *There's nothing there.*

But what if there was, and if, given the correct circumstances, it could speak? What might there be to learn from the dead? Men had been trying for thousands of years to answer the question of what happened when one died, and here he might have a firsthand witness lying by his side, begging for attention.

No, he would not let curiosity prod him into speaking aloud again. His reasoning told him ghosts did not exist, and whatever his misguided senses might tell him, he needed to stay with the logic of the mind until he had proof to the contrary.

He closed his eyes and imagined a heaven full of stars, and began to count those that fell. Within minutes he felt himself losing track of his self-made heaven as sleep overtook him. The presence was still there by his side, inactive, for all the world as if it, too, were weary and in need of rest. His last thought as he slipped into unconsciousness was that it might as well have been a house cat beside him, for all the harm it did.

He was exploring the ruins of Maiden Castle again, as he had when he was ten years old. The long stick in his hand was his sword, and he used it to poke the ground and through patches of overgrowth, seeking the clang of buried metal armor, although his older mind knew he would find nothing.

Alex, a soft female voice said, the sound speaking in his head. There was no intonation, no emotion, no direction from whence it came. *Alex.*

He raised his eyes from the ground and saw a woman sitting on the ruins of the garden wall. She was dressed in a pink underdress, with tight sleeves. Over it she wore a long white and gold sleeveless tunic, a golden girdle around her hips. Her hair, long and pale, hung in tangled locks down to the top of the wall, pooling there and spilling off in snaking rivulets of hair.

Alex, she said again, and this time he saw her lips move, although still the sound came from inside his head.

He walked toward her. "Do I know you?" he asked.

Alex, she repeated.

He stopped a couple feet in front of her. "What are you doing here, in these ruins?"

She held out her closed hand, palm up, then slowly opened it, finger by finger. Pink blossoms spilled out, carried away by the breeze. She left her hand there, holding it out as if in invitation.

He looked into her eyes. The irises were black, indistinguishable from her pupils, telling him nothing. He had never seen such dark eyes. Her face was long and narrow, attractive in an unusual way, her features somehow working together to create an impression of otherworldly beauty. A straight scar ran from her forehead through her eyebrow, then picked up again across her cheekbone, adding to the unusual quality of her face.

Alex.

He put his hand in hers, feeling the cold pressure as her fingers closed around it. He felt her strength as she drew him toward her; felt her size as he stood pressed against the side of her thigh. Sitting on the wall she was higher than him, and he knew that standing next to him she would be nearly his own height. She smelled faintly of dry, sweet hay.

"What do you want of me?" he asked.

Touch me, she said, and lay back, stretching herself atop the uneven wall. Her hair trailed down to the grass and he noted the pull of fabric outlining the gentle thrust of hipbone and thighs.

His eyes dropped to her full breasts, obviously loose of any stays, the nipples hard nubs beneath the layers of cloth. She took the hand of his she still held and brought it to her chest, laying it palm down between her breasts.

Touch me, she said again, her voice in his head soft and placid. She released his hand, laying her own arms at her side and closing her eyes.

He did not move for a long moment, then carefully slid his hand over her breast, feeling the soft give of flesh and the hard cherrystone of a nipple. He rubbed his hand in light circles over it, feeling the path her nipple traced across his palm and fingers, and feeling the answering arousal in his own loins.

He ran his hand over her collarbone and up alongside her neck, holding the side of her jaw as his thumb swept over her cheek, brushing the tail of the scar. He bent his face down close to hers, breathing deeply of her sweet scent, brushing his lips lightly against her own, just a feather's touch, then pulling back.

She opened her black, fathomless eyes. *Touch me,* she said yet again, and bent one knee, her skirts tenting around her leg, leaving no question to what she asked.

"Who are you?" he asked.

She pulled at her skirts, sliding them up to her thighs. *Alex,* she said softly, arching her neck and raising her other knee. *Take me.*

He got up on the wall, kneeling between her curtained thighs, and unbuttoned his clothes, uncovering his aroused flesh to the summer air. He pushed the hem of her skirts the rest of the way up, so that they pooled across her hips.

Her nether hair was dark gold, the flesh between a crimson pink, parting like the petals of a rose as he gently pushed her thighs apart. He leaned over, holding himself above her, bracing on one hand on the wall along her side. Her own cold hands came up to reach inside his drawers and around to his buttocks, squeezing gently, urging him forward.

"Tell me your name," he said, needing to know it, even as he used his other hand to guide himself to her.

Serena, she whispered, just as his manhood parted her and slid inside. Her hands on his buttocks pulled him hard into her, forcing him to plunge all the way home.

It was then that the cold hit him.

She was ice inside, his manhood gripped in a frozen glove. He tried to draw out, but she wrapped her legs around him, holding tight, lifting off the wall to wrap her arms around his body. She moved against him, undulating, rocking, creating against his will an answering, perverted pleasure that both repulsed and drew him.

"Let go of me!" he cried, struggling against her entangling limbs. They both fell off the wall, landing on the springy turf, and still she clung to him, drawing forth a response despite his protests, her hips fastened to his, stroking and massaging him until he found he could not help but give in to her rhythm.

You are mine, she said, as he thrust within her, unable to stop, the cold climbing from his loins up toward his heart.

He looked at her eyes, and there were no whites now. They were black from lid to lid, a shining midnight in which distant stars shone.

He screamed, and made one last frantic struggle to

escape, to pull himself from her body. He woke tangled in bedsheets, covered in sweat. After a moment to gain his bearings, he lay his hand over himself, absurdly certain he would find it ice-cold. It was warm with life, hard, and tingling with arousal.

His breath left him in a long sigh, and when his heartbeat quieted in his ears he tried to relax again. The faint light from the windows and the birdsong told him it was near dawn. He had been asleep for only a few hours.

And still he felt the presence beside him.

Chapter Ten

"Are you enjoying the stables? Sleeping well?" Woding asked Underhill. Serena thought he sounded a bit testy, not quite his usual self. Perhaps it was the pile of paperwork he was trying to get through that soured his mood. He was sitting behind the desk in his little-used office, the one reserved, she had gathered, for his business affairs. Like most rooms in the castle, it had a beautiful view of the countryside.

"Not as comfortably as I would in my own bed, truth be told, but I am content to stay where I am," Underhill replied, setting down the post. "If I may say so, you do not look particularly well rested yourself."

"Bad dreams, is all," Woding said, smothering a yawn. He leaned back in his desk chair, rubbing his eyes. "My body refuses to accept that I want it to sleep during the day, and revenges itself upon me with nightmares."

"No noises disturb your slumber?"

"Not a one. It's beginning to seem more and more as if we had a prankster in our midst. Either that or our ghost has found something better to do with her time."

Serena narrowed her eyes. That was not what she wanted to hear. For three days she had been Woding's shadow, and he had not once looked directly at her, or in any other way revealed that he was aware of her presence.

Perhaps he wasn't.

The only unease she saw in him was while he slept: every time he closed his eyes he was plagued by nightmares. Even that, though, she could not be certain was because of her presence. Certainly she was not doing anything to interfere with his dreams.

At first she had thought he was deliberately trying to ignore her, but now she could not be certain. She slipped off the windowsill and came around to where she could see his face. Was he lying to Underhill? Or did he really think she had gone away, or never been here to begin with?

She couldn't tell. She reminded herself that he was a sly man. He could be taunting her, telling her that he was winning, and that he thought her beneath his notice.

Or maybe he really could not sense her presence anymore.

She sat on the desk, propping her foot on the arm of his chair.

"Before I forget," Underhill was saying, "Daisy Hutchins has asked to speak with you. Shall I send her up?"

"Yes, do," Woding said, pushing back from the desk, forcing Serena to drop her foot. "I've had enough of these papers."

"I'll send her right up."

Woding didn't reply, instead picking up the post and flipping through the letters, sorting them into piles, frowning at one in particular. Underhill left, and a few minutes later the cook stood in the open doorway, giving the frame a rap to announce her presence.

"Mrs. Hutchins, please come in," Woding said. "There was something you wished to discuss with me?"

"There is, Mr. Woding," she said, stepping into the room and standing squarely in front of the desk, her solid frame looking as movable to Serena as a block of stone. She had dark brown hair drawn back in a bun, covered in a white cap. She wore a short brown loose gown over a quilted blue petticoat, the loose gown held shut by the apron tied around her waist. A large white kerchief was crossed over her ample breasts. Marcy, the housemaid, wore a similar outfit, albeit in brighter colors, and Serena guessed it was the usual attire for a country laborer nowadays.

"Won't you sit down?" Woding asked.

"Thank you, sir." Mrs. Hutchins sat, suddenly looking a trifle uncomfortable, seated across the desk from him as she was. It was obvious to Serena that the woman felt more at ease on her feet.

"Have you been settling in all right?"

"Yes, sir. I like my quarters very much, and am enjoying my work. I am proud to have charge of an entire kitchen, and the buying of goods. Such a position is not easy to come by for a woman of my age, and I thank you."

Serena guessed her to be in her late twenties, and imagined she was right to be honored to be given such responsibility, especially considering the man she had replaced.

"What can I help you with?" Woding asked.

The cook took a breath and began. "It's like this, sir. I don't want to be saying anything against anyone, but when I went with Mr. Sommer with the wagon down to buy supplies in Bradford-on-Avon, we came back with everything like I'd asked, except for those things what will be delivered later, but then Mr. Sommer refused to bring the wagon all the way up to the castle. He said he'd go no farther than the stables, and that the horses would not either. He had Dickie and Marcy load hand-carts with the goods, and haul them up through the tunnel.

"Marcy didn't complain—she's a good, strong girl, a good worker—but I confess I do not see the purpose to it. Dickie at least was quick about it, but was useless for hours after, blathering on about the evil atmosphere of the tunnel. I've been through that tunnel a dozen times myself, sir, and have never had a moment's fright."

"Are you asking me to have Mr. Sommer drive the wagon up to the castle in the future?" Woding asked.

"No, sir," Mrs. Hutchins said.

"Ah," Woding said, and wisely closed his mouth.

Serena had known an old man at Clerenbold Keep much like this Daisy Hutchins. He often had a point to make, but there was no way on God's good earth that he could be rushed to it. His mind had not functioned without sidetracks, and one could only sit and wait and try to look patient while he rambled toward his conclusion.

"My eldest sister married a man who owns a livery stable, and who does farrier work as well. They have seven children, the oldest of whom is Nancy. She's just turned eighteen. They've tried to raise her good and

117

proper, but Nancy was never one to be kept away from what she wanted."

"Oh?" Woding said.

"It's the horses, sir. Nancy loves the horses. They gave up trying to turn her away from them long ago, and so she's worked side by side with her father since she was old enough to stand."

Serena rested her jaw in her hand, watching Mrs. Hutchins talk. She was guessing that some of the woman's volubility was because she didn't expect Woding to like her point, once she got to it. Woding seemed to be getting the same idea: Serena thought she saw his eyes widening.

The cook abruptly stood. "Nancy!" she called toward the open door. "Come in here, girl."

Nancy did as bidden. She bore a strong resemblance to her aunt, with the same wide-spaced, downturning eyes and dark brown locks. Her hair, however, was pulled back in a long braid, and the dress she wore was several inches too short, revealing heavy boots on her feet. She wore a thick cotton smock over the dress, like a workman. She was of average height, but broad-shouldered, and Serena guessed her hands would be rough.

"My idea, Mr. Woding, is that Nancy might be allowed to work in the stables with Mr. Sommer. She has a way with horses, and could take them through the tunnel when the carriage needed to be brought round, or the wagon. The horses would not spook with her, sir."

Serena thought the cook might be right. Nancy exuded the solid calm of warm porridge. Even looking at her was somehow comforting. Serena doubted the girl had ever made a sudden move or a shrill sound in her life, and it was quite possible she might be able to keep the horses in line even if Serena was there trying to spook them.

"You want your niece to be a stableboy?" Woding asked, his incredulity barely concealed.

"I intend one day to be a coachman, sir," Nancy said on her own behalf. Her voice was low and calm, and she apparently saw nothing strange in her statement.

Serena laughed, delighted. She could not have foreseen that her torturing of Sommer would have given a young woman the chance of a paid position in a stable.

"Hush, child," her aunt admonished. "Don't be putting the carriage before the horse."

"I'd never," Nancy said, affronted.

"She wouldn't need much," Mrs. Hutchins said to Woding. "Room, board. She's a good worker, sir. You would not regret taking her on."

Woding held up his hand, stopping her. His eyes went from her to Nancy, studying the girl. Serena felt her heartbeat quicken. Was he actually considering it?

"The stables have always been the domain of men," Woding said. "I have never heard of a female coachman, footman, postilion, stableboy, or groom." He paused, still looking at Nancy, who for her part was doing an admirable job of displaying calm composure.

"However," Woding said, and with that one word a warm light flared to life in Nancy's eyes, "it is also true that women work beside the men in my mills, and women have always labored in the fields at harvest. If you can show me that you can indeed bring the horses through the tunnel without their shying, then you have the job. Room, board, and the going wage for stableboys."

Nancy nodded her head in a male gesture of thanks. "Shall I bring them through now, sir?"

"In a bit. I have some letters to attend to; then I'll join both you and your aunt in the courtyard."

Nancy nodded again, and let her aunt guide her from the room.

Serena followed the women to the door, then a few steps down the hall. The reaction she'd been waiting for came as, once out of sight of Woding, Nancy turned and enveloped her aunt in a rib-cracking hug, lifting the stout woman almost off her feet. "Thank you, Aunt Daisy," Nancy said, and kissed the woman on the cheek. "I shall never forget this."

Mrs. Hutchins shook out her skirts and rearranged her apron when Nancy released her. "Make me proud, dumpling. 'Tis all I ask."

Smiling, Serena returned to the office.

Woding was reading a letter, a grimace on his face. When he reached the end of the second page he tossed it to the desk, then for a moment looked right at her, accusation in his eyes.

Her lips parted in surprise. What? What had she done?

Alex looked away from the presence that he now called Serena in his mind, remembering his determination not to acknowledge her in any way. It was hard, though, when her little game of touching Beth's hair had led to the letter now sitting on his desk.

Little sister Sophie was coming to visit, and God only knew who or what she would bring with her. He would count himself lucky if it was only a crackpot priest to do an exorcism of the castle. Sophie's fascination with the supernatural was a great annoyance to both himself and his other sisters.

He pushed the thought from his mind. He had a bit of time left before his peace was disturbed, and he wouldn't have it ruined by borrowing trouble from the future.

He went to go join Mrs. Hutchins and her niece in the courtyard, wondering as he went down the stairs what had overcome him in regard to *that* situation. A stablelass? Sommer would not be pleased.

On the other hand, he himself was not pleased to hear that Sommer's nervousness had made it necessary for supplies to be hauled by hand up through the tunnel. He'd known the man wouldn't bring the horses through, but hadn't realized it was causing inconvenience to others besides himself.

If Sommer didn't like having a stablelass on hand, then he had better start doing his job properly.

Alex came out into the sunlight of the courtyard, his eyes wincing at the brightness. He was getting too used to the half-light of indoors, and the soothing darkness of night. Daylight glared, as painful as lemon juice to his eye.

"Why, hello, puss," he heard Nancy say. She was squatting down, the hem of her smock pooling on the paving stones, looking at something he could not see. "Where did you come from? I didn't see you there."

Alex stared at the girl.

Otto, who had been sleeping in a patch of sunlight in the courtyard, lifted his head, and then came completely awake, scrambling to his feet with a "Woof!"

Nancy's head turned, as if watching something streak away, and for a moment from the corner of his eye Alex thought he saw a blur of orange down near the ground. Otto, barking madly, went galloping in the same direction.

"Oh, now that's funny," Nancy said, standing up, her

placid brow showing only the slightest sign of consternation.

"What's that?" Alex asked, at the same time sensing Serena's presence by his side.

"That orange cat. I don't know where it went." She walked several feet in the direction Otto had gone, looking about her feet, tapping the paving stones with her boots as if seeking a hollow spot. Otto could be heard somewhere along the curtain wall, still barking.

"Cat?" Mrs. Hutchins asked. "I didn't see a cat."

"Sure you did. A big orange one, with tattered ears."

"I didn't see any cat," Mrs. Hutchins repeated.

Both the women turned to Alex, as their master and therefore the authority on the disagreement. "I wasn't really paying attention," he said. "It sounds as if Otto saw a cat, though, doesn't it? Hmm?" He smiled at them and changed the subject. "Shall we get on with it, then?" he said, and set off toward the tunnel, his mind clanking along on gears suddenly thrust out of sync.

A ghost cat? Serena *and* a cat? This was the time for him to start giggling like a lunatic. Maybe there were ghost horses, ghost dogs, ghost chickens, even. The whole mountaintop could be infested with ghosts. It was no wonder Otto went wild when it looked like nothing was there.

He blinked, shaking his head. Somehow he was beginning to both believe and disbelieve in ghosts at the same time. How could his brain hold such opposites within its bounds, allowing them to coexist?

The cool darkness of the tunnel was a relief after the bright sunlight, and the muscles around his eyes relaxed. The two women followed behind, their footsteps echoing his. As they wound down and around, for the first time in several days he felt Serena fading away, and by the time the sunlight of the lower entrance was visible, he had lost the sense of her entirely.

Interesting.

Sommer, predictably, did not like the idea of a stablelass, and liked even less that Nancy was to be allowed to try to bring the horses through the tunnel. He turned a frightening shade of red when Nancy had the temerity to suggest that he stay behind, as his nervousness might infect the horses.

Logic forced Alex to agree, although he was already regretting giving Nancy this chance. Sommer spewed some particularly rude comments about women and then stomped off to sulk in his quarters, leaving Alex with the distinct sense that if Nancy passed her test, he might soon be short a coachman.

Ten minutes later, he had a new stablelass. The horses had shown not the least hint of shying anywhere in the tunnel, nodding their heads and blowing, ears forward, completely at their ease all the way up to the courtyard.

As soon as Nancy disappeared back into the tunnel with the horses in tow, Alex felt Serena return to his side. It took all his willpower not to look toward her, not to acknowledge in some way what that return told him. If not for her deliberately staying out of the tunnel just now, Nancy would likely be on her way home, jobless.

What they said was true: Serena hated only men. Furthermore, there was some form of intelligent awareness to her.

Movement from behind the gate to the walled garden caught his eye, and he tried to shrug off thoughts of Serena. If that was Ben Flury at work, he wanted to talk to him.

He found the elderly man kneeling beside a flower

bed, his hands gently massaging the dirt, pulling out weeds without disturbing the plants that grew there. His grandson did the same on the opposite side of the bed, albeit with a little less grace.

"Mr. Flury, hello," Alex said.

"Mr. Woding." Flury sat back on his heels, then pushed himself to his feet. The process was slow and painful-looking.

"The gardens look wonderful, all of them," Alex said. "I am glad that you've stayed on to work them."

The older man gave a gentle smile. "I couldn't leave you to a houseful of women, now, could I?"

"I would certainly hope not," Alex said, although he thought Serena would enjoy having Maiden Castle live up to its name by having a female gardener as well. "You wouldn't have happened to have seen an orange cat about anywhere, would you?" he asked.

"With chewed ears? Aye, I've seen him once or twice."

"You *have?*"

"Never lets me get close enough to touch him, but aye, he's been around."

John spoke up from behind his bush again. "I've never seen him."

"Since when do cats like noisy young boys?" Flury asked his grandson.

Alex chewed his upper lip a moment, thinking how to phrase his next question. "Do you know to whom it belongs?"

"No, sir," he said. "But I should think the only owner possible is Serena."

Alex blinked at him.

"You do know it's a ghost cat, don't you?" Flury asked, as matter-of-fact as you please.

"Er, I had rather suspected, yes."

"Well, there you are then. It won't hurt you none, if that's what concerns you. Harmless little beast. Seems to enjoy tormenting that hound of yours, though."

"Yes." Alex stood silent, staring at the unruffled man, the machinery of his mind again clanking off-kilter. "Yes, well, thank you for clearing that up. What I truly wanted to ask you, though, was a question about the cherry tree."

He and Flury followed the path over to the gnarled tree. Flury reached up and touched a dead branch, bits of bark crumbling into his hand. "It doesn't look good," he said.

"I was thinking it was unlikely it would last more than another year or two," Alex said. "But I don't know much about trees. What do you think?"

"This branch was alive a few weeks ago. See the leaves? It looks as if it may have caught some disease. Do you want me to take it down?"

Some small movement from the corner of his eye caught Alex's attention. He turned his head, but saw nothing amiss. He turned slowly back to the tree, and as he did so a tall figure became vaguely visible, at the very corner of his vision. He stood stock-still.

"No, I was wondering if there was some way to save it," Alex said, absurdly trying not to move his mouth while he spoke. The figure started coming closer to him, still out of focus, but from the shape of her silhouette, a woman. A very tall woman.

"I don't know if that's possible," Flury was saying. "It's quite old."

"It has the most unusual blossoms I have ever seen," Alex said, trying to sound normal. "I had hoped that there might be a way, if not to save it, then at least to reproduce it." The figure stopped right beside him, and he caught his breath, feeling that heavy sense of presence that Serena gave him, stronger than ever.

Flury rubbed his chin. "We might try grafting a branch onto another tree," he said. "Or we might be able to start one by seed." He looked down at the ground, clear of any cherry debris. "If we can find a seed, that is."

The figure still hovered at the edge of his vision, only barely holding the form of a woman. He thought he might be able to see the garden through her, but could not be certain.

"Try whatever you can," he said. And then, tentatively, "Do you ever see anything besides the cat?"

"What, you mean like Serena herself?"

Alex raised his eyebrows in confirmation.

"Just the cat."

"Ah. Well, thank you. Try whatever you can with the tree."

"Is Serena giving you trouble, Mr. Woding?" Flury asked, concern on his brow.

"No, no, not at all."

"They do say as that Briggs had a bad time of it while he was living here. I shouldn't be surprised to see her play her games with you, as well."

"You seem remarkably unconcerned about it all," Alex said, his throat dry as the figure hovered in the corner of his vision.

"Aye, well. I've seen a ghost or two in my time, and never known them to do any real harm. As far as Serena is concerned, my guess is she likes her flowers, same as any other woman. I figure that's why she leaves me alone."

Alex nodded his thanks to the man and started back

to the castle. The figure vanished from his periphery when he turned his head away, and he felt the presence following behind him as he walked back to the castle. At the door he paused and turned, as if taking a last glance outside. He held still when the faint shape came into view, again from the corner of his eye. She was definitely there, not two feet from him.

Either he was having hallucinations now, to go with the imaginary sense of a presence, or he was seeing the ghost that followed him day and night.

Neither explanation gave him comfort.

Chapter Eleven

Woding seemed more tense than usual, Serena thought. His eyes had the wide watchfulness of a wary horse, as if he was expecting something to jump out at him from behind every corner. It was what she wanted, but she wished she knew what had brought it on so suddenly. Maybe it was that whole incident with Beezely.

The cat even now brushed up against her leg, and she bent down to pet him. "Naughty kitty," she said, scratching him under his chin, feeling his purr rumble against her fingers. "Do you appear to them on purpose?"

She followed Woding to his bedroom, where he shucked off his shoes and lay down on the bed. She knew his habits well enough by now to know that he must be intending to watch stars tonight, and sought to prepare himself with a nap. The clear sky boded well for stargazing.

He didn't look in the proper state of mind for napping,

though. He lay flat on his back, his hands clasped together on his belly, his ankles crossed. She sat down cross-legged on the empty half of the bed, pulling at her skirts so they were loose over her knees. She put her chin in her palm, her elbow on one knee, and settled in to wait.

This was her least favorite part of haunting Woding. Observing him sleep was entertaining for only the first few minutes, and then she began to get both jealous and bored. Jealous because she no longer knew the joys of sleep: she could fade into oblivion easily enough, but it was a black and empty oblivion, devoid of dreams or the luxurious sensations of slumber. The boredom came because he did nothing but lie there. The thrashings of his nightmares held a certain interest, but even that was a frustration, as she had no way of knowing what images tormented his mind.

Woding was staring at the fabric lining the underside of the tester, a vein throbbing in his temple. She leaned over to look directly into his face. It was not a bad face, she had to admit. She wondered what he'd do if she touched it, maybe brushed her fingertips across those tightly closed lips.

Her fingers tingled with the desire to do it, but she held back. She had to remember she did not like the man. She should not be having thoughts like this about him.

Eventually he closed his eyes, and bit by bit his breathing deepened. She stretched out beside him on the covers, her fingers playing with the ends of his hair on the pillow, passing through without disturbing them.

He wasn't an entirely bad man, she reluctantly admitted to herself, watching him sleep. She could imagine no other hiring a stablelass. She still couldn't quite believe that he had done it. Maybe all those times she thought he was being manipulative of servants, he was instead being kind.

No, that couldn't be right. Manipulative and sly fit her vision of him much better than did generous and kind. He might use the carrot instead of the stick, but he still managed to get his own way. Her brothers would have underestimated him, thinking him weak and laughing at his methods. But who would have laughed last? Woding probably had much in common with Hugh le Gayne, and there was no question of who had won that battle of wits, Hugh or she and Thomas.

Alex woke feeling more tired than when he had laid down, restless images from his dreams flitting into his disjointed memory. *She* was the cause of his poor sleep; he was certain of it. Daytime be damned, it was Serena who had him thrashing and sweating when he sought calm slumber. He turned his head, catching the pale shape in the corner of his eye.

He needn't have checked. She had been staying so close to his side these past days, it felt as if she were attached to him—and always would be. He wondered which of them had the greater stamina to endure such closeness. He feared anyone who had hung around a pile of ruined rock for half a millennium might have already proved her staying power.

The thought made him groan, and he quickly masked it with a stretch, easing his stiff muscles. If he knew what she wanted, he would give it to her, if only she would go away. Of course, that was probably just what she herself wanted from him: his departure. And that was the one thing he would not give. He could not imagine explaining to his fellow amateur astronomers that he had left his perfect tower because a female ghost insisted on sleeping beside him at night and watching him at his bath.

His bath. What was he going to do about that? It had been bad enough when he only felt her presence in his room, but could still force himself to dismiss it as his imagination. To actually catch glimpses of a watching woman while he bathed . . . that would be a different experience.

Perhaps going mad was the best solution. He would simply never again change his clothes or wash his body.

He checked the clock and saw that it was time for dinner under the watchful eyes of the Canadian caribou. The presence tagged along, and as he sat down at the head of the empty table he gave a moment's thought to what Serena might think of this new version of her castle. Did she like the caribou? The castle must not look much as she remembered. Briggs had not cared much for historical accuracy, and even the flight of stone stairs that Serena had supposedly fallen down was nowhere to be seen. For all he knew they'd been pulled up and the stones used in the walls.

The table was already set, and a ring of the bell brought Marcy and Dickie, carrying the dishes that held his dinner, lamb stew, a pudding, and an overabundance of boiled peas. Daisy Hutchins was not an imaginative cook, but he would not be left starving. And, truth be told, he rather preferred plain fare to some of the elaborate, sauce-drenched dishes that Leboff had forced on him. He would miss the ice cream, though.

Marcy and Dickie left him alone to fill his plate and eat, and he soon found his mind wandering off into the starry skies, far beyond the realms of stews and puddings. He ate by rote, fork and knife working together without his interference.

Then he noticed the peas. Two of them, sitting on the tablecloth.

Had he done that? He didn't think he'd been so careless. His sisters had ensured that his table manners were impeccable, even when he was not paying attention.

A third pea hopped off his plate, making a little splat of gravy as it landed on the linen. He stared at the offending legume for a long moment, then from the corner of his eye caught the white movement of a presence.

Serena.

A pea suddenly shot off the table, much as if someone had flicked it with a finger. With his knife and fork, he carefully picked up the two remaining peas, depositing them back on his plate.

Yet another pea inched up the edge of the plate and dropped over the edge. It slowly rolled toward Serena, then took off across the dining room, hitting one of the leaded-glass windowpanes with a soft pat and dropping to the floor, leaving a smudge of gravy on the glass.

Alex took a deep breath, watching as a fifth pea made its escape from his plate. He didn't know if this came under proper ghostly behavior, playing with someone's food. It seemed more like something a bored child would do. It certainly was not frightening, although he would admit it was plenty annoying.

The pea took flight, landing in the flower arrangement at the center of the table. Another dropped off his plate.

He turned his eyes away, until he could catch in his peripheral vision the cloudy outline of Serena, her arm extended as she made the pea dance a gravy gavotte on the tablecloth. Still looking away, he readied his fork in his hand, and then—*whap!*—he slapped at where her hand should be with the flat of the utensil.

The shape leaped backward, but not before the fork bounced off something solid. His lips were curling in boyish victory when his entire plate violently upended, sending stew and peas all over the table. He shoved his chair back, standing just in time to save himself from being dripped on by a rivulet of gravy.

He stood surveying the mess, aware of the white figure and unwilling to give her any satisfaction for such a childish display. He rang the bell, and in a minute Marcy bobbed in, her hazel eyes going wide at the mess.

"Please bring a fresh plate," Alex said.

"Yes, sir," Marcy said, having the good sense not to ask the obvious question. "I'll have Dickie come help me remove the cloth."

Alex nodded, and waited while the two young people cleared away the mess, resetting the table with fresh dishes and cutlery. Dickie knocked over the empty wineglasses twice, obviously having suspicions about what had occurred. When they'd finished, Alex sat down again as if nothing had happened, and served himself small portions of each dish. He would not let a petulant ghost deprive him of his pudding and peas.

He could see the figure move back into place at the seat to his left, and when that vague white shape of a hand moved toward his plate, he lifted his fork in a threatening manner, making it very clear he knew what she was about. The hand stopped.

He ate the remainder of his meal in peace.

How had he known what she was about to do? This was no good, Serena fretted, chewing her upper lip, sitting with crossed arms watching Woding eat. Was his sense of her that good, and he had been pretending otherwise all this time?

Or—horrid thought—what if he could see her, the way Ben Flury could so often see Beezely? Her fingers went to the scar across her face, tracing the path. No, he couldn't see her. Even the thought of it made her feel sick to her stomach. Almost no one had seen her for centuries, and that was the way she liked it. No one knew what a lumbering giant she was, or that she had an ugly face. It had been one of the few benefits of her undead state.

Maybe it was something with his astrology that helped him to gauge her so well. She would have to watch him more closely, and pay more attention to what he did. It would help vastly if she could read, but even had she been taught, she doubted she would be able to decipher his scratchings. What flowed from his pen bore little resemblance to the thick script she had seen in her family's Bible.

Woding finished his main course, and Marcy and Dickie returned to clear away the dishes and serve his dessert, a bread pudding with custard sauce. She really couldn't let him win like this, sitting there smugly eating his sweet.

Dickie was almost to the door with a trayload of dishes. Serena snuck up to him, took two peas from the dish, and popped one into each of his nostrils.

The resultant crash of dishes snapped Woding's head around, and had Marcy giving a shriek of surprise.

"My nose!" Dickie cried, stumbling amid the fallen crockery, treading in stew. "I can't breathe!"

Woding rose, but it was Marcy who reached Dickie first, grabbing him by the shoulders. "Let me see!" And then, when she did, she let go of him, stepping back.

"Oh, Dickie," she said. "That's not funny. You fright-ened me."

Dickie gasped for air through his mouth, his lips hanging wide like the mouth of a fish. "I can't breathe." His fingertips touched his nose, jerking back at the smooth, firm texture of the peas. "What is it?" he yelped. "What's in there?"

Marcy turned away from him, shaking her head in disgust, and began to clear up the mess on the floor. It was Woding who answered him, his face hard. "You have peas in your nose. Go find a mirror and remove them."

He then stepped past Dickie, leaving the dining room and his dessert.

Serena followed, feeling rather pleased with that bit of mischief. She punched imaginary peas into noses all the way up to Woding's tower room, wondering what would have happened if she'd used his nose instead of Dickie's.

He sat down at his desk, placing both hands flat on its surface, staring at the papers scattered there. She could see his chest moving with his breathing under the white folds of his cravat.

"Serena," he said, raising his eyes and looking straight at her.

She froze, her eyes wide, a fist in mid–pea punch, and just managed to keep herself from answering. She sud-denly had the same feeling of dread and fear that had come with being called in front of her father for a mis-deed.

"I have had enough of your childish games."

Good. Maybe he would leave.

"For a while, I admit, I was growing curious about who you were," he went on. "I have felt you following

me, lying beside me in my bed, and watching me bathe."
He leaned back in his chair. "I have even dreamed about
you, and what you may look like." He looked at a spot
in the distance, his eyes going vague as he recalled. "It
seemed you were a tall woman, with long, pale blond
hair flowing down past your hips."

Her lips parted, a chill running up her body.

"I even thought, once or twice, about how fascinating
it would be to speak with you, and to hear you talk about
your life."

What?

"Now, though, I am not at all certain that I want to
know anything about you. I have doubts that you retain
any more of your humanity than its worst qualities, par-
amount among them cruelty and violence. I fear you
may be nothing but the echo of a disturbed mind."

She was not disturbed! That was unfair. And she was
more human than not—why else would she feel this pain
when the living were near? He did not understand her,
did not understand the purpose of her haunting, did not
understand that it was in self-defense. He understood
nothing!

He sighed. "Which are you, Serena? Are you a beautiful woman caught halfway between life and death, or
are you nothing but an echo of the ugliest parts of humanity?"

Silence stretched to the corners of the room, trapping
her mute in its bonds. She was neither, but she wished
she could be one of those two, wished it as she always
had, with all her heart. She wanted to be a beautiful
woman about whom men dreamed.

"If you are indeed a woman, I should like to know
you," Woding said.

Serena drifted a few inches off the floor and sat in a

nonexistent chair, trying to make sense of all this. People had but rarely spoken to her during her years as a ghost, and most often when they did they said things like "Stop it," or "Don't hurt me." No one tried talking to her as if she might have something to say. Except for Thomas, no one in her lifetime had, either.

Woding had dreamed of her as a beautiful woman.

Stuffing peas up a boy's nose suddenly seemed a petty thing to do, much more shameful for her than for poor Dickie, stumbling around with his green-plugged nostrils. For a moment she got a glimpse of how Woding must perceive her—not as a force to be reckoned with, as she had intended, but rather as a spiteful child.

He had dreamed of her as a beautiful woman. He guessed, or knew, that she was tall, with long, pale hair. He must not have seen her face in his dream.

She drifted backward, half disappearing into the stonework of the fireplace as she thought on his words, her mind trying to encompass this shift.

He claimed he wanted to know her.

Had anyone ever wanted to know her?

Chapter Twelve

The night of stargazing was long, but peaceful. Alex could still feel Serena close by, and could still catch glimpses of her from the corner of his eye, but there were no disturbances as there had been at dinner. She did not play with his pen, did not blow on his hair, and did not make thumping noises. She was as well behaved as he could expect. Better, really.

He hadn't known if his ploy would work, but apparently it had, at least well enough to keep her quiet for a few hours. Serena had shown him that force or insults from him only led to grand, violent retribution from her. While chewing his lamb stew he had accepted that he was basically powerless when it came to the ghost. She could do whatever she wished, and he had no way to stop her.

And yet he had not grown up in a house of women without learning a few things. His sisters, even as chil-

dren, had been able to wrap his father around their
dainty little fingers, obtaining whatever they wished with
an adoring look, a bit of flattery, and an astonishing
aptitude for creating practical reasons where no such reasons actually existed.

The lessons had served him well. He might not be a
fearsome warrior, but warriors did not rule the land.
Warriors got their limbs chopped off and died on battle-
fields. A warrior was but a pawn to those wily enough
to rule.

He leaned on the parapet, watching the deep blue sky
catch the first hints of sunrise to the east. Demands had
not worked with Serena, but it was looking as if flattery
might. He caught pale movement from the corner of his
eye. She appeared to be pacing back and forth, parapet
to parapet, right through the end of his reclining chair.

It had been somewhat of a lie he had told her. Part of
him did not want to know who she was, as her visits to
his dreams were unsettling, and she had done nothing to
make him think her company would improve upon further acquaintance. She was, quite literally, the stuff of
which nightmares were made.

On the other hand, what man of either science or phi-
losophy would not seize the chance to speak with the
dead? There were so many questions she could answer,
so many things she could explain, if she chose to com-
municate. And besides that matter, he actually did feel
curiosity about who she was personally, and wanted to
know if the eerily erotic woman in the dreams was her.

The eastern sky was turning a vivid pink as the sun
crept toward the horizon. A breeze ruffled his hair.

If Serena chose to talk, he would learn the answers to
questions of life and eternity that man had asked since
first he walked the earth.

He would also have to accept the possibility that he had gone stark, raving mad.

Serena followed Woding down to his bedroom, still undecided about what she would do. His words had the distinct odor of manipulation, and yet she found herself tempted by them.

Wily devil.

What would it hurt, to talk a bit with the man?

It would hurt the cherry tree, true enough, to use its energy to create a voice he could hear. The expenditure would be less than that of moving objects or making great, thudding noises, though. Maybe if he knew her, he would understand why she needed him to leave.

She scratched that thought. Whatever Woding's ways, he was still a man. He would do as he wished, regardless of her desires.

But to spend even as little as an hour in conversation with another person, as if she, too, were real . . . The thought made her heart ache with such longing, she doubted she could survive if she rejected it. She doubted she could survive stopping if she acted on it.

She could instead fade into oblivion, and wait there until Woding had left the castle, as he eventually would. If he didn't move out, he would at least die of old age. But then the chance would be lost completely, perhaps never to come again, or the cherry would die in the interim, making waiting him out pointless.

Her fretting distracted her until she saw that he was heading for his bathroom. She made to follow, but then he stopped in the doorway, turning to look over his shoulder toward her.

"Serena," Woding said. "Would you do me the great kindness of waiting here while I bathe?"

She stood in her tracks, her face flaming, as he shut the door behind him.

Damn Woding. He had already taken away the pleasure of spying on him in his bath, and she had not even agreed to speak with him yet.

Serena went to sit on his bed and wait, nervous as a bride. She listened to the running of water, and then the splashes as he bathed. She felt as if some of her power in their encounters was already slipping away.

He was a wily, sly creature. Even as she felt the first ebb in her determination to be rid of him, felt the faint shift in the tide against her, she was unable to crush the desire to hear him speak to her again.

He came back in, wrapped in a dressing gown, a nightshirt visible at the neckline. Was she not even to have a glimpse of his bare shoulder while he slept? This was too cruel.

"Thank you," he said, looking briefly toward her, then turning away.

She stood up, her hands clasped tightly before her, watching as he moved about the room. He went to the windows first, pulling shut the curtains against the morning light, sending the room into twilight. The half-dark soothed her somewhat, making her feel less visible to him, although she knew the thought was ridiculous. His seeing of her, however strong it was, likely had nothing to do with light.

He came back to the center of the room, then stopped. "Do you wish to speak now?" he asked.

No.

Yes.

She did not know. She wanted him to keep talking, and then perhaps later she would have the courage to join in.

He listened, his head cocked to the side. "I suppose I shall have to take that as a no." He took off his dressing gown and got into bed, the mattress sighing as his weight pushed out the air amid the feathers. He pulled at his nightshirt as it twisted around him.

She sat at the corner of the foot of the bed and leaned against the post, trying to calm herself. She would have liked to see him propped up by pillows, comfortable and ready to entertain her, rather than lying on his side, hunched up and stiff, pulling occasionally at his recalcitrant nightshirt.

The quiet lengthened, and it became apparent that he would not break it. But he didn't pull shut the bed curtains, either. He did not look like one ready for sleep, but neither did he look like one who was going to break into the long tale of his boyhood and coming-of-age for her amusement.

Odious man. Why didn't he make this easy for her?

Why didn't he look at her and ask her questions?

His eyelids lowered to half-mast.

Alex, she said, on a breath as soft as the beating of a moth's wings.

His eyelids closed.

Alex, she said more loudly, a wren's wing beat of air. No response.

"Alex!" she said, and this time her voice was a swan taking flight. She heard it vibrating through the air, reflecting off the walls and floor. It was a much different sound from the snow-forest muffling she usually heard when she spoke, in the plane of the dead.

His eyes came wide open, and he sprang to a sitting position, up against the headboard. "Hello, what?"

"Alex," she said again, and her voice settled into the right range, a pheasant or a hawk, clearly heard but not overloud. "Did you have a pleasant bath?"

He looked slightly away from her, as if watching from the corner of his eye. "What?"

"Did you have a pleasant bath?" she repeated carefully. She had grown used to listening to the modern way of speech, but her own words formed themselves as they always had, her vowels stretching and shaping in a manner that must sound foreign to him.

"Yes, thank you," he said, his eyes still wide.

"That is good." She sat in silence, trying to think of something else to say. Everything that came to mind seemed inane, although perhaps no more so than breaking centuries of silence with an inquiry about a man's bath.

"Are you Serena?" Woding asked, perfectly motionless, as if moving might bring her down upon him.

"I am Serena Clerenbold," she confirmed slowly, enunciating each syllable with pride. She felt her eyes sting, to say her full name, and hear it echo in the air. "I am the fourth child of the warrior Robert Clerenbold, and his only daughter. I had four brothers, each of whom were as gifted with the sword as my father, and only one of whom survived the Great Mortality."

"The Great Mortality? Do you mean the Black Death?"

"The Pestilence," she said, her mind going instantly back to those dark days. How could speaking of it have the power to carry her there so swiftly? "It destroyed without favor. My family. Our peasants. The sheep, cattle, chickens, even the dogs lay dead in the fields, black and corrupted. The scavengers themselves would not touch the corpses, so foul and reeking of evil they were."

"But you survived it?"

143

"Aye, I survived. And Thomas, my younger brother. We were all that was left."

"What happened to you? Why do you haunt the castle?"

"I was murdered!" she said, speaking loudly again. "Murdered by that filthy brute le Gayne. The lying, thieving, stinking bastard, may he rot in hell."

"The legend says that you killed him."

"Lies!" she exclaimed, and crawled across the bed to him. A muscle in his face twitched. "Do you see me?" she asked, leaning close.

"Barely."

"Do you see my face?"

"I cannot distinguish it."

She sat back on her heels, relieved on that score. "Le Gayne murdered me upon our wedding night, and stole our lands from my brother, who was foolish enough to believe such a trickster's words."

"Is that why you became a ghost, because you were murdered?"

She did not answer.

"Serena?" he said.

"I do not know," she at last replied.

"Isn't there something you want, like justice or revenge? Or maybe that the truth be known? There must be some reason you haunt this castle."

"I do not know! All I know is that I want to be alone again. This is my home, and you have invaded it. I want you to go, you and all the rest."

He leaned forward and reached behind himself to rearrange the pillows, making a comfortable support for sitting up. He straightened the blankets and coverlet, then leaned back and looked toward her.

"Why did le Gayne kill you?"

"I do not wish to speak of it."

He was quiet a moment. She could see that he was thinking of what next to say. The startled look had gone from his eyes, although she thought his relaxed pose was a lie.

"What became of Thomas?" he asked at last.

She sighed and moved back to her place at the foot of the bed, leaning against the post. "Thomas went to fight under the Black Prince," she said. "He came home four years later, and was told that I had run off to join a nunnery, but that I had died on the road and been buried in an unmarked grave. Le Gayne invited him to spend the night, which he did, not yet knowing that le Gayne had stolen all his land while he was gone."

Alex listened, astonished by what was happening here within the confines of his bed, and as Serena spoke he began to realize that he could see her, faintly, in the center of his vision. The more she talked, the clearer she became. On impulse he reached over to the bed curtains, pulling them shut. Her image grew clearer in the darkness, glowing faintly in contrast.

She was transparent, and her colors palely luminous, yet he could see that she was the same woman as in his dreams, with the same strangely beautiful face. She sat leaning against the bedpost, her long, tangled hair draping her shoulders and coiling on the coverlet.

"I woke Thomas in the night," she was saying. "I showed myself to him, and told him I had been murdered the very night he had ridden off to war. I bade him to flee, and come back with an army to wreak his vengeance, but he would not wait. He set fire to the castle that very night. When le Gayne came running out from the fire, Thomas handed him a sword and offered to fight to the death, to right the wrong that had been done.

"Thomas killed le Gayne for me, but not before himself receiving a wound that shortly proved his own mortality. I saw him fall, and be hacked to bits by le Gayne's men-at-arms, the castle burning down around them, casting a bloody glow upon it all."

"Good God," Alex said, appalled. He saw that she was looking at her hands, lying palms-up in her lap. Then she raised her gaze, looking at him, her irises black as night.

"He was dead before they put the first blade to him. I saw him standing beside me, looking down on his body. He turned to me and smiled, taking my face in his hands. He kissed me once, with such gentleness as I had never known from him. And then he was gone."

"I'm sorry."

She shrugged. "So that is how I know it is not vengeance that keeps me here, or a search for justice. I have had that."

"Why did you stay on the mountaintop, while your brother was able to leave?"

"I do not know."

"*Where* did he go?"

"I do not know!"

"You must have some idea," he said.

"No more than you, or any other."

"But you're dead!" he said, exasperated. "How can you not know what happens when someone dies?"

"Do you know where your soul came from?" she asked.

"What? No—"

"How can you not know that, and yet live?"

He opened his mouth to argue, then shut it again. She

146

had him there. "Will you remain a ghost forever?" he asked, expecting the same answer she'd been giving to every other question: "I don't know."

"Why are you not married, Woding?" she asked instead. "You are well past the age when you should have been."

"I was once," he said. Her change of topic had caught him off guard.

"What happened?"

"You are avoiding my question," he accused.

"She must have died. Did you love her?"

"I am not going to talk about Frances with you."

"You would have me tell you of my life. Why can I not hear of yours?"

"Why do you not show yourself, instead of coming as a voice out of the darkness?" he challenged back, knowing she was unaware he could see her quite as well as he did. "Why do you hide? What are you afraid I'll see?"

"I no longer wish to speak with you," she said, and then vanished.

Alex blinked, looking at where she had been. The sense of her presence was gone, as well. It was as if she had never been there at all: not even the bed curtains wavered at her passing.

He blew out his breath in a noisy, horse-blowing sound, and sank loosely into the pillows. He flopped his hand onto his forehead, holding it while he shook his head back and forth.

She looked like a ghost. She moved like a ghost. She talked like a woman Geoffrey Chaucer would have met on a pilgrimage to Canterbury. So was she a ghost? Or was he out of his mind?

He very well might be stark, raving mad. Crazier than

147

a bedbug. 'Round the bend. Crackers. He admittedly felt a few buttons short of fully dressed—but he was in bed, after all.

He gave a shout of incredulous laughter. The deuce of it all was that she had told him nothing that he could use to prove to himself they'd had their conversation. She had not told him where she was buried, and had revealed no secret passageways leading to long-forgotten dungeons. For all the information he had gleaned from her descriptions of being dead, he might as well have been talking to himself. "I do not know," she had said. Again and again.

His heart had quit beating when she first spoke his name. It was a miracle that he'd survived the shock of it. Actually hearing a voice was a step beyond vague anxieties and seeing a figure in the corner of one's eye.

He pulled his constraining nightshirt off over his head, flinging it to the foot of the bed. Whether she was real or not, she was gone. His bath had been particularly enjoyable, since he'd known there was no one spying upon him, although he would admit there was a very small, extremely vain part of him that had taken a certain pleasure in her interest.

On the other hand, sometimes a man wanted to scratch himself in ungentlemanly places.

If he was a lunatic, at least he seemed to have found a way to gain some control over his delusions. If he were being completely reasonable, he would do the wise thing and move to Bath with his sisters, and surround himself with the company of others with their feet firmly upon the ground of reality. He would watch stars from a town house rooftop, and for only a few hours of the night. He would go back to hands-on management of the mills, he would attend the rounds of house parties, he would seek out a wife and have children, and he would forget he had ever thought he had conversed with a beautiful ghost sitting at the foot of his bed.

He thought of the gruesome tale Serena had told of her brother's demise, and of the Black Death. They were gruesome tales, yet fascinating.

He thought of Bath, and of the elegant assemblies his sisters adored. Elegant, and stupefying.

He grinned into the dark. He might be mad, but he was miles from being bored.

Chapter Thirteen

Now who was this arriving? Serena wondered, looking down on the courtyard from an upstairs window of the castle. It had been over a week since Woding had seen any visitors.

The rattling carriage drew to a halt; the door was opened and the step lowered. A man got out first, dressed in somber colors, then turned to give a hand to a woman. Her hat was bedecked in feathers and fake flowers, all flattening in the wind of the gusty, unseasonably drizzly day. A second woman climbed out after the first, dressed more simply, and then a third, this one wearing no hat at all. Her gown, even from such a distance, looked cheap, garish, and well-worn.

As the small group went inside, Serena left the window, heading for the main staircase. She had been avoiding Woding for the past few days, feeling as though she had presented herself as an utter idiot in their conversation, being either unable or unwilling to answer any of his questions to his satisfaction. She felt as well that she had revealed too much that was personal about herself, speaking of Thomas's death as she had. Then his prodding for her to show herself—and her scarred face—had panicked her, and she had fled.

She had lost the knack of talking with another human being.

She had been practicing what she would say the next time, for she knew there had to be one. Her mind had been going nonstop, and she'd been mulling over every word they had exchanged, choosing words that would have been better, grimacing at those she had actually said. Their conversation, even as poorly as it had gone, had been like the first bite of food taken after a day of fasting. She couldn't stop now. She was only surprised she had not approached him again already.

The group of visitors had congregated at the foot of the stairs, in the entry hall between the library and the blue drawing room. Serena stopped at the landing half-way down the stairs, under the rose window. She could see now that the young woman in the feathered hat was Sophie, Woding's younger sister—Serena remembered her from her first visit here, with Woding's other sister, Philippa. She could only suppose that the man with her was her intended, the vicar. She had heard about him from the staff. He looked an earnest, fairly foolish young man, all long limbs and buggy eyes, obviously entranced by his dark-haired, dark-eyed fiancée.

She heard Woding coming along the upper hallway, and met his eyes as he stopped at the top of the staircase, noticing her presence. For a moment she had the sensation that he could see her much more clearly than he had let on, but she dismissed the idea. No one had been able to see her clearly without her either being in great distress or intending to be seen.

He nodded to her, then gave a slightly pained smile and looked over the rail at the group below. She didn't know if the pain was for her or for them. Perhaps both, given his solitary ways.

"Alex!" Sophie cried, looking up and seeing him. She dashed to the bottom of the stairs, waiting as he came slowly down them.

Serena watched him as he reached his sister and gave her a kiss on the cheek. "Sophie," he said. "I hope your journey was pleasant."

"I hardly noticed, I was so eager to get here. I wanted to come last week, as soon as I received Beth's letter about your ghost actually touching her, but Philippa would not allow it. She insisted I complete my dress fittings first. Dress fittings! When we have proof there are spirits abroad in your castle!"

Woding shook the man's hand, calling him Mr. Blandamour, and greeted the older woman in plain dress, Miss Silverlock, whom Serena guessed must be a nurse or chaperon to young Sophie, who was continuing to talk. "Of course I knew there were ghosts here the moment I saw the place. There is such an air of brooding, so many dark rooms that quite give one a chill. I know I am more sensitive than most to the energies of the other side, but surely you too have felt the presence of those who lived here before."

"Josiah Briggs, you mean?" Woding asked. "I feel his presence in every molding, every carving, every bit of black marble and fragment of stained glass."

Sophie made a pouty face. "You're making fun of me."

"Do forgive me. I fully recognize this is an ancient

structure, with walls dating all the way back to the 1820s."

"Al-*ex*." Sophie groaned.

"You have not introduced me to your companion," he said, nodding toward the woman in garish clothing.

Sophie gave a smile like all of sunlight. *"This,"* she said, going to the woman and leading her forward, "is Madame Zousa."

"How do you do, sir?" Madame Zousa said, giving a shallow curtsy while looking at the floor. She was of an indeterminate age, her coarse black hair peppered with gray that could have come at thirty-five or sixty-five. Her face was brownish and lined, but whether from age or sun Serena could not tell. Her expression revealed nothing of what she thought or felt.

"How do you do, madame," Woding said to the woman.

"Madame Zousa is a *Gypsy*," Sophie said in a loud whisper, as if it were a secret the woman did not already know. "She is going to help us to contact the ghost."

"Is she now?" Woding did not sound amused.

"I tried to talk her out of it," Blandamour complained, "but she was intent on bringing her."

Miss Silverlock nodded her head in distressed agreement. "She was not to be dissuaded. There will be trouble when Mrs. Stearne hears of it, I have no doubt."

"Oh, pish," Sophie said. "Philippa makes a fuss no matter what I do. I can hardly wait to be married and in charge of myself."

Serena saw the eyebrow Woding raised toward Blandamour, but the man was gazing cow-eyed at his fiancée, obviously no threat to her independence.

Underhill appeared, and soon was ushering Madame Zousa and Miss Silverlock up the stairs to their rooms, his pursed mouth indicative of his disapproval of the Gypsy. The threesome passed right by her, but the Gypsy did not so much as flick an eyelid in her direction.

Huh, Serena thought. *So much for the Gypsy's supposed powers.*

She descended the remaining stairs and followed Woding, Sophie, and Mr. Blandamour into the blue drawing room, so named for the powder blue velvet upholstery on all the chairs and settees. The floor was an eye-crossing geometrical design of five different woods, the walls above the wainscoting covered in gilded paper, and the fireplace a black marble beast surmounted by a mirror, which in turn was topped by carvings of Gothic arches and the figures of saints. As with most of the other rooms, the view from the windows was the only place an eye could find peace and joy.

Unless one were a Sophie or a Briggs. Serena listened in disbelief as the young woman sighed over the details of the room, declaring to Blandamour that she should very much like to have a similar room in the vicarage.

Sophie sat at the end of a settee, untying her hat and setting it next to her. Serena went and sat several inches away from the girl on the same settee, wanting to get a better look at this bit of frippery that shared blood with Woding. She looked closely at the features of the girl's face, assessing the lines of brow and nose, then looked back at Woding.

He was staring at her, a bit of white showing round his irises. She gave a little shrug of apology, and moved away from his sister. She got a minuscule nod of his head in thanks, and she wondered once again just how well he could see her.

Sophie continued to chatter on, seemingly needing no more than an occasional murmur from her male com-

panions to keep going. She had the same hair as Woding, and there was a similarity about the nose and mouth,
but that was all the resemblance Serena could see. Certainly the effect of those features was much different
when the lips would not stop moving than when they
held still, as did Woding's much of the time.

The aimless chatter grew quickly boring, and Serena's
mind began to wander. Sophie seemed a harmless
enough sort, but she felt sorry for Blandamour, who
would be listening to her for the next few decades. She
was contemplating whether to stay for the sake of watching Woding, or go to preserve her sanity, when Woding
spoke, drawing her attention back to what was being
said.

"You were a fool to hire that Gypsy woman, Sophie,
and you had no right to bring her to my home."

"She comes very highly recommended."

"She comes recommended by imbeciles. The woman
is without question a charlatan, and the only feat she
will accomplish is bilking you out of several pounds.
Good lord, Sophie, when are you going to grow up and
start acting as if you had an ounce of sense in your
head?"

"That isn't fair, Alex," Sophie said, her voice trembling. "I was only trying to help."

"You wanted to entertain yourself, and without giving
a thought to how your actions might affect others."

"But Beth is certain the house is haunted—"

"What if it is? Do you think a ghost would take kindly
to having someone like Madame Zousa here? All that
hiring a fake like her will succeed in doing is making
matters worse."

"Madame Zousa's not a fake," Sophie tried again, obviously hurt. "She can talk to Serena and find out what

it is that has trapped her here on this mortal plane. Once she knows that, she will have the power to send her on to her final rest, and your castle will be haunted no more. It will be like an exorcism—only much more humane."

"From the glee you've shown at the thought that the castle is haunted, I should have thought you would want it to remain so," Alex said.

" 'Twould not be Christian to know a soul was suffering in such awful torment and not try to help it onward, isn't that right, Mr. Blandamour?" Sophie said, turning to her fiancé for support.

"Surely the greatest hell is to be held away from God's love," Blandamour agreed.

Serena rolled her eyes and heard Woding give a snort. She saw him glance over at her before addressing his sister again.

"Perhaps Serena does not wish to go. She may not be feeling particularly tormented by the absence of God's love."

Sophie laughed, the sound slightly teary. "You're teasing me now." She gave a quivering smile, evidently deciding that her brother could not be as angry as he seemed. "Beth told me you insisted it was a prankster causing all the fuss. Perhaps Madame Zousa will be able to locate him, if she fails in her search for Serena. I did not tell her Serena's name, by the by, or even that it is a female ghost with which we are concerned. I am not a complete fool, you know. When she discovers the information on her own, we will know for certain that she is not taking advantage of our trusting natures."

Woding shook his head, apparently abandoning hope of making an impression on his younger sister. "Speaking of Beth, when I received your letter I asked her and Rhys to join us for dinner tonight"—he was interrupted by a shriek of delight from Sophie—"knowing how much you two enjoy one another's company."

After another ten minutes of prattle from Sophie, the young couple left to freshen up and change for dinner. Woding then surprised Serena by addressing her.

"Would you be so kind as to follow me to my study?" he asked in a low voice, glancing about to be sure no one was listening.

"Most happily," Serena said in the voice he could hear, and then mentally berated herself for not just saying yes. She should not let him know how eager she was to speak with him again. One's enemies should never know where one's heart lay.

When they reached his tower study he closed the door, then went to lean against the edge of his desk. Serena sat in the window embrasure, there being no other chairs than the one behind his desk. She did like to stick to the conventions of being a living person, subject to gravity. Nonexistent chairs were to be used only in times of distress.

"I want to ask you a favor," Woding said.

"Yes?"

"I'm sure you know as well as I do that that Gypsy woman is a fraud, and intent only on putting on a convincing performance to earn herself a few coins."

"She walked right past me without so much as blinking an eye," Serena confirmed. Really, the woman should have learned a bit of her trade. It was insulting to be passed by in such a manner.

"There, you see? She is undoubtedly harmless, her only threat being to the silver, which I am certain Underhill has already locked away. What I ask is that you refrain from doing anything to improve the Gypsy's per-

157

formance, and most especially that you do not do anything to frighten or harm Sophie."

"You know I would not harm a woman!" Serena cried, offended.

The corner of his mouth jerked in a quick smile. "I wanted to be certain you had not changed your mind, after hearing Sophie wanted to have you exorcised. That could be perceived as a direct provocation."

"She's a foolish girl," Serena said. "Neither she nor that Gypsy woman are any danger to me."

"Then you will stay away from Madame Zousa's performance tonight?"

"I did not say that."

"The last thing I need is for one of them to somehow catch a glimpse of you during it, or for you to go touching someone's hair again."

Serena clasped her guilty hands together, holding them against her stomach. "No one will see me. And I have no need to touch women's hair."

He looked doubtful, but let her protestations pass, changing the subject. "I had wondered where you had been these last few days. I thought you might have gone."

"I won't be so easy to get rid of as that, Woding," she said haughtily. "I was thinking about our conversation, is all. I told you much about myself. It occurs to me that there is much I would like to have you explain about yourself, in turn," she said, gesturing slightly with one finger toward the many-armed brass contraption.

His eyes followed the small movement, and he turned to look at where she pointed. *The wily scoundrel!* It was as she had feared! "The devil take thy guts!" she cried. "You lied to me, Woding! You see me much more clearly than you claimed!" She hopped off the embra-

158

sure, stalking toward him, her hands fisted at her sides.

He stood up, facing her as she approached.

"Forsooth, how much of me do you see?" she asked, horrified at the thought that he could see the scar that blazed its deep pink trail across her face.

"I see you as a transparent woman, with your own illumination, as if glowing from a candle within."

"What else?"

"I see the faint colors of your dress, and of your hair. You wear a girdle of some fashion. Your hair reaches to your thighs. I do not know the color of your eyes, or"—he hesitated, and she got the feeling he was changing what he was about to say—"or if you have wrinkles 'round your eyes. I cannot see you that well."

"In truth?"

"Do you have wrinkles?"

"Marry, I would not tell you if so." She pursed her lips a moment, then backed off. If he was lying, he would not admit it. She could best judge the truth of his statements by his behavior. If he could see her scar, he would not long have an interest in her. She had no control over it one way or the other, a realization that made her stomach roil. She stared at him for several long moments, digesting that, then changed the subject. "Why do you humor your sister, letting her play her foolish games?"

"Because they are just games," he said, going toward the door. "I save my strength for the battles worth fighting."

And with that he left, leaving her to wonder if he referred to her.

"Silence!" Madame Zousa said. "We must have total silence!"

"The ghosties have fragile nerves," Rhys said to Alex in a stage whisper. "They need their quiet." Both Beth and Sophie hushed him with furious hisses.

"If she thinks that, she knows nothing of our Serena," Alex whispered back.

"Alex!" Sophie said in a hiss.

"So sorry."

Alex leaned back in his overstuffed seat in the blue drawing room, watching with some amusement as Madame Zousa set up her paraphernalia. The gaslights and candles were all out save for a single fat candle in a dish, set in the center of a swath of black silk on the floor.

At least the cloth saved him from having to look at the marquetry.

Madame Zousa dumped the contents of a charm-bedecked cloth bag onto the edge of the cloth, revealing what looked to be a pile of barely clean chicken bones, bits of dried brown flesh still clinging in a few spots. A shriveled chicken head and one withered claw emerged from one of Madame Zousa's pockets, and then a small pouch, contents unknown.

Alex couldn't help but wonder if these were the usual tools of her trade, or if instead she was making good use of last night's supper.

A familiar pale illumination caught his eye as Serena came into the room, an appearance that brought him a conflict of emotion. She came directly to his side, then knelt down on the floor, her eyes on Madame Zousa.

When he had first seen her on the stairs after her three-day absence, he had been both dismayed and relieved. Dismayed because it meant he had not somehow effected a cure for the insanity of thinking he had talked with a ghost. Relieved because as inharmonious as their acquaintance was, it was obsessively fascinating.

Those three days without her, his mind had gone again and again to their encounter: to what she had told him; to the medieval accent of her voice, which he thought he could gladly listen to for days; to how she had looked, so eerily similar to what he had dreamed; and most of all to how strangely human she seemed, her emotions rich in her voice, her gestures and movements no different from those of a living woman except in their intensity.

He had gotten next to nothing done with his star charts, his mind had been so filled with Serena and with worrying—absurdly!—that she might not come back. He was tempted to blame her for draining him of his intellectual energies; only honesty forced him to admit it was his own lack of mental self-discipline that was the culprit.

But then, what did it matter if he let his mind dwell on her for a few days? He had no deadlines under which to work. Why shouldn't he allow himself a minor obsession, especially one so intriguing and unusual?

The days of unwashed clothing and lunatic ranting were obviously fast approaching. He could see it now, mothers telling their children to beware of Mad Woding of Maiden Castle, who conversed with spirits. His sisters would have him crated off to the asylum—or worse yet, Bath.

Ah, well. He glanced at Serena, at her profile, so clear to him in this near-dark. The candlelight had the odd effect of making each place it reached on her slightly more transparent, leaving the back of her head more clearly defined than her face. It was as if her own light struggled to complete with light from other sources.

What did she make of these goings-on?

Madame Zousa arranged her chicken bones in a star pattern on the cloth, then cast her dark-eyed gaze on each of the guests in turn. They all sat in separate chairs around the cloth, too far from each other to touch. Alex wondered if that, and the dark, were meant to increase their unease and susceptibility to Madame Zousa's tricks. The candle on the floor underlit their faces, making the familiar eerie. Sophie herself looked ghoulishly sinister, with the dim orange glow touching under her chin, nose, and eye sockets, her normally rounded cheeks deeply shadowed beneath her eyes.

Serena was the only one of the lot who looked almost normal. Madame Zousa was positively troll-like in contrast, her black hair hanging loose and wild. God only knew what the woman had in mind, or of what she was capable. Sophie, when pressed, had admitted to having hired her through a friend of a friend, who claimed the woman lived in the woods.

"A harpsichord should be playing off-key," Rhys said. "To complete the mood."

Madame Zousa pointed a bony finger, and gave a glare that silenced him. He looked over at Alex with raised eyebrows, his fingertips to his pursed mouth like an old woman caught gossiping. Alex smothered a smile.

"The spirits," Madame Zousa said, her voice low and portentous, "are everywhere." She waved her hands over her chicken-bone star, and started speaking in what he assumed to be her native Romany tongue, rolling her eyes up into her head, the whites glimmering beneath her half-closed lids. She rose up on her knees, swaying back and forth, her chanting guttural and loud.

The swaying slowed, and Madame Zousa's eyes rolled back and forth. Her voice decrescendoed to a soft, childish tone, and she switched back to English.

"Spirits, hear my call," she said, then rolled her head on her neck, her eyes unfocused, staring into the dark. "Spirits, come to me. Tell me who haunts this house, and what deeds he has done. Tell me what holds him from the world beyond."

Despite himself, Alex felt a shiver go through him, the dark room alive now with anticipation. He glanced at Serena, who was watching the display intently but otherwise seemed unmoved.

"Spirits, move through me," she said. She opened the small pouch and upended it over the pattern of chicken bones. A matted clump of orange-brown chicken feathers landed on the bones with a *poof,* breaking apart like a poorly packed snowball. "Spirits, move through air."

The feathers stirred, as if touched by an unseen hand. Alex saw Serena's eyes widen, and she crossed herself. She glanced up at him, as if for reassurance.

For heaven's sake, what was he supposed to do? If anything, he should be asking *her* for protection. This was her realm, not his.

Madame Zousa held her arms out wide in front of her, as if waiting to embrace someone. She leaned back, kneeling, her knees spread wide under her skirt. It looked as if she were expecting the spirits to come to her in more than one sense.

Serena was reminded of how she must have looked to le Gayne, at the stream, inviting his attentions. The thought seemed to call to some unseen spirit, and she heard, as if from a distance, a female voice begin to sing:

> "There were three ravens sat on a tree,
> They were as black as they might be,
> With a down, derry, derry, derry, down, down."

A frisson went up the back of her neck, and she shifted slightly closer to Woding, suddenly not so certain that Madame Zousa was a complete charlatan.

"Aaaaa," Madame Zousa groaned, and undulated her arms and shoulders in a rippling wave, as if they were a snake. "Aaaaa . . ." She let her hands drop down to her groin, clasping herself there. "I feel you," she said.

Beth and Sophie gasped, and Rhys and Blandamour let out grunts of surprise. Serena's muscles tensed, but she saw that Woding just watched, his eyes narrowing in the look she knew meant he was suspicious.

The thought that he doubted was almost a comfort, but then she saw *it*; a shadow in the dark, a shapeless form, rising above the candle and then moving toward Madame Zousa.

> "Then one of them said to his mate,
> 'Where shall we our breakfast take?' "

The female voice sang again out of the darkness. The others seemed not to hear it.

Serena scrambled to her feet, her eyes on the black cloud. Everyone else's eyes were on Madame Zousa. Was she the only one who could see it? She could feel evil coming off the shadow, deep and corrupted, as foul as the corpses of the Pestilence. It moved toward Madame Zousa, then covered her.

Madame Zousa groaned again, her hips jerking forward in a rhythmic motion, as if she were being held and mounted by a man. Her eyes turned to Serena, focusing on her for the first time, and in their depths Serena saw both fear and a desperate plea, her body continuing to jerk under the thrusts of the assault.

"Stop him," Serena said in a hiss near Woding's ear.

All the others were staring with fascinated eyes at the groaning Madame Zousa, writhing on the floor.

He looked up at her uncomprehendingly.

"Stop him!" Serena repeated, trying to keep her voice low, but feeling it rising with her panic. "Don't you see what he's doing to her?"

"Who?" Woding asked.

He didn't see the shape, didn't feel the evil.

Oh, God, that poor woman. She couldn't just stand there and watch.

She did the only thing she could think of, leaping to the center of the black cloth and kicking the chicken bones apart. The shadow dropped Madame Zousa, who collapsed to the floor like a boiled cabbage, and then it turned to Serena and began expanding, filling her vision in a claustrophobic cloud of evil.

"Holy Mary, Mother of God," Serena recited desperately in Latin, her voice loud and audible in the room of silent observers, her heart thudding. "Pray for us sinners now and at the hour of our death, Amen!"

The black shape gave a shuddering bellow that vibrated down to her bones, calling forth the memory of le Gayne's howls on their wedding night. She continued quickly through her rosary, her muscles weak with terror, and the shadow began to fade away, dissipating with each word she spoke, and then it was gone.

Serena dropped to her knees beside Madame Zousa, her hands fluttering helplessly over the woman's slack face. She looked imploringly to Woding, whose expression of confused anger changed to one of deep concern as he finally understood that something had gone wrong, and Madame Zousa's collapse was not part of the performance.

"Rhys, get some light in here!" he ordered, lurching

from his chair and coming to kneel beside Serena. He pulled Madame Zousa's upper body onto his lap, cradling her head in his arm, lightly patting her cheeks. "Madame Zousa!" he said. "Madame Zousa!" And then, to Sophie, "Smelling salts! Do you have any?"

"What? Salts?"

Beth took Sophie's reticule from her, and started digging through it, coming up moments later with the salts. She gave them to Woding, who opened them and waved them under Madame Zousa's nose.

Sophie was still flustered. "What's happened? I don't understand. She was in a trance, wasn't she? Isn't she all right?" Blandamour came and put his arm around her, half lifting her from the settee and forcing her to accompany him from the room.

"Hush, sweeting," Serena heard him murmuring to her. "Madame Zousa has had a fit. Leave her to your brother and the Coxes. They will know what to do."

"But she did contact Serena, didn't she?" Sophie asked. "The voice. Whose voice was that, praying? I didn't see Madame Zousa's lips moving."

"Hush, dearest, and don't think of it. We'll see if Cook can make you a toddy."

Madame Zousa began to come around, blinking, closing her mouth and reaching up to wipe at the saliva that had dribbled down her chin. Woding pulled out a handkerchief and helped her. The room brightened as Rhys got the gaslights back on, and several candles lit.

"Where is she?" Madame Zousa asked weakly.

"Where is who?" Beth asked, wrapping her own shawl around the woman's shoulders as Woding eased her into a sitting position.

Madame Zousa looked around, her eyes passing over Serena without seeing her. "The tall, pale woman, with the long hair." Her voice had lost its Romany accent, and begun to take on a distinctly Cornish hue.

"I saw no one," Beth said, "but I heard a woman's voice speaking Latin. Did you hear it, too, Rhys?" she asked, turning to her husband.

"I heard someone," he said, "but I'm not saying I know who it was." His tone of voice suggested he was holding much of his opinion back, and none of it was kind toward Madame Zousa.

They all looked toward Woding.

"I think we had best get you tucked up in bed," he said to Madame Zousa. "I'll ring for Marcy to keep an eye on you. We can discuss this all in the morning."

Marcy was duly called for, and Madame Zousa taken away. Serena caught Woding's eye and she pointed to the black silk, candle, and chicken remains. He took her hint and blew out the candle, then gathered the silk, bones, and feathers together and tossed the lot into the fire.

Serena stood and watched the materials go up in flame, wanting to be certain that every last scrap was burned to cinders. It was only when she heard the others leaving the room that she pulled herself away, unwilling to stay in the drawing room alone.

"I've never seen anything like it," Beth was saying as the threesome crossed the entry hall and went into the library. It was a far cozier room, the fire already burning merrily in the hearth, the spines of the books giving the room a sense of comforting familiarity.

Rhys and Woding pulled three chairs up around the fire; then Woding served them all brandy, Beth included. Serena wished she could have some herself, her body was still trembling with the aftereffects of fright.

Woding pulled an ottoman to the side of his chair,

167

seemingly without purpose or intent. She was standing to the side, watching them all settle in with their drinks and beginning to feel very much the lonely, frightened outsider, when she realized that Woding meant the ottoman for her.

She sniffled once, feeling a pathetic hint of grateful tears in her eyes, and sat down.

The rehashing of the séance was about what she expected, Beth excited, Rhys trying desperately to pass much of it off as a performance, and Woding largely keeping his own counsel. Blandamour appeared shortly before the group broke up, telling Woding that Sophie had been reluctantly put to bed under the care of her nurse. Serena rather felt for the poor wench, foolish though she might be, if she were going to have to spend the rest of her life mollycoddled in such a manner.

As they parted for the evening, Serena stayed close to Woding's side, visions of the black shadow haunting her thoughts. She followed him to his room.

Alex closed the door and went to his bed, setting his candle on the small table beside it. He waited a few more moments to be sure that the others were out of earshot down the hall, and then turned to Serena, standing alone and pale across the dark room. She glowed with the self-contained luminescence of foxfire, visible herself yet illuminating nothing around her.

"What the hell happened down there?" he asked, feeling a confused ire that had no proper target. Somehow, he was certain her presence had brought about the fiasco tonight, only she seemed as shaken by the events as was Madame Zousa.

"I do not know," she said.

Predictable.

"Enough with 'I don't know'! You said you would

not interfere tonight. I want to know why you broke your word, and why you spoke. For God's sake, everyone heard you!"

The full implications of her speaking and being heard by others suddenly dawned on him as he said it: he was not crazy. She did exist. He had proof now, of a sort, for they had heard her, too. He sat on the end of his bed, struck silent by the realization.

He watched her come toward him, stopping a few feet away.

"Forsooth, you did not see him?" she asked.

"See whom?"

Her hands were clasped tight in front of her. "I think it was the spirit of Hugh le Gayne."

"In the drawing room? Why? Have you seen him here before?"

"No, but it felt like him, and what he did to that woman . . . It could only have been le Gayne. It had to have been!"

"Serena," he said in a low, calm voice, sensing the depth of her distress, "tell me from the beginning. What did you see?"

She described a darkness upon dark, a shadow of some evil presence that had taken Madame Zousa and made of her a toy for his pleasure, raping her as they all sat and watched. He felt his skin go cold, tightening in belated goose pimples.

"And you think this shadow was Hugh le Gayne?"

She wrapped her arms around herself and gave a shiver. "It must have been."

"But he's gone now, right? You got rid of him with that prayer you said."

"I think I did."

"Think? Or know?"

"I do not know! One moment he was there; the next he was gone." They were both silent a long moment, and then she added, "I am afraid he might come back."

The thought gave him no small unease. "The bones were burned, and I doubt Madame Zousa—or whatever her name really is—will be calling upon the dead anytime soon."

"Perhaps he will not need her next time. Perhaps she has shown him the way to escape the bounds of hell and come after me!"

"Serena, stop it," Alex ordered. "You're frightening yourself. It—or he—is gone."

"He has been burning in hell all these years, waiting for a second chance at me. How do you know he will not return? He did it once! Maybe he's still here in the castle, waiting for me to be alone, or waiting until I go to that place between wakings, where I shall be helpless."

"What place?"

She fluttered a hand impatiently at him. "When I am not here. It is like your dreamworld, only with no dreams. It is nothingness. There would be nothing to stop him if he came after me there, no way for me to defend myself!"

She was nearly as bad as Sophie, Alex thought. She was talking herself into a terror. Who ever heard of a ghost afraid of a ghost? And this behavior from her was unexpected for another reason: even though frightened, he would have thought she would take an offensive position against the shadow. Hugh le Gayne must have been a monstrous man to have so devastating an effect on her so many years after his death.

"Do something, Woding," she said suddenly. He could feel her gaze intently on him. "You have the power. You can guard us all against him."

"I have no power against such things. You are proof enough of that."

"The stars! You understand the stars, you are an astrologer, you must know how to keep le Gayne away."

"An astrologer?" He laughed. "I am no astrologer, Serena. I do not seek the future in the stars."

"But why else would you spend your nights in study of the heavens?"

"I seek knowledge, but not of the kind you mean. I am trying to decipher the riddle of falling stars. I am an amateur scientist, is all. An astronomer."

"Do not the stars tell you what will happen, and explain what has?"

"Not in any mode I can understand."

"The men of greatest learning in my day were the astrologers," Serena said. " 'Tis well known that the fate of man is writ in the stars and planets. Why do you not know this as well?"

He chewed the inside of his lip a moment, thinking on how best to explain himself. She wouldn't hear him at all if he started by totally refuting her beliefs. "There are those who still believe that truth can be read in the heavens," he began. "That is not, however, the type of truth I am seeking. What I want to know is what causes those streaks of light that we call falling stars. I want to know what they really are, not just what they appear to be. I am curious."

"You are going to a lot of trouble to satisfy your curiosity, Woding." She narrowed her dark eyes at him. "There must be more to it than that. If it is not to seek power, it is something else."

"I do not know why there should be anything else."

"Is this because of what happened when you were

here as a boy, the night the stars fell?" she asked.

"What do you know of that night?" he asked carefully.

"What do you?" she countered.

He tread carefully. "Rhys has always said you tried to kill me. He would have me believe that you pushed me from that wall."

"I did not!"

"But you *were* here."

"Of course I was here. By Saint Stephen, where else would I have been? I have not left the place for nigh on five centuries."

"Did you see me fall?"

"I—" she started, then stopped.

"Did you see me fall?" he repeated.

"For God's love, I did not mean to hurt you," she said quickly, softly. "I do not even know what happened, not entirely. I saw you there, gazing up at the night sky, and I reached out. . . ." She paused, her eyes focused somewhere in the past.

"And?"

She came back, looking at him again. She shrugged. "And somehow you must have seen me. I did not mean to frighten you."

"Why did you reach for me?"

"I do not know!"

"Serena, I grow tired of that answer."

"Why should I know the answers to all your questions?"

"I am asking why you reached for me."

"And I am telling you, I do not know! There was something about your face, the expression in your eyes, as if your soul had suddenly expanded in a flash of wonder. I do not know. Perhaps I thought . . . thought I could somehow touch what you felt. I wanted to be a part of your wonder, if only for a moment."

This was not what he had expected to hear. Where was the rage, the hatred, the murderous passion? All he heard was a heart-wrenching longing. He could hardly believe that he had been the boy to rouse such feelings in her.

"And then I think you saw me, and were horrified, and you lost your footing and fell," she said. "I woke your cousin, and held my gown against your cut until he gained his wits and came to help you. I do not believe I meant you any harm."

"You have doubts?"

"Envy does terrible things to a person, Woding. You were more alive on that wall than I could remember ever being. I wanted that, but if I couldn't have it, how do I know that part of me did not want to be certain that no one else had it, either?"

A faint understanding of her nature and her experiences began to flicker beneath his consciousness, softening him toward her even as her complexities took him aback. "Do you still envy me?"

"I will not harm you."

"That is not what I asked."

"What do the envies of a mere spirit, insubstantial as air, matter? Why do you ask anything about me at all? I cannot matter to you. Perhaps you seek only to pacify me by playing to my vanity."

The remark was close enough to his original intent to make him uncomfortable, but his interest in her had since taken on a life of its own, an interest that seemed more valid than obsessional now that he had trustworthy witnesses to her existence. "Perhaps it is the other way around, and *you* are blackmailing *me* into talking with you," he said, avoiding her accusation. "If I ignored you, by morning I might have no male staff left at all."

"They may leave you anyway, after they hear what happened tonight. And most assuredly the women will leave you if Hugh le Gayne returns. He would not be so gentle with your servants as I."

"That is not a pleasant thought," he said.

He did not know for certain what had happened tonight, even after Serena's explanation. Madame Zousa might have only had a fit, and not called any spirits at all. He did believe that Serena thought she had seen something, though. He knew now that she would not have spoken otherwise, and she most certainly would not have admitted her fears to him if something had not truly, deeply frightened her. That much, at least, he understood about her.

"Then do something about it, Woding. Search your books. Find something to keep him away."

"Mr. Blandamour might be the better source of help."

She made a disparaging noise with which he could not help but agree. One did not easily imagine the gangly vicar in a spiritual duel with the likes of a shadowy le Gayne.

He went on. "You seem to have done an admirable job of banishing the spirit yourself."

"You're not going to help me," she stated flatly.

"Serena, I am not what you think. My charts and my telescope have nothing to do with magic."

"Astrology is not magic."

He sighed. "I'll tell you what. When we have a moment to ourselves, I'll take you to my study and explain what I do there. Maybe then you will understand what I'm trying to say. If there is any magic to be had, you can find it and use it yourself."

She nodded, quick and firm. "I will do so."

"All right then. Let's call it a night, shall we?" He stood up, leading the way to the door.

She didn't move.

"Serena? Good night."

She stayed standing there.

"I want to take a bath and go to bed. I'll see you in the morning."

She only looked at him.

He held on to his patience. "What is it?"

"I want to stay here tonight."

"I beg your pardon?"

"I don't want to be alone. I won't bother you. I've spent the night here before, and never troubled you."

He'd been plenty troubled. He did not relish the idea of repeating those erotic nightmares. "I would rather you did not."

"He may still be here."

"If he returns, you may come wake me."

"I pray thee, please?" she asked softly. "May I stay?"

The plea sounded as if it cost half her soul. It occurred to him that she must have rarely asked favors of anyone. He was also aware that she could stay whatever his protests. Her vulnerability defeated him in a way her aggression never had.

"All right." He sighed.

"Thank you."

Was that a smile he saw on her face? "Make yourself comfortable. I'm going to take my bath."

She looked worried, and opened her mouth to speak.

"Alone," he said, before she could even ask.

"I won't look."

"No."

"I promise."

"No."

"Prithee, please?"

"Those words are not a magic incantation to get whatever you wish," he said sourly.

She kept looking at him.

He had created a monster. It had been easier to have her do as she wished than to have to consent to it, making himself a willing partner. "Oh, fine," he said at last. "Do as you will. But keep in mind that I can tell when you're watching me."

Good God. He sounded like a virgin protecting her modesty. Why should it matter even if she did look? he wondered as she followed him into his bathroom. She made a show of staring closely at a landscape painting while he ran the water and undressed.

The problem was, a part of him almost wanted her to turn around and stare, as he knew she had done before. A very small part of him, to be sure, but it was there nonetheless.

He slipped into the hot water, aware of her presence and her every movement as she went from painting to dresser, displaying unnatural interest in the contents of the room. There was, he admitted to himself, something strangely arousing about bathing in the presence of a woman. It was even more perverse that he should be getting even the hint of a thrill from that, considering that she was a ghost.

The nightmare in which he had made love to her on the ruined wall flitted back to him in disjointed, half-remembered images. Would she truly be cold to the touch? A tingling memory of unwanted pleasure shimmered through him, stirring his manhood.

He was a sick devil, no question about it.

As he dried off, he watched her from the corner of

his eye, trying—or hoping?—to catch her breaking her
promise. She was as good as her word, though, completely turning her back as he toweled off. He put his
arms in his dressing gown and tied it shut, disdaining a
nightshirt. If she was going to behave herself, there was
no point in putting himself through the torture of twisted,
clinging fabric.

Serena noted the lack of nightshirt with a bare quirking
of the corners of her lips. Good, she thought. At least
while he slept she would have the delight of looking at
his neck and, possibly, a bit of shoulder. Get him warm
enough and even some chest might become visible. It
was a great pity he was not as free with his person as
her brothers had been with theirs.

She followed him back into his bedroom. He raised
an eyebrow to her when he reached the side of his bed,
and she obligingly turned her back once again, listening
with a tingling awareness in her loins as his dressing
gown was removed and the sheets drawn back.

This was most unlike her, lusting after a man—and
tonight of all nights, after that encounter with le Gayne!
Perhaps she could blame it all on that first view of his
bare buttocks. Or maybe it was his hiring of that girl to
be a stablelass, such an unexpected, admirable thing to
do. Or maybe it was that he showed an interest in her,
and noted her presence when no one else did.

He was a civil, responsible man, and therefore a new
creature to her acquaintance. Surely her fascination
could be attributed to that alone.

Somehow, though, that didn't explain why the very
thought of lying next to him on his bed made her want
to touch herself between her thighs. She flushed with
embarrassment at even admitting the thought to herself.

177

Stupid man. She would be wise to avoid him.

"You can turn around now."

She immediately did so, and climbed onto the foot of the bed, finding her accustomed place leaning against the post. As he blew out the candle and pulled shut the curtains, her eyes ran along the muscled contours of his arm and up to the pocket of black hair in his armpit. She wondered if it would be soft, if she touched it. The thought of his reaction if she were to do such a thing made her giggle inaudibly.

He looked at her suspiciously, then said, "Good night, Serena."

"Good night, Alex," she said, using his Christian name like a taunting caress.

He frowned, his expression easily visible to her in the dark. She wondered if he knew she could see it.

He settled down to sleep, and she held to her position, distracting her mind by gazing at what little she could see of him. She felt safe here within the confines of the bed curtains with him, as if they were in their own little world, and the very fact of Woding's existence would somehow keep le Gayne—or whatever that shadow had been—away.

Funny, but a month ago the thought that she could feel safe in the presence of a man would have been un-believable. More than that, it would have been repulsive. She had grown up thinking of males as the ones com-peting with her for whatever it was she wanted, be it attention or the last piece of cake. They were to be dealt with and outsmarted, but never to be gone to in search of aid, except as a last resort. Help was something they gave her only when it suited their own purposes.

Perhaps Woding had purposes of his own, of which she was unaware. His thinking often confounded her, his logic convoluted and indirect compared to her own. It would be wise to expect the unexpected where he was concerned.

His breathing deepened, and soon she was certain he was asleep. She drifted up off the bed, her hair flowing out around her as if she were suspended in water. She stretched out above him, matching the length of her body to his, and let herself drift down until she was only inches above him.

He shifted, rolling onto his back, the covers coming down to just below his collarbone. *Ah, lovely bone, so gently curved and strong.* She bent her head down, daring to let her lips run above it, only a breath of air away from touching. She followed his neck to his ear, his face close beside hers, his stubbled cheek nearly touching.

She brought her face back above his. What would it be like to kiss him? To have him kiss her? What was it like between a man and woman who did not despise each other? She had heard there was pleasure, but did not believed it possible for the woman.

Could Woding, who already seemed to be showing her that a man could be good, also show her the good that was possible between a man and a woman?

Her eyes went to the streak of white in the dark hair at his temple. That had been his first reaction to seeing her: utter horror.

She drifted upward, away, until her back was against the tester, and looked down at Woding with the new sting of tears in her eyes. He would never show her anything about the physical love between men and women. Even if she had not been a ghost, he would never feel any desire for such a great, lumbering ox of a woman as she, with a scar more suited to a soldier than to a maiden.

179

Shadow of le Gayne or no, the confines of the curtained bed were no longer a comfort, and Woding no longer a source of reassurance. She did not belong with one such as he, with his gentle speaking ways and his handsome face. He was meant for a softer sort of woman, one with grace and a sweet temper.

She drifted through the curtains and stood upright on the floor outside the bed. The room felt colder than it was inside the bed curtains, although she knew that was just her imagination: she was long beyond sensing warmth. She searched the shadows of the room for any hint of movement, or of a darkness darker than it should be, impenetrable to her vision, but the room was as inert as it ever was. At least for the moment, there was no shadow waiting to take its revenge on her.

The appearance of nothing amiss did little to allay her fears, but she'd had a lifetime and more of mastering her innate cowardice, and would manage to do so again. Bravery was not found in the fearless: it was in those who went on regardless of their fears.

Where she needed to go right now was to talk to Madame Zousa.

This would likely be her only chance to speak to the woman alone, before she was in the company of others or she left the castle entirely. Serena still thought it likely Woding had something in his books on stars that would help her, but obviously the best source of information would be the woman who had opened the path for le Gayne in the first place.

She would have realized that sooner, if she hadn't been sidetracked by fantasies of Woding's bathing body.

She squared her jaw, crossed herself, and headed out to find the Gypsy.

*　　*　　*

He was dreaming.

He stood at the entrance to the castle garden, the walls only partially ruined, the grounds covered in a meadow of sweet wildflowers and grasses. At the end of the garden, the cherry tree stood in full bloom, its trunk slender with youth, its branches long and limber. Beneath the tree, in dappled sunlight, sat Serena.

He walked through the grasses toward her, blue butterflies flitting around him, bees humming in the yellow and pink flowers. As he approached, he saw that she wept.

He went down on one knee beside her and reached out, brushing back one of her tangled locks and tucking it behind her ear. She turned her face away, but he placed his fingertips on her chin and turned it back. Her skin was warm to his touch, supple, alive. Her lovely face was blotched from crying, her eyelids red and swollen.

"Serena, what is it? What has happened?" he asked.

"Dead, all dead," she said.

"Who is dead?"

She wept, shaking her head.

"Who is dead?" he repeated.

"We all are," she said at last, her eyes meeting his. They were black again from lid to lid, leaking diamond tears. She held up her hands, and when he looked at them they were coated in crimson blood. "I killed us all."

He woke with a start, his eyes coming open to the darkness of his curtained bed. It took him a moment to realize what was amiss: Serena. The familiar sense of her and the softly illuminated glow of her presence were gone.

Her worries about the shadow conjured by Madame

Zousa leaped immediately to mind, and fear for her ran like an electrical current through his body. He yanked back the bed curtains and leaped out of bed, throwing on his dressing gown as he ran across the room to the hall door. He had to find her.

Madame Zousa, Serena said in her ghost voice, hoping the Gypsy woman had the spiritual ears to hear it. *Madame Zousa! Wake up!*

She was in the bedroom allotted to the woman, one of the nicer servants' rooms on the top floor. There was a fireplace and a desk, in addition to the wardrobe. The iron bedstead was not overly large, but the housemaid Marcy shared it with the Gypsy woman regardless. Apparently Madame Zousa, too, had been unwilling to sleep alone.

Madame Zousa! She did not want to wake Marcy. Despite her earthy cheerfulness, the maid would likely not be amused to find a ghost in the room in the dead of night. Serena didn't want her screaming and bringing the whole house upon them.

The Gypsy woman showed no signs of having heard her. How could she sleep like that after what she'd been through?

There was no helping it. Serena drew on her precious energy and manifested a hand with which to shake the Gypsy's shoulder.

"Mmmmuhh," Madame Zousa grunted, and rolled over, her back to Serena.

Serena gave her another shake, and added in an audible, exasperated voice, "Madame Zousa, wake yourself! God's heart, woman, what type of seer are you?"

"Who is it?" Marcy asked blearily from her side of the bed, raising her head. After a moment with no answer she dropped back again and fell back asleep, never having been fully awake. The disturbance did at least stir Madame Zousa, and she rolled back over, opening her eyes.

Serena, after a moment's indecision, let just her face show to the woman.

"Jesus Christ preserve me!" The Gypsy gasped.

"Shhh!" Serena hissed, and let her hands show, flagging the woman to be silent. "I won't hurt you. Do you remember me? From this evening?"

Recognition finally came. "It's you!" the Gypsy whispered, and sucked in her breath, her eyes widening.

"Yes, 'tis I. I need to speak with you," Serena said urgently, quietly. "Come out into the hall."

Fear flickered in the woman's eyes, and she gripped the covers tight in her hands, tucking them close under her chin. "No."

"I must speak with you!"

"You sent that thing to take me! I will go nowhere with you!" she declared, her voice dangerously close to breaking a whisper.

"I did no such thing! I didn't send it; you summoned it yourself."

"It came from you, and it left when you told it to. Do not think you can trick me!"

Serena frowned. This made no sense. Had the woman been deranged by her experience? "By Our Lady, I did not call it," she tried again. "If my presence somehow made it come, that was not my wish."

The distrust in the woman's eyes was still there, but the fear lessened a hair. "Mayhap you tell the truth," she said doubtfully. "You may speak to me here, if you must, but I will go nowhere with you."

Serena held back her exasperation, drawing on the

techniques of Woding. He would not shake the woman by the shoulders, or drag her out into the hall by her hair. He would not slap or pinch her until he got what he wanted. No, he would flatter and cajole and play the gentleman. And in the end he would get what he came for.

"It is clear that you have a talent that others lack," Serena said, the words as sour to her tongue as vinegar. "You have the true gift of vision." *And walked right by me while I stood on the staircase. Aii! How does Woding stand it?* "You are a woman of great knowledge and power, and I come seeking your help." It was a miracle Woding did not make himself ill with such tactics.

The woman's hands on the blankets loosened under the sycophantic words. "You need my help?"

"I want you to tell me what you know of conjuring spirits, and of sending them back to the place from whence they came. I need to know what charms or spells you use to protect yourself from them."

"You are a spirit yourself. Why would I tell you? You may use it against me."

"I swear before God, I would not do so."

Madame Zousa's mouth pinched, as if by doing so she could hold in the precious information.

"I pray thee, please?" Serena tried, making her expression as meek and helpless as she could.

"Well . . ." Madame Zousa relented.

Apparently those pleading words did have a certain magical effect. She would have to remember that, nauseating as it might be to beg. The ploy opened all kinds of doors.

"I cannot tell you the secrets of my trade," the woman went on, bringing up short Serena's celebration. "But perhaps I can give you a charm to ward off evil. Step back," she said, shooing her away with her hand.

Serena obeyed, and the woman got out of bed, careful not to disturb her sleeping companion. She went to her bag, sitting open on a chair, and rummaged through it in the moonlight coming through the window.

"Ah, here we are," she said, coming up with a small silver medallion on a fine chain.

Serena stepped closer, reaching out to touch it. The moonlight reflected off the medallion's surface, limning the contours of a woman's profile. A narrow band of some sort held the woman's curls close to her head and off her neck, a crescent rising above her forehead. "Is it a coin?" Serena asked.

"A sacred coin, forged in the fires of time," Madame Zousa said. She turned the medallion over, revealing the image of a woman seated on a throne. "This is the goddess Diana, known by the Greeks as Artemis. She is ruler of the moon and of the hunt. She will protect you."

" 'Tis a heathenish thing," Serena said doubtfully. No priest would have approved. " 'Twas calling upon the Virgin Mary that sent the shade back to whence he came."

Madame Zousa let the medallion twirl in the moonlight. "Diana is from a time before time, before Christ's name was even known. Her power reaches beyond the realms of Christianity to touch every man, woman, and child, whether they believe in her or no. She is a warrior, a goddess." Then Madame Zousa shrugged. "But if you do not want it . . ."

"She is a warrior, you say?"

"And a huntress. See here?" Madame Zousa said, holding the profile of the woman close for Serena to see. "Do you see the crescent moon above her forehead? It

185

is her symbol. The moon holds a woman's power, and Diana holds the moon."

"Give it to me," Serena said.

"Gladly," the gypsy said, holding it up, a full moon tethered to a chain. "Only one thing. There is the matter of the price."

"Price? What price? I have no coins to give you. I have nothing even to trade with you!" Hadn't the woman noticed she was a ghost?

"You have information."

Serena frowned at her. "What type of information are you seeking?" She would not help this woman to steal from Woding, if that was what she had in mind. Neither would she allow her to blackmail or otherwise cause harm.

"Tell me your name, and tell me something about yourself that no one knows," Madame Zousa said.

"Why?"

"I fear I will not be paid for my time if you do not!" Madame Zousa said frankly. "Things did not go as I had planned this evening. No one wants a Gypsy who tells them nothing, or worse, who has a fit and collapses in the middle of the drawing room. Give me the information that I ask, and perhaps I shall be paid well enough to feed myself for a few weeks."

That was a plea that Serena could understand, and there *was* something she would like everyone to know. She told that fact to Madame Zousa, along with her name.

The Gypsy laid the chain across her outstretched hand.

Marcy screamed.

Serena and Madame Zousa both jumped, startled. Serena went invisible, still holding the chain with the medallion, and Madame Zousa rushed back to the bed, trying to shush Marcy. The maid continued to scream.

The door opened and Serena ran for it, intending to pass right by whoever was there, her body solid now so she could hold the chain in her hand.

It was Woding, his hair mussed, his dressing gown barely closed. "Serena!" he said, and stepped toward her as she was trying to pass through the doorway. Too late to stop herself from colliding, she went formless and passed through him.

The medallion dropped to the floor, and her body filled with stars. It was the only thought that would come to her as she drifted, stunned, in the hall just past him. He looked equally stunned, leaning against the doorjamb with a vacant expression on his face.

It was nothing like passing through others had always been. Instead of cold nausea, warmth was what she felt, warmth and a tingling sense of life glittering up and down every fiber of her being. Mixed impressions of Woding himself flitted through her mind: memories of people she did not know, circumstances she had never experienced, sensations she had never felt. For a brief moment she saw herself from his perspective, drifting stunned and pale in the dark of the hall, her hair a weeping willow about her.

Alex was dimly aware of hysterical sobs coming from the room, and distant-sounding voices. "The head! I saw the floating head!" one cried, while the other soothed and hushed in crooning tones. It was as if someone else, not him, were hearing those sounds. His whole body was too busy trying to make sense of what had just happened.

The closest thing to it in his experience was that moment immediately after reaching sexual satisfaction, when the pleasure was still filling one's senses, but the physical efforts have ceased. It was not the climax itself, but the languorous bliss that followed. Coupled with it was a sense of sharing—of having blended souls with a person—in a way that was not humanly possible.

Wild emotions not his own flamed and died in fireworks throughout his awareness. Fear, anger, determination, lust. He sensed a will that was stronger than steel, tempered by soul-searing hardships. He saw visions of green pastures, and the valley below Maiden Castle in a lonelier time. He saw a smallish keep that was cold, stark, and unyielding. There were men who were equally so, as well as a brief glimpse of a worn woman with love and softness in her eyes. Death. Corruption. Flames and blood and the clash of swords.

He heard a woman's voice singing in his head:

> "There were three ravens sat on a tree,
> Down a down, hay down, hay down,
> There were three ravens sat on a tree,
> With a down."

The sensations and images began to fade, and he pushed himself upright against the doorjamb, his head still feeling drunk with the essence of Serena's soul. He saw her a few feet away, floating just above the floor, her hair a wild waterfall around her. She had been, for a moment, part of him, and her thoughts had been his.

He saw her begin to take notice of where she was, and for an instant saw himself as if through her eyes, leaning against the jamb like a man who'd been punched in the gut.

She bent down and picked something silvery up off

the floor, but before he could tell what it was, she had regained her senses and was away like a deer, her pale form disappearing around a corner.

He took a step to follow, then realized the futility of it. If she had needed his help against the shadow, she would have stayed and asked him for it. She could be anywhere in the castle—or out of it—by now. He pulled his dressing gown more securely closed, and turned his attention to the two women in the room.

Chapter Fourteen

It was, Alex thought, like a group of judges convening to discover and decide the fate of an accused criminal. Sophie and Blandamour, the nurse Miss Silverlock, Beth and Rhys, Marcy, Dickie, Underhill, Sommer, and even Otto were sitting spread around the blue drawing room, looking variously curious, frightened, affectedly bored, or self-righteously angry, depending upon their individual character and purpose. It had seemed only right to include the servants, as they'd had their own ghostly experiences, and if left out of the convocation they would most likely have come up with something worse in their own imaginations.

Madame Zousa stood by his side, the center of their attention, dressed in a gown equally as old and garish as her last one had been. It was, he noted, suspiciously clean and well mended for a garment belonging to a supposedly nomadic woman living in a caravan in the forest. Madame Zousa, he suspected, was most likely known at home as Mrs. Penryhn, or some similarly Cornish appellation. She probably had a pilchard fisherman for a husband.

He couldn't blame the woman for trying to earn some extra money, though, however much he disapproved of her fraudulent methods, and at least in this case he knew that she had been in contact with Serena last night, just as she had been hired to be.

"Madame Zousa has informed me that the name of the ghost of Maiden Castle is Serena Clerenbold," Alex said to the assembled group, eliciting a collective intake of breath, followed by much whispering.

"We knew it was Serena already," Rhys said. "That information is not new, and certainly not worth Sophie's wasting her money."

"You *did* contact her, Madame Zousa!" Sophie said over Rhys. "I knew you would! Tell us, what did she look like? What did she say?"

"Clerenbold, did you say?" Blandamour asked.

Madame Zousa chose to answer the vicar first. "That is what she told me. Serena Clerenbold."

"Interesting," Blandamour said.

"What is?" Sophie asked her fiancé.

"The name. It is not a common one, but I think I may have come across it once or twice before, in records of the area. It caught my eye because it seemed such an appropriate name for an age that valued chivalry. It means 'bright and bold.' There are some parish records in this county that go all the way back to the eleventh century. I studied them once while tracing my family's history."

That caught Alex's interest. "Do you think you could find the reference to the Clerenbold family again?"

191

"I might be able to, given time."

"I should very much appreciate it," Alex told him. Here would be written confirmation of her life, and perhaps further clues to what had brought Serena to the state she was in now. The images she had left by passing through him had played and replayed in his mind the remainder of the night. He wanted to know what the reality was behind them. He wanted the whole story, both from her words and from history.

"Even if there is a Serena Clerenbold somewhere in the records, it does not prove anything," Rhys said, apparently having decided to take on the role of devil's advocate.

"Miss Woding asked of Serena's appearance," Madame Zousa said, leaving the sentence dangling and effectively silencing Rhys. Even he was not immune to curiosity on that score. "Marcy will be able to confirm what I am about to say, for she, too, saw Serena in my room last night."

Dickie's eyes went wide, his mouth dropping open as he turned accusing eyes on the girl. "You didn't tell me!"

" 'Tis true; she came in the middle of the night," Marcy said.

"Most likely a dream," Rhys muttered, only to get a not-so-subtle nudge from his wife.

"Hers is a unique face," the Gypsy said. "Long, with high cheekbones and black eyes that tilt up at the corners. There is a mark of some sort across her face," she said, and drew the line of the scar with her fingertip across her own skin.

Alex was glad that Serena was not present. He had intuitively sensed that her scar was part of what made her so unwilling to be seen. She would not have appreciated having its presence announced to this group. He himself had not known that Madame Zousa had seen Serena quite so clearly.

"Her hair is long and wild, of a pale blond. Her skin is white as milk, transparent in the dark. I could see the shadows of the wardrobe through her."

"And she had no body, just hands!" Marcy added. "Her head floated, glowing like a lantern held high in the dark." The maid sounded as though she was enjoying herself. "She about scared the life out of me, but I scared her, too, for she vanished like *that,*" she said, snapping her fingers. "The moment I opened my mouth to scream. She must have hit Mr. Woding on her way out, though. Didn't she, Mr. Woding, sir?"

All heads rotated back to him. "I am not certain what happened," he said, in a slight stretching of the truth. "Madame Zousa, you said that there was a message that Serena gave you to tell us?"

No matter his blandishments last night, Madame Zousa had refused to divulge this one part of her conversation with Serena until she was before the assembled group this morning. The woman had a sense for the dramatic, and fully intended to take advantage of her treasured information.

"She said that she wanted it known by one and all that on her wedding night her husband did not bed her. She insists that she died a maid, as chaste as the day she was born."

"Then why would she kill her husband?" Sophie asked.

"Maybe she had been longing for her husband to exercise his marital rights, and got upset when he didn't," Rhys said, causing Beth to give him a reproving frown.

"Why would that be what she wished us all to know?" Beth asked.

Madame Zousa shrugged. "She did not say."

"There must be a reason," Beth said.

"You're a woman," Rhys said. "Why would you do such a thing, if you were her?"

"To regain my honor if it had been unfairly besmirched," Beth said.

"For respect," Sophie said. "No one cares a whit for a fallen woman."

"To catch a man!" Marcy said loudly, then slapped her hand over her mouth, her face going red.

"Come, what man is there for her to catch?" Rhys said. "She's dead."

Beth and Sophie looked at each other, brows raised, then turned their eyes to Alex. Rhys saw the look and followed it to its target, and everyone else's eyes slowly followed suit.

"Don't be ridiculous," Alex scoffed.

A wicked light entered Rhys's eyes. "Perhaps it *would* make a sort of sense. She went after you the first time you were here, after all. Maybe it was love at first sight. It could be she has become obsessed with you." He leered. "You are, after all, a fine figure of a man. What woman could resist?"

There was muffled laughter from the group.

"What rot," Alex said, growing uncomfortable under the teasing. It would have helped if he hadn't had so many dreams where Serena lay beneath him, her legs wrapped around his hips.

"Have you not seen her even once?" Beth asked.

"I have had no problems with her," he said.

Rhys grinned. "That is not what she asked, cousin mine."

"Oh, Alex, you mean you *have* seen her?" Sophie complained. "I cannot believe you would be so cruel as not to tell me!"

"Mr. Woding," Dickie asked from behind the others. "Is it true you have seen her?"

"She was in your bedroom, wasn't she?" Underhill asked, then said to the group, "I heard her in there, pounding on the walls."

They were all staring at him, waiting for his response. He found, rather to his surprise, that he did not want to tell them what he knew of Serena. It felt like a violation of the fragile bond they had formed to repeat in front of a group the things she had told him.

"I have seen her, yes." He could admit that much without harm.

"Where?" several voices asked.

"On the stairs. In the hall. Various places. Mostly she seems to be watching whatever is going on, that is all. I do not believe she means to harm anyone, despite her earlier activities. She may simply have regarded us as uninvited guests."

"And now?" Rhys asked. Alex noticed he had gone a shade paler than when he had been so gleefully poking fun. "What was she doing up in Madame Zousa's room, scaring the daylights out of the maid? That does not sound particularly friendly to me."

"She came to give me the message," Madame Zousa said. "I asked that she show her face, and she did. It was only unfortunate chance that Marcy should wake."

Alex knew the real story from the Gypsy, and was glad that she had chosen to keep it quiet, whatever her motives. He doubted she wanted it known that she had called up uncontrollable, molesting phantoms that had even a ghost frightened. It would not be good for a fortune-telling business that catered to women.

"Was she in this room with us last night?" Sophie asked Alex.

He made a noncommittal sound and directed the conversation elsewhere, relieved when the discussion began to devolve into a rehashing of last night's events. Madame Zousa reshaped events to her own benefit, and Alex was inclined to let her. She might not be precisely what she said she was, but he would not forget what she had endured, according to Serena, and that she had given Serena the medallion to help soothe her fears.

He quietly excused himself from the gathering, his own curiosity satisfied as to what message Serena had given Madame Zousa.

Rhys followed him out of the drawing room, joining him on his way out the door. "Do you need some fresh air after all that nonsense?" Rhys asked, sounding as though he wanted very much to believe it had indeed all been untrue. "That supposed Gypsy is quite the talespinner."

"She does have a talent for drama," Alex agreed.

Rhys walked quietly beside him across the courtyard and to the path atop the lower wall, then spoke again. "You meant what you said in there, that you have seen her several times?"

"Whether for good or ill, I did." He would not prevaricate with his cousin.

"Then you should leave this place, Alex. Much as I like the thought of Serena spying on you, I have a bad feeling about it."

"She is not going to harm me. She did not even push me from that wall when we were children."

"You do not know that." When Alex did not answer, Rhys looked at him. "Or do you?"

Alex shrugged.

Rhys laid his hand on his cousin's shoulder, stopping him. "How do you know that she did not push you?"

"She told me." He would not lie to his cousin, but neither did he wish to explain. Serena's confession was too personal for that.

Rhys's hand dropped, his face going sickly. Alex thought that Rhys, for all his childish ghost-story glee, was not adjusting well to this situation. "My God, Alex," he croaked out, "you've been talking to her."

Alex resumed walking, heading for the corner bastion. He felt curiously distanced from Rhy's concern. It was more of an inconvenience than a warning that he should be cautious. He knew Rhys had no way of understanding his unique relationship with Serena. No one could understand.

"Alex, this isn't right; it's unnatural," Rhys said.

They reached the bastion, and Alex went to lean against the parapet, gazing out over the distance. The valley below was hidden beneath a low-lying layer of fog, making the castle seem to float upon a dreamworld. Like a memory of sex, thinking about the encounter with Serena in the doorway brought back an echo of the sensations. It was too overwhelming an experience to willingly do again, yet its effects entrapped his mind with a compelling fascination.

"Are you listening to me?" Rhys asked.

"Of course."

"You're not behaving normally. This . . . this *thing,* Serena, she is doing something to you. Leave this place. Go back to Bath. You are spending too much time alone up here."

"I'll think about it," Alex said. He could feel Rhys frowning at him.

"I have to go back to the farm today, but Beth would like to stay on as long as Sophie is here. Would that be all right with you?"

"You and your wife are always welcome," Alex said, turning his attention to his cousin and smiling. "You know that."

Rhys sighed, abandoning his earlier arguments. "I almost think it is worse leaving you with the two of them than leaving you alone with your ghost."

"Serena doesn't talk half so much," Alex agreed.

Rhys gave a short laugh, without much humor. "I might feel better about this all if I had seen her myself. It's beginning to seem as if I am the only one who has not had some encounter."

"But you have," Alex said. "The night I fell, she woke you up. She was afraid I'd lie there the rest of the morning and bleed to death."

"*She* woke me?" He grunted in astonishment. "I never knew."

"She's not evil, Rhys."

"Just . . . be careful. That's all I ask."

"I can take care of myself."

"I know, Alex. God, I'm sorry. I sound like an old woman. I should stay out of your affairs."

They walked the perimeter of the castle together; then Rhys went inside to gather his things. Alex continued on to the garden, the latch of the iron gate making its familiar clank as he opened it.

No one was working in the flower beds today, and the walled space was quiet in the noontime sun. The craggy cherry tree stood on solitary watch over the lesser plants and blooms. He followed the path toward it, and stopped underneath its sparse branches. Another limb was showing signs of disease, the leaves withering away.

He tilted his head back, looking for further signs that the tree was moribund. A twinkling of silver caught his eye. He squinted at it. Hanging from the topmost branch, the small silver medallion twisted at the end of its chain.

It dawned on him then that there had to be some connection between Serena and the cherry tree. The hints had been there since he first saw the tree as a child and felt that it watched him. Could it be that she was buried nearby? The thought that even at this moment he might be standing over her remains unsettled him. It was an unwelcome reminder that she was no longer of this life, however strong her reality felt in the night.

Rhys's concern might have a note of truth in it. For someone who called himself a man of science, he was proving himself quick to abandon thought in favor of emotion. He was beginning to think of Serena as a real woman, and surely that was as illogical as a man could get.

Perhaps it would be a good thing to have Sophie and Beth here for a few days. They would remind him of what was real and what was not.

The only problem was, comparing the two in his mind, it was the unreal that he preferred for company.

Chapter Fifteen

"No, that cannot be," Serena said, looking in dismay at the many-armed brass contraption in Woding's tower study. "God did not create the universe in such a manner. The earth is at the center. The stars and the sun revolve around it. Everyone knows that!"

Woding raised an eyebrow at her. "Do you want me to explain day and night again?"

"No. No!" She glared at the brass orbs, the one depicting the earth half-illuminated by the small lamp within the ball Woding said was the sun. "It makes more sense for the sun to rise and set around the earth," she argued. "Who is there on the other planets that they should be treated the same? No one! The heavens revolve around us. 'Tis how they have such a great influence upon events."

"Have you ever ridden a horse, Serena?" Woding asked.

"Yes, certainly."

"When you rode the horse, did you move across a stationary field, or did the field move past you while you stood still?"

" 'Tis a foolish question. How could the field move around me?"

He said nothing, apparently waiting for her to work it out for herself. She looked back at the orbs. It was most unsettling, almost unbelievable, and yet . . . And yet, for a moment, she imagined she was on a horse, and for a moment held the illusion that she was the one stationary while the field moved past her.

It was ridiculous. And it was what he implied she had been thinking of the earth and heavens. She looked at the contraption that he called an orrery again, and visions of revolving circles within circles filled her head.

"If the earth spins," she said, placing her finger on the orb and spinning it, "and if it and the other planets in turn circle the sun," she continued, moving each in its orbit, "then does all of it together in turn circle something larger?"

He raised his eyebrows at her and gave an approving nod. "That is an excellent question, Serena. It is thought that the solar system does indeed move through space in an orbit, along with the stars."

"If they do, then perhaps at the center of that circle is where God resides," she said. "Mayhap 'tis indeed presumptuous of us to believe that the heavens would circle those who had come from dust."

"There may be God or some other force, or nothing at all."

"Or that circle may be inside circles larger still," she said, ignoring him, her mind stretching into the concept of infinity for the first time. She looked at him. "I suddenly feel quite small."

"Is that comforting or frightening?"

"I do not know." She smiled with him, recognizing her stock answer, and for that moment felt not so alone in the vastness of the universe. "Does it frighten you?"

"It reminds me that my troubles are not so large as I might think. When I look out to the stars, it is as if I leave this planet and the petty details of life. I forget for a time who I am."

She tilted her head, studying him. "Do you not like your life?"

He gave a quick smile, a flash of white gone as fast as it had come, like the tail of a deer bounding through the woods. "I have everything I need," he said.

"You have no wife. Surely a man needs one of those. Why have you not married again?"

"That's a rather personal question."

She raised her eyebrows and gave him the same waiting look he had given her.

He sighed. "It never felt like the right time, or like I had met the right woman. I got caught up in building the family's business, and forgot about building a family, telling myself that there would be plenty of time later for that."

"Is it later now?"

"Not yet."

"Then when will later be?"

His smile this time was tinged with emptiness. "I expect I shall know the time when it comes."

"I do not think so, Woding. I think you are hiding from your heart up here in your tower, staring at your heavens. Your heart cannot see the time to have a wife and children if it is out beyond the moon, chasing stars."

"Did you follow your own heart when you married le Gayne?" he asked.

She walked over to the window, looking out over the night-cast valley. Although she could not see it, she knew exactly where the ruins of Clerenbold Keep stood, and imagined the last of the foundation stones standing strong against the grasses and vines.

"No. I followed my head, treating my heart as if it knew nothing of what was best for me. You can see what a success that was." She turned her back to the window and gazed across the room at him. His hair was tousled, bits of it standing up. He had run his hands through it several times while explaining the workings of the heavens to her. "You waste the treasure you have, Woding."

"Which treasure is that?"

"Your life. You live, yet you do not. There are only traces left in you of what I saw when you were a boy. Sometimes, when I watch you, I think I am the one more alive. I do not understand why you shut yourself up in this castle and try to surround yourself with men. I do not understand why you choose to live with cold stars instead of a warm wife and your family."

"Tell me about le Gayne. Tell me why you married him," he countered. "Do not expect me to bare myself to you and your criticism while you remain silent, holding your secrets close."

"I was not criticizing. I married le Gayne because he was rich and I was afraid Thomas and I would starve. I wanted children, and le Gayne could give me those, no matter if I loved him or no. Thomas and he struck a deal, Thomas signing over several acres of land to le Gayne as my dowry. In return, le Gayne outfitted Thomas for fighting under the Black Prince."

"That sounds a story too common to end in murder."

"Christ's curse, you did not know le Gayne!" she said, the old hatred coming up in a flood. "He wanted only the land. Neither Thomas nor I could read, and did not know that the deed le Gayne wrote up for the land gave him not only the acres Thomas had promised, but all of the Clerenbold lands. 'Twas why he was so happy to send Thomas to war: chances were that he would die by another's hand before discovering the trickery."

"But why kill you? There was nothing you could have done against him, once the deed was signed and you were married. You might never have even known, if Thomas had died in battle. The land would have gone to you anyway."

"He did not want me for his wife."

"There must be more to it than that. Certainly more to explain why the man could not wait past his wedding night to kill you, if that was his plan."

"He could not bear me," she said slowly, the words a mix of pain and anger. Even now it was humiliating to recall the insults he had cast at her. "He told me he could not stand the sight of me. He said I was a great lummox of a woman, an ox, fit only for pulling a plow. He said my face could frighten children, and give them nightmares."

"The man had no taste. You have a beautiful face."

"What?" she said, startled out of her remembrance. "What do you know of my face? You said you could not see it clearly."

A twitch of guilt played across his face, telling her the truth before he himself could. "You have become more and more clear as we have talked. In the dark, especially, you look almost like a living person to me, and are equally as clear."

"What do you mean, in the dark?"

He shrugged, a child trying to minimize his crime. "In daylight you are transparent, but in the dark you are opaque, and illuminated as if from within. I can see you even when I can see nothing else."

"Ohhhh," she moaned. How could this be? God's heart, what manner of fool had she been making of herself while he could see her expressions so well? All this time she had thought she'd been somewhat protected, yet she had been completely exposed to his scrutiny.

"I've guessed that it is the scar you did not want me to see."

"Devil take you, Woding!"

"Serena," he said, coming toward her, his hands out and open, as if asking her to put hers in his. "You are beautiful. Le Gayne was wrong in what he said."

She backed away from him, her eyes wide, her head shaking from side to side in denial. He cornered her against the wall, and although she could have sunk back through it, she did not, watching him come closer and closer. He stopped when he was only a foot from her.

A strange, unknown sensation ran through her, a quivering tingle that could have been fear or dread, but was neither. It made her heart thump, and her breath come heavy in her chest.

He reached out his hand toward her face, and she closed her eyes, allowing herself to become solid enough to touch. His fingertips lightly grazed her skin, at the start of her scar, and then traced it across her face, gliding tenderly over her cheek.

"It is as unique and beautiful as you are," he said. "It sets you apart."

She opened her eyes, feeling his fingertips still on the

edge of her cheek. "I have always been apart," she said. "Even before this marked me."

His eyes were dark, looking at his own hand upon her face, and he seemed not to hear her. "Your skin is soft," he said, and moved the back of his fingers along the edge of her jaw. "And warm."

The strange sensation tightened in her gut, sending a flutter to her loins, and making her half close her eyes in this unknown pleasure. "What are you doing to me?" she asked softly. His hand moved down her neck, lightly tracing the curve to her shoulder. "Woding? What is happening?"

"I have seen nothing like you in all my life," he said, and bent his head down and laid his lips against the curve of her neck.

Her knees went weak, and she lost her ability to think. Time stopped, and all awareness left her except of those lips against her skin, pressing softly, damply, moving up toward her ear.

A knock at the door startled them both apart, and Serena went insubstantial, falling into the wall. She emerged confused and befuddled in the night air outside the tower, and drifted around to the window, watching from outside as Underhill brought in a tray with coffee and a late supper for Woding.

Woding himself looked as disoriented as she herself, distractedly ordering Underhill where to set the tray. Otto came in the room, sniffing around as if aware of her recent presence, and after going to Woding for an absentminded scratch on the head, went to go settle his large frame in the corner as Underhill left.

Half of her wanted to rejoin Woding, and feel him again touch her, kiss her, stroke her. It was like the lure to drink too much wine and become intoxicated. The other half of her sought separation, to make sense of what had just gone between them. She could not believe it had happened, and could not believe that he had meant anything he said.

He looked toward the window and saw her. Even through the glass, she heard him say her name, calling softly to her, "Serena."

It could have been the devil calling, the temptation to go back was so strong. A fear of the unknown possessed her, and although she knew it was the cowardly choice, she left him there.

Alex went to the window, searching for one last sight of Serena. She had pulled him to her with a magnetic force, his body acting of its own will to approach her, to touch her, to kiss her. It was as if some silent part of him had grown frustrated with the erotic dreams and sought to make them real. He desired her.

Whether that was for good or ill, he could not say. He went and sat behind his desk, staring blankly at the tray of food and coffee, the objects making no sense to his mind. All he could think of was the feel of her skin beneath his lips, and the sweet scent of hay that came from her.

Lust was something he had not felt for a long time. Too long. That a dead woman with violent tendencies should arouse it in him was almost beyond comprehension. Perhaps Serena had hit on a truth when she said that she was more alive than he was, except when looking at the stars. It was as if his body sought her out to return it to life.

He poured himself a cup of coffee, and let it steam in the cup in front of him, untouched.

Untouched.

That was what Serena claimed to be. Did the rules of honor apply here as with a living woman? Common decency demanded that he not toy with her emotions by indulging his desires. For all her strength, he sensed she was fragile when it came to relating to men. She said she had been murdered by a man—one who had claimed she was undesirable. She would be slow to trust one again.

It would be unfair to continue any form of dalliance with her, for surely, at some point, it would have to end. What future was there to be had with a ghost? He couldn't very well introduce her to friends, or have her acting as hostess at dinner parties. She couldn't go anywhere with him. He couldn't ever marry her. He seriously doubted they could have children.

He had a sudden image of ghost babies winking in and out of sight, and shuddered.

Beyond the practicalities, wasn't there something simply wicked and perverted about sleeping with a ghost? For all that he usually spared few thoughts for his immortal soul, a small part of him wondered if it wouldn't somehow be damaging to it to have sex with a dead woman.

Obviously it could never work out with Serena. He would eventually move on to someone living, and she would be left here, alone again with the stones of the castle.

He drank the coffee, his thoughts miles from his charts and stars.

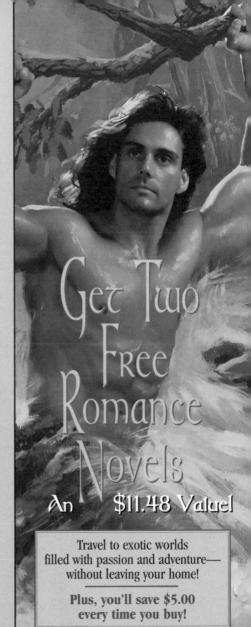

Thrill to the most sensual, adventure-filled Romances on the market today...

FROM ✦ LOVE SPELL BOOKS

As a home subscriber to the Love Spell Romance Book Club, you'll enjoy the best in today's BRAND-NEW Time Travel, Futuristic, Legendary Lovers, Perfect Heroes and other genre romance fiction. For five years, Love Spell has brought you the award-winning, high-quality authors you know and love to read. Each Love Spell romance will sweep you away to a world of high adventure...and intimate romance. Discover for yourself all the passion and excitement millions of readers thrill to each and every month.

Save $5.00 Each Time You Buy!

Every other month, the Love Spell Romance Book Club brings you four brand-new titles from Love Spell Books. EACH PACKAGE WILL SAVE YOU AT LEAST $5.00 FROM THE BOOKSTORE PRICE! And you'll never miss a new title with our convenient home delivery service.

Here's how we do it: Each package will carry a FREE 10-DAY EXAMINATION privilege. At the end of that time, if you decide to keep your books, simply pay the low invoice price of $17.96, no shipping or handling charges added. HOME DELIVERY IS ALWAYS FREE. With today's top romance novels selling for $5.99 and higher, our price SAVES YOU AT LEAST $5.00 with each shipment.

AND YOUR FIRST TWO-BOOK SHIPMENT IS TOTALLY FREE!

IT'S A BARGAIN YOU CAN'T BEAT! A SUPER $11.48 Value!

Love Spell ✦ A Division of Dorchester Publishing Co., Inc.

GET YOUR 2 FREE BOOKS NOW—AN $11.48 VALUE!

*Mail the Free Book
Certificate Today!*

TWO FREE BOOKS

Free Books Certificate

YES! I want to subscribe to the Love Spell Romance Book Club. Please send me my 2 FREE BOOKS. Then every other month I'll receive the four newest Love Spell selections to Preview FREE for 10 days. If I decide to keep them, I will pay the Special Member's Only discounted price of just $4.49 each, a total of $17.96. This is a SAVINGS of at least $5.00 off the bookstore price. There are no shipping, handling, or other charges. There is no minimum number of books I must buy and I may cancel the program at any time. In any case, the 2 FREE BOOKS are mine to keep—A BIG $11.48 Value!

Offer valid only in the U.S.A.

*Name*_____

*Address*_____

*City*_____

*State*_____ *Zip*_____

*Telephone*_____

*Signature*_____

If under 18, Parent or Guardian must sign. Terms, prices and conditions subject to change. Subscription subject to acceptance. Leisure Books reserves the right to reject any order or cancel any subscription.

A $11.48 VALUE

Get Two Books Totally
FREE —
An $11.48 Value!

▼ Tear Here and Mail Your FREE Book Card Today! ▼

PLEASE RUSH
MY TWO FREE
BOOKS TO ME
RIGHT AWAY!

Love Spell Romance Book Club
P.O. Box 6613
Edison, NJ 08818-6613

AFFIX
STAMP
HERE

Chapter Sixteen

"Dickie, stop it," Marcy complained, raising her shoulder to shrug him off her neck. Serena watched with interest, unseen a few feet away.

"What's wrong with you?" Dickie complained. "You never let me touch you anymore."

"It's not fitting," Marcy said, a touch petulantly.

"It never bothered you before."

"I just don't want anyone to see you doing that. I could lose my place."

"Then meet me tonight, out in the garden," Dickie said. "No one will see you there."

"Mrs. Hutchins might find me gone. No, I shan't risk it," Marcy said primly. "Now go back to work and stop following me around."

Dickie sulked off, casting backward looks to Marcy, but the maid went about her business with unnatural absorption, cleaning out the fireplace as if it were a challenging task.

Serena stayed near, watching the girl. She had no personal experience to compare to Woding's unexpected advance a week ago, and thought that watching Marcy and Dickie might teach her something of what was normal. All she had seen all week, though, was Dickie panting after the maid, and Marcy coming up with excuse after excuse for why Dickie should leave her alone.

At first Serena had thought the girl was being coy, but now she suspected that she truly did not want Dickie hanging around her like a dog after a bitch in heat. Whenever Dickie touched her, there was annoyance and a hint of repugnance on the girl's face.

Serena thought the girl would be kinder to tell the boy flat-out that his attentions were not wanted.

As supper approached she followed the maid toward the kitchen. Beezely appeared, and she picked him up, scratching him around the ears. Nancy the stablelass joined Marcy, and Serena eavesdropped with interest on their conversation. The two were of an age, and although disparate in temperament and interests, they still managed to find companionship with each other, becoming fast friends in the short time that Nancy had been at the castle.

"Dickie's becoming quite the pest," Marcy told her friend.

"I had thought you liked him well enough."

"I thought I did, but that was when I hadn't seen anything of the world."

Nancy snorted, rather like a horse. "There is not so much here that could have impressed you, unless you speak of the master."

"No . . . he's fine-enough looking," Marcy said

vaguely, "but I think he is too high above me to be what she meant."

"What who meant?"

Marcy's eyes lost their vagueness, becoming sharply mischievous with untold secrets. "Promise not to tell?"

"On my word," Nancy said solemnly.

" 'Twas Madame Zousa, that night I spent with her," Marcy whispered eagerly. "She said that I could do better than Dickie, that I should aim higher."

"Did she mean someone here?" Nancy asked, and Serena thought she detected a trace of apprehension in the girl's voice.

"I don't know," Marcy admitted. "But I saw the truth of her words the moment she said them. Look at Dickie. He's nothing but a scullery maid. Madame Zousa was right: I can do much better than him, I am sure of it. I only wish she could have told me *who*."

"You've only a few choices here," Nancy said. "The master, Mr. Sommer, and Mr. Underhill. I'm sure you don't want to count the gardener and his grandson."

"Sommer is too old, Mr. Woding too rich. No, it must be Mr. Underhill. Do you think he's handsome?"

Nancy's cheeks turned pink. "I don't know. He's fair enough of face, I suppose. A bit thin, though."

"Yes, rather gangly about the arms and legs, I agree. But still, he has a good position, and is not so terribly old."

"You are not going to pursue him, are you?"

Marcy tossed her brown curls. "I may take a look at him and see if he is worth it."

"Oh."

"I don't know that I'll want to keep working," Marcy said as the two went into the kitchen where supper was waiting. She lowered her voice so as not to be heard by

211

the others. "And I would want him to be head of a much larger household than this one."

"Ah," Nancy said, to no apparent end. To Serena's eyes, the stablelass did not look particularly happy with her friend's declarations of intent.

The supper table was a full one, with everyone except the Flurys present. They went home at dusk every evening. Sommer was there, and Underhill. Dickie, Mrs. Hutchins, Nancy, and Marcy made up the remainder.

Serena sat on a cupboard to the side, a fine seat from which to watch the interactions. Beezely jumped down from her arms and up onto the table, walking among the dishes and stopping to investigate those that looked tempting, although Serena was certain the cat could no more smell the food than she could.

The servants were putting on a fine dramatic performance this evening. Sommer, it appeared, had eyes only for Nancy, a most unexpected development. He seemed both drawn to and angered by her presence. Marcy made a show of flirting with Underhill, causing resentment to smolder in Dickie's eyes. Mrs. Hutchins watched the display with disapproval. Nancy watched her plate for the most part, but every now and then her eyes, too, would flick to Underhill, and Serena felt certain it was longing she saw there.

Underhill seemed interested only in discussing the larder with Mrs. Hutchins.

Serena left them as they were finishing their puddings, and went out to her garden. Dark was coming sooner each night, the flowers in the garden becoming scarcer and scarcer. In another month the leaves would be turning and falling to the ground. She always worried about the cherry tree in the winter, feeling the sap hiding in the trunk and branches of the tree, waiting out the cold.

It was always a relief when the weather warmed again, and the tree began to form its first budding flowers.

The sky was slightly lighter than it would be a few hours hence, and a smudge of orange and green remained above the black line of the horizon. She went to the cherry tree and climbed up it, sitting among its branches near the medallion that twisted in the gentle breeze, its metal dully reflecting what little light remained.

She had spent most of her evenings this past week here, it being the only place she felt safe at night from the shadow form of le Gayne, with the exception of Woding's presence. Woding's company held other dangers, though, that she was too cautious to venture into without full thought.

So she had spent hours upon hours gazing at the sky, knowing Woding was likely doing the same from his tower, and replayed in her mind again and again the touch of his hand on her face. She repeated and tore apart his words, looking for the flaw, looking for the clue that would tell her he had lied when saying he thought that she was beautiful.

When she was certain he was asleep, she would go look in on him, staying just long enough to renew his features in her mind. His eyelids would flutter when she was near, as they always did, making her wonder if he dreamed of her. And what he dreamed, if so.

Any thought of chasing him from the castle was long gone. All she could consider now was whether she should go to him again. It seemed that to do so would be a blatant invitation to his touch. It was unthinkably forward, and a priest would have said immoral. And yet, it was the most magical thing she had ever experienced, better even than her first ever taste of the rare and precious sugar her brother had once brought home.

If she were honest with herself, she would admit that she wanted him to touch her again. Not only that, but she wanted him to kiss her. She wanted him to do to her what a gentle man would do with his wife on their first night of marriage.

It was immoral, yes, but what use were morals to a woman who was all but dead? She had her doubts there was a hell waiting to burn her for eternity, for surely she would have gone straight there upon the death of her body, if there had been one. Who was watching her, who would punish her for her sins? No one.

And yet she could not believe that Woding would want to teach her anything of the ways between a man and a woman, no matter his touch upon her face and his soft words. He would want someone living, who would not fade away at the end, leaving him alone in his bed. He would want someone with whom to build a life, someone to bear his children, never mind his obsession with stars and things not of this earth.

It was fruitless thought. How could she decide what to do when she did not even know if he would be willing? It would be a far greater humiliation to have Woding reject her, than le Gayne. She had expected le Gayne's hatred, and protected herself as well as she could from it. Le Gayne she had not cared for.

Woding, in some way she could not recognize, she did care something for. His opinion of her mattered. A galling thought, to be sure.

What she wouldn't give to have Thomas here to talk with! He might not have been wise or keen-witted, but he had been a man, and his perspective on this matter would have been welcome.

She cast her mind back to the crude conversations the men at Clerenbold Keep had carried on around her, having grown used to her presence. Even her father had ceased shielding her from their words. Those men had spoken of women they would slake their lusts with and then discard. They spoke of women who wanted a man between their thighs, and how those women could not get enough of sex. The men said that if a woman offered herself free of charge or ties, then it would only be natural—nay, only courteous!—to take her, and give her the pleasure of their manhood in return.

Perhaps it was true that all a woman had to do was offer, and a man would willingly join with her, but she did not want to be taken for one of those sorry wenches who would hike her skirts with no more than a wall at her back, not even caring if there were passersby.

It was a dilemma. She wanted to behave like a loose woman, but she didn't want to be one.

Alex looked over the parapet of his tower, and saw the faint glow in the branches of the garden cherry tree that told him Serena was spending yet another night alone there, next to her dangling medallion.

He had scared her, hurt her, upset her somehow with his words and his touch a week ago, and she had avoided him since. He had passed a restless week, getting little accomplished, his thoughts going to her, and to the dreams that haunted his sleep.

They had been short, fragmented dreams of the sort easily forgotten if one did not hold tight to them upon waking. Always she was in them, often far off, a tall figure across a field or a formal garden, standing still as a deer, waiting for a sign that she should flee. And always, when in his dream he moved to approach her, she would vanish into the woods or behind a yew hedge, slipping from sight, not to appear again.

215

He didn't like having her avoid him like this! It was senseless. He was a grown man and should be able to keep his hands to himself. He simply needed to reassure her on that count. For all he knew, le Gayne had tried—albeit unsuccessfully—to rape her on their wedding night. The very touch of a man's hand might be painfully repugnant to her.

He left the tower and traced his way through the dark halls of the castle, and then out into the courtyard and garden. He did not bring a candle or lamp with him, as his eyes were fully adjusted to the dark. The garden gate was open, letting him slip silently inside. Serena had not moved from her spot, glowing like the moon behind the branches and leaves of the cherry tree.

He came to the trunk of the tree and looked up, shifting around until he could see part of her face. She seemed to be staring, entranced, at the medallion, although he thought it likely her thoughts were a thousand miles away.

"Serena!" he whispered loudly.

She jerked, startled, and grabbed tight to a branch to keep from falling. "Woding?" she whispered questioningly back, peering through the leaves.

"Yes. May I speak with you?"

"What about?" she said.

"Serena, please. Come down from there. I cannot speak to you when you are hanging from the branches like a monkey."

"You have seen a monkey?" she asked, and he smiled at the note of interest in her voice. Here he was worried about unspoken currents between them, and it took only the mention of a monkey to bridge their distance.

"Yes, several times, although never in the wild."

"I should like to see a monkey," she said. "And a lion.

216

I have never seen a lion, nor even a bear."

"I have seen all manner of strange creatures in menageries," he said. "Come down, and I will tell you about them."

"Did you see a unicorn?"

"Come down and I will tell you."

She moved silently through the branches, climbing down them as if she were solid and at risk of falling. He wondered at that—why she so often maintained the conceit of being human. Was she solid now, or only pretending?

"Where did you see the unicorn?" she asked, dropping down lightly to her feet, bending at the knees as if from an impact, and then straightening.

"I never did see one," he admitted. "I should have thought that if there were any, you yourself would have been more likely to see one, living when you did."

"Oh."

He led the way out from under the tree, into the star-bright garden. "I have, however, seen a tiger. Do you know about tigers?"

"No," she said, following him out of the shadows. "What manner of creature is it?"

"An enormous cat, striped in black and orange, with a white belly. It lives in the jungles of the east, and in hot weather is said to cool itself in pools of water."

"A cat in water!"

"Indeed. In Africa there are birds that are as tall as you and I, and which cannot fly. They are called ostriches, and they lay eggs as big as your head."

"Where is Africa?"

"South of the Mediterranean Sea. And the Americas! You know nothing of those lands! They are beyond the ocean to the west, an endless expanse of land only par-

217

tially settled by the English, French, and Spanish. Wild tribes of half-naked savages still roam there, mounted bareback on their ponies and hunting buffalo with bow and arrow."

"The world seems to have grown very large since last I heard of it," she said in some confusion.

"Larger still than I've told you," he said.

"Tell me no more," she said. "It aches to hear of such places, and to know that I will never see any of them, nor the creatures who live there."

"Ah, Serena, do not look at it that way. I will likely see none of those places, either."

"But you know it is possible. If you wished, you could leave this mountain tomorrow and board a ship for any of those lands. It is different when even the possibility is not there. It hurts."

"The hurt is in your mind, Serena. It need not be. Come, look up at the stars," he said, putting out his hand for her to take. After a moment's hesitation she did so, her fingers warm and firm against his palm. He pulled her to his side, close but not touching. "Look, up there, at Cassiopeia," he said, pointing. "Are not the stars beautiful?"

"Yes," she agreed.

He ran his eyes over her pale profile, lovelier even than the stars. Her irises were as black as in his dreams, and he imagined for a moment that the heavens above were reflected therein, shimmers of far-off worlds dancing in her eyes.

"I have no hope of ever visiting those stars, and no hope of going even so far as the moon. The lowly clouds themselves are beyond my limit, except when they sink below the castle. That does not stop me from wanting to learn of them, or finding wonder in their presence, though. My world is larger simply by knowing they are there. There is not time enough in a man's life to explore all the universe, but there is space enough in his mind to hold it."

"My mind holds my own experiences, my own past and present, no larger world than that," she said. "How can America or Africa become part of it, when I have never seen the ostriches or the savages?"

"They already have become a part of your world. You have imagined how the bird looks; you have seen for an instant the wild men hunting. It's part of your universe now. You do not need to be trapped by this mountain, Serena, no matter that you cannot leave."

"But who will tell me of the world beyond it?"

For a moment he saw himself as her teacher, opening the modern world to her medieval eyes, and sharing the vastness of man's learning. It was a heady thought, and quickly became an overwhelming one. There was so much to share, so much she did not know. She had a quick mind and a fierce determination, and deserved better than having him in his vanity think he could teach her all she could know.

"Books."

She took her hand from him. "I cannot read. You know that."

"Children can learn how to read and write. So can you. You have intelligence that should not be squandered in illiteracy."

"But who will teach me?" she asked softly.

There was only one answer to give. "I will."

She turned her eyes to him, and for a brief instant he thought he saw the blackness shift, turning a lighter color, a gray-blue, and then they were dark again. "Thank you," she said on a whisper, and leaned forward and pressed her lips softly against his cheek.

He was too startled to move, the warm pressure sending shafts of tingling warmth through his body and wrapping his heart in a tender embrace. When she pulled away, it took him several seconds to recall where he was and of what they had been speaking.

"You may not be thanking me after your first lesson," he said, trying for a wry tone, trying as well to shake off the feeling of closeness between them as they stood alone in the nighttime garden. "I may be an impatient taskmaster."

The smile she gave him was plainly disbelieving, giving him pause to wonder what manner of impressions she had formed of him.

"When do we start?"

He cast his eyes up at the clear night sky. He should take advantage of the weather. With the advent of autumn, he could expect fewer and fewer nights such as this one. "Late tomorrow afternoon, a few hours before dusk."

She gave a shiver.

"Are you cold?" he asked. He had never considered that she might be capable of such a thing.

"No. I am happy," she said. "So very happy. Is this what you wanted to talk to me about?"

"Excuse me?" he asked, lost, but then remembered what he had said when he first came out here. It would be awkward and, apparently, unnecessary to inform her of his intentions to keep his hands off her. He wanted to do nothing to bring dark thoughts to the light shining now from her face. "I had wondered at your absence, is all," he said in a half-truth. "I've grown accustomed to your company."

She seemed as willing as he to avoid mention of the

last time they had been together. "I will not leave you again," she said.

Her words sent a touch of anxiety through him, at the same time that he enjoyed their sound. There was a part of him rational enough to wonder what the hell he was getting himself in for . . . and why he seemed to care nothing for the insanity of his actions.

He was going to teach a ghost to read, and he knew already he would take every opportunity to lean over her shoulder and smell the hay-sweet scent of her hair, to brush against her, to lay his hand over hers and direct her use of a pen.

He *was* mad.

Chapter Seventeen

"Alex, it is three-thirty, the same time it was when last you looked," Beth said, feeling a bit put out by his inattention to her and Sophie. It made one feel very much like an unwelcome burden. He was usually so attentive: she had even thought, in passing, that he might have something of a care for her. She loved Rhys, of course, and would never think of betraying him, but Alex's fondness for her had been flattering, and gave her an easy confidence in his presence. "One would think you had a pressing engagement, the way you keep checking the clock every half minute."

"Truly, Alex, it is most rude," Sophie said, setting her flowered teacup into its saucer with a tiny clink. "One would think you were not desirous of our company, although I cannot imagine whose company you *do* desire. You have not had a single visitor since I came here myself."

"I do apologize," Alex said. "I am waiting for nightfall, is all. I hope to have a clear night for stargazing."

Sophie made a delicate snorting sound of dismissal. "I do not see how any person could find such interest in a bunch of dots in the sky, whether they streak prettily or no."

"Sophie, you must admit it is a romantic notion," Beth said. "Lovers and poets become obsessed by the stars as well, so one can only conclude that astronomers must have something in common with them."

"I assure you, I shall not be writing poetry anytime soon," Alex said.

"Pish," Beth said. "I'm certain you already have some stashed away under your star charts and tables."

Sophie daintily picked up a triangle of cucumber-and-salmon sandwich, and nibbled on the edge. "I think it is high time my brother stopped looking at stars and found himself a wife," she said, sitting straight-backed and superior, aping the attitude of her eldest sister. "It will settle him down," she said to Beth, as if Alex were not sitting right there.

"He does not need settling," Beth said.

"Hear! hear!" Alex agreed, raising his teacup to her.

"I will say, though, that he needs a female in his life," she added.

Beth caught the mock frown Alex gave her, and raised an eyebrow in reply, giving her curls a slight toss. She might miss his flattery, but she was not so shallow a friend that she did not want the best for him.

"He won't likely find one up here," Sophie said. "Unless you want to count the ghost. I still do not forgive you for making me go to bed, Alex, while the rest of you sat around discussing it all that night. I do not see why I had to wait until morning, like a child. I am not

223

a child. I am about to be a married woman."

"So you are," Alex agreed. "Yet surely you agree that you are not one yet."

Sophie made a moue, her face turning a bit ducklike in the process. Beth hoped her friend would not engage in the practice too often, once married to Blandamour. When his infatuation faded, he might not think it so charming, and one must ever remain charming to one's husband.

"To return to the subject," Beth said, interrupting the bickering, "Alex is settled and responsible enough as it is. His wild hairs only add to his appeal to the fairer sex, as he well knows." She caught him rolling his eyes. "All that stargazing is of little use, however, if he does not have a female audience to appreciate his romanticism. Mooning about looking poetic is rather pointless if there is no one to see you and give a sigh."

She was stretching the truth of her own feelings: she was uneasy about Alex's nights in the tower. Although it had started as a bit of a joke, he was getting a reputation as an eccentric in the county, and becoming the topic of much speculative gossip. A wife to share his bed and see to his well-being might keep him tethered closely enough to earth that neither ghosts nor stars could pull him away.

She had no real concerns that he was losing his mind. She just couldn't shake the feeling that much went on here that he did not tell, and that the ghost Serena was a part of it. No friend would sit idly by while a man spent his nights in contact with the spirit of a dead woman, and she did consider herself a friend.

She was intrigued by the idea of Serena, but uneasy about it as well. What could one know of the mind of a ghost? Were her intentions evil? She was finding that ghost stories were exciting and romantic only as long as they stayed stories, and on the outer edges of experience. She did not like to think that Serena might possibly be the cause of Alex's glances at the clock.

"I shouldn't much like a sighing female hanging about," Alex said. "They cost too much in smelling salts."

"Then what type would you prefer?" she asked, smiling, aware and a little embarrassed that she was hoping he would describe someone like her.

"Well," he said, setting his cup on the table and leaning forward. "First, she must be tall, with a strong body. Frances was as lovely as a porcelain doll, but I felt equally likely to break her."

Beth felt a remembered twinge of sadness. Frances had indeed proved too frail to overcome her fever. It made a certain sense then that Alex would want a woman healthy as a horse. "A woman can be of smaller stature without being fragile," she reminded him, thinking of how Rhys was surprised in bed by the strength of her thighs, and her ability, when she wished, to overpower him. Admittedly, he let her do so, but still. . . .

"Ah, but with a tall woman one does not need to cramp one's neck with bending down to kiss her. She can look you straight in the eye."

"That does not sound very feminine," Sophie said, "a woman being as tall as a man."

"She would have strength of will, as well," he went on, ignoring his sister's comment. "She would say what she thought, and go after what she wanted. She would let nothing defeat her, and yet would retain a tender heart beneath the steel."

"It sounds as if you want one of those horrid Greek goddesses, who trounce upon mere mortals as they pursue their desires," Beth said. "And you know what happens when a man displeases a goddess. He ends up turned into a tree or a rabbit, or comes to some equally unpleasant end."

"You must admit it would be glorious while it lasted," he said with a smile.

Sophie sniffed disapprovingly. "It's not terribly realistic of you, though, Alex, to be casting your sights on ancient goddesses. They simply do not frequent the assembly rooms of Bath."

Beth laughed. "No, how very true." And how ironic to have Sophie lecturing Alex on the nature of reality.

"I do not understand why it matters in which order the letters go," Serena complained.

"This is the way it is done. Everyone knows them in this order."

"That does not mean I have to," she said.

He sighed in mild exasperation, a sound that encouraged rather than chastised her. "It's the alphabet, Serena. It goes in alphabetical order. Later on, when you learn to use the dictionary, you will need to know the letters in this order."

"What is a dictionary?"

"A book for finding the meanings of words you do not know."

"How would I know which word to look for, if I did not know it?"

"Are you being deliberately difficult?"

She blinked innocently at him.

"You are a wicked woman. Your brothers must have had a terrible time with you."

"I gave as good as I got, is all I will say," she pronounced primly, and turned her eyes back to the sheets of paper on Woding's desk in his tower study. "Show me which ones make my name. I will learn those first, and they will be my landmarks. I cannot make sense of all of these at once."

He bent down next to her and wrote out her Christian name beneath the rows of letters. "That is how I imagine Serena is spelled," he said. "I do not know for certain."

"And Clerenbold?"

"Learn this first, and then we will tackle Clerenbold. It uses some of the same letters." He spelled out loud the letters of her name for her, and had her repeat them until she could do it by heart. He gave the letters their sounds, showing her how they went together to form the one word: Serena.

"These 'e's, they do not sound the same," she protested.

"No. The same letter can have different sounds, depending upon the word."

"I do not like that."

"Neither do schoolchildren."

She made a noise to show what she thought of that comment. She stared at her name on the paper, then formed the sounds, her lips moving as she went through the letters. "It's quite a lovely name, isn't it?" she said.

"If you do say so yourself."

She leaned away from the desk, and pointed at the paper. "Write yours there, beneath mine."

He bent forward again and picked up his pen, then stopped. "Which would you prefer, my Christian or my surname?"

"Christian."

He bent to his task, and muttered to her under his breath, "I do not see why, when you insist upon calling me by the other, without even the courtesy of a 'Mr.' "

"Nor have I heard you call me 'Lady Serena,' Woding."

"Your pardon, madame."

"Mademoiselle, if you please."

"Do you speak French, then?"

"Doesn't everyone know a little of it? Thomas loved to practice swearing in that language. He imagined using it to curse the French in their own language while he ran them through with his sword."

"Mm. I am not sure I regret not having had the chance to meet him," he said, beginning to write out his name.

"He would not have liked you, at least not at first," she said.

"Why is that?" he asked, looking up from his careful penmanship.

She gestured to the room at large, the telescope, the orrery. "He would not have understood all this. He did not like what he did not understand."

"He is not alone in that."

"No. 'Tis a great fault of human nature."

He stared at her, then said, "You surprise me. Up until yesterday I would have thought you were of the same opinion as Thomas."

"I have no fondness for ignorance. It weakens one. Thomas and my brothers understood that concept in relation to warfare, but to nothing else. I, however, felt that I learned that lesson a hundred times over. It was my ignorance on a dozen scores that was partly to blame for what happened to me."

"That cannot be an easy admission to make."

"Rest assured, I blame le Gayne for most of it," she said, and bared her teeth in a false smile.

She did blame le Gayne, but since Woding had first started conversing with her, she had felt flickers of her

228

own guilt flaring up whenever she thought about what had happened, what she had done. Ignorance had not been enough to bring her and Thomas to their end. Le Gayne had not been enough. Something had had to bring the two together, and a very dark part of her, hidden away beneath the rest, was beginning to say that she herself had been the key to the disaster that had followed.

That could be why le Gayne's shadow had appeared. It could be a reason for it to come back. Madame Zousa's medallion seemed to be working so far, though, keeping her safe. She had seen flickers of darkness suggestive of that evil spirit, but so far had been in no danger that she knew of.

"Spell your name for me," she said, and listened while he did so, trying to distract herself from her own dark thoughts. As Woding explained the letters of his name and pointed them out in the alphabet, the vast collection of squiggles began to take on a sort of sense. She still could not recall most of the letters, but they were now looking less like spilled worms and more like something with meaning.

She saw him glance out the window, and followed his gaze. It was full dark.

"We'll stop here," he said, "and resume tomorrow."

She didn't want to stop, not now when her brain was beginning to put the first hint of order to it all. "Can we not continue up there?" she asked.

"I cannot have the lamp uncovered."

"Woding," she said, shaking her head. "Do you think I will have trouble seeing without a lamp?"

He flushed, caught out in his foolish error of thought. "You're right, of course. I warn you, though, I shall be looking at the skies. You will have to spend your time reciting the letters of the alphabet."

"S, E, R—"

"In their proper order."

"Were you always like this, Woding, or did you only become so exciting in your old age?"

"Sarcasm does not become you."

"I was not being sarcastic. Spirits do not stoop to such modes of expression."

He grunted and held his arm out, directing her to precede him to the steep steps to the roof. She obeyed, rising from her chair, and once at the steps lifted her skirts to climb them. He started to follow, but she pointed back at his desk. "You'll have to carry the paper for me."

He did as she bade, but said, "I thought you could carry some things. I thought you carried that medallion that Madame Zousa gave you."

"I did, but it is much easier for you than for me. I find it . . . quite fatiguing." She did not want to tell him of her connection to the cherry tree: whatever trust she had in him, it was not yet that strong. To tell someone of the tree was to give him the power to end her existence.

She stopped when she was far enough up the steps that the trapdoor would have pressed against her head. It would be indelicate to continue, showing a headless body to him as she went through the closed door.

He came up beside her, the two of them standing close on the steps, and raised his arms to push open the trap. His nearness made her dizzy with the possibility of his touch, and with his arms raised she was tempted to wrap her own around his chest and press her face into his neck.

The trapdoor fell open with a loud thud, and the moment passed. She climbed out onto the roof, her lips curving in a smile as the world spread out beneath her and the night breeze blew through her body. Perhaps she could understand a little of what drew Woding to this tower.

She looked up into the deep eternity of the heavens, and in a flashing leap of thought, understood some of what Woding had tried to explain to her about what he felt when gazing at them. "It's an oblivion within awareness that you find here, isn't it?" she asked, hearing him come up behind her.

"What was that?"

She tilted her head back, the world falling away around her, her eyes seeing nothing but sky, and felt her soul lift up into the infinite midnight blue of the heavens. "It is like walking in the pitch-black across an open field, your eyes wide, your senses awake to every sound. You know there are things out there, yet you feel you are the only creature on earth, the only solid object in the night. It is as if the world has disappeared." She brought her gaze back down and turned to look at him. "That is what you feel when you look into the night sky. Am I right?"

His gaze on her was thoughtful. "It is a better description than I have ever come up with," he admitted quietly. "You have a gift for putting intangibles into words, when you choose to use it."

"Thomas said I liked the sound of my own voice," she said.

"I have difficulty imagining you as a chatterbox."

She laughed. "No, never that. 'Twas more a matter of beating down my brothers with words until I got my way. Big as I am, I still could not best them in brute strength."

231

"I'm sure you had your ways. I grew up with a household of sisters, and I've seen the trickery of which they're capable."

"Subtlety was always my last resort," she said.

"So that's what it's called."

She smiled. "You have stars to watch."

"And you have letters to learn."

"That's right, easy there," Sommer said, his hands hovering above Nancy's as she pulled the team of horses to a halt outside the stables. His right side was pressed up against her, and it was all he could do not to grab hold of her and push her down upon her back upon the short coachman's bench, and smother her in the kisses of his pent-up desire.

"You have a gentle hand with the horses; there is no question there," he said, and was rewarded by her warm gaze. He thought she had grown fond of him, especially since he had started training her to drive the teams of horses. She had claimed to know how already, but there was no way on God's green earth that he would let her lay hands to the reins except under his tutelage. Well, except for in the tunnel. Admittedly, she did a decent job there, but that was a limited circumstance. It was nothing like an open roadway.

Ah, she was something special, his Nancy. Yes, he had resented her at first, but her quiet, solid ways reminded him too much of a sweet-tempered horse to let that resentment last. She was like the earth itself, patient and calm, all-accepting. She was not the giggling, high-pitched female he had feared would wreck the peace of the stables.

It had been no trouble to receive the permission from Mr. Woding to teach her to handle the teams and the carriages. This nighttime excursion had been his own idea: night driving was a necessary skill, but the romantic part of him he had not known existed had been what urged him to it.

He and Nancy, under the stars, high upon a coachman's seat, his hands over hers on the reins . . . He had held hopes that a kiss might follow, or at least a touch of the cheeks. It had not happened, but he had confidence it would, in time.

"Nancy, may I have a word with you?" Underhill asked, coming out of the part of the stables where they had their rooms.

Sommer cursed under his breath. *Damn Underhill.* He was the only fly in the horse ointment of his plans. The manservant had been sniffing around Nancy's skirts, making eyes at her when he thought no one was looking, and generally making a damned nuisance of himself.

It was a hellish thing for the three of them to sit in the small common room of the stables, in front of the fire late at night, as they sometimes did. Underhill tried to charm Nancy; Sommer could see that plainly enough. He told jokes and anecdotes, trying to coax a smile from her. And Nancy, sweet Nancy, she smiled at his antics even though Sommer knew in his heart that she did it only to humor Underhill and preserve his feelings.

A jewel such as she would not be taken in by one such as Underhill. No, she needed someone who understood horses the way he did, and who could understand the workings of a horse-lover's mind.

"One moment," Nancy said to Underhill, and then turned her soft brown eyes to him. "May I?" she asked simply, her expression revealing nothing of eagerness, only the desire to do as someone had asked. Underhill was technically in charge of all the staff, answering only to Mr. Woding. She need not have even asked his permission to obey Underhill's request.

"Aye, but be quick about it. I won't be rubbing down these horses all by myself."

She nodded her assent.

Ah, beautiful lass. Brushing the horses was one of his favorite ways to spend time with her. The smell of horse sweat, the close, steamy heat, the sight of her body at work upon the massive frames of the animals . . .

He sometimes imagined his own sex growing as large as those on the horses, and her waiting for him on hands and knees, her rear legs spread slightly apart. She would squeal as he mounted her, his teeth bared, nipping at her neck.

He watched from the seat as she went with Underhill into the living quarters. What could the man wish to speak with her about that could not wait? Likely he thought his own whims more important than the needs of the horses. *Selfish bastard.*

Minutes went by, the horses growing restless in their traces. He wanted Nancy to help him remove them. He could have done it himself, but it was a good excuse to have her by his side. He liked to correct her, or show her better ways to do things. He knew she appreciated his expertise. She might even make a fine coachman someday.

He shifted on his seat. What were they doing in there? And what did Underhill need from her, anyway?

Dark suspicions began to fill his mind. Was Underhill cooing in her ear, while he sat out here like a fool? Was he making advances toward her? Unwanted advances? Perhaps he had her up against a wall even now, his hands on her while she protested in that deep, gentle voice. It would likely spur the whoreson on.

He secured the reins and leaped down from the coach seat. He stalked over to the building, jealousy flaring through his blood, anger at Underhill's affront cloaking his vision. The horny son of a . . .

The room was orange to his dark-adjusted eyes, the lamplight bright after the night outdoors. It was sound that told him where to look.

"I couldn't wait for you to return," Underhill was saying. "God, Nancy, you feel so good." He had her pinned beneath him on the wooden settee, only her legs and skirts visible as they fell half off the hard piece of furniture. Underhill had his hand halfway up her thigh.

Sommer launched himself at that writhing back with a roar of rage, and pulled the gangly man off his Nancy. He barely knew what he did, barely felt the thud of his own fists against the bony frame, and did not hear Nancy's shouts and cries. It was only when Underhill was unconscious beneath him, his face bloodied, that he became aware that Nancy was clinging to him, trying to stop the assault.

"You're killing him! Stop!" she cried, her lovely voice scratchy with tears.

He stumbled back, away from the crumpled form of Underhill, and Nancy released him, dropping down beside the fallen man, cradling his head in her lap. Her fingers gently touched his damaged face, his blood marring her white smock.

"What have you done?" she asked, looking up at him, tears streaking down her face. "Why? He did nothing to you."

The sickening truth came home to him as he watched her coddle Underhill. She had not been a victim, but a willing participant. The thought made him ill, made him

235

want to kick Underhill again, or slice his throat and finish the job.

But Nancy was there, looking at him with wounded eyes. She had a reason to hate him now, whereas before there had been only respect, and perhaps a chance of turning her affections away from the unworthy.

Ah, God. What had he done?

He turned and walked from the room, his arms hanging loose at his sides, his eyes seeing nothing until he found himself in front of the stables and the carriage with the still-hitched horses.

He couldn't stay here, couldn't look again at Nancy's face. He climbed into the coachman's seat and felt a cry of despair trembling up from inside. He bit down on it, picked up the reins, and released the brake.

"I am not certain he is quite normal, with his kisses," Sophie said.

"Ah? How so?" Beth asked. They were in the blue drawing room, their chairs pulled close to the fire, a tray of biscuits and cakes on the table between them. It was far too late in the evening for tea goodies, but there was something temptingly delicious about eating such fare while talking with a good friend into the wee hours.

"He is such a mild-mannered man in all other respects, I had rather expected him to be mild-mannered in his affections, as well. Such has not proven to be the case. Why, before he left here he had me all but pinned against the books in the library, and . . . and . . ."

Beth raised an eyebrow. "And?"

"And—this is quite embarrassing—he put his *tongue* in my mouth." Sophie widened her eyes in remembered shock.

"Did he, then?"

"And . . . and . . . he moved it. In and out."

Her friend's eyes looked very much like those of a frightened rabbit. Beth smiled. She was glad to hear that Blandamour had some male animal instincts under all that genteel infatuation. He might stand a chance against Sophie, after all.

Voices and a clattering of footsteps drew both their eyes to the half-open door that led to the entry hall. A moment later the stablelass, Nancy, appeared in the doorway.

"Excuse me, madame, miss," Nancy said, "I am looking for Mr. Woding."

Beth rose from her chair, sensing the tension in the normally placid girl. "I believe he is in his tower. What is it? What has happened?"

"There's been a fight between Mr. Sommer and Mr. Underhill."

"Oh, dear me. Are either of them hurt?"

"I am afraid that Mr. Underhill may be badly so," Nancy said, and Beth was surprised to see the sheen of tears in the girl's red eyes. "My aunt, Mrs. Hutchins, has gone to tend to him. Please, could you take me to Mr. Woding?"

"Yes, certainly," Beth said, hurrying over to the girl, and taking her hand and giving it a brief squeeze. She looked in need of more comfort than that, but first things first.

"What was the fight about?" Sophie asked, following behind them.

Nancy's answer was a gurgle of sound that neither of them could decipher. Beth patted her back and hurried her up the stairs. *Poor child.* Horses were surely much easier to deal with than men.

*   *   *

"A, C, E, G, B, F, D," Serena sang. "J, K, M, N, L, O, P."

"Close, but not quite," Alex said, turning his eyes from the sky to her. She was sitting on the floor beside his reclined chair, facing him, the sheet of paper with the alphabet on the ground next to her. The red light of his small lamp cast a faint pink glow onto her luminous skin. "It's A, B, C, D, E, F, G. Try again."

He saw her frown down at the paper, her lips moving in silent repetition of his example. The frown got deeper, and aloud she went through the first seven letters, slowly and carefully.

"Perfect!" he said. "And now—"

"No, no, let me stop there for now," she said. "I am beginning to confuse myself. P, T, C, D, G, they all sound the same. I am making myself dizzy."

"You are doing remarkably well."

"I feel like an idiot."

"I imagine that even some idiots learn a little of how to read."

"How reassuring. Thank you ever so much, Woding."

He shrugged, hiding a smile, and looked back up at the stars, her glow visible at the edge of his vision. She was like a star fallen to earth, his Serena.

"What is it you are looking for in the falling stars?" Serena asked after several minutes of silence had gone by. "Why do you chart their paths?"

"Because they are not really falling stars," he said.

"They aren't?" she asked, obviously surprised. "Then what are they?"

"That is precisely what I am trying to find out. What do you think they are?" he asked.

"I do not know. I had always assumed they were what they appeared to be."

He looked at her. "But do they really appear to be stars that fall from heaven? Where do they come from, if so, and where do they go? There are neither more nor less stars above no matter how many seem to fall."

She turned her face up to the sky, considering. "The stars have not changed at all since I was a child," she agreed. "Maybe those that fall are stars from too far away to be seen, and they pass by to someplace equally distant, beyond our sight. Perhaps they travel so quickly we can see them for only an instant."

"That is not a bad theory," he said, her ideas meshing with some that he himself had devised. "It sounds much better than some of those that other scientists have suggested, like that in certain weather plants release gases at night that react with the air."

"I should think that the plants themselves would be glowing, if such were the case. No, my idea is much better."

"Naturally," he said. "You become an expert upon things with remarkable swiftness."

"Alex," she said with a touch of timidity that caught his attention. She almost never used his Christian name, and being timid was not one of her problems.

"Yes, Serena?"

"Would you teach me something else, if I asked?"

His mind went racing. What lessons of the modern world could make his warrior ghost blush? Questions of procreation came immediately to mind. *Please, no.* He couldn't draw her pictures of men and women and what they did in bed. "Certainly. What is it?"

She was quiet. "Oh, never mind," she said after a bit, and looked down at her knees.

"All right." Whatever it was, he was happy not to push.

"Will you teach me how to kiss?"

He jerked upright, staring down at her. "*What?*"

"Never mind! Never mind!"

"No, wait, you asked me to teach you to kiss. Why? Do you want me to kiss you?"

"No!" Her hands were up, fluttering around her face, not knowing what to do with themselves. "Why would I want that? No, of course not. You think too highly of yourself, Woding."

"Why did you ask?"

The hands went through another confused flight. "I'm curious. That's all. I've never truly been kissed before, on the lips."

"Never?" he asked, some of his shock dying down. He remembered clearly enough listening to his sisters talk on and on about what it would be like to be kissed by a man. They had even gone so far as to try to practice on him. He had fled the house in horror. He had never quite understood how they could despise so much that was male, and yet seem to center their lives around finding a man for their very own.

"Well, le Gayne did, if you want to count that. I don't."

"If you want a kiss, I can give you that, to satisfy your curiosity," he offered. "You don't have to pretend to want to learn how to do it."

"I do want to learn," she mumbled.

"But why? You're not going to—" He stopped himself. She did not need him to remind her that she was never going to have a lover or a husband.

"Maybe . . . maybe it is part of why I am still here," she said. "I did not care for le Gayne, but I wanted to be a wife and mother. I wanted to *live*, as fully as I could. Even while I was dying I wanted that. I wanted to experience everything I never had a chance to."

"So I kiss you, and poof, you're gone to the afterlife?"

She shrugged, her face half turned away. She looked human to him in that moment, completely a woman who had made herself vulnerable to a man by revealing some secret part of herself, and making a request that embarrassed her. Frances had made the same movement when they had talked about lovemaking.

He swung his legs off the chair, and she scooted out of the way as his feet came down beside her. He reached for her, and for a moment his hands tingled with warmth as they went through her; then she solidified, and when he tried again he felt the give of supple flesh.

He pulled her gently toward him, until she was sitting sideways on the ground between his legs, one of her long thighs covering his right foot in heavy warmth. Her eyes were open wide, watching him warily. She held perfectly still as he bent down toward her, his hands on her shoulders holding her in place if she should suddenly bolt.

Her sweet, warm scent filled his head as he came close to her, his lips hovering less than an inch above hers. He closed his eyes and breathed deeply, inhaling her, feeling the gentle touch of her breath on his skin, and then he set his lips lightly on hers.

They were slightly parted, and smooth like the skins of cherries. He felt the quiver of her body in his hands, and in the irregular breath she let out. He moved his head, brushing his lips across hers with a light touch that set his own nerve endings shimmering. With the tip of his tongue, he lightly stroked her full lower lip, then took it between his own lips, pulling at it gently before letting it slide free.

He moved one hand along her shoulder, and then up

under her hair to the nape of her neck, the silky strands against the back of his hand warm from her heat. He felt her hands settle on his knee and thigh, tentatively, almost as if she was afraid to touch him. He bore down firmly on her mouth, and supported her head with his hand as she bent back under the pressure. The hands on his leg squeezed. He eased off and nipped at her lips with his own, then forced her mouth open and thrust his tongue inside, rubbing it against the texture of hers, letting her taste him as he tasted her.

She made a soft cry deep in her throat, and the sound went straight to his groin.

Beth knocked on the door to the tower room. "Alex? It's Beth." She waited, then knocked again. Sophie and Nancy rustled behind her, huddling close, eager to escape the dark coolness of the tower stairs. "Alex?"

She lifted the latch and pushed open the door a few inches, peering into the room. She doubted he would welcome three women invading his private study without invitation. "Hello?"

She opened the door all the way, seeing that the room was empty. There were no lamps or candles lit, her own candle throwing the only light over the desk and gleaming orrery. They all three stepped into the room, and then Beth's candle guttered in a draft.

"He must be up top," she said, going toward the steep stairs to the roof.

"This is worse than visiting a sorcerer in a novel," Sophie complained, following with Nancy. "Why couldn't he have left a lamp burning?"

A sound caught Beth's ears. "Shh!" Beth hissed, hushing her friend. "Do you hear voices?"

They all three held motionless at the foot of the steps,

listening. "If you want just a kiss," Alex was saying, "I can give you that."

They turned wide eyes on each other. A female voice answered, and in a hope against hope, even as the hairs on the back of her neck began to rise, Beth asked Nancy, "Is that Marcy?"

Nancy shook her head no. "I don't know that voice," she said.

"Then who is it?" Sophie whispered.

"Shhh," Beth commanded, and they all continued to listen. "Even while I was dying I wanted that," the woman was saying. "I wanted to experience everything I'd never had a chance to."

"So I kiss you, and poof, you're gone to the afterlife?" Alex replied, and then there was silence, followed by a shuffling of movement and the peculiar, heavy-breathing quiet that comes when two people kiss.

Beth handed the candlestick to Sophie, grabbed her skirts in one hand, and climbed quickly up the steps, her heart thudding in sick terror. Her head came out the hatch, and she saw Alex in the red light of his lamp, leaning forward from his chair with his arms entwined with a shining white light, formless and inhuman.

"Alex!" she cried.

Immediately he jerked back from the light, which vanished the moment he released it.

Beth scampered up the last few steps and dashed over to him, reaching out as if to take his hand, and then at the last moment refraining, some instinctual part of her not wanting to touch him. He looked stunned. "Alex? Are you all right? Alex?"

He seemed to gather himself together, then scowled up at her. "Yes, what is it?" His eyes slipped away from

243

her face, going to a corner to Beth's right before coming back to her again.

She straightened, every hair on her body standing stiff, the skin of her face fairly crawling with the sense of being watched by the unseen.

"Alex, come down from here," she said with false calm. "Underhill needs your help. He's been badly beaten by Sommer."

"What?" Alex all but shouted, coming quickly to his feet. "Where is he?"

"Nancy is below. She'll explain everything. Mrs. Hutchins is with him now." She gestured for him to precede her down the stairs, and he quickly obliged, his concern for his manservant evident.

She stood for a moment longer than necessary on the rooftop, her eyes scanning the empty darkness that was alive with awareness. She shivered, and then followed Alex below.

Chapter Eighteen

"Otto, here, boy, come on," Serena said softly, crouching down and holding out her hand to the hound. "Come on, I won't hurt you." The dog, head and tail down, ears back, gave her a wide-eyed, distrusting stare and slunk off down the hall.

Serena sighed, straightened, and followed. She had been at it for over an hour, and was coming to the conclusion that Otto was a cowardly, dim-witted creature only barely worth his feed. Her attempts to befriend the beast were getting tiresome, but she had decided it was in her best interest to do so, and she would not give up, however difficult the loathsome canine was being.

Surely there must be some intelligence in the animal, some redeeming feature. Woding doted on the thing, after all, and that in itself was her primary motivation.

She tracked Otto into the library, through the entry hall, and then up the stairs. He didn't run so much as keep up a slow trot, pausing occasionally to see if she still pursued. He was probably getting as weary of the game as she was. *Stupid dog.* If he'd just sit still and let her pet him, they could both be done with this.

The door to Woding's bedroom was ajar, and Otto pushed his way inside. Serena followed, closing the door behind her, trapping him inside with her.

"Ot-tooooe," she crooned. "Ot-tooooe."

The dog went from door to door, pawing at the wood, looking for an escape as she came closer and closer. "Woo woooo!" he cried.

"Ot-tooooe, nice doggie, come make friends. I won't hurt you."

"Woo wooo!"

The whites of his eyes were showing, and she could see his flesh quivering. Maybe if she pounced on him and held him tight, he would eventually give in through sheer exhaustion.

She was about to act on the thought when he made a dive for the bed, scrambling beneath it, making the mattress buck and bounce as his back hit against the underside. "Wooo oo ooo," he cried from his cave.

She rolled her eyes. Beezely would never be such a coward. She went and sat on the bed, looking about the empty room, wishing Woding were there even as she was glad he had been gone for two days. She had a certain nervousness about seeing him again, after such an intimate encounter. She worried that he might regret it, or might have found her kisses unskilled and repulsive. He might never want to repeat the experience.

There had been a great deal of activity in the house since Beth interrupted their kiss. The doctor had been sent for, and had declared Underhill to have a few cracked ribs and bruised internal organs, but to otherwise be in working order. He would, of course, require a great deal of rest and care, but still he refused to stay anywhere but in the stables.

Sommer had driven the carriage at a reportedly hell-bent pace to an inn on the far side of Bradford-on-Avon, and there proceeded to drink himself into a near stupor. Unfortunately, he had been conscious enough to climb back into the coachman's seat. No one knew quite where he had been headed, but he took a corner on one of the country lanes much too fast, and was thrown from his seat, landing in a watery ditch, where he promptly passed out.

The horses had had the wit to stop, and when the next passerby came some hours later, the abandoned carriage prompted him to check for injured persons. He found Sommer half-dead from the chill of the water, and back in Bradford-on-Avon a doctor was again summoned.

Woding had had no choice but to release Sommer from his employ, both for the attack on Underhill and for his recklessness with the horses and carriage. Much to Nancy's delight and Woding's surprise, Nancy out of necessity became coachman, and Woding had accompanied her on her first outing, returning Beth and Sophie to their respective homes.

Serena had stayed away from the turmoil except for moments of spying to check in on events and Woding's whereabouts, and spent most of her time in the garden. She needed the time alone to sit in solitude and obsess over those moments in Woding's arms, and on what might or might not happen between them in the future.

Her first true kiss. She forgot about Otto under the bed as the scene replayed itself again in her mind. She found that she could re-create some of the sensations just by thinking about it, feeling the same paralyzing sense of being the helpless recipient of his touch. It was as if all thought, all ability to control her own actions had left her, leaving her mind consumed by the sensations of her body. She could have sat there all night, between his knees, letting him kiss her as he wished.

She was a shameful, wanton creature, and what was worse, she did not care. After many hours of careful consideration, she had decided that her possible eternal damnation did not matter so much as the chance to feel Woding's naked body against her skin. If his kisses were so wonderful, then surely sharing his bed would be paradise on earth. She had no reason to preserve her virginity any longer, so why not? And perhaps it would be only as real as sex in a dream, where one woke with the lingering sensations and a sense of guilt, but nothing had truly changed.

The room was dimming as the sun began to go down behind the heavy blanket of clouds that had concealed the sky all day. The shadows in the corners began to grow and darken. Otto's whining settled into an exhausted quiet.

Why shouldn't she experiment with sex? It would hurt no one, least of all Woding.

A shadow moved. She saw it from the corner of her eye, and jerked her head, staring wide-eyed. Nothing. Then, as if with a pulse that pumped it larger, a shadow swelled.

Serena crawled backward to the head of the bed, her skin going cold and sweaty at the same time, her breath seizing in terror. The shadow, expanding to fill half the room, floated toward the bed, stopping at the foot and then pouring itself between the posts toward her.

She screamed, her cry changing from one in the silent ghost realm to one that the living could hear, a scream of utter terror. Otto came bumping out from beneath the bed, his claws scrabbling on the wood floor, and once on his feet began to howl. "Aaa rooo roo roo!" he bellowed, adding his voice to Serena's.

The roiling shadow paused as if distracted, giving Serena a moment's sanity within her terror. In that moment she remembered the prayer that had worked before, and shut her eyes, clasping her hands before her and bowing her head. "Hail Mary, full of grace . . ." she recited, going through the rosary with a desperate hope that it would again drive away the shadow. Her sinful thoughts of moments earlier weighed on her mind, creating a crevasse of doubt in her worthiness.

She felt a cold, damp touch over all her skin at once, as if the shadow were enveloping her. She felt it begin to seep into her skin, pressing inward. "Nooo!" she cried, breaking her prayer and opening her eyes. Blackness was all around her, and it filled her mouth as she screamed.

Dimly, she was aware of Otto lunging at the shadow, biting at the insubstantial shape, and then she knew nothing.

The castle was quiet as Alex came inside. It felt vacant to him, and perhaps it was, he realized. Sophie was on her way home, Beth was back on her farm, and Mrs. Hutchins was down in the stables tending to Underhill. Marcy and Dickie had the day off, and as far as he knew had gone home to the village to visit their families.

He stood still a moment, feeling the emptiness around him, and savoring what it meant. No more interruptions, and he would have private time with Serena. That kiss they had shared—it had been like nothing he had ever experienced. Beth had not made reference to what she had seen, but the look in her eyes had told him that she was frightened, although whether *of* him or *for* him, he did not know.

Neither did he care. All he could think at this moment was that he felt more alive than he had in years, and felt the blood coursing through his body as if he were a youth again, his body aching to touch the female form. He had thought himself long through with such lustful obsessions.

He started up the stairs, and then a sound caught his attention. He paused, listening, and it came again. It sounded like Otto howling softly, a plaintive, forlorn cry.

Frowning, he jogged up the stairs and down the hall, following the sound to his room, where it barely penetrated the thick door. The sound stopped as he put his hand on the latch and opened it, and then Otto almost knocked him down, leaping upon him.

"Here, boy, how did you get locked in my room?" he asked the dog, who licked his face and then dropped down and trotted over to the bed. The curtains were half-closed, so all Alex could see was that Otto stared at something, and then began again his plaintive cry.

Curiosity and apprehension crept up his spine as he approached, and then he saw that it was Serena who lay upon the coverlet, her limbs as lifeless and broken as a rag doll's. Her eyes were partially open, but no white or iris showed, only an orb of blackness beneath the lid. Her usual illumination was dimmed, and she looked as if she were fading into the shadows.

It reminded him of his last sight of Frances, pale and spent in their bed, the fever having drained the life from her.

"Serena!" he shouted, breaking free of the spell of

horror in which the sight of her had caught him. He knelt on the bed and reached out to shake her, but his hand went right through her. "Serena!" he yelled again. "Wake up! Do you hear me? Wake up!" He brushed his hands through her, trying to stir some reaction, his hands feeling only a faint tingling as he did so.

There had to be a way to revive her, to wake her. He couldn't just sit here and watch her fade away, as she seemed to be doing before his very eyes, as if she were dying. A ghost could not die!

In a fit of desperation, he threw his body through hers, stretching out so that his own form occupied and surrounded every inch of her own, bending his arms so that they matched the pattern she made on the bed. A slow tingling went through his body, a faint echo of what he had felt that time they had crossed through each other in the hall.

"Come on . . ." he urged her in a whisper. "Wake up."

He closed his eyes, concentrating on his breath and heartbeat, willing them to fill her with whatever life it was she needed. The tingling grew stronger, becoming an electric current over his skin, then undulating through his muscles. He felt his manhood grow hard, and then bits of her memories began to fill his mind, and she moved, sitting up through him, gasping.

He rolled away and sat up beside her, shaking. "Serena?"

She turned her eyes to him, and they were normal now, and her glow once more illuminated her fine skin. "Woding?" she asked, her voice quavering. "What are you doing here? What happened?" Before he could answer, her eyes widened, and she said, "Le Gayne."

"Here?" he asked, his short-lived relief turning quickly back into alarm.

"Otto saw him and tried to chase him away." She turned to the dog, then crawled across Alex's legs to the edge of the bed, where Otto sat on the floor, his sad eyes watching everything. The dog's tail thumped on the floor as Serena reached out and petted his head. "You are such a good dog," she said softly. "I'm sorry for ever being mean to you." She lowered her face, and Otto tried to lick it.

She materialized, and Alex felt a quivering in her body, where it half lay against his legs. She had her face down, letting Otto lave her cheeks. "Serena?" The quivering continued.

Ah, damn. She was crying.

He pulled her up into his arms, sitting across his lap with her buttocks wedged between his thighs. She wrapped her arms around him and wept into his neck, her tears silent except for the harsh gasps of her breath.

"It's all right; he's gone," Alex murmured to her, rocking her back and forth as he'd seen his sisters do with their children.

A bone-jarring shudder went through Serena, and then a high, keening sound emerged from deep within her throat, sending the hair on the back of his neck straight up. He grimaced, holding her more tightly.

He did not know how long they had been sitting that way, or how long ago her tears had stopped, when he noticed that her lips were pressed against the bare skin just below his ear.

It was an innocent touch, surely. She moved her head, her mouth now ever so lightly touching moistly upon his ear, her breath a soft, warm whisper. That gentle exhalation of air traveled right into the core of his brain and snaked in a spiral down to his groin. How could she be so *warm?*

She shifted in his lap, and he became aware of her breasts, rubbing him through the layers of her garments. He had never felt her against his body like this, except for dim memories in dreams. She felt so solid, so real. Her body had the heavy weight of flesh, and her arms around his neck were strong with muscle. A deep, rich, feminine scent of skin rose from her to mingle with the sweet-hay scent of her hair, and he held her close, pressing his face against her cheek and into her hair.

He let his hand rub against her back, feeling for the first time the heavy, silken texture of her white surcoat. It moved against the pink woolen underdress, and he did not know if there was yet another layer beneath that. If he pressed hard enough he could make out the ridge of her spine, the angles of her shoulder blades, and the narrow hills and valleys of her ribs. She arched her back in response, pressing herself against him, her mouth opening on his ear.

Her tongue came out and traced lightly over his lobe. The sensation made him groan, and made him want to hear a similar response from her.

From behind he gently gathered her hair and pulled it away from the side of her neck, letting his fingers get lost in the warm, silken locks. She shivered in his arms, her neck bare and exposed, the neckline of her garments not starting until her collarbones. Her skin was as pale and smooth as custard, the only thing he could see in a room that had grown completely dark as they sat in each other's embrace.

He parted his lips and laid them where her neck curved to meet her shoulder. Her hands gripped the back of his jacket, her fingertips digging into his flesh, and the rest of her remained perfectly motionless, waiting.

He pressed his lips more firmly against her skin and

253

kissed her gently, then moved his kisses up the side of her neck. He heard her drag in a shuddering breath, and she tilted her head farther to the side, giving him more room, laying herself bare to his mouth. He made his way up to the bottom of her jaw, and reached up to brush back stray strands of pale blond hair from her cheek and forehead, leaning back a bit so he could look her in the eyes.

Her eyes were half-closed, but she met his gaze without reservation. He saw the willingness there, the lack of resistance. He tilted his head to the side and laid his lips against hers, letting her feel the touch of them as he had the other night, letting her grow accustomed to the sensation. He wrapped his arms more closely around her and held her tight, feeling her breasts flatten against his chest.

He felt his manhood swelling further against the confines of his trousers, and the pressure of her hip wedged so tight against him. Her hands went up to the back of his neck, her fingers playing in the short hair that brushed his collar.

He put his hand on the back of her head, lightly stroking her hair and then cupping the back of her skull and holding her as he deepened the kiss, urging her mouth to open beneath his. As she gave way beneath him and allowed his entrance, he shifted and maneuvered her to the side, rolling over so that she was beneath him on the bed, her body half under his.

She made a noise of protest and pain, and he immediately pulled back. She struggled for a moment, her hand going behind her neck as she strained to rise, and he realized that she had become pinned by lying on her own hair. He eased her up, and with a practiced flick of her hand she swept her hair out from under her shoulders, to where it spilled like turbulent water over the coverlet and down the side of the bed. He had a sudden image of himself, naked, bathing in that hair, long strands of it twisted around his member.

She smiled up at him and raised her arms back to his neck. He needed no second invitation.

Distant echoes of propriety rang in his head, like the bells of a church from across the valley, but they seemed to have little to do with the moment at hand or with either him or Serena. How could the rules of behavior for maidens apply to this? Serena was not of this world, and all that mattered was the pleasure they both desired.

He laid one leg between hers, pressing his manhood against her hip, his thigh tight against her sex. He massaged his hand in circles on the side of her waist gently, moving the fabric against her skin, encouraging her to writhe beneath him, to forget herself and enjoy the pressure of his body against hers.

He slid down several inches, bending his leg to keep it in contact with her, loving the feel of her long body against his. There was so much more of her to touch than with any other woman—it was like having a banquet set before him, after a lifetime of dainty teas. When his face came even with her breasts, he took the erect nipple of one into his open mouth, sucking at it through the layers of cloth, and pinching it gently with his teeth.

She arched beneath him, her hands falling to her sides. He looked up under his brows at her face. Her eyes were closed, her concentration all on her body and the sensations he gave her. He knew she had never felt anything like it in all her life, and the knowledge fueled a desire to see her reach the ultimate bliss in his arms.

He slid his hand under her buttocks, cupping one of the mounds, molding it with his hand, squeezing and massaging it as his mouth pulled harder against her breast, his breath and tongue dampening the cloth. He pressed his fingers into the soft flesh of her buttock, holding it in his hand and pushing it in a circle, knowing that the motion would pull indirectly at her sex, the flesh rubbing against itself and his thigh.

Her lips parted, and soft, involuntary moans rose from her throat. He reached down and gathered some of her skirt in his hand, pulling it up to where he could reach the bare skin of her knee. His fingertips pressed lightly under her kneecaps, and her leg tensed in response, her hips rubbing against him as he let his fingertips move on, trailing lightly over her warm skin, her fine hairs teasing his nerve endings.

Her thigh was both muscled and soft, padded with a silken layer of fat that sent primitive messages to the core of his brain. She was ripe for sex, her body fertile ground waiting for the plow. He could lose himself in the warm wealth of her, plunging full-bore into the cradle of her hips, her softness capable of receiving and embracing every inch of hardness he gave to her.

He moved his hand upward and found the damp heat of her curls and the mound that rose above her sex, still hidden between the twin cushions of her thighs. He put his hand over the mound, fingers pointing downward, and moved his palm in a slow circle, pulling against the folds of her sex.

With his hand in constant motion, he moved back up her, to where he could again reach her neck with his mouth, his kisses this time harder, his tongue moving hard and fast against the bend of her neck, and upward to the small space behind the lobe of her ear.

When she gasped he moved to her mouth, his tongue going inside her as his fingers pressed between her thighs, covering her nether lips, the tip of his middle finger pressing into her opening. She was already growing damp, his finger finding a hot spring of slick wetness. He took it on his fingertip and spread it, moistening her, then laid his fingers against her again, catching the folds between them as he gently stroked up and down.

Her thighs parted of their own volition, opening like the door to a secret cavern. He rubbed his tongue against hers, and after a moment she responded, moving hers against his, then pushing forward to gain entrance into his own mouth. Her arms came up to wrap around his neck, her body arching toward him as she began to suck at his tongue, her hips moving in rhythm with his hand as he stroked her.

He let his hand move down at the end of a stroke, his finger sliding within her, feeling the heated walls of her passage, the slick flesh springy with softness over the powerful inner muscles. His manhood ached to be inside that tight hallway, clasped by her strength and wetness as he thrust in and out. There was none of the cold here of his nightmare, none of the fear. She was burning with her own desire, her flesh as hot as that of any woman in the throes of passion. The faint, lingering dread of the nightmare was dissolved by the heat against his hand.

He took his finger out and rubbed the wetness in tight circles over the bud of her desire, feeling the hard nub beneath its hood. Her legs began to twitch, jerking with each touch, her body flexing against him. As her tongue stilled, he plunged his own back into her mouth, moving it in and out to match the rapid motion of her hips. He thrust his finger full-length inside her just as she found release, feeling the contractions of her muscles squeezing his finger.

Her thighs closed tight over his wrist, her body's jerking slowing and then stopping. After a long moment she relaxed, and he carefully removed his finger from her. He looked at her, a smile of satisfaction pulling at the corners of his mouth at what he had done, but it was not over yet. When he took her a second time, this time with his manhood, she would be screaming with pleasure.

"Alex," she said, and opened her eyes and pulled his face close to hers, sprinkling it with fairy kisses. She then held him still while she stared deeply into his eyes, her own appearing a deep gray-blue. She brought his head down with her hands and slowly, reverently, kissed each of his eyelids shut.

A quiver went through him, her lips upon him filled him with an emotion gentler than any he had ever known. It was as if she touched him with her soul, her heart speaking to him through her lips and hands.

The realization of her depth of caring shook him. A moment ago all he had wanted was to continue his seduction of her, taking her to the heights of what her body could feel, but now he could not do so. He had not considered that this was more to her than bodies in the night. She was a virgin who had never known love, and to continue would be dishonorable if he could not give back to her the same depth of feeling she gave to him. He did not want to hurt her. She was too precious, too fragile. Satisfying his animal desires was not enough of a reason to cause her heart further pain.

Damn his conscience. He wished it could have waited another half hour before coming awake.

Alex pushed Serena's skirts down, then gathered her close in his arms, pulling her to lie snuggled against his side. He brushed the hair back from her forehead and kissed her softly between the brows. Her hand on his chest gripped him once, then relaxed, her whole body following suit, as she was apparently oblivious to the fact that there was a whole world of experience she had not yet had.

He closed his eyes and tried to think of other things, and to ignore the manhood that lay stiff and yearning against his belly.

Chapter Nineteen

Bath

"I'm glad that's over," George Stearne, Philippa's husband, said, as he leaned on the billiard cue clasped in both his hands. There was a chorus of agreement from the small group of men assembled around George's billiards table, their jackets off, their cravats loosened. None of them took a woman's delight in weddings, and Sophie's wedding today had been no exception.

Alex made a grunt of agreement to match those of the rest of his close male relatives: in-laws, mostly, except for Rhys and one other male cousin. His young sister and her beloved Blandamour were now safely on their way to his vicarage, there to share their first night of connubial bliss.

"Alex, did Blandamour ever make good on his offer to look up the Clerenbold family in parish records?" Rhys asked from across the table, a wide glass of dark amber whiskey in his hand.

Alex tried to read Rhys's expression through the haze of smoke in the room, but the dim light and his own consumption of drink this day defeated him. He had not spoken privately with his cousin since Beth had interrupted his kiss with Serena, and did not know what Beth had told him. He had been avoiding Rhys, not wanting to hear whatever lectures he had in mind to deliver, and in no mood to discuss anything of what had passed between him and Serena.

After that night when he had brought her to ecstasy, he had left Maiden Castle. He'd used the semivalid excuse of required attention at the mills, forging new business acquaintances, and then being in town for the final preparations for Sophie's wedding. The one obstacle that might have kept him from going—the danger of le Gayne's return—she had removed herself, saying that she would be safe if she stayed near the medallion Madame Zousa had given her. That had been all she had said to him, and she had stood cold as stone as he gave her a peck on the cheek in farewell.

It was a surprise that she had even allowed him to touch her that much, given his transparent excuses. As lacking in tenderness as his parting had been, it was the best he could manage. The thought of having her hold him and whisper endearments in his ear had terrified him more than any of her ghostly antics ever had.

It wasn't that he didn't want to spend time with her. He just didn't want her to feel anything for him beyond the friendship and sexual desire that was all he himself was capable of giving.

261

"Who are the Clerenbolds?" George asked. He was a portly man, balding, with colorless eyes, and was a bad businessman when left to his own devices. Philippa held a firm hold on the purse strings in the family, as well as on the strings that controlled George's actions in commerce. Alex had to give the man credit for being married to Philippa and still retaining his basic good humor.

"The Clerenbolds," Alex said, deciding it was best to keep control of the conversation, "are a family who lived in a keep a few miles from my present home, in the fourteenth century. According to what my new brother-in-law was able to discern, the family died out around the time of the plague. There has been speculation that Serena Clerenbold, the last daughter of the family, married the man who lived in the original Maiden Castle, but unfortunately this remains speculation only. Blandamour could find no proof of such a marriage, although he is determined to keep looking."

"The ghost!" Percy Cletch said. He was married to Alex's second-oldest sister, Constance. A tall, skinny physician with a fondness for studying both insects and human parasites—and drawing them in great detail—Percy was the only relative who had seemed to understand Alex's wish to study falling stars. Alex often thought Percy would be happiest giving up his doctoring and going to live in a tropical jungle teeming with bugs and worms. "I hadn't wanted to bring her up myself, but I say, I've been dying of curiosity to hear about her."

"Does she have anything to do with that coachman you have?" Harold Tubble asked. Married to Alex's gossipy sister Amelia, Harold was a less-than-brilliant squire with an unfettered love for dogs. On the rare occasion Alex had been to their country home, the smell of dog had all but overwhelmed his normally undiscerning nose. "Who ever heard of a woman driving a carriage! What's next, a female ship's captain?" he said, and gave a belly laugh that the others joined in.

"My wife says she feels much safer with Nancy Clark at the reins than she ever did with Sommer," Rhys said when the laughter died down. "She says the girl has a gentle hand with the horses."

Alex shot his cousin a look, surprised by the defense.

"Likely drives them at a pace even an old woman would like," Harold said.

"I beg your pardon," Rhys said stiffly. "My wife is no old woman."

"I don't care about the coachman—coachgirl—whatever she is," Percy interrupted impatiently. "I want to hear about the ghost."

"Philippa about burst her corset when Sophie told her about that gathering you all had," George said, his eyes glowing. Alex doubted very much whether Philippa would appreciate having any undergarment of hers mentioned aloud.

"My aunt Millicent had a ghost in her house," Harold said. "Used to scare the wits out of me as a child, although all it ever did was move things around when no one was looking. Uncle Frederick said he thought it was Millie herself, forgetting where she'd put things, and there was no ghost a'tall."

"I saw a ghost once," one of the other cousins said. All eyes turned to him, and he continued, "A lady in gray, going down a staircase. I wasn't more than six or seven years old. My family was visiting friends in their country house, an old place falling down around their ears. She looked real as day, and it was only when she vanished at the bottom of the stairs that I knew she wasn't. We later found out that she had been seen there several times. No one knew who she was, although one

guess was that she was the wife of the man who originally built the house."

"Gray ladies, white ladies—why do they always wear
those colors?" Rhys asked the room at large.

"Women like to dress alike," Harold said. "Just look
at the lot of them at any assembly here in Bath. If they
can't think for themselves while alive, they certainly
won't when dead."

"Ah, so there are afterlife fashion plates for them to
follow. I should have known," Rhys said. "That explains
it."

"Could we please return to the subject at hand?" Percy
asked in pained tones.

"Very well," Rhys said. "Alex, what color dress does
Serena wear?"

Alex let his glance play over the faces watching him,
waiting for an answer. The alcohol in his blood had loosened some of his self-control, and begged him to abandon his habit of remaining quiet on personal matters.
They were looking for an entertaining story, something
to while away the time before they had to go back to
their wives—many of them his own sisters, poor fel-
lows—so why not give it to them? Let them go back to
their marriage beds with a tale to tell, rather than the
endless speculation they were so fond of. Besides, it
would be a wonderful thing to see Rhys's eyes go wide.
He still had not forgiven him for all those pranks as a
child.

"She wears white," Alex said. "A white sleeveless
surcoat with gold embroidery, and a gold-link girdle.
Beneath it is a pink underdress, fitted tight to her body
so that you can see every curve. She wears no corset,
her breasts shaping her clothes themselves, no stiff fabric
between them and the outside world."

He smiled at the room of men. They stared back.

"Have you touched them, then?" Harold asked. "Her breasts."

"You can't touch a ghost," Percy said dismissively. And then, "Can you?"

"What if I said you could?" Alex asked. "If you were given the chance, if she came to you in your bed while you lay undressed and reached for you, would you let her do as she wished?"

"Not with Philippa by my side," George said sadly. "I'd pay for it the rest of my life."

"Depends if she's a comely wench," Harold said. "No use having a go at a phantom hag when you could find plenty of living ones the next house over."

"Say you are bachelors still," Alex said, to a chorus of ayes. "Say she is long of limb, with pale gold hair that brushes her thighs, and dark eyes that are like looking into eternity. What would you do then?"

"Give it to her!" Harold cried.

"I wouldn't want to deprive the unfortunate woman of her one joy," George said solemnly.

"For curiosity's sake, I'd have to give in to her demands," Percy said. "It would be a unique experience, well worth studying."

"It's not that simple," Rhys said, interrupting the voices that were speaking over each other with descriptions of what they'd do to such a ghostly figure in their beds. "The ghost haunts the house you live in. She is always there. She attacks people she doesn't like. She can follow you day and night, never leaving your side. She can hear every word you say, and see everything you do."

"Sounds like Philippa," George said gloomily.

"Now you're talking about marriage," Harold agreed.

"You can leave the house whenever you wish, and she won't come with you," Alex said, knowing that such would appeal to them. Personally, he would like to take Serena places. "She doesn't spend money: she never buys new clothes or furniture, she never plans parties, she never insists on taking a trip or going to a play or the opera." There were grunts of approval from his audience. "Certainly she does not plan 'musical evenings' in the drawing room. She has no relatives living." That got a surprised laugh, all of them in the room in-laws or relatives of each other. "She cannot be unfaithful, or bear children." What would the children of himself and Serena look like? Tall and strong.

"That's more a mistress than a wife," a cousin said.

"Only she can't give you the clap!" Harold threw in. "Won't cost you gewgaws and upkeep, either."

"She's always there when you want her," George said wistfully. "And always willing."

"She never grows tired," Alex said.

"No headaches?" Harold said. "There's the gal for me."

"Physics would suggest that a female ghost could assume all manner of unusual positions," Percy said. The room was quiet for a moment as male minds went to work on those possibilities.

"She'll always stay exactly the same," Rhys said into the quiet. "She'll never grow old, never grow fat." He looked directly at Alex. "She'll never die."

"I'd pass her on to my son," Harold said, oblivious to the undercurrent that had just passed between Rhys and Alex. "Like an inheritance. Better for his first experience than a whore, I'll warrant."

"No, she won't, will she?" Alex said to Rhys, ignoring Harold's comment. "She'll never get sick, or catch a fever that wastes her body away to nothing. She'll never be thrown from a horse, fall down a flight of stairs, or have so much as a toothache. Wouldn't you wish the same for Beth, if you could?"

"What joy is there in living if you never change?" Rhys said. "I don't think Beth would like to stand by and watch me grow old and die."

"That's what you think!" Harold said. "She'd find another to replace you soon enough."

"It does seem a trifle vain of you to assume you are her only reason for living," Alex said.

"Women!" Harold said. "They have the world fooled. We're told they are the romantic ones, but I tell you, they are mercenaries at heart, every one of them. My body wouldn't be cold before Amelia would be tallying my assets and planning a tour of the continent. I, on the other hand," he said, putting his hand over his heart, "worship the very ground her dainty foot sets sole to."

Several gazed incredulously at Harold; then George said, "That is the purest bucket of drivel you've ever let pour from your mouth, Harold. I know for a fact that your dear Amelia and my precious Philippa have the same size feet, and they are not a one of them dainty. You show more devotion to your dogs than to your wife."

Harold shrugged. "They do just as good a job of keeping a man warm at night, and they don't complain about the snoring."

"Is this all talk, Alex," Percy asked, "or do you actually see this ghost, this Serena?"

Alex looked blankly at his brother-in-law, his mind still caught up in swirls of drunken anger at Rhys's comments. What did his cousin know about losing a wife? What state would he be in were something to happen to

Beth? Pray God nothing like that ever happened, but if it did . . . ? Alex doubted Rhys would be willing to suffer such a loss again, if ever. How dared he judge his actions?

"Alex?" Percy repeated. "Do you see her?"

"She comes to me every night," Alex said, throwing caution completely to the winds. "She is as solid as you, Percy, when she chooses, yet I warrant her touch is far more pleasing." *Let Rhys chew on that. Let them all chew on it.* His brothers-in-law, whose income was partially dependent upon him, could worry that he'd lost his mind and that the money would soon follow.

He was sick unto death of behaving as he was supposed to. They all—his sisters, his cousins, too—wanted him to *behave*—meaning live as they lived. They wanted him to get married again, to "settle down," to have a family. He suspected the men wanted that as well, if only so he would stop being a silent taunt to them with his freedom.

Toe the line, Alex. Be responsible, Alex. Don't let us down. Make money. Be a gentleman. Don't be crude; don't upset anyone. Behave.

To hell with that. He'd lived up to his responsibilities, and now that the last sister was in someone else's hands, he'd do as he pleased, and be damned with what anyone thought.

"She's actually a fascinating young woman," Alex said. "I'm thinking that I'll leave the lot of you to provide the descendants, and spend my remaining years with Serena. She'll make a far more interesting companion than any of the bits of fluff floating around Bath, and I don't even have to marry her." He frowned up at the ceiling as if in contemplation, then continued. "Although I suppose that could be arranged, if she felt it necessary. She comes from an era more devout than our own, and she is Catholic, after all. Perhaps I should ask her when I return."

A few uncertain chuckles greeted his words. He looked around the room and saw that no one knew quite what to think of his proposal. Unlike Rhys, he was not known for his stories and jokes, and they clearly did not know if he was serious, or only speaking from his cups.

Let them wonder. Marriage was the last thing on his mind, but they didn't need to know that. They didn't need to know that he had fled from Serena when she showed signs of caring for him, fled with all the grace of Dickie with peas up his nose. Let them wonder; let them think he was cavorting with legions of the dead up in his castle on the hill.

God, he was drunk. A niggling instinct told him he was going to regret all this in the morning.

He rose carefully from his chair and set his drink on a small table. "I do hope I have satisfied your curiosities," he said, giving them a formal, somewhat listing bow. "Now I am afraid I must retire for the evening. I will need to get an early start in the morning if my coachman, Nancy, is to return me to the loving arms of my ghost before nightfall. And so good night, gentlemen."

He had made it to his bedroom and begun to undress with the ineffectual help of Dickie—standing in for the recovering Underhill—when there came a quick knock on the door, followed immediately by the appearance of Rhys.

Alex raised an eyebrow at his cousin. "I believe the ritual is for the knocker to await a response from the knockee before opening the door. Or were you longing to see me in my drawers?" he said, standing up and stepping out of his trousers.

"You'd have to pay me," Rhys said. "It's a sight that could frighten horses."

Alex pretended to look down at his drawers in wonder. "I had not realized I was so impressive."

Dickie snickered, reminding Alex he was still there. "You go on to bed," he told the boy. "My dear cousin will make certain I am tucked safely to sleep."

When the boy had gone, Rhys lost no time in coming to the point. "Alex, what's happening to you? Do you have any idea how crazy you sounded in there?"

"Crazy as a bedbug," Alex said, and sat on the edge of the bed to remove his socks. The room tilted and swayed around him, and he felt a hiccup of bile in his throat. He grimaced and swallowed it down. "Mad . . . as . . . a . . . hatter," he said, pulling off his sock and letting his foot drop to the floor with a thud. He looked up at Rhys. "They say if you know you sound crazy, then you aren't."

"You're not crazy, but from the sound of it you're treading a path that may take you to the edge."

"Ah. So she did tell you."

"About the kiss, or whatever it was? Of course. She was pale as candle wax when she described it. I had to hold her for an hour until her shaking stopped."

"How nice for you."

"Damn it, Alex! Will you be serious for just a moment? This is not a joke. You are playing around with something very dangerous."

Alex undid the cuffs and neck of his shirt and pulled it over his head, tossing the garment toward a chair. It hit the side and slid to the floor. It looked very comfortable there.

"I don't want to tell you how to live your life—"

"Much appreciated," Alex mumbled.

"But if I were in your shoes, I would hope that you would try to slap some sense into me. Don't tell me you wouldn't be concerned if I showed every sign of becoming obsessed by an affair with a ghost."

"It's not as if she were a monster," Alex said.

"Like hell she's not!"

"True, she has been known to go bump in the night, but she's stopped that now. I'm teaching her to read."

"Will you ask her to pour tea next?"

Alex frowned. "I don't think she eats."

Rhys let out a cry of frustration, throwing his hands up into the air. He took several breaths, then placed his hands on his hips and stared seriously at Alex. Alex returned the frown, trying to look attentive.

"However real she seems to you," Rhys said, "she is still a ghost. She is *not* a living woman. I don't know where she came from or where she's going, and neither do you. You don't know what she wants from you, or what she might do to get it."

Alex widened his eyes in mock terror. "You don't mean she's after my virtue?"

Rhys shook his head in disgust. "Go to bed. I'd forgotten what a jackass you can be when you drink."

"Yes, Mother."

When Rhys had gone Alex forced himself to get up and use the water closet, then blew out the lamps on the way back to bed. He all but collapsed onto the mattress, pulling the covers up around him, too tired to crawl beneath them.

A scant two hours later he awoke, his dry tongue stuck to the roof of his mouth, his bladder protesting. He rolled off the bed and went to relieve himself and

271

get a glass of water from the nightstand, then got back into bed the proper way.

This time sleep would not come so easily. He was still half-drunk, but clearheaded enough to know that he had not been as far into his cups as he had allowed himself to pretend in the billiards room, and then later with Rhys. His cousin was right. He *was* a jackass when he drank, as if the whiskey gave him license to be the bastard he rarely was in normal life. The truth was, he had been in the mood to be obnoxious, and had needed an excuse to act on it.

He stared into the unremitting dark, absent of any presence but his own. Even in his facetious words to the other men, there had been an element of truth. He wanted Serena in his bed. He'd been fighting against that desire for three interminable weeks, and the battle had made him bad-tempered.

Enough of being noble. What was the point of it all, anyway? He was unhappy; she was probably unhappy; it did no one any good.

If she wanted his body, she could have it.

Chapter Twenty

Serena stood in the corner bastion, practicing the moves of swordplay that her brothers had taught her. *Parry, thrust, retreat, lunge. Whack, chop off an arm. Slice, off with his head.* She held her imaginary sword before her, picturing Woding standing motionless with fright.

"But darling," he would say. "You know I care for you. I truly needed to be gone for three weeks. I missed you the entire time, and regret going. Please, can't we kiss and make up?"

"You're a lying, scum-sucking, dog-licking bit of scrunge wiped from a pig's trotters," she said to the imaginary Woding. "Death would be too good for you. So take that!" she said, and stabbed at him, the sword piercing his thigh.

The pretend Woding slapped a hand over the wound. "Ow!" he cried. "That hurts."

"Good! Take that!" she said again, and poked the

blade between his ribs, puncturing a lung. "And that! And that!" She stabbed him full of holes, leaving small wounds dripping blood down his neat clothing.

"Ow! Ow! Ow!" Woding said, dropping to his knees and cowering, his arms crossed protectively above his head. "Please stop! Forgive me! You're beautiful and wonderful, and I was an idiot to go away. I am not good enough for you. Please let me kiss the hem of your gown," he said, crawling toward her.

"Kiss my shoe," she ordered.

He did so, bending low to press his lips against the toe of her worn leather shoe.

"Now you may kiss my hem."

He obeyed.

"Kiss my knees."

Still kneeling, he pressed a kiss against each of her knees through the cloth.

"My hand."

He took her hand, kissing the back of it, and then turning it over and pressing his face into her palm. One by one he undid the tight buttons that went up the side of her arm, his lips touching each new inch of skin as it was exposed.

"Damn it all," Serena complained to herself, and pulled her hand away from the imaginary Woding. He and the sword vanished as she banished the fantasy.

"What are you looking at?" she asked Otto, who lay on the sun-warmed stones, watching her. Since the day the shadow had come after her, the Great Dane had lost his fear of her, even taking on a protective role. The slavering beast probably thought he was better than her now. *How humiliating.*

Not half so humiliating, however, as being left by that bastard Woding after he'd had his hand on her most private of places, making her thrust and moan against him. Oh, God, she'd never be able to bury the shame of that. It had felt so *good* at the time. How could he have been so unaffected?

She must have done something wrong. She must have repulsed him by her reaction, or maybe she smelled bad. Whatever it was, he had been eager enough to get away the next morning.

The worst of it was, as angry as she was at him for abandoning her, she wanted him back. She wanted to feel his hand on her again, his mouth on her breasts, his lips on her neck. She wanted him to slip his finger inside her again, and bring her to that place of passion she had only guessed at having existed, too afraid to have explored her body on her own.

Damn the man. And damn her own body and its desires. She'd think being a ghost would be some protection against such things.

She left the bastion and continued around the lower wall walkway, making the round she had made several times a day for the past three weeks. She wandered the halls of the castle; she wandered as far as she could in the tunnel; and she wandered the path in her garden. There was nothing to do but think about Woding and worry about a reappearance of le Gayne. There wasn't even anyone left at the castle worth frightening. The only males were Ben Flury and his grandson John, and she cared too much for her garden to distress them in any way.

Otto followed her as she headed back to the garden, as he had been following her on most of her wanderings these past weeks. He was probably hoping to get a better chance at catching Beezely, the stupid hound.

The garden gate was open, Ben's gardening tools on

the path. She soon found the gardener and his grandson putting into place a stone bench near her cherry tree. She watched as they finished, and then they sat on the bench to enjoy the fruits of their labors. John looked up at the branches of the old tree, frowning.

"Shouldn't we cut off those dead branches? They don't look very good. The whole tree looks in sad shape. Maybe we should cut it down."

Serena's eyes went wide. She would strangle the boy before she'd let him touch her tree. Her heart started to race and a sweat broke out over her skin. They would not touch her tree!

"Not without Mr. Woding's say-so," Ben answered, stopping Serena where she had begun to move forward. "He wants to reproduce it, if he can. Which reminds me, I should be making a cutting soon. We'll have to find a suitable sapling on which to graft it."

"We'd better hurry," John said, looking up at the cherry. "It doesn't look like it's going to survive much longer. It didn't look this bad at the beginning of the summer, did it? I can't remember."

"No. But trees can surprise you. They can keep a spark of life long past when you're certain it's gone."

Serena went to her tree and laid her hand against its trunk, hoping Ben's words were true. Well over half the branches were dead, the leaves shriveled and brown where they still clung at all. She had been taking a terrible toll, what with her reading lessons and her touches exchanged with Woding. Had it been worth it?

It took only a moment to know the answer. *Yes.* Even the anger and humiliation she felt now, the lust and yearning, the distrust and confusion, it was all worth it. It made her feel alive. She would gladly trade another five centuries of merely existing for one more day of feeling that she lived. Well, make that one week of feeling that she lived. If it was all she was going to get, she wanted as much of it as possible.

Ben soon set John to work pruning one of the vines that grew against the wall. The older man knelt down beside one of the beds and started weeding and removing dead plants, a task that seemed never to end. Serena sat on the new bench and watched them, having nothing better to do. Also, she'd grown fond of Ben and his quiet ways.

A minute later a clatter of wheels and hooves in the courtyard drew her attention, and Otto's ears suddenly perked up. He was instantly up and galloping out the gateway. Serena's heart fluttered in her chest.

Woding. He was home.

"A, B, C, D," Serena recited under her breath, "E, F, G." Night had fallen, and still she had not summoned the courage to face Woding. With his ability to see her when no one else could, it was impossible for her to spy on him, which she thought was a most lamentable circumstance.

She hadn't greeted him upon his return because she didn't want him to know how impatient she had been to have him back. Neither did she want him to know how angry she had been at his leaving, how hurt. Going to him for a resumption of her reading lessons was the only plausible, unembarrassing excuse to see him she could think of.

Perhaps she had waited long enough. She would not appear eager, and she would not seem to be avoiding him. She moved through the house, checked his room, then headed for his study in the tower.

She found him at his desk, papers spread before him

but his eyes focused on something in the distance, unseen by any eye but his own. It was only a moment before he saw her.

"Serena!" he said, jumping up and coming around the desk toward her. "Where have you been? I was hoping to see you the moment I arrived."

She looked at him sideways, not trusting this enthusiasm, and not certain what to make of it. Glad to see her, was he? "I was working on my letters," she said, stepping around him and going to the desk, pretending to look at the papers there. "Did you have a good trip?"

"Good enough," he said, coming back toward her. She saw from the corner of her eye that he was going to put his hands on her shoulders, so she stepped away to the side, and went to the window to look out at the night.

"You're upset, aren't you?" he asked, speaking to her back.

"Whatever do you mean?" She turned and raised an eyebrow innocently. "Upset? Of course not. You're back, and I'm very happy."

"No, you're not. You're angry as a wounded boar with me for leaving you so suddenly."

"I do not know of what you speak," she said haughtily. "I'm sure I barely noticed your absence."

"How foolish of me to have been concerned!" he said, and she could not miss the irritation in his tone. "In that case, I certainly do not need to offer you any apology." He sat down again and picked up a paper, studiously ignoring her.

The horrible man. She stood for several long, silent minutes, waiting for him to ask her again what was wrong. He sat there, shuffling papers, glancing at her once or twice but showing no interest in her pout.

She wanted to kick him. He was supposed to force her to accept his apology, not sit idly by leaving her to ask for it herself. She wanted groveling! Agonies of regret! She wanted him to suffer.

He began to hum under his breath, a jaunty little tune that she recognized, and then he softly sang the words.

> "There were three ravens sat on a tree,
> Down a down, hay down, hay down,
> There were three ravens sat on a tree,
> With a down."

"Why are you singing that?" she asked sharply.

"Excuse me?" he said, looking up from his papers.

"That song."

He hummed a few bars. "I don't know," he said. "I don't even know the name of it. I've had it stuck in my head for weeks now. Why, do you recognize it?"

"Don't sing it anymore."

"Why not? I rather like it. I wish I knew the rest of the words. " 'There were three ravens—' " he sang.

She hurried over to him and put her hand over his mouth, her flesh becoming solid in order to silence him. "Don't sing it, Woding," she said threateningly.

He took her hand and pulled it down from his mouth. "Or what? You're going to give me the cold shoulder again?"

She tried to jerk her hand out of his grip, but he tightened his hold and then yanked her off balance, tumbling her into his lap. She grabbed for his shoulders to steady herself, and found herself exactly where she wanted to be: wrapped in his arms.

"It's about time you found an excuse to come to me," he said.

279

"It wasn't an excuse. I loathe that song. It brings up all manner of unpleasant recollection."

"Like what?" he asked, brushing his cheek lightly against her own, his mouth near her ear.

"It doesn't matter."

"Tell me," he said, and nibbled her earlobe. His hand went to the side of her rib cage, gently massaging her flesh.

"Not now."

"I want to know what goes on in that mind of yours," he said, and moved his hand up to cup her breast, his thumb rubbing over her nipple.

"Ah, I cannot think," she said, her eyes going half-shut. His hand and lips felt so good, so very good. Her disgruntlement with him got shunted away, unimportant compared to continuing this pleasure. She was tired of being angry, anyway.

He slid his arm beneath her knees and stood, lifting her in his arms. She clung tightly to his neck, feeling his muscles flexing against her weight. Embarrassed by her size, she made herself less substantial to lighten the load.

"Stop that," Woding said. "I want to feel you as a solid woman."

She did as he bade, and he kissed her on the forehead and then released her legs, allowing her to stand, pressed up against him, her arms still around his neck. His hands went down to her buttocks, and he molded them in his palms, pulling and shaping them as he pressed his hips against hers. She opened her mouth and kissed him, playing with his lips as he had played with hers, and pressing herself against the ridge of hardness she felt against her belly.

He parted from her and took her hand, leading her out

the door and down the stairs. She followed willingly, albeit with her heart beating rapidly in her chest. She knew he was taking her to his bedroom, to repeat what he had done there before, and perhaps more. She felt the urgency in his strength as he led her, and knew that he would be asking more of her this time.

The thought frightened her, and that same fear sent ripples of excitement through her body. Each tug on her hand was a message that he wanted her, and that if she did not protest too hardily he would be having her.

They came to his room and he kicked the door shut behind them, pulling her to the edge of the bed.

"I want to see you naked," he told her, and releasing her hand he stepped back, his eyes roving over the length of her body.

She crossed her arms, holding them tight against her chest. "You first."

He shook his head. "You've seen me dozens of times. Fair is fair. It's your turn." He sat in the chair beside the bed and gazed at her. "Undress for me, Serena. Let me see you unadorned, as God made you."

" 'Twould be indecent!"

"I would enjoy it very much."

She shifted from one foot to the other, trying to find a way through her conflicting emotions. It went against all habit and experience for her to willingly bare her body before the eyes of a man: the very thought was mortifying. And yet part of her wanted to do it, wanted to be wanton as a whore and flaunt her body to him, if she could be certain that his reaction would be lust and not laughter.

"It will give you pleasure?" she asked.

"Did it give you pleasure to watch me take a bath?" he asked back.

She kicked off her shoes in answer.

"Slowly, Serena," he chided softly.

She put her hands to the clasp of her golden girdle, feeling suddenly unfamiliar with the task of undressing. How did one do such a basic thing slowly, and in a manner more erotic than mundane? "I have not undressed for a very long time," she admitted. She had not removed her clothes in all the time that she had been a ghost. There had been no reason to, for they remained as clean as they were the day she died.

"If you forget how, I'll be glad to help," he said, and smiled.

She smiled back, reassured slightly that he did want to see her. She unclasped the girdle, holding one end as the chain fell from around her hips with a quiet, rippling series of clinks, then pulled the girdle through her other hand, as if playing with a snake. She felt a bit foolish, but a quick glimpse at Alex showed that he was watching every move.

She coiled the girdle around her hand, then let it slide off into a neat circle on the corner of the bed. She put one foot up on the edge of the mattress and slowly pulled up her skirts, past her knee, where her woolen stocking was tied in place with a worn garter. She pulled on the edge of the bow, loosening the knot, then dropped the garter atop the coiled girdle. She slanted a look at Alex, then inched the stocking down her calf, past her ankle, and lifted her foot off the bed to push it down over her heel and off her toes.

She was distracted momentarily by the sight of her own feet, and checked them over to be certain there were no unseemly spots. They looked remarkably good, considering the length of time they had been untended. She repeated the stocking routine with her other leg, then stood facing Alex.

There was a faint smile curling his lips, and his eyes were gleaming.

She knew of no attractive way to remove the white surcoat, so she did it in the usual way, straight over her head. She folded it neatly once it was off, the silk garment still precious to her as a link to her mother.

She stood before him in her tight pink underdress, and one by one undid the buttons that molded the material around her forearms, still feeling embarrassed but beginning to enjoy the look in Alex's eye. When that task was complete, she swept her hair around to one side, twisting it over her right shoulder to hang down her chest, and then went to Alex and turned her back to him.

"I cannot reach the lacings," she told him. It was only partially true. She had managed well enough on her own in the past, but it didn't seem to fit the mood to twist awkwardly in front of him, her arms bent at unnatural angles as she struggled with the cords.

He stood to untie the knot, and she could hear his breathing as his fingers worked at the cord, then loosened it as it crisscrossed down her back.

"Thank you," she said, stepping away. She looked at him over her shoulder, commanding him with her eyes to resume his seat.

His smile was crooked and rueful this time. "You are growing sure of yourself," he said, sitting down.

She flashed her eyebrows up and down, a saucy response requiring no words. She flipped her hair back behind her, and with it concealing most of her body she pulled the underdress down over her shoulders, off her arms, then down past her hips, letting it drop to the floor.

The cool air of the room sank through her thin linen

chemise, the loose garment all that she wore now. She stood still, her body unaccustomed to freedom from the tight heaviness of her dress. She raised her arms to the side, no wool pulling at the movement, the chemise unsticking from her body, the creases falling loose. Her breasts felt weighty on her chest, unsupported and unbound, and she could feel the cool air rising up her chemise, drying the slight dampness beneath them.

She reached up to the thin ribbon drawstring below her collarbone and tugged it loose. Already low on her shoulders, the chemise gave in to its own weight, the neckline gaping wide and sliding off her body. It caught for a moment over her wrists and hips, and she brushed it past, the garment falling to join its sister around her feet.

Her chin rose, her lips curling in a smile, her eyes narrowing like a cat's as she felt her body nude in the air for the first time in hundreds of years. She did not need to look down to know that her breasts were still high and full with youth, her limbs long and strong, supple with muscle and the layer of silken fat that she had not completely lost, despite the deprivations of her last months alive.

She forgot that she was taller than she was supposed to be, bigger boned, stronger than a lady, and felt instead the glorious freedom of a butterfly emerging from its cocoon. She spread her arms, like wings drying in the sun, and felt the stretch of unencumbered muscles.

She let her arms float back down to her sides, and then, her chin high, turned to Alex, feeling her hair brushing at her shoulders and buttocks.

"Good God in heaven," he said beneath his breath, and rose to his feet. His hands held a fine tremor as he reached out to touch her, his palms over her breasts. He stepped closer, kissing her lightly on the lips, putting his face beside hers, his breath touching her cheek, then her neck. He laid light kisses on her shoulder, then cupped her breast in his hand, holding it as if raising water from a stream to drink.

She put her own hand on the back of his shoulder to balance herself as he laved her breast with his tongue, making her unsteady on her feet. His other hand went down around her hip to her buttock, stroking and massaging. The pressure of his mouth on her breast had her arching backward, and she brought her other hand around to his shoulders as well, afraid she would fall over. Her legs began to quiver.

"You, too, Alex," she said hoarsely to him. He moved his kisses up her neck, the pressure harder as he held her close to him, pressing her naked hips against his clothed ones. "Let me see *you* naked," she said, and brought her hands around to his chest, sliding them inside his jacket and pushing it to the sides.

He stepped back and yanked at his clothes, showing none of the slow deliberation he had asked of her. Her body tingled as she saw each bit of his body unwrapped, knowing that it soon would be pressed against hers, skin to skin. Her lips crooked as he hopped on one foot, removing stockings, her own reaction surprising her. She had not thought there would be room in her for humor during lovemaking.

The smile lasted but a moment, as that was all it took for him to divest himself of the remainder of his clothing. Her eyes moved down his body, familiar to her yet not, its angles and lines endlessly fascinating and new. Her gaze came to rest on his manhood, engorged and pointing upward toward her. She felt a flush of answering wetness deep within her, a contraction of muscles that said her body knew where he belonged.

She closed the short distance between them, her arms going lightly around his chest, and they held each other, their bodies lightly touching. She looked into his dark sapphire eyes, level with hers, as he gazed back, holding her eyes with his own for several long moments. It reminded her of when they had passed through each other in the hall, each learning the nuances of the other's soul—only this time it was an intentional learning, anchored in what was real and possible.

She broke their gaze and closed her eyes, laying her head upon his shoulder, her face tucked into his neck. She could feel the hair on his chest brushing her breasts and nipples, a soft tickling that made her move against him, increasing the sensation. He laid his own head against hers, his hands going up and down her back, stroking her, calming her remaining nerves at the same time he aroused her. His manhood was a warm rod against her lower abdomen, his thighs strong and rough with hair against her own smooth legs, scissored between them.

Some primal part of her knew that this was right, this was how a man and a woman should be together, skin to skin, body to body. Clothing and the shyness that went with it were mere obstacles to overcome.

As if given some silent cue, they separated and went to the bed. Alex took her folded clothes and set them on the chair, then pulled back the covers, revealing the clean sheets, their bare whiteness a silent invitation.

The truth of what she was about to do began to send sharp jabs of nervousness through Serena. She had no cares at this moment for what was morally right or wrong; it was the sheer vulnerability of laying her body open to the intimate touches of a man that made her hesitate, a quiver working through her nerves to betray her hesitation.

As if sensing that she needed help in making that motion of acceptance, Alex wrapped her in his arms again, and kissed her gently on the lips. His lips caught and released hers, distracting and soothing her as he pulled her with him slowly down onto the bed, his hands stroking over her back and down her buttocks to her thighs.

She let him persuade her, let him take charge, needing the assurance that he knew what he was doing and would guide her.

She lay beside him, feeling him shift as he shoved the covers down to the foot of the bed; then, with his arms around her, he rolled her on top of him, her thighs parting over his. Her hair draped in a curtain around their faces as she lifted her head to look down at him.

"Kiss me, Serena," he told her.

She obeyed, tilting her head to the side and lowering her mouth to his, mimicking the gentle way he had kissed her. Alex shivered.

He broke away then and moved her body up until her breasts were near his mouth. She supported herself on her elbows as he reached down and let his fingertips play with her from behind, stroking her lightly, and the pleasure of it made her forget the awkwardness of the position and turn her cheek against the crown of his head. Her lips parted as she breathed, her eyelids shut. All her concentration was on those fingertips, and the swirling, stroking patterns they made on her. She felt him touch the opening to her core, his fingertip gently exploring the sensitive, untried flesh.

He rolled her onto her back again, and kissed his way down her body, swirling his tongue in her navel, making her smile at the playfulness of the gesture. She loved the look of the top of his head, the black waves of his hair so dark against her skin. She brought her hands down to run them through his hair as he trailed kisses over her stomach, making her squirm with the sensation.

The part of her that burned with need for him was pressed against his chest, and she could feel the top of her sex rubbing against his skin as he moved, the friction rough with his chest hair. She liked the way she was hidden against him, and yet so intimately revealed.

He slid lower, and her eyes widened as he lifted her thighs over his shoulders, his face between them. She squirmed, embarrassed, but he held her still, looking up at her from between her legs, commanding her with his eyes to submit.

"Alex, please," she pleaded, feeling exposed.

He looked down at her, and she felt his fingers parting her folds, moving aside the curls that covered her, the air cool on her damp warmth. She closed her eyes and turned her head to the side, unable to watch.

Suddenly a warm, wet touch stroked her, and her eyes came open. The stroke came again, then centered on her most sensitive point, an infusion of liquid heat surrounding the working of that magical touch. She looked down, seeing only the top of Alex's head, but knowing now that it was his mouth he used on her, exchanging kisses with her sex as he had with her mouth.

Thoughts of embarrassment fled from her mind as his tongue and lips massaged and suckled her, the sensations overwhelming her ability to think or feel anything but pleasure. She dropped her head back down, her eyes closed, her neck arching. She didn't care what he did to her, as long as he kept on doing this.

The pleasure built inside her, making her strain her muscles against him, as if reaching for that peak she knew existed. Just when she was sure it was in sight, he took his mouth from her.

She wanted to protest, but already he was moving up her body, his hips holding her thighs wide. He rested one elbow beside her, and with his other hand brushed a few stray hairs back from her face. He looked into her eyes, then reached down between them, and a moment later she felt something hard and blunt pressing against her.

Alex kissed her gently on the mouth, and she was aware of her own faintly salty, woodsy scent on his skin. When he raised his head, he looked into her eyes again, as if asking her to trust him, to stay there with him as he completed this act they had begun. She clung to that look, keeping her own eyes wide open as he pressed harder against her, her body reluctant to open to this new force.

She felt a burning pain as he pushed his way inside her, and clenched her jaw hard against it. He held still, half in her, and kissed her cheeks, her eyelids, and then her mouth. He pulled out slightly, then moved back inside her, deeper this time. The hand that had been directing his manhood moved up to tease at the nub of her sex, creating new pleasure to mix with the pain of his entry.

She didn't know whether she wanted him to stop or to continue, his fingers creating a maddening desire in her for the blunt force that was burning its way inside her. The stretching discomfort of his entry was somehow also the answer to the tingling desire roused by his fingers.

As she gradually grew accustomed to him within her, he began to move more easily, his thrusts longer and faster. His hand left her, his weight coming down on both arms now on either side of her. He shifted his hips, moving them up her body slightly to a new angle, and slowed his strokes. She found herself moving against him, his position allowing her to massage her most sensitive places against him, the discomfort not absent but mingled with the pleasure.

She wrapped her arms around his back, and entwined her legs with his, joining him stroke for stroke, her muscles tensing once again in pursuit of the peak. His thrusts grew fast and hard, and she urged him on with her fingers digging into his back, her hips rising to meet him.

He reached down and touched her, setting her off just before he himself reached his own peak. He clasped her to him, squeezing her tightly as he held himself within her, his mouth finding hers and kissing her frantically between gasping breaths. She felt the pulsing waves of his release in her delicate flesh, the waves mingling with the rhythmic contractions of her own pleasure.

"Serena," he said into her hair, still holding tight, and then he relaxed on top of her, his weight greater than she had expected, pressing her down into the mattress. A moment later he rolled to his side, taking her with him. He was still inside her. "I didn't mean to crush you," he whispered.

"You didn't," she said equally softly. "If you have not noticed, I am not a fragile little thing."

He smiled and kissed her. She felt his manhood begin to withdraw from her, softening now that it was spent. It was a peculiar sensation, and when she wriggled slightly it came all the way free, nestling between them as she tucked one of her thighs between his. They rested that way, the silence between them warm and full.

"You are bold and beautiful," he said to her when their sweat had dried and their breathing slowed, and he kissed the scar on her forehead, where it began.

"Not that," she said, tucking her face down.

"Yes, that, too. It makes you look rather like a pirate. Did I ever tell you that when I was a boy I had a fascination with pirates? Especially female ones."

"I know nothing of pirates," she whispered.

"If you tell me about your scar, I will tell you about them."

She reached up and pulled the pillow more comfortably under her cheek, where it rested on Alex's arm. She still felt the hesitation in her chest that had kept her from speaking of the scar, but it was not so strong now. He had seen it and wanted her anyway. She could not believe that indifference completely, but it was so much better than loathing that it seemed worth the risk to talk of it.

"I was training with my brothers in the use of swords, and in fighting. I didn't enjoy it much—have you ever been near a true swordfight, or a battle?"

"No, fortunately not. Only fencing done more as an art than for practical use."

"Then perhaps you do not know how frightening it is, the clash of metal on metal, and sharp edges swinging through the air, wielded by a powerful arm. You sense how vulnerable your flesh is, how easy it would be to become seriously injured in even a mock fight."

"Why were you joining in? Surely your family did not expect that of you."

"No, of course not, not if they stopped to think about it. They sometimes seemed to have forgotten, however, that I was not male. I think they looked more on me as an untried youth than as a girl, and they teased and competed with me as if I were one of them, only a very poor specimen with peculiar habits and weak arms. My father

291

remembered my gender only when he thought of possible alliances he might make by marrying me off."

"What of your mother?"

"She died when I was very young. It was largely a household of men, with the occasional serving wench or spinning woman thrown in, and I am afraid I did not do much to encourage their motherly attentions. I saw soon enough that favor fell to the strong, not the weak."

"And so the sword practice," he said.

"Yes. My brothers were usually somewhat more careful with me than with each other. They would knock me down and thwack me cheerily enough, but deep down something kept them from doing me any serious harm. I was as tall as or taller than most of them, a circumstance that made it all the more amusing for them to see me eating dirt when I tried to play at their games.

"One thing at which I excelled, however, was archery. On a hot, sunny afternoon, after he had called me a clumsy cow one too many times, I challenged William to a match. He was the second oldest, and had a fearsome pride."

"You beat him," Alex predicted.

"Oh, yes. To the cheering and jeering of half the keep. One of his arrows had missed the target entirely, while I had one of those days of marksmanship where it seems that no arrow can fly wrong. Even so, I was tired by the end, for he had insisted on going two out of three, three out of five, and on and on until the humiliation of it became too great.

"All was fine that night, although William was more sullen than usual, quieter. He was not one to take the jibes of others well.

"The next day on the practice field, he insisted on being my training partner, although I was admittedly poor with a sword. However much practice I had, I could not be as strong as any of my brothers, and my arm tired quickly."

She shrugged within Alex's arms. "William wanted to prove that he was better than I was. In swordplay it would have taken little for him to do so, but with his anger from the day before he lost that care that even he usually had with me. In his determination to best me, he accidentally struck me upon the face."

"Accidentally?" Alex asked doubtfully.

She snuggled more closely against him. " 'Tis perhaps part of why I do not like to speak of it, the thought that my own brother may have scarred me on purpose, to teach me a lesson in humiliation."

"What happened to him?"

"He was scolded soundly by Father. But then so was I, for being so stupid as to try to fight him, and for getting myself a scar that would make it that much more difficult to wed me. Years later I watched William die . . . during the Pestilence. With his last words, he cursed that I should be the one besting him yet again, by surviving."

He kissed her on the forehead. "We should have exchanged houses, you and I. I thought I was in hell surrounded by nagging, primping, manipulating girls who would rather I had been a caged canary than a brother."

"Is that why you had a household of men here?"

"It was an experiment meant to produce peace and quiet. I had not, of course, counted upon you."

She smiled, recalling the uproar she had caused.

"Do you want to hear about the pirates now?" he asked, stifling a yawn.

She stroked her fingers along his side, enjoying the

lazy feel of their embrace. "You can tell me later," she said. "Sleep now, if you want."

He smiled and his eyes closed, and within minutes she heard his breathing deepen. A lassitude was creeping through her own limbs, but it had nothing to do with sleep. She had remained "real" for far longer than she usually did, draining energy, and there was not much time left in her tree for her to squander. She felt warm and secure in his arms, but it was a comfort she would have to dole out to herself in sparing portions.

She gave him one last kiss upon the lips, and faded from his arms into the oblivion that was her only form of rest.

Chapter Twenty-one

When Serena roused, she found herself standing in the garden, as she always did when she came back to the conscious world. She was not certain how long she had been drifting in the realm of nothingness as she tried to let her tree recoup some of its losses. That nowhere world was as timeless as it was formless.

The season had already stripped the tree of its leaves, so they could give her no clue to its state. She ran her hands over the trunk, and felt that there was still a pulse of life within it: not as strong as it had once been, but neither quite as feeble as it had been after she had slept with Alex.

She had no precise gauge for these things, but she doubted she would be able to expend herself in such a way more than two or three times more. What would happen then, she did not know.

The garden looked far closer to winter dormancy than

it had when last she'd seen it, and a frisson of worry went up her spine. Had she been out for only days, or was it weeks that had passed? What would Alex be thinking?

She made her way quickly to the castle, noting that night was falling. She went through the kitchen, pausing briefly to observe the staff assembled for the evening meal.

Underhill appeared fully recovered from his ordeal, not even the trace of a bruise remaining. Nancy sat across from him, but kept her eyes on her food, not returning any of his longing gazes. A quick glance under the table confirmed, however, that Nancy's stockinged foot rested quietly atop Underhill's own.

Marcy and Dickie sat side by side, and he looked pleased with himself, while Marcy looked decidedly pouty. She leaned away when Dickie stretched across her to reach the bowl of potatoes.

Mrs. Hutchins ate her dinner as if it were fuel for work, and nothing more. Serena caught her sending a supervisory glance at her niece and Underhill, checking that all was in order.

Otto, who had been lying by the fire, saw her and got up, padding after her into the hallway. As she reached the stairs in the main entry hall, she spotted Beezely napping upon a step halfway up. Otto barked once, and the cat's eyes popped open.

Beezely stretched, his claws coming out, his eyes closing tight as his mouth gaped wide, needle-sharp teeth displayed as he tilted his head back. Otto woofed again, his tail wagging. Beezely stretched out on the stair, lying on his side, the tip of his tail flicking negligently.

Otto's own tail slowed like an unpowered pendulum,

finally resting at midpoint. He whined impatiently, shifting. Beezely rolled onto his back and started to purr.

"Give it up," Serena told the dog. "He's not in the mood to be your prey today."

Otto galloped up the stairs to the feline, putting his jowly face down to him. Beezely licked his cheek and Otto withdrew, sneezing dramatically.

Serena left them to continue on their own, and went first to the dining room, and then to the tower. There she finally found Alex poring over his papers, his hair a rumpled mess, testament to the fingers that had run repeatedly through it. In a glass dish on his desk were several dozen burned wooden matches.

"Alex," she said, in the voice that he could hear.

His head jerked up, and then he shoved back from his desk, his chair falling over behind him as he stood. "Serena! I thought you'd gone."

"I've been resting. I do not judge time well when I do that. How long has it been?" she asked. As he came around the desk she let herself go solid, anticipating his embrace.

"Nearly three weeks. I didn't know what to think," he said, stopping in front of her.

He looked too surprised to do anything but stare, so she closed the distance herself, wrapping her arms around his rigid body and laying her head against his shoulder. "I'm sorry," she said. "I did not know so much time had passed. It tires me to be real, and I must rest." It was the truth, although not the whole of it. She did not want to tell him of the dying tree, and her tie to it. It would destroy the time she had left.

"You should have told me," he said, his arms finally coming up and holding her in a tentative hug. "I didn't know what to think when I woke and all trace of you was gone. Your clothes, your shoes—even any stain of blood. For a moment I thought I had dreamed it all."

"I won't go away so long again," she said. "I lost track of time, is all."

"I should not have tired you so."

"Don't say that," she said, touching his lips with her fingertips. "It is the most wonderful tired I have ever felt. I would not give up a moment of it." And it was true. She would have to ration what time she had left, ration what she could share with him through touch, but it was worth the cost.

He smiled, but there was something uncertain in his eyes, and he released her and moved slightly away. Her own happiness at returning faltered as she realized he was holding back, and she went immaterial again, conserving strength. She stepped over to his desk. "Tell me what you have been working on while I was away," she said, running her fingers over his papers. If he was talking, maybe she could subdue this painful tightness in her throat that said he did not seem entirely happy to see her.

"You must have little interest in that."

"On the contrary," she said, going around the desk to where she could look at his charts right-side up. "I want to know what occupies your mind, and I very much enjoyed our last conversation about astrology." And she wanted to know what had happened to draw him away from her. Or had he never been as close as she had thought to begin with? Maybe he had been hoping she really would disappear after losing her virginity.

"Astronomy."

"They are the same," she said, not bothering to look up.

"As you will," he said.

She heard the hint of humor in his voice, and a little of the tightness loosened. If she could amuse him, then at least he did not hate her. "Why the dish full of spent matches?" she asked. Matches were one of the more wonderful new things she had seen since Maiden Castle was rebuilt. She would like to strike and burn a hundred of them herself, but she doubted that the delight of such a novelty had been Alex's motivation.

"It was a thought I had while lighting a lamp in the dark," Alex said. "Here, let me show you." He picked up a new match, then blew out the oil lamp that had been burning on his desk. She saw him look at her and frown. "You can still see me, can't you?"

"As well as I suppose you can see me," she said, remembering what he had said about how she seemed to glow. "Or perhaps better."

"Well, pretend all is dark, as dark as the night sky. You see stars burning at their appointed places, and perhaps you see a sliver of moon near the horizon, but all else is blackness. Nothing moves. You see nothing approaching, and then . . ." He scraped the match across a striking plate, and the head burst into flame. "There, did you see it?"

"I see it," she said. "I do not understand your point, but I do see the flame."

He snapped his hand, waving out the match, and dropped it in the dish with its siblings, then brought out a fresh one. "Not the flame," he said. "It is the moments before." He again struck the match against the plate, a trifle more slowly and weakly this time, causing the head to spark where it scraped along, but not to catch fire. "There, you see?" he asked excitedly.

"I see no flame."

"But did you see the fraction of a second before there was no flame?"

"The spark?" she asked.

"The sparks." He repeated the demonstration. "Do you see?"

"It looks a little like a glowing streak."

"Yes! What if what we see as a streak of light across our sky is something similar to what we see when we strike a match across a rough surface? What if it is the heat of friction causing something to catch fire, and then burn its way across the heavens?"

"But what is the match head, and what does it strike against?" Serena asked. "There is nothing up there."

"There are planets and stars and comets, and pieces of them sometimes fall to earth. In 1803 just such a stone was seen to fall from the sky, near a village in France. That is the match head."

"But then rocks should be falling upon us every time we see a star fall, and such is not the case."

"Perhaps they are too small. Perhaps they are no bigger than the head of this match, and burn themselves into nothing before they can reach the ground."

"And against what does it burn?"

"The very air we breathe."

She chortled. "I think not."

"Have you never felt the wind blow upon you with such force that it was as if something solid pushed you? What is wind but air? It can wear away mountains, given enough time. It is possible, Serena. And look at this," he said excitedly, lighting the lamp and coming around to her side of the desk. He pulled out a star chart with many lines upon it, all intersecting at almost the same point. "I did not see it for so long: my attention was all on numbers and durations and times. I was obsessed with calculations, when simply looking afresh at my own dashes across the chart could have told me so much more. I had these short lines that marked the path of a falling star, and then it struck me that if I extended them, back to whence they came . . . You can see yourself."

"They all come from the same place," Serena said. "Every falling star?"

"No, only those on the same night, or a series of nights one after the other. They all come from the same place in the heavens! Do you see?"

"But what does it mean?"

He ran his hands through his hair. "Ah, well, I don't know about that. I have ideas, but I don't know. I am trying to tie this theory of the striking match to the patterns of when there are showers of falling stars throughout the year. How I wish I had a thousand years' worth of observance to sift through, to find the key. If there is one."

"You make me wish I had paid closer attention to the heavens," she said. "I sought solace in them as something eternal, but cared little for keeping note of what they did."

"There are precious few who have, however long their existence," he said, and gave her a grin. "We all of us look to the sky, but what we each want from it is as different as each man from the other."

She was silent a moment, her mind circling around a new understanding of his nature. "I think that you believe that if you could unravel this mystery, you would be unlocking a secret of the universe. I think you believe that if you could understand this, you could understand what your place is on this earth."

"This is about science, and discovery," he said.

"No," she said, shaking her head slowly, "it's not.

And it's not about losing yourself in the vastness of the heavens, either, like you told me before. It is quite the opposite." She looked into his eyes as she spoke, and saw a puzzlement deep within the sapphire, a puzzlement that was laced with hurt, as of an ancient wound that he barely knew existed.

After a moment he shook his head, breaking their gaze, and turned his attention back to the confusion of papers on his desk. "Whatever it is, 'twill be a long while before I find my satisfaction. I will not be getting any closer to a solution in the next few weeks."

"Why is that?"

He sighed, sitting down and leaning back in his chair. "I have received a letter, most elegantly penned, from dear sister Philippa. She and my sisters Amelia and Constance have elected to visit me, along with their families, and doubtless with a friend or two as well. For all I know, Sophie and Blandamour may join them. They should all be here tomorrow. I've let Rhys and Beth know, and invited them to stay as well, if they dare."

Her lips parted, the corners of her mouth turning the slightest bit down in disappointment.

"Exactly," he said. "We shall have little time to ourselves, and certainly I shall be unable to put to use whatever clear nights we may have."

"But why do you allow them to come?" she could not help asking.

He grimaced. "To repair the damage I myself did. Apparently I did a fair job of convincing them I was dancing on the edge of lunacy, and they are descending en masse to ensure that such is not the case. As I won't go to them, they have decided to come to me."

Serena pulled in her chin, indignant at the idea. "You do not need to be coddled like a baby. You are not mad."

302

He shrugged with one shoulder. " 'Twill make them feel better."

"You are a most generous brother to sacrifice yourself in such a way."

"You are partly to blame for my allowing their visit, you know."

"Me? How?" she asked, appalled.

"It is what you have told me of your own brothers, especially Thomas and William."

"I don't know why any of that should make you wish to have your sisters here."

"Don't you?" he asked, looking at her with a mirror of the same intensity she had used on him. She felt a tingle in her nose, and an ache in the muscles of her face that spoke of long-hidden tears. "You watched them both die," he said. "You lost all your brothers."

"Let be!" she said, feeling the wetness in her eyes.

He cocked his head slightly to the side, and she saw the understanding sympathy in his eyes. "My sisters yet live. However much they annoy me—and they do annoy me greatly—I still care for them. I sometimes forget that."

She wandered over to the telescope, not wanting him to see the jealousy on her face. Whether it was jealousy of the affection he showed for his sisters, or envy that he had living siblings, she was not sure. At this moment she was jealous even of his own living body. He would go on to a normal life, with family and love and laughter, whereas she never would.

She closed her eyes, her own envy making her feel ill. With effort she smothered the sensation and turned to face him again, a false smile on her face. "Enough of this serious talk. Weren't you going to tell me all about pirates?"

"That depends," he said, arching an eyebrow at her. "Are you going to keep your gown on all night?"

She laughed through the remnants of her tears, even as she recognized that an offer of sex from him was not the same as an admission of affection. She knew, however, that she would rather have his body close and his heart far than go back and spend a lonely night in her garden. She had had thousands of lonely nights in her existence already. She needed no more.

She walked toward the tower door, casting what she hoped was a seductive look over her shoulder. "Are you going to sit at your desk all night?"

He was out of his chair and halfway across the room before she had time to react, startling all thoughts of envy and loneliness from her head. For the moment, there were much richer emotions to consider.

Chapter Twenty-two

It was clear enough what was going on. Woding's brother-in-law Harold Tubble, the stupid, red-faced squire, had brought his equally stupid niece Felicia as a marriage prospect.

Serena stood in a shadowy alcove of the music room, watching the assembled guests as Felicia pounded her plump fingers upon the piano keyboard and trilled along with the song. The girl had a bosom it was hard for even a woman to take her eyes from, all pillowy masses of white flesh pushed up over the neckline of her off-the-shoulder evening gown, rippling and jiggling as she moved her arms.

And worst of all, behind the wench on the piano bench, Woding stood adding his own rich baritone to the birdlike chirpings of the girl. There must be a fantastic view of that jellied cleavage from up there, Serena thought. She had not seen him cast even a single glance at her where she stood in the alcove, his attention all on his performance and the bouncing, pink-cheeked Felicia.

The guests had arrived yesterday, spaced over hours, keeping Woding constantly busy. Every spare room was filled, even the servants' quarters, and there seemed to be no place where quiet could be found. People were invading her garden, children running wildly along the paths, jumping off the bench, and falling into the flower beds. They were walking along the lower wall, they were talking in the kitchens, and their noises could be heard in every nook and cranny of every hall and room. Even Woding's tower had been invaded, becoming a lookout for attacking armies or the crow's nest of a ship to the minds of several nieces and nephews, a lantern-wielding troupe of whom had even explored the cellars, in search of the ghost they had all heard about.

She could bear nearly all of it. She was strong. She knew how to endure. It was understandable that Woding needed to direct his attentions to his guests: they did not give him a chance to do otherwise. She also understood that he had been too worn out to do more than hold her as he fell asleep last night. In a way, his attention being given to others had been of help to her, as she had been able to conserve her energies and recover from the quick, playful lovemaking of two nights ago. It had not been as exhausting as that first time, but it had been draining nonetheless.

She could bear nearly all of it, except for Felicia. It was eating her away inside to have that bouncing breeding machine present when there was yet an uncertainty in Woding's feelings for her. The looks exchanged among Woding's sisters and brothers-in-law, the flirtatious sparkle in Felicia's gray-green eyes, the subtle manipulation of seatings and activities to push the two of them together, it was all as corrosive as acid on her heart.

Woding was laughing now with the trollop as the others applauded their duet, and with her plump little hand on his he raised Felicia from the bench so she could curtsy as he bowed. She was a short creature, all hips and bosom, with a squeezed little waist in between. Her thick brown hair reminded Serena of Beth's, but she had none of the intelligence in her eyes that Beth had.

No, Felicia's eyes glittered with imbecilic humor, and a hunger for Woding. Serena's Woding. And Woding let them glitter at him to the girl's heart's content. Was he thinking what that plum pudding of a girl would be like in his bed? Was he thinking of the children he could beget from her fertile loins? Maybe he was thinking of how he could mend the tattered ties with his sisters, by acceding to their obvious wish that he marry a living girl and settle down into family life.

Felicia was a sponge-headed lackwit who would never care about his falling stars or challenge his ways of thinking. Didn't he see that?

The chairs were pushed back to the walls, and Philippa took the place of Felicia at the piano. She ran through a quick series of scales, then started in on a rousing melody, revealing a musical talent that Serena would never have guessed resided in such a stern woman. Soon the lot of them were prancing about the floor, arms catching and swinging, skirts swaying, smiles all around.

Woding protested at first, but soon he, too, was among them, being passed around the women like a new baby to be cooed over by all, and of course most especially by Felicia.

Serena left the room, revolted and sick, angry and

helpless all at once. Woding seemed not to mark her leaving.

In the main entry hall, several of the children, their ages ranging from four to fourteen, were huddled at the foot of the stairs. The blond-haired daughter of Philippa, Louisa, had their attention as she told a story in low, breathy tones, her eyes wide, her hands telling the tale alongside her words.

"And on her wedding night she vowed her husband would never touch her!" Louisa said to the pale little faces all around her.

Serena knew what story the girl told, the same way a young Rhys had told a tale to Woding, the same way countless other children had told each other tales over the years, to frighten one another in the ruins of Maiden Castle. She felt an urge to make herself visible to them, preferably with a dagger dripping blood in one hand, le Gayne's severed head in the other. *That* would give them something to whisper about under the covers at night.

She resisted the urge, never having enjoyed the hysterical shrieking of frightened children. She was not a monster. Instead she climbed past them up the stairs and went down the hall to Woding's bedroom.

Otto was lying in the middle of the bed, Beezely— unbelievably—curled up nearby. Serena crawled onto the mattress and lay down beside them, resting her cheek on her folded arms, watching the animals sleep. She would wait here for Woding to tire of that dancing pudding and come to her, where he belonged.

Alex finally escaped from those few relatives still awake, and from Felicia, who seemed to have made it her mission of the day to take any and every excuse to bump into him, touch his arm, sit beside him, and give him views of her prodigious bosom, all the while gazing up at him with invitation in her eyes. She was a foot shorter than he was, and he felt in constant danger of stumbling over her, the way one stumbles over a spaniel that in its adoration stays too close to one's feet.

She was a sweet girl, but quickly becoming a bit of a pest. He knew why she was here, and knew equally well that there was no chance in hell that he would find her acceptable wife material, even if there had not been someone else.

Serena. He had seen her watching from alcoves and doorways, from corners and shadows, silent and still. He wondered what she was making of all this, and whether she wished to chase them all from his house.

When Philippa had started playing music for dancing, he had rather wished Serena *would* appear, and send them all running. He had always loathed dancing.

He began to climb the stairs to the upper floor. He was impressed with Serena's forbearance this past day and a half. Given her behavior when he had first moved in, her admitted abhorrence of noisy guests, and most of all her temper, it was a minor miracle that she had not found it necessary to vent her frustrations in some unearthly manner.

Sometimes he felt that he hardly knew her, for all the time they had spent together. Sometimes he felt he did not know himself, or what he wanted. When she had vanished for weeks after their lovemaking, he had at first gone half-mad with the torture of not knowing where she was. He hadn't known if she was gone for good, if she was avoiding him, or if she were paying some unknown ghostly price for engaging in physical love with a living person.

Her unexplained absence had made her an obsession

in his mind for several days, until he had finally sought a return to sanity in his work, into which he diverted all the passion that had been devoted to her. It had been effective, and he had been able to convince himself that it was a good thing she had disappeared when she had. If she had remained, he might have become even more deeply involved with her. How much worse it would have been if he had been in love with her when she had vanished.

There were risks enough in loving the living. Loving the dead was as good as issuing an invitation to pain.

And then she had returned, suddenly and without warning, as if no more than a day had gone by, and as if they could pick up where they had left off. His emotions, so briefly ordered during her absence, became again a turbulent jumble. He wanted her as much as he had before her disappearance, but now he had the fresh memories of the pain of her absence to hold him back. His rational mind told him he would be an utter fool to risk his heart on a woman who might vanish from his arms even as he held her.

He opened the door to his room and went in, seeing Serena at once, then Otto and the orange cat, all spread out upon his bed. He smiled despite himself, liking the cozy scene, thinking of how much cozier still it would seem through the winter to have so many companions on or in his bed. If they stayed.

Serena rolled over to face him, propping her head on her hand, her elbow making no dent in the mattress. "Done with them for the night, are you?" she asked.

"They've mostly gone off to bed."

"I wish they'd go off home."

"Want me all to yourself, do you?"

"You think very highly of yourself, Alex Woding," she said, looking haughtily at him.

He came over to the bed and sat down beside her. Otto and the cat both raised their heads at the disturbance, cast accusing looks at him, and then got up and thumped—at least, Otto thumped—onto the floor. He spared the animals a brief scowl, then looked back to Serena. He hesitated a moment before placing his hand on the curve of her hip. Would she be solid? His hand touched warm flesh, and he saw that she was now pressing into the mattress as much as he himself did.

"I could wish them gone myself," he told her, running his hand up her side. She rolled onto her back, half closing her eyes as his hand made its way up to her breast, cupping and massaging the soft mound.

"What of your plans to renew the bonds of family?" she asked, although he could tell her interest was far more on what his hand was doing.

"Perhaps that is something better done one at a time. All of them here at once is a bit overwhelming." He prodded her to roll onto her stomach, and then raised her skirts, dotting kisses up the backs of her legs.

"You would not have liked living in my day," Serena said, her voice slightly muffled by the arm her face rested upon. He felt her shiver as he opened his mouth against her tailbone, on that small, flat triangle of skin directly above her buttocks. He flicked his tongue against her. "Everyone ate in the hall, most everyone slept in the hall—there were always people about, and little privacy. At least, until they all died."

His tongue stopped for a moment, but then he realized she was stating a fact and was not distressed. He continued his quest up her backbone, his hands searching over her body as he came up beside her and lay on the bed facing her.

"Do you prefer it in this time?" he asked.

She smiled, her eyes crinkling although her mouth was hidden by her arm. "I prefer your bathtub to mine."

Her answer was unexpected. "Don't tell me that is why you took to watching me at my bath: envy over modern plumbing."

"You thought I liked looking at *you?* What pride you have, Woding," she said, and he knew she was teasing.

"We could share a bath," he suggested.

Her head came up off her arm. "Now?"

He raised his eyebrows at her.

She climbed over him in a flash, her knee digging into his belly, and let out whooping cries of joy all the way into his bathroom. After a stunned moment awaiting the return of his breath, he rolled off the bed and followed.

Chapter Twenty-three

Serena listened to one side as Ben explained to his grandson about his plans for the sapling they had just unloaded off the wagon in the courtyard. John was maneuvering it into the wheelbarrow, to be transported to the garden.

"This is the right time of year for it. We'll cut this sapling off about six inches from the ground, and then make a split in the trunk. We'll cut a small branch of newer growth from the old tree, and wedge it into the split. The key is in lining up the inner portion of the bark of each tree. That's where they grow, you see. You don't have that lineup, you don't have a graft. We'll seal it all with wax when we're done."

John nodded through all this, as did Serena, following them to the garden. They must be talking about taking a graft from her tree. She didn't particularly like the idea of a small living branch being cut from it, but she trusted

Ben Flury to take only the minimal amount. It would be good to know the rare and beautiful cherry would have an offspring.

"Hey, there, what are you doing?" Ben suddenly shouted.

Startled, Serena looked up and saw what the normally gentle-voiced man had seen. There were children all around her tree, and one, a boy, was up in the branches, climbing right for her medallion.

She flew through the garden in an instant, and up into the tree.

"Stop!" she yelled, her voice supernaturally loud.

The boy started, surprised, and for a moment lost his balance. He grabbed for the base of the slender branch that held her medallion, and the slightly wider branch it grew from, but his weight was too much and there was a sickening crack as the wood gave way. The limb bent down at a broken angle, still attached to the tree by only its flexible bark.

The boy gave a yelp and tried to cling to the branch as it broke and bent, but he began to slide off the end of it, his legs kicking madly at the air trying to find purchase. He caught the medallion with his frantic flailing and held it tight in his grip as he came to the very end of the branch.

Serena made herself solid and lunged for the boy, snagging him by the arm just as he began his plummet to the ground. She saw startled brown eyes look up at her, but she was not visible, and to him and to the children below it must look as if he were hanging in midair. He howled, the screech echoed by those of the terrified children below.

She made herself visible, and that only increased their bellowing. She didn't care, her only thoughts of the branch the idiot child had broken, and on the medallion that, somehow, he still held in his dangling hand.

"Give it to me!" she yelled at him. "The medallion!"

He only looked at her with wide eyes, making no move to raise the hand with the medallion. Was her accent too thick for him to understand?

She shook him a bit to get his attention, sending gasps and shrieks through the audience below. "Hand it over!"

"Let me go!" the boy suddenly screeched. "Mother! Mother!" he screamed.

Strong as she was, Serena realized she couldn't haul the boy up one-handed, and solid like this she needed her other hand to keep hold of the tree. They were not that far off the ground, as she had caught him when he had already begun to fall. Keeping a tight grip on the boy's wrist, she began to carefully move down the tree a few feet. Bending low with the boy dangling from her long arm, it was only a few moments before he was low enough that the drop would not hurt him.

She released him, and he screamed again, as did his cousins, and then he was safely on the ground, falling over as he landed. Serena leaped down after him, her wild hair and skirts billowing about her, and she straddled his prone form. The other children all ran screaming from the garden.

"Give it to me!" she ordered. "The medallion!"

When he only stared at her with terrified eyes, she bent down and pried the charm from his fisted hand, then climbed off him. "Go!" she told him. "Shoo!" she said, waving her hand at him, and then went invisible again.

She was only dimly aware of him scampering to his feet and following his kin, for she was too busy examining the medallion for damage. The fine silver chain was broken, part of it no doubt still wound around the broken branch. The medallion itself had a few new scratches, but other than that seemed all right.

She looked up at the broken branch, wincing. She closed her eyes for a moment, and could feel the life— her life—already beginning to drain from it. The limb was connected to the tree by only a bit of bark now.

She climbed back up into the tree and, finding a new branch, wound what was left of the silver chain around it. This was the only place it made any sense to her to keep the medallion, where it could guard the very essence of her against the reappearance of le Gayne.

She looked down and saw Ben Flury at the base of the tree. Remembering what he had said about cutting a small branch for the graft, she reached out to the one that had originally held the medallion, and snapped it off of the larger, broken branch. It would die soon anyway.

The sound of the snap drew his eyes, and she let the small branch fall. He picked it up from where it fell, looking up into the tree once more before nodding. He moved off toward where the wheelbarrow and sapling had been abandoned. His grandson was nowhere to be seen, doubtless having led the charge from the haunted garden.

All was quiet now, the only sounds the growing breeze and Ben's snips and sawing. Serena rested in the branches, insubstantial as the wind, feeling shaken by what had happened. She didn't think she would be able to relax again until all of those relatives were gone.

Ben was sealing the graft with wax when Woding appeared at the entrance to the garden. Serena lifted her head, watching him, feeling a tremor of anxiety move up her chest. He didn't look happy, and after he exchanged a word with Ben, the older man left the garden.

He did not like what had happened; she could see that from here.

She came down from the tree and sat on the bench, waiting as he approached. Her legs were wobbly enough that she did not think it wise to stand on them.

He stopped in front of her, his face set in hard, dark lines. She had seen him annoyed, but never had she seen him angry like this. Not with her. This was the look he had given Sommer while berating him for his attack on Underhill.

A sick feeling churned in her stomach, and sweat broke out beneath her arms and on her forehead. Even her father's wrath had not caused her the distress that Woding's did now. So this was the price of caring.

He glared down at her, and the seconds stretched into eternity as she stared at the folds of his cravat, unable to raise her eyes all the way to his face.

"Why, Serena?" he said at last, just when she thought the silence would kill her. "What could have been so important that you had to frighten a group of children?"

"The medallion," she said quietly, still not meeting his gaze. "A boy climbed the tree to take it."

"So you had to scare him out of the branches, then dangle him above his cousins? You had to drop him, then attack him while he lay on the ground?"

Her eyes flashed up to him at that. "I didn't attack him, and I didn't mean to scare him out of the branches. That was an accident. I was only protecting what was mine."

"You said last night you couldn't wait for them to be gone. Was this your way of ensuring it? Frightening children? Endangering their lives? My sisters are now more determined than ever to have me leave this place, and I can hardly blame them."

317

"I had to get the medallion!" Serena protested. "I wasn't trying to scare them away."

"How can I believe that, when you could have come to me and asked for the charm back? I would have retrieved it for you immediately. You know that."

She felt his statement hit home. She had not even thought of going to him; she had simply been intent on getting the medallion at whatever cost. Did she still feel she could rely only on herself, or had she deep down wanted to scare those children and send them running to their mothers? "Le Gayne could have come back for his revenge on me in the time it took you to get it," she argued, the excuse feeble even to her own ears. "He's been waiting centuries to get back at me!"

"Revenge?" Woding asked. "You told me he hated you, not that he wanted revenge for something," Woding said. "He killed you. What reason for revenge would he have?"

She clamped her mouth shut.

When she didn't answer, his eyes widened. "*Did* you kill him?"

"No! I told you before I didn't. How could you even think that, knowing me as well as you do?"

"Knowing you! What do I know?" he asked. "There are a dozen topics you will not let me bring up, a thousand questions to which you answer 'I do not know' or 'I don't want to talk about it.' How well *do* I know you?"

"I am not a murderess."

"Then tell me why he would want revenge on you. Tell me why you are so connected to this tree," he said, gesturing above her at the branches. "Tell me everything that happened between you and le Gayne. You *were* guiltless, weren't you?"

She shifted on the bench, her eyes going to her palms in her lap. She heard the wind, and heard his breathing as he waited.

"I thought that *you* knew *me* well enough to understand you could trust me with whatever you had to say," he said at last. "How can there be anything worth preserving between us, if we cannot trust one another?" he asked.

He waited a long moment, giving her one more chance to speak, but when she remained silent he left her without a word, his footsteps loud on the path. She looked up and saw his back as he retreated, his stride quick. He did not look back.

She sat motionless on the bench, her mind numb and unthinking, her world feeling as if it had fallen apart in the space of an hour. The sky began to darken, the wind to pick up, swirling dead leaves around the legs of the bench and through her feet.

With the coming of darkness she began to shake off the spell of numbness, Woding's words becoming something he had said to her, and not something heard from a distance, as if he spoke to someone else, someone who had no heart. The breach the argument had opened between them felt like a chasm through her soul.

She had no one but Woding, and now she might have lost even him with her ruthlessness with that boy in the tree, and with her unwillingness to share with him all that had happened with le Gayne. She would lose him, with no one to blame but herself.

There must be something constitutionally wrong with her, that she destroyed all that she touched. Perhaps there was too much bile in her nature, or she was too choleric. The forcefulness and stubbornness that had seemed to guarantee her survival amid her brothers and during the

Pestilence now seemed to be what would guarantee losing Woding, and alienating any with whom she came in contact.

The air around her began to condense, the growing darkness forming a mass in front of her. She rose slowly to her feet, trembling, as the thing formed, becoming a massive, hulking figure, only vaguely human in shape. She stared up at it, feeling bare of defenses. A voice from deep inside her told her that she deserved this, that there was no use fighting it any longer.

"Is it you, le Gayne?" she asked the shadow.

It shifted, then pulsed, as if breathing, but there was no answer.

"What do you want of me? Haven't you done enough to me already?"

The shadow expanded, its sides stretching out and around her. She spun around, and saw the walls close behind her, trapping her within the cloud of darkness.

"How many times do you have to kill me?" she shouted at it. "I know it's you, le Gayne!"

The shadow began to swirl around her, slowly at first, then faster, and as it spun it shrank, closing in on the space where she stood, the sound of wind loud in her ears. She felt the vast, cold darkness of it only inches away, blowing by her skin, catching her hair in its currents. It was a malevolent presence, full of hellish secrets and tortured thoughts.

Terror rose up in her throat, making it impossible now to speak, and she wrapped her arms over her head and crouched down on the ground, tucking her head down on her knees, whimpering.

She felt it coming closer, the cold blackness reaching its fingers through the crooks of her arms and bends of her knees, finding each crevice and opening, and worming its way through. She felt it find her face, like dead hands touching her, and she remembered that she had done the same thing to poor Dickie in the beer cellar.

She remembered stuffing peas up his nose, and pulling him out of bed. Biting Leboff on the calf. Putting the male maid's cleaning bucket in the tunnel for Sommer to trip over. Spying on Woding in his bath and bed. Accidentally scaring him off the wall as a child and nearly causing his death.

She remembered appearing to her brother Thomas, and setting in motion the confrontation with le Gayne that had caused both their deaths. She remembered her wedding night—oh, God, her wedding night. Locking le Gayne in the storeroom and refusing him food or water. Luring him to the stream, and having Thomas strike him with a pot.

She remembered throwing her cup at Thomas, and leaping over the table, threatening him with a knife.

Her mind went back, and back, and back, recalling unkindness after unkindness, each one of them motivated by her obsession with her own needs, whatever the cost to others.

It had all led to destruction. Herself, dead. Thomas, dead. Le Gayne, dead. Clerenbold Keep a pile of rubble, as well as Maiden Castle. She had thought she was fighting for her survival, struggling to live, but all she brought was death, to herself and to others. Her blood and theirs was on her own hands, not le Gayne's.

She threw back her head, opening her eyes to the blackness, feeling tears trickle out the sides and down her temples. Evil had been done to her, but even more, she had done evil to others. The cloud was not just le Gayne but was herself as well, every violent and selfish act she had ever committed, every dark thought, every wish for harm to befall another.

The shadow was every trace of evil that had touched her life from outside, and that she had drawn from the depths of her own dark soul. It had come to take her to the hell that she so richly deserved, and which had been waiting for her for nigh on five hundred years.

She closed her eyes in surrender, wanting the evil to take her and claim her as its own, to give her the punishment that she deserved but had been seeking to escape by clinging to the edges of the mortal world.

Cold and darkness sank into her, robbing her even of her illusion of breath, reaching toward her heart. As her mind began to go black she conjured an image of Woding's face, wanting in this final moment to cling to the one good thing she had had, for however brief a time. She sent a prayer heavenward that he would find someone to love, and that he would be happy in his life.

The cold that had been so steadily advancing through her body stopped. She did not notice at first, her awareness focused all on Woding, on holding his image in her mind and feeling for these last seconds the love that had grown in her heart for him. The cold began to retreat, slowly, then more rapidly, draining out of her limbs like water. The howling sound of wind died away.

All became quiet, the only sounds those of the insects in a nighttime garden. Slowly she opened her eyes, almost afraid of what she would see. The shadow was still there, but smaller now, no longer surrounding her. It stood in front of her, no larger than a man.

Serena rose unsteadily to her feet, watching as the shadow grew yet slimmer, taking on the slender form of her own self, tendrils of shadow hair lifting in the breeze. She reached out her hand tentatively, and the shadow mirrored the movement until they were touching fingertips, sisters of light and dark. Serena jerked her hand away from the cold touch.

"You needed me once," the shadow said. "Why do you cringe from me now? I am part of you. The strongest part."

Serena shook her head. Her heart, filling with a new understanding, knew that was untrue. "You would have taken me if that were so. You're not the strongest part: you never were. Love was always strongest, only I let you convince me otherwise."

"Love would never have kept you from starving," the shadow said.

"I would have died a better death from starvation than I got from you."

"Love will buy you nothing, if that's what you're hoping. Your darling Alex doesn't want you. No one wants you. You belong with me, and with others of your kind." The shadow came closer, its toes touching coldly against Serena's, its otherworldly breath shivering against Serena's skin. "You cannot escape me."

Serena closed her eyes and felt the warmth of love inside her, a warmth that expected no recompense and made no demands. She opened her eyes and gazed straight at the shadow. "I already have."

The shadow shook its head. "I'll always be a part of you."

Serena felt a shiver of truth to those words, but she knew it was her own choice how large the shadow loomed in her. The shadow was le Gayne, and Thomas, and herself—it was all she regretted, and all the sins she could not bear admit were her own. "Why after so many years on this mountain did you try to destroy me now?" Serena asked.

The shadow did not answer, its empty eyes narrowing in unspoken frustration. It took only a moment for Serena to find the answer herself. While she was alone here, she had not changed, and this evil had been happy to watch her torture herself with loneliness and hatred. Yet when Woding had brought a ray of light to her dark heart, it had feared losing her to something brighter.

As it had.

Serena turned and looked at the cherry tree that was so near to dying. Only one main branch still lived. She did not need the shadow to tell her that her time here was almost over. She knew it in her buried bones, just as she knew that she need no longer fear moving on from this world.

Serena turned back to the shadow. "I love Alex," she said. "With all my heart."

And with a howl of dismay, the shadow vanished.

Chapter Twenty-four

Serena sat very still as Dickie approached the fireplace, bucket in hand. It was early morning, and most of the household was still asleep. Dickie's morning chore was to clean out the fireplaces of accumulated ashes and lay new fires. She had chosen her ambush accordingly, in the dining room. The morning sun was barely over the horizon, yet this room with its many windows and cream plaster walls was already lightening. It seemed the least ghostly of places that he would go on his rounds.

He moved nervously, no doubt having heard of her exploits in the garden the day before. He had likely spent a sleepless night.

"Good morning, Dickie," she said to him in a voice he could hear, trying to sound cheery and harmless. "Looks like we'll have a lovely day, doesn't it?"

He dropped his bucket, spinning around, his eyes

searching the gloom. His eyes finally found her, sitting very still in one of the chairs at the table.

"I'm sorry; I did not mean to startle you," Serena said calmly, her hands together on the tabletop. She had run her fingers through her hair and braided it into a thick—albeit messy—rope down her back, in hopes she would look a little less wild, a little less frightening.

"Your pardon, miss," Dickie said uncertainly. "I did not know there was anyone in here. Breakfast will not be served for a bit yet."

He must think she was a family member, or perhaps a lady's maid to one of the sisters. "I came to talk to you, Dickie. I wanted to say how sorry I am for the way I've treated you. It was most unkind of me, and I wouldn't be able to rest without tendering my apologies."

"Your pardon, miss?"

She sighed. This was not easy. "I am the one who put the peas up your nose, and pulled you out of bed. I scared you in the beer cellar."

His eyes about popped from his head, and a queer squeaking sound emerged from his throat. "You're the ghost?" he asked.

She nodded.

He grabbed a poker from near the large fireplace and brandished it at her like a sword. "Don't you touch me!"

"I'm not going to," Serena said. "I'm here to apologize for treating you so badly."

"Don't think I won't use this," Dickie said, slashing the poker through the air. The barb at the end caught on the carved back of a chair, gouging into the wood and knocking the chair over backward. Dickie yanked at the poker, casting frantic glances at her between tugs. "I can take your head off with this!" he said, his voice screeching up two octaves. The poker remained stuck.

"You don't need to be afraid of me. I won't hurt you."

With a final, full-body tug from Dickie the poker came loose, the sudden release surprising him. His arms came up and he lost his grip on the poker, the metal rod arcing up over his head and behind him as he staggered backward.

Serena watched, stunned, as the poker flew up and thwacked the mounted caribou that hung on the wall across the snout. One eyeball came loose, falling with the poker toward the floor as the entire head creaked, twisted, and then pursued its fleeing eyeball to the ground. The poker hit first, its clanging quickly dampened by the *whump* of stuffed caribou.

The eyeball rolled slowly across the wood floor, its passage the only sound in the now silent room. It came to rest against Dickie's shoe.

Dickie looked from the eyeball up to her, and gave a little moan. He was trembling all over.

"I'm sorry for all I did to you," Serena repeated. "Please accept my apologies." She pushed back the chair and stood, and, walking very slowly so as not to further distress him, she left through the door, opening and closing it as a normal person would.

The children would be going nowhere near the garden, so she sat on the bench in the corner bastion and waited. Fretting mamas or no, a sunny late-October day would draw them outside. She had seen before how the boys liked to play Defender of the Keep here, and how the girls took up housekeeping in the small stone guard shelters.

A few of Woding's sisters and brothers-in-law went by, but she remained out of sight to them, content to wait. It was past noon when her patience was rewarded, and she heard the first piercing shrieks of children.

She checked first for maids watching them. There were two, young women dressed in drab clothing. They were engrossed in their own conversation, not much interested in the children, and eventually took a seat at the edge of sight, on a bench in one of the other bastions. Serena let herself become visible. Her hair was not only braided, but knotted up behind her head. She wanted to look as unlike before as she could.

The children avoided her at first, with the natural avoidance of little ones for a silent adult in the middle of their accustomed play space, doubtless wishing heartily that she would get up and leave. Eventually a pair of girls came close by her, heading for the guard shelter that looked out over the valley.

"Would you like to hear a story?" Serena asked.

The girls, perhaps aged eight and nine—Serena knew she was not good with children's ages—stopped and stared at her, little frowns marring their smooth brows.

"It's about this castle, and about another one across the fields out there, crumbled now to nothing and hidden in the woods."

"Is there a princess?" the slightly taller of the two asked.

"You might say so, and there are several princes, some good and some bad."

"All right, then," the girl said, and without hesitation sat herself down at Serena's feet. Her companion followed suit.

"Are there others who might want to hear the story?" Serena asked them.

The older girl gave an exaggerated sigh, and got up

from her place on the paving tiles. "Michael! Louisa! Penelope!" she hollered, making Serena wince. The girl had a strong pair of lungs. "Gertrude! Mary! Sarah! David!"

There was fussing and place-changing, and much running back and forth to gather other cousins. The boy who had been in the tree slowed his steps when he saw her, stopping several feet away. Serena smiled and gestured to him, then turned her attention to the others, counting on his curiosity to drag him toward the forming group. A few of the others gave her funny looks, but they had seen her for only a moment, and her hair had been loose, wild, and doubtless the most memorable part of her appearance.

She saw the boy resume his movement forward, finding a place at the edge of the group. He looked around at his cousins, but with them so blatantly unafraid Serena knew that he would not dare to let out a shriek and be called a sissy for it. Any boy who would climb for the medallion while others watched had pride in his courage.

It was not long before the lot of them were settled around her, fascinated—even the oldest, although that girl tried, unsuccessfully, to look superior to what was going on. The lure of a story had not lost any of its power over the ages, Serena realized. They were as avid as if they did not have a roomful of books at their disposal.

The gossiping maids looked over once from their bastion but apart from the absence of shouting, they found nothing amiss with the children's activity, and went back to their conversation.

"I know you have all heard the legend of Serena, the ghost who haunts this castle." Serena said carefully, speaking slowly so they could understand her despite her accent. "I know you may have caught a glimpse of her in the garden yesterday. What I want to tell you is the *real* story of Serena Clerenbold: how she lived, how she died, and all about her time as a ghost."

"She murdered her husband!" Louisa put in.

"Did she?" Serena asked, raising an eyebrow at the girl. "Perhaps the truth is different than you expect.

"Serena lived in a keep across the valley, with her four brothers and her father," Serena began, "and from them she learned the way of warriors."

She told the entire tale with little of it censored. It took a long time to get to the end of the story, which included everything that had happened in the garden yesterday. She looked at the boy from the tree while she told much of that, trying to make it clear to him that it had been an unfortunate mistake.

"So that's the truth of the ghost of Maiden Castle," Serena concluded.

"So where is she now?" one of them asked, a cute little girl of maybe six, with blond braids.

Louisa elbowed the girl and rolled her eyes. "Where do you think, nitwit?" she said. "Who do you think has been telling us the story? Don't you see the scar, and the way she's dressed?"

A smart girl, Louisa, Serena thought, although apparently with the disposition of her mother.

The eyes of the children turned back to Serena, as the youngest who had not figured it out for themselves now realized who she was. Unlike Dickie, they showed no fear, looking more curious than frightened.

"You're a ghost?" a boy asked.

"I am," Serena said.

"Prove it!" another little boy shouted.

She smiled wickedly, then made her head disappear. The children gasped. One of the braver girls sitting near her stood up, and to the hooting encouragement of her cousins inched her hand toward the space where Serena's head should have been. Serena popped her head back and snapped her teeth at the little girl's fingers.

The girl shrieked, then laughed in delight. "Again!"

The other children all clambered up and pushed to get close to her, many little hands reaching out to touch her. Serena stood and let them pass their hands through her arms, through her skirts, through her hair.

The boy she had frightened in the tree inched his way toward her. She held her skirt up to the side, making a curtain, and nodded toward it. He gave her a dubious look, then sucked in his lips, narrowed his eyes, and barreled through it. He turned once he'd come out the other side and looked up at her, surprise and a growing confidence on his face. She wiggled the skirt in her hand in invitation, and he ducked through it again, laughing this time.

She dropped her skirt and let her hand go substantial enough that she could stroke him lightly on the cheek. "I'm sorry for what I did," she said softly to him, bending down, and he nodded his head once, quickly, in acceptance.

"Do you want to see one more trick?" she asked the children, straightening to her full height.

The answer was a chorused, "Yes!"

She smiled at them, and then slowly faded into nothing. Insubstantial, she moved away from the bench and watched them feeling around in the air as if they could tell from touch where she had gone.

"Serena, where are you?" Louisa asked. "Come back."

Lisa Cach

"I have to go now," she said, her voice coming out of the air.

The children responded with a collective groan of disappointment and complaint. She even thought she heard a whine. There seemed no better possible farewell than that.

Woding would not look at her. The foul man saw her—he could not help doing so—but he would not look at her. She could make a fuss and force him to, but that would only push him further away. Dogging his heels as she once had would be another form of force, as well. She'd had enough of trying to force people to do as she wished.

She left his office without a word, leaving him to the pile of business correspondence on his desk. She tried to tell herself that he was just being a man: it seemed an innate characteristic of the sex not to talk about anything that troubled them personally.

She didn't have much time, though, to sit around waiting for him to speak to her again. Her tree had reached a point where its decline had taken on a force of its own. It would die soon no matter how she conserved her strength, and she could not bear the thought of having that happen while there yet remained a rift between her and Woding.

These were her last good-byes, she supposed. Her deathbed farewells. She could tell him that, and put a blanket of guilt on him, forcing him to talk to her that way. *No.* She wouldn't do that, no more than she would stand in front of him and scream until he acknowledged her.

Although she'd like to.

He had to want to do it himself. She would make as many overtures as it took, but the olive branch would still fall to the ground if he was not willing to take it from her hand.

It was a brave thought, braver in its way than her kidnapping of le Gayne, and doubtless a far wiser decision, but it left her sick with fright that it might come to nothing. She felt as though all her shielding had been torn away by her confrontation with him, and, later, with the darkness that was in herself. She felt naked and exposed, vulnerable, and it was hard not to pick up her armor again, and bang her shield with her sword, crying out for battle.

Sitting quietly in his office with him had not worked to get him to talk to her. She knew no other way to show she was penitent, and was asking for rather than demanding his attention.

Even the years alone on this mountain had not been so lonely as sitting in his office, ignored by him. It was a personal rejection, more painful than any other because he knew her as no other person ever had.

She reminded herself again that he was male, and this was the male way. She had seen it in her brothers, and in the silent men-at-arms when their love affairs, so proudly boasted of, had gone awry.

She reminded herself, but it still hurt.

She wandered down the hall, wanting to find a quiet place to sit and think.

Then she saw Beth heading toward her—or, rather, toward the room she shared with her husband, the door to which was near where Serena stood. As she watched the woman approach, it occurred to her that here was someone who would know what she should do. Beth had known Alex for years, and would know how best to approach him. Also, she had never seemed *completely* opposed to Serena's existence. Perhaps she could be persuaded that helping her would do Woding no harm?

She followed her into the room.

Chapter Twenty-five

There was something strange going on. He could tell. His nieces and nephews were invading every nook and cranny of the castle as if they were termites, searching for Serena. They claimed she had sat and told a story to them out on the lower wall, and they wanted to hear another. They also wanted to see her do more wonderful ghost tricks.

Dickie, Underhill reported, was the new king of the servants' hall, repeatedly recounting a bizarre encounter with Serena in the dining room in which she had apparently begged his forgiveness for being such a rude ghost. No one entirely believed him, but the cocky change in his manner argued that he told the truth.

Sophie and Blandamour had arrived, and Beth had immediately spirited the new bride away, ostensibly to chat about married life, but there seemed more going on than that, given that they spent almost all their time shut up in Beth's room with Marcy, the maid, who when she did emerge looked as if she were a cat holding a live canary hidden in her mouth. Rhys complained that he was not allowed in his own room except at night.

And where was Serena herself? For two days he had not caught so much as a glimpse of her. He had had time to cool off and collect himself since he had so harshly berated her in the garden, and now he wanted to talk. He wanted to apologize for ignoring her in his office, when she had so clearly wanted to try to make amends. At the time, he had feared he was incapable of being civil to her, and had gone on the assumption that saying nothing was kinder than saying something he would regret. Later consideration had made him realize how cruel a thing that was, to her especially.

He was worried about her. Worried about that shadow she said was trying to harm her, worried about that dying tree to which she seemed somehow connected, worried that, however right he might or might not have been in their argument, he had hurt her and pushed her away. He had the uncomfortable sense that in his eagerness both to be right and to protect himself against an attachment to her, he might have come perilously close to losing something precious.

He remembered the half-drunken conversation with his brothers-in-law after Sophie's wedding, discussing the merits and problems of having a ghost for a lover. No one had thought to mention that she could disappear completely whenever she wished, and he would have no way to follow.

He heard the pounding footsteps of children in the hall, running past the library door. He wanted to talk to Serena, but he also wanted to know what the hell was going on in his home.

The answer came after dinner that evening. He and the other men had rejoined the women in the blue drawing room, to spend yet another evening in games and talk. At least there would be no dancing tonight, as the piano was safely in another room.

He noticed both Beth and Sophie leave the room together, and several minutes later Sophie returned alone, her eyes shining, her body fairly quivering with excitement.

"Excuse me," she said, loudly enough to carry over the murmur of voices. "Excuse me! May I have your attention, please?"

Conversation stopped and all eyes turned to her.

"Beth and I have a special friend whom we would like to introduce to you all. You've all heard a great deal about her already, but I'm afraid that much of it has been untrue, and you may have formed a mistaken impression of her."

Alex found himself rising from his seat, his eyes going wide. They couldn't mean— No, they couldn't be about to— Surely she herself wouldn't—

Sophie turned slightly and nodded to someone beyond their line of sight, and a moment later Beth walked in, her hand holding that of Serena.

Serena as he had never seen her before.

Gone was the long, wild hair, replaced by an elaborate coiffure of ringlets, braids, and a chignon, pinned atop her head and decorated with pale silk flowers. The arrangement emphasized the long, graceful stretch of her neck, and the elegantly sculpted form of her cheeks and chin. The scar was still present on her face, but even less noticeable than usual. His eyes were drawn back and forth between her dark eyes and her pink lips, both emphasized, he was sure, by a touch of subtle makeup.

Gone, too, was her medieval gown of pink, white, and gold, replaced instead with a modern dress that was cut low on her shoulders, with tiny puffs of sleeve that left her arms bare. The fabric was of pale blue and white stripes with pink flowers worked between, the delicate shades complementing her complexion. The bodice fit tightly, the slightly high waist belted in the same fabric, the square buckle made of paste diamonds. The skirt belled gently over petticoats, not nearly as full as those worn by his sisters, but it reached only to her ankle, as the current fashion dictated. On her white-stockinged feet she wore black silk slippers, laced in crisscrosses over her feet and around her ankles.

He thought he recognized the gown as one of Sophie's favorites, one that had previously had enormous, full sleeves and an equally full skirt. They must have completely undone and reworked it, he thought, and made the shoes themselves. They had transformed his ghost. Her height would still make her stand out in any group, but other than that, the only thing unusual anyone would find in her appearance was her astonishing beauty.

It was more than a matter of features. A critic would say that her face was too narrow, her nose too long, the bridge too low. Together, though, her features fit, and add to that the elegance of her carriage and her pose of complete confidence, and she could silence a room. As she was doing now.

Philippa was the first to speak. "Sophie, dear, I'm afraid you will have to tell us a little more. Kindly do give us a proper introduction."

Sophie's eyes danced with mischievousness. "Certainly. Philippa, I would like you to meet Serena Clerenbold. Serena, my sister, Mrs. George Stearne."

"It is a pleasure to finally meet you, Mrs. Stearne,"

Serena said into the utter silence of the room, her accent faintly audible. She must have practiced those words.

"I say," Harold Tubble declared, his brow puckered. "You can't be *that* Serena, can you?"

"If you mean the one who has been haunting the castle, I'm afraid so," Serena said. "I am the ghost."

Felicia gave a little shriek, and covered her face with a handkerchief.

Alex's frozen brain began to work again, a thousand thoughts jumping in at once: He had to stop this before chaos ensued. He wanted to see what would happen. He didn't know what Serena meant by this. He had to talk to her. He wanted his family to talk to her. A thousand thoughts jumbled in his brain, and among them a theme became apparent.

He cared about her, in a way he hadn't cared about anyone since Frances had died. His brave ghost, Serena, who had enlisted the aid of living women in a crazy plan he was not sure he wanted to see brought to fruition. What did the three of them think they were doing, bringing her into the drawing room like this?

He began to move toward her, wanting her out of this crowd, wanting to be alone with her, to talk with her, to take those silly flowers from her hair and have her be with him as she used to be, unbound by pins and corsets and black laces around her ankles. She didn't look right to him dressed like this, however lovely she was. He wanted to have her all to himself, to lie with her in the curtained intimacy of his bed through the night. She was his Serena, his nighttime passion, his secret under the stars.

He should not have pushed her about her past, about what she may or may not have done, or she could not yet tell him. When she was ready, she would. He had his whole lifetime to work on gaining her trust, and maybe even longer. She was making herself vulnerable by appearing this way to him, and to his family. She must trust him enough to think he would not let her come to harm.

There was a shifting movement of confusion among his relatives. "Ghost" plainly was not a fitting description of the young woman standing before them. Alex came out of his tunnel vision of Serena as Percy spoke.

"Is this some manner of joke?" his brother-in-law asked.

"That's a damned solid piece of female, for the dearly departed," Harold said a trifle more loudly than he should have, considering his wife was sitting next to him. Felicia was now peering over the top edge of her hankie, her eyes round and bovine.

Beth spoke to them all. "Serena wanted to dispel some of the worry you have had about Alex. That's why she is here tonight."

"I wanted to be able to tell you all in person that I want only the best for him, and shall do nothing to harm him," Serena said. "I also wanted to apologize for the unfortunate incident with the children the other day. I know you were all frightened by that, and I am sorry."

"You, my dear," Philippa said to Serena in her haughtiest voice, "are no ghost. I should think I would know a ghost when I see one. I am not at all certain of what you three are up to, but I think this is a very rude sort of prank you girls are trying to play on us."

"It is no prank," Alex said, turning to look at Philippa. "This *is* Serena Clerenbold, who died in 1350."

"Alex, you are not funny," Philippa said.

Alex felt the grin on his own face. This was too much. They wanted to protect him from his obsession with a

340

ghost, and when introduced to her face-to-face, refused to believe she was real.

"Beth?" Rhys asked his wife, his tone speaking the entire question for him. Alex saw her give him quick, shallow nods in the affirmative, her eyebrows raised, her eyes as bright as Sophie's. The two women were enjoying this.

"Alex?" Rhys asked him, his hand on his arm, stopping his movement forward. His face was a mask of shocked surprise.

"It truly is Serena," Alex said. He took Rhys's arm off of his, but kept his own hold on his cousin and friend, gently pulling him forward. "Let me introduce you. It is only fitting, since you are, in a sense, the one who first introduced her to me."

Serena's lips curled in a small, shaky smile as they approached, and he saw that beneath her confident exterior she was nervous, anxious about the reception she was receiving. It occurred to him that up until the last couple of days, she had avoided showing herself to anyone for centuries. He recalled how disturbed she had been when she realized he could see her, and her sensitivity over the scar that painted its faint trail across her face. Mending the rift between them must mean a great deal to her.

He realized then that her caring for him, and her trust, went far deeper than he had suspected, even that first time he had brought her pleasure and been discomfited by her tenderness. This time, though, the realization brought with it a warming sense of wholeness, as if an answer he had been asking the universe had finally been answered.

He made the introduction, and Serena held out her hand to Rhys in the way that Beth and Sophie must have taught her. Rhys hesitated, then gingerly took her fingers and bowed, kissing the air just above the back of her hand.

"I just don't understand," Alex heard his sister Amelia complaining behind them. "So all along this Serena has been a real person? Why was everyone saying she was a ghost? That's not a new euphemism for a mistress, is it?"

"Amelia! Really!" Philippa huffed.

Alex couldn't fail to notice that Rhys was staring agog at Serena, for once left with nothing to say. Beth released Serena's other hand and took her husband's arm. "It's all right, darling," she said to him. "I assure you, she will not throw you off a wall."

"I remember you as a little boy," Serena said to him, smiling. "I can still see some of the imp that you were in your face."

Rhys at last found his voice. "That is a most startling thing to hear from a woman who looks to be at least ten years my junior."

"I am fortunate that I do not show my age."

Rhys gave a startled laugh. "Indeed."

"If you will excuse us," Alex said, "I would like to speak with Serena alone."

"Of course," Rhys said.

Sophie and Beth both gave Serena encouraging smiles, and then he took her arm and led her out of there, away from them all. A threesome of children saw them, and stopped in their tracks.

"Serena! We've been looking all over for you," Louisa said earnestly. "Where have you been? And why are you dressed that way?"

"I've been here, there, everywhere," she said, gesturing about in the air. "Your aunt Sophie and cousin Beth dressed me like this, so I could meet your mama and papa without scaring them."

"I should have liked to have seen their faces if you came in with a sword!" a boy said. "That would have been grand."

"Perhaps another time," Alex said, pulling her away.

"Will you come back and tell us another story?" Louisa asked.

"If I can," Serena said over her shoulder.

He led her up toward his room, but she resisted, saying, "Could we go up to your tower? I should very much like to see the stars tonight."

He nodded his assent, and they went together up to his study, and then up onto the roof. He grabbed a blanket from the study on the way, knowing the air would be crisp.

"I am not used to my arms being bare," Serena said, rubbing them with her hands after they had both come out above. He shook out the blanket and wrapped it around her shoulders, then pulled her to him, holding her against him. After a moment she put her arms around his waist and laid her head on his shoulder. "You're not still angry with me?" she asked.

"Shhh," he said. "It is forgotten, except that I am sorry to have treated you so poorly. You deserved better from me."

He felt her squeeze him once, a silent acceptance of his apology. "I don't want to waste time talking about it," she said, and Alex thought that that must be the first time he had heard such words from a woman. "There are other things I want to tell you about my past. The things I was unwilling to before."

He leaned back and tilted her head up so he could look at her. Even solid as she was now, she still had that luminescence that spoke of unworldly origins. "Don't feel that you must."

"No, I want to," Serena said. "It is important: I want you to know all about me. How can I ever know that you cared for me if you never knew who I really was?"

"I know who you are," he said. "Whatever your past, I know the woman who is standing in my arms—although I'm not entirely certain of what went on between you, Beth, and Sophie."

"Isn't Beth wonderful?" Serena said. "When you wouldn't speak to me, I went to ask her advice. She said that I should continue what I had already started with Dickie and the children: showing people that I was not a monster, and apologizing. She said you would never leave someone you had any feelings for alone to face your sisters."

"She's far more devious than she looks," he said, frowning. He thought he had learned the sly ways of women, but obviously he was still an utter amateur at their games.

"And Sophie is smarter than she appears, when she wants to be," Serena added. "It took a clever mind to rework a dress to fit me. 'Twas a good thing she could find so much extra fabric in it."

"You like your new clothes."

She shrugged. "I like that I have this chance to finally wear something different, but I do not much like this hairstyle. My head is aching from the weight of it. But Alex," she said, changing her tone. "I do want to tell you about what happened with le Gayne."

"The shadow that has been following you?"

She grimaced. "Ah, that. I may tell you of that as well. But first, there is so much else. . . ."

He sat on the reclining chair that was still up there,

the back half-raised, and settled her across his lap leaning against his chest, both of them covered by the blanket. The sky above was dark and clear, the stars shining brightly in the firmament.

"Do you remember that song you kept singing after we passed through each other in the hallways, the song with the ravens?" she asked him.

"Yes, of course. 'There were three ravens sat on a tree—' " he sang.

"Now let me tell you why that song has stayed with me through all this time," she said, and then began her story.

He was mostly quiet throughout it, except for murmurs expressing that he listened and the occasional question asked for clarification. She told it with a touch of self-deprecating humor that only emphasized the desperation she must have felt while she lived, and while she and her brother plotted and carried out their foolish plan.

As she talked, the pieces of memory that he had involuntarily received from her in the hall that night, and briefly again when he had tried to revive her on his bed, played through his mind, serving as illustrations for the events she described. He could feel echoes of the emotions she had had, and see through her eyes. He understood why she had kidnapped le Gayne, and imprisoned him in hopes of a marriage.

"Thomas, properly outfitted, went off to war, and le Gayne took me home to the castle that used to stand here," Serena said. "He was reasonably civil to me, giving me no cause to be on my guard other than the truth of the situation as I knew it. In front of all the castle people he treated me as if it had been a marriage like any other, a practical agreement that demanded only that husband and wife play the roles prescribed. He was remarkably good at playing that game.

"I only wish he had kept on with it.

"I retired to our room early, and as I had no waiting woman to attend me—and le Gayne had not arranged for one—I set about preparing myself for our first night together. I took down my hair, but could go no further. I could not bring myself to undress and bare my body to his touch.

"I paced and I argued with myself. I had known this time would come. I had known what I would have to do. I had even, before, persuaded myself that it would be worth it, in order to have children. But now, faced with the reality, I could not do it.

"I don't know how long I walked the length of that room, with its new tapestries on the walls, its huge wooden bed with no sign of woodworms or bedbugs. He was as rich as Thomas and I had suspected, and his chamber was furnished in a manner Clerenbold Keep had never seen.

"He finally came in. He had been drinking with his men, but not so much that he was impaired—just enough that he felt free to do whatever he pleased, which he was free to do anyway, short of killing me, now that I was his wife in the eyes of God.

"If he was surprised I was still dressed, he did not show it. 'Take off your clothes,' he said. 'Let me see the mare I've been forced to purchase.'

"I shook my head no.

" 'Looks like you've got a fine pair of breeding hips on you,' he said. 'Now it's time to put them to use. You can't have crops without first planting the seed.'

"I backed away from him.

" 'What's the matter?' he asked. 'Isn't this what you

wanted? Isn't this why you were so wild to get me as your husband? You've got what you wanted: you'll be ridden from sundown to sunrise, and at noon, too, if the mood hits, and I expect you to bend over and lift your skirts and say, 'Yes, master, please,' every time you see me.'

"The facade of civility was gone now, and I could see the look of hatred in his eyes that he'd had when he was locked in our cellar. He continued to insult me, telling me how ugly I was and how grateful I should be that he would deign to mount me. He said he couldn't stand the sight of me.

"I had signed myself over to him, and he knew it. The only thing that surprised me was that even while trying to intimidate me he made reference to siring children. It gave me a shred of hope that whatever else he might have planned for me, he would at least keep me sufficiently intact to bear his child, and would care for that child when it came.

"Not that it was a great comfort, at the moment. That would be many months ahead at the soonest, and for the present I was terrified of what he planned to do with me.

"I didn't know much of lovemaking, but I did know that if the woman was unwilling, it would go badly for her. I had even heard of young girls who, taken repeatedly against their will, had died of the experience.

"He came at me. I dodged, sidestepping him, my training with my brothers finally coming to some use. He came at me again. I feinted, and then he snatched me by the arm. Even half-drunk, his skills at battle were far better than mine.

"He kicked my feet out from under me, and we went down on the ground. I was as helpless beneath him as I had been on the bank of that stream, his weight holding me however hard I bucked or kicked, his strength under that fat greater than mine would ever be.

"I stopped thinking. There was no thought of submitting left, no thought of future children or filled larders, no thought of starving in the winter. All I knew was that I was trapped and the creature atop me was going to harm me.

"Is that how men in battle feel?" Serena asked him suddenly, and he shook his head, for he didn't know. "Or perhaps it is closer to what an animal feels, put at bay by the hunters with their hounds.

"I had one arm free, and in my scramblings I caught hold of something familiar: the hilt of a dagger. It was tucked into his belt, the same as any man wore, and most women.

"I yanked it out, and stabbed it into his shoulder.

"He screamed and rolled off me, his hands reaching for it, seeking to pluck it from his body.

"I saw what I had done and lay stunned, awakened for a moment from the blind panic that had possessed me. He started cursing—terrible words, threats, worse than I had ever heard from my own brothers—and I saw that he was in no mortal danger from his wound, but was instead furious.

"I feared for my very life. I scrambled to my feet and ran out of the room, bumping into and then rushing past a serving wench who had been closest, and the first to respond to the shouts of her master. I could hear others coming down the hall, and the bellowing rage of le Gayne behind, coming after me.

"As I came to the head of the stairs I turned to see how close he was, and he was right there. He reached for me and caught at my arm. We struggled, and he struck me across the face with his good hand. His other arm was too weak from his wound to hold me, and I came free of his grasp. He struck me again, and I lost my balance. That is when I fell down the stairs, to the hall below.

"It didn't hurt," she said, looking at him now. "Isn't that strange? I felt the impacts as I tumbled down the stairs, the force of my body against the stone, but I didn't feel the pain.

"I lay there for I don't know how long, not thinking anything, not moving. Then I saw myself lying there, as if I were a person standing above my body, looking down at that poor half-dead thing. I was still part of that body, though. I knew I wasn't completely dead.

"Then le Gayne, bleeding shoulder and all, was above me, and his men, too. He went down on one knee and held his hand in front of my mouth, feeling for my breath. I don't know if he felt anything. My eyes were closed, and I could not open them, could not move.

" 'She's dead,' I heard him say. He ordered most of the men away, but kept two by his side, who helped him to carry me out into the garden. There were saplings there waiting to be planted, and a hole half-dug for a cherry tree. The men dug it larger, and dumped my body there on le Gayne's orders. They began to fill it in with dirt, and to place the sapling atop me.

"Le Gayne stood at the edge of the hole while they worked, staring down at me. 'If you want my castle so badly,' he said to me, 'have it. You can spend all eternity here, for all I care, and may the devil eat your soul.'

"He wouldn't give me a proper grave, would not bring his priest to pray over me. I think he knew I was not dead, however close I may have been, and this was his vengeance for everything I'd done to him.

"As I was buried in the dirt I felt my last ties to my

body loosening, breaking up. Soon I would be free of it, as the last of my life left it. At the same time I could feel the roots of the sapling spread around me, full of new life, and the power to grow and endure. I clung to those roots. I refused to go. I could not let le Gayne win, and I could not let it all end this way. It was unfair. I had fought so hard to survive for so long, I could not give up. I still wanted to live, still wanted to have children, and to experience everything that a life was supposed to hold. I simply could not let go.

"Somehow I became entwined with the cherry sapling. My soul, or life—I don't truly know what—became dependent upon it, like mistletoe on an apple tree. As it survived, so did I."

"But it's dying now," Alex said, a sick knot forming in his gut.

"Every time I appear to someone, or speak so they can hear me, every time I move an object or make a noise, I take strength and life from the tree. It supports me, but it is fragile. When I draw too heavily upon it, I hasten its end."

It made sense to him now, her tie to the tree, and why she would hang the medallion there rather than anywhere else. "Ben Flury has grafted a branch onto a new sapling. Will you be able to draw from that as well?"

She shook her head, a silent no. "I would have felt the change if that were so. It is the tree whose roots go through my soul that matters, and that cannot be replaced."

He sat forward abruptly, holding her in his arms. "You're killing the tree right now, by being here with me, aren't you?" How long had he let her sit there, talking? It felt like it must be well past midnight now. How much time did she have left?

"It doesn't matter anymore. It will die soon whether I hasten the end or not."

"You can't hurry it along! Go transparent, or invisible—whatever it is you do."

She touched his temple, smiling gently. "It cannot be stopped. Let me end the way I wish, with you, here."

"But you can't go! It's too soon."

"Too soon for what?"

"For you. For me. You can barely write your name. There is too much yet for you to learn," he protested, unable to say what was in his heart, barely recognized but there.

"I think I've learned what I needed to."

"What was that?" he asked, but just then she turned her face upward, her lips parting in surprise.

"Look, Alex! Look!"

He tilted his head back, and saw a shooting star streak across the heavens, and then two more. Several began falling at once. "It's like the night I first saw you," he said in hushed awe. He looked at her. "I was thinking this evening, when I saw you come into the drawing room, that that faint scar on your face looks like nothing so much as the trail of a falling star."

She reached up and touched the line on her face. "You make it sound almost beautiful."

He leaned back in the chair, pulling her with him, until they were close against each other, gazing up at the raining storm of stars overhead. He tried not to think of the future or of how long they might have left together. He simply tried to stay where he was, right now, Serena in his arms, silent streaks of light above them in a moment that was, he hoped, perfect enough to last an eternity.

She began to lighten in his arms, to grow less dense,

his hold on her slipping; then she lost all solidity and his arms fell closed on nothing.

"Serena?" he asked, turning his eyes from the stars.

Her hair was loose and flowing again, its tangled strands spread around them, floating on the night air, and she was wearing her old white and pink clothes. The blue-and-white gown she had been wearing lay beneath her, flat and empty, the silk flowers from her hair lying now on his shoulder.

"Do you know what it is I learned?" she asked him, her voice a whisper on the wind. "I learned what it is to love. I love you, Alex Woding."

And then she was gone, her face fading into the streaking stars, her dark eyes blending into the eternity of night.

"No!" he shouted, the suddenness of it, the reality of it ripping at his heart. "Nooo!" She couldn't be gone, not yet. It was too soon.

There was no answer to his cry, the night silent under the streaming light of the stars, the vast emptiness of the heavens stretching above him. The skies held no magic without her, had no wonders to compare to her. "I love you, Alex Woding," she had said. Those words were more miraculous than any number of falling stars, and they pulled at his heart in a way that no astronomical marvel ever had.

He remembered something else she had once said to him, about his quest to decipher the workings of the heavens. "You believe that if you could unravel this mystery, you would be unlocking a secret of the universe. You believe that if you could understand this, you could understand what your place is on this earth."

He hadn't comprehended her meaning at the time. He thought he did now. Her love for him had unlocked the greatest secret of the universe, the one he had utterly failed to understand: that a life without love was not a life worth living. It was love that gave life meaning, love that gave one a place on this earth.

"Come back to me, Serena," he said softly into the night, his voice rough with tears. Let it be even a day more with her, he would give his very soul for it. "I love you. Come back."

And as if in answer one star, a brilliant fireball, suddenly fell directly toward him, its brightness making him throw up his arm to shield his eyes as he stumbled to his feet. He heard a sound like the crackling of flames, and in a brilliant flash the fireball streaked past where he stood atop the tower, so close he could feel the heat of it, and before he could even turn to follow its course, it had struck with a crashing roar that shook the very foundations of the castle.

The cherry tree in the garden was aflame, the ends of its dead branches burning like torches. The trunk was partially split, half the tree listing at an angle. On the far side of it a large section of the garden wall was missing, the ground a furrowed crater.

"No!" he cried out in horror. Not the tree, not the cherry! Whatever trace of Serena that might remain was in it, in the very flesh of the bark and the roots that reached into the ground.

He ran for the steps, half fell down them, ran through his study, downstairs, through halls where people were emerging from doorways, questions on their lips, downstairs again and out the door to the courtyard, barely aware that Rhys followed behind him, tying shut his robe. He sprinted across the cobbles, through the garden gate, and to the flaming tree.

"Serena!" he screamed at the flames. "Serena!"

And then he saw it, in the center of the black crack of the trunk that had been partially split by the fireball. There was a wedge of paleness, bare and new as a baby's flesh, something there inside the trunk that could not be part of the shattered wood.

He lunged for the trunk, grabbing the opposing sides of the split in his hands and pulling them apart, forcing the split wider. Rhys grabbed at him, trying to pull him away, but he snarled, shaking his cousin off. When the wedge came wide enough he jammed his foot in, using the strength of his leg to pry the wood apart. It cracked under the pressure, sparks and cinders falling on him from the burning branches above. Rhys was shouting something, but he did not know what, and did not care.

At last the tree fell wide open, half of it crashing to the ground as Serena, naked as the day she was born, fell out of the burning wood and into his arms. He heard a shout of surprise from Rhys, and then his friend was beside him, helping to pull Serena out and away from the falling sparks, her body covered in sticky sap, her lovely hair gone, only the short blond fuzz of a babe covering her tender scalp under a coating of sap.

"Serena," Alex said softly, cradling her in his arms, wiping at her eyes and mouth as Rhys draped his robe over her. "Serena. My love."

Her eyelids fluttered, then opened, and her irises were as blue as a butterfly's wings.

Epilogue

Spring

Serena walked the garden path to where the grafted sapling had been planted, where the old cherry had once stood. Its unusual pink double blossoms were on schedule with those of the other fruit trees, the grafted branch strong and healthy on its new base. Alex had finally found the tree in a book of botanical prints: the cherry hailed from the Far East, the lands of China and Japan. How le Gayne had ever gotten hold of such a specimen, she did not know.

The charred remains of the other tree had been hauled away many months since. She hadn't liked to see it go, but the new tree that was part of the old softened the loss. Alex had hesitated about having the stump torn out, roots and all, fearful of what might be found entangled underneath. She had insisted, though, knowing somehow that whatever had remained of her old body was part of her now, used in the forming of this new one.

She touched the place on her face where the scar had been. It was no longer there, nor were any of the scars she had gained over the years of her previous life, however small or large. It was as if she had been born anew, a babe full-grown emerging from the womb of the cherry.

Instead of a skeleton, what they had found when they pulled up the stump was a golden chain: the girdle that had belonged to her mother. She wore it now, loose around the waist of her pale blue gown. Beth and Sophie had assured her that it was all the fashion to add medieval touches to one's wardrobe—which was a good thing, as she still could not bring herself to dress completely as most women did, with their corsets and ridiculously full sleeves.

She was learning, however, the beauty of shopping, and of female friendship as well. Alex sometimes gave her a mock-frightened look that had nothing to do with her past, and everything to do with packages and a growing fascination with dress designs. It was as if she had spent her life locked away from girlish pleasures, and had finally been set free.

Clothes were only a small part of what she was discovering, though. Her reading skills had progressed rapidly, and half of any given day found her in the newly filled library, stacks of volumes around her, bits of this and that stuck between the pages to mark her place.

The other half of the day invariably found her on the back of a horse, Alex riding at her side. The valley she had watched from above for so long she now knew again from up close. They had ridden to what was left of Clerenbold Keep, as well. As she suspected, nothing was left of it under the trees and shrubs except for a few stones. It didn't sadden her, as she thought it might. It was too far in the past for her to feel that, and she'd had too much time already to dwell on what was lost forever.

Beezely suddenly appeared out of nothing, sauntering down the path toward her. He brushed against her skirts, passing through the edge of them. "Meow?" he asked up at her, purring.

She squatted down, holding out her hand, and Beezely tilted his head, trying to rub the top of it against her. He went through her hand, but didn't seem to notice, his purring uninterrupted. He lowered himself to the ground and rolled onto his back, his belly to the sun.

Serena stood, feeling the breeze ruffle through her short white-blond hair, paler now than it had been when she lived, more the color it had been when she was a child. Sophie had bought her a beaded net to wear over it until it grew out, as well as a number of pretty white caps, but she rather liked the feel of it blowing free, so light after the heaviness of her long hair.

"Serena?" Alex called from the courtyard, where she knew the carriage was waiting, Nancy at the reins. They were to leave today for Bristol, and from there they would take a ship to the Americas. It was his wedding present to her, a trip to see the world, although she knew it was something he himself had longed to do since a child.

Alex's sisters had eventually come to accept their marriage, although they thought of her as a woman from no family—all except Sophie refusing to believe what she had been. His brothers-in-law, from what Alex said, tried not to think about it at all. Rhys believed she was who she said, though, and after several weeks of looking wide-eyed at her whenever she was near, had eventually begun to relax in her presence.

She turned, smiling, and saw Alex come to the garden gate. He looked more handsome to her now than he had the first time she'd seen him. She didn't know if it was the deepening of her own feelings that made him look more appealing, or the sparkle that now lit his eyes, even when he wasn't talking about shooting stars and the vastness of the universe. It was as if he had come back to life after a sojourn in his own purgatory, just as she had.

"Everything's ready, Mrs. Woding," he said, coming toward her. "Are you?"

"The question is not if I am ready, Mr. Woding," she said, taking his hands as he reached her. "The question is, is the world ready for me?"

"God help it if it's not."

She laughed and let him lead her toward the garden gate. "I do hope we get to see a pirate while in the Caribbean."

He groaned and squeezed her hand. At the gate she stopped to take one last look at the garden, with its beds of flowers in bloom.

"We'll come back," Alex said.

"I know we will," she said, turning to him. "I know."

AUTHOR'S NOTE

Meteor storms such as those described at the beginning and end of this story do indeed occur. In 1833 the Leonid meteor shower was so bright that it woke many of the inhabitants of Rhode Island. It was estimated that 60 meteors per second were visible. At the time, the connection between meteor showers and the paths of comets was unknown, as was the precise nature of falling stars themselves.

Bewitching the Baron

Lisa Cach

Valerian has always known before that she will never marry. While the townsfolk of her Yorkshire village are grateful for her abilities, the price of her gift is solitude. But it never bothered her until now. Nathaniel Warrington is the new baron of Ravenall, and he has never wanted anything the way he desires his people's enigmatic healer. Her exotic beauty fans flames in him that feel unnaturally fierce. Their first kiss flares hotter still. Opposed by those who seek to destroy her, compelled by a love that will never die, Nathaniel fights to earn the lone beauty's trust. And Valerian will learn the only thing more dangerous—or heavenly—than bewitching a baron, is being bewitched by one.

___52368-X $5.50 US/$6.50 CAN

Dorchester Publishing Co., Inc.
P.O. Box 6640
Wayne, PA 19087-8640

Please add $1.75 for shipping and handling for the first book and $.50 for each book thereafter. NY, NYC, and PA residents, please add appropriate sales tax. No cash, stamps, or C.O.D.s. All orders shipped within 6 weeks via postal service book rate. Canadian orders require $2.00 extra postage and must be paid in U.S. dollars through a U.S. banking facility.

Name_____
Address_____
City_____State_____Zip_____
I have enclosed $_____ in payment for the checked book(s).
Payment <u>must</u> accompany all orders. ❑ Please send a free catalog.

Elaine Fox
Untamed Angel

Bestselling Author of *Hand & Heart of a Soldier*

With a name that belies his true nature, Joshua Angell was born for deception. So when sophisticated and proper Ava Moreland first sees the sexy drifter in a desolate Missouri jail, she knows he is the one to save her sister from a ruined reputation and a fatherless child. But she will need Angell to fool New York society into thinking he is the ideal husband—and only Ava can teach him how. But what start as simple lessons in etiquette and speech soon become smoldering lessons in love. And as the beautiful socialite's feelings for Angell deepen, so does her passion—and finally she knows she will never be satisfied until she, and no other, claims him as her very own...untamed angel.

___4274-6 $4.99 US/$5.99 CAN

Dreams Of An Eagle

Lori Handeland

After losing everything in the War Between the States, including her husband and young daughter, Genny McGuire is haunted by the dream of a white eagle who takes her to the heights of happiness, then leaves her in despair. Frightened, yet compelled to learn the truth behind what she believes is a prophesy, Genny heads for the untamed land of Bakerstown, Texas—and comes face-to-face with Keenan Eagle, a half-breed bounty hunter as astonishingly handsome as he is dangerous.

___52276-4 $5.50 US/$6.50 CAN

Dorchester Publishing Co., Inc.
P.O. Box 6640
Wayne, PA 19087-8640

Please add $1.75 for shipping and handling for the first book and $.50 for each book thereafter. NY, NYC, and PA residents, please add appropriate sales tax. No cash, stamps, or C.O.D.s. All orders shipped within 6 weeks via postal service book rate. Canadian orders require $2.00 extra postage and must be paid in U.S. dollars through a U.S. banking facility.

Name_____
Address_____
City_____State_____Zip_____
I have enclosed $_____ in payment for the checked book(s).
Payment <u>must</u> accompany all orders. ❏ Please send a free catalog.
    CHECK OUT OUR WEBSITE! www.dorchesterpub.com

JAGUAR EYES

Casey Claybourne

Daniel Heywood ventures into the wilds of the Amazon, determined to leave his mark on science. Wounded by Indians shortly into his journey, he is rescued by a beautiful woman with the longest legs he's ever seen. As she nurses him back to health, Daniel realizes he has stumbled upon an undiscovered civilization. But he cannot explain the way his heart skips a beat when he looks into the captivating beauty's gold-green eyes. When she returns with him to England, she wonders if she is really the object of his affections—or a subject in his experiment. The answer lies in Daniel's willingness to leave convention behind for a love as lush as the Amazon jungle.

___52284-5 $5.50 US/$6.50 CAN

Dorchester Publishing Co., Inc.
P.O. Box 6640
Wayne, PA 19087-8640

Please add $1.75 for shipping and handling for the first book and $.50 for each book thereafter. NY, NYC, and PA residents, please add appropriate sales tax. No cash, stamps, or C.O.D.s. All orders shipped within 6 weeks via postal service book rate. Canadian orders require $2.00 extra postage and must be paid in U.S. dollars through a U.S. banking facility.

Name_____

Address_____

City_____ State_____ Zip_____

I have enclosed $_____ in payment for the checked book(s).

Payment <u>must</u> accompany all orders. ☐ Please send a free catalog.

DARK DESIRE

CHRISTINE FEEHAN

The stranger silently summons her from across the continents, across the seas. He whispers of eternal torment, of endless hunger...of dark, dangerous desires. And somehow American surgeon Shea O'Halloran can feel his anguish, sense his haunting aloneness, and she aches to heal him, to heal herself. Drawn to the far Carpathian mountains, Shea finds a ravaged, raging man, a being like no other. And her soul trembles. For in his burning eyes, his icy heart, she recognizes the beloved stranger who's already become part of her. This imperious Carpathian male compels Shea to his side. But is she to be his healer...or his prey? His victim...or his mate? Is he luring her into madness...or will his dark desire make her whole?

___52354-X $4.99 US/$5.99 CAN

Always Faithful

Julie Miller

When Jonathan Ramsey disappears in a covert operation on the dark isle of Tenebrosa, nothing can keep him away from his family—not even death. But the guardian angel who gives the marine his life back blunders: Jonathan Ramsey is born again as someone else.

Emma never questions that she will again see her beloved husband. But the man who comes to her has a different face and an unknown name. Suddenly, Emma knows this wonderful stranger is the man she's waited for. But to rediscover the man who won her heart so long before, Emma has to learn that true love never   dies—and that the greatest hearts are always faithful.

___52374-4 $5.50 US/$6.50 CAN

STRANGER ON THE MOUNTAIN
Linda O. Johnston

The mountain lion disappeared from Eskaway Mountain over a hundred years ago; according to legend, the cat disappeared when an Indian princess lost her only love to cruel fate. According to myth, love will not come to her descendants until the mountain lion returns. Dawn Perry has lived all her life at the foot of Eskaway Mountain, and although she has not been lucky in love, she refuses to believe in myths and legends—or in the mountain lion that lately the townsfolk claim to have seen. So when she finds herself drawn to newcomer Jonah Campion, she takes to the mountain trails to clear her head and close her heart. Only she isn't alone, for watching her with gold-green eyes is the stranger on the mountain.

___52301-9 $4.99 US/$5.99 CAN